CRIMSON
THE CHROMAVEILED

C. BRITT

CBRD PUBLISHING

COPYRIGHT

Cover art by:
Indie Bubble
Dragon, wyvern, and wygon artwork by:
Lizzie DeLano
Map drawings by:
C. Britt (map drawings created using Photoshop Elements and The Map Effects Fantasy Map Builder)
Formatting by:
C. Britt (Created with Vellum)

https://www.cbrdpublishing.com

To those who dream of being in a fairy tale, waiting to be rescued.
To those who dream of being the hero and saving the day.
To those who dream of being both.

TABLE OF CONTENTS

CONTENT WARNINGS

Crimson the Chromaveiled is written with older teens and adult readers in mind. Romance scenes are not explicit and are fade-to-black style. This story contains scenes of violence, gore, battles, and death, including death of people and of fantasy creatures.

MAPS OF FENGLAURIA

North S
Dividing Sea
The Nortgren
Midstrytch
Dry Cliffs
Rundish
Long Waters Edge
Rockthorn Coasts
Pahnzelias
Kandreolos
The Dreadlands
Tumultuous
Ocean
Fenglauria
Drawn by Alicia Derriny - Fenglaurian year 1367

Vakandya
Losmchayos
The Twains
Westerlands
Nurthahrya
The Whitnalls
Grand Basins
Duldurk Ocean
Bottomless Ocean
The Pailwall
The Scoplands
Weidlahnt
Southern shores
Sunderlands
South Sea
N

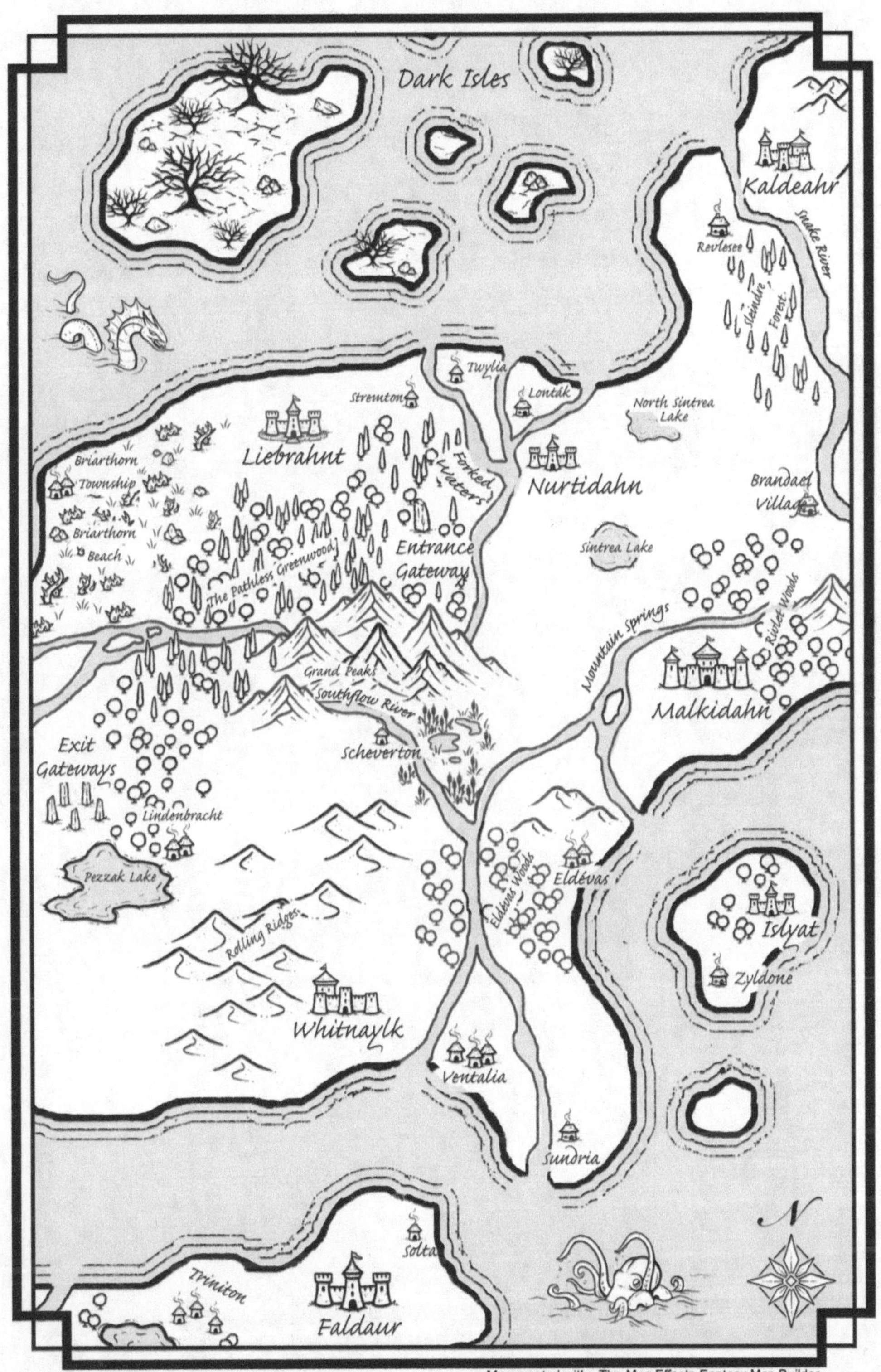

Map created with: The Map Effects Fantasy Map Builder

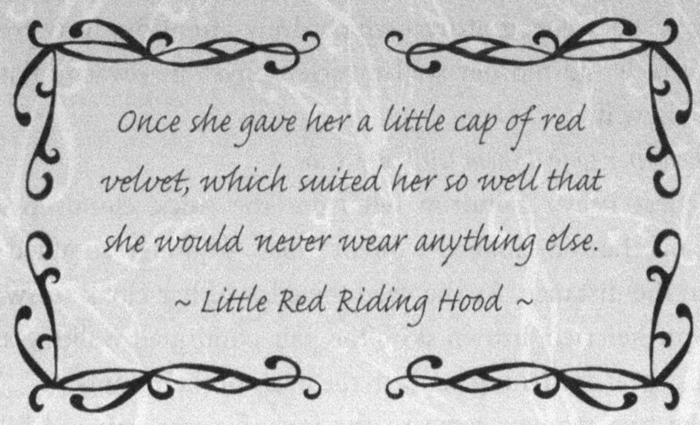

wo figures strode down the narrow, rutted cart path, ignoring both the darkening sky and the wind that had begun to tug at their cloaks. Their quest had been assigned. These two knew they would have no rest until their task was done, and neither would the growing storm.

The first of the pair was a tall woman with bright green eyes who was nearing forty years of age. Over her pale yellow dress, she wore a narrow belt that accentuated the slenderness of her waist. Her shoulders were draped with a midnight-blue cloak that stopped at the tops of her ankle-high, black boots. A simple plait of long, straight, blonde hair hung down her back, resting atop the unworn hood of her cloak. And although she was quite stunning, the jagged scar across the pale pink skin of her cheek hinted at a less-than-easy life. Still, the slight disfigurement did nothing to diminish her beauty.

All the better to lure them with, my dear.

The second woman could hardly have looked more different than the first. She was barely past her twenty-third birthday. In addition to the difference in their ages, she was several inches shorter than her companion, and the lower edge of her blood-red cloak brushed across the dusty ground as she walked. Coils of shoulder-length black hair bounced slightly with every step. She wore an ill-fitting, torn dress made of pale gray cotton. Her mud-stained boots came halfway up her calves. The ragged attire—which drew attention away from her beautiful face and hid her well-muscled physique—wasn't flattering, and she knew it.

All the better to fool them with, my dear.

The first heavy raindrop fell from the thick clouds overhead, landing on the red-cloaked woman's face. Thunder rumbled somewhere in the distance. As she used the edge of her cloak to swipe the droplet off her rich, brown skin, the pair continued walking steadily onward, gravel crunching beneath the heels of their boots.

As the two women came to the top of a tree-covered hill, they stopped. The quiet village of Eldévas sat in front of them, no more than half a mile away now. Simple, wooden structures—a church, a stable, a pen for goats and chickens, a few houses and shops—lined the sides of the cart path. A few dozen villagers milled around the buildings, buying things from the shopkeepers, sweeping their front steps, or simply visiting with their neighbors to share the latest gossip.

The ocean lapped at a narrow, wooden dock on the other side of the small cluster of buildings. A rowboat bobbed on the water, rocking a bit faster as the wind and waves gradually increased.

In the center of the village was a circle of stones topped by a small roof with a bucket hanging from it. Ezmaunda shrugged one side of her blue cloak behind her shoulder to free her arm, then gestured toward the well. "Melzia, you wait for me there until you see the mark. Aye?"

"Aye." Mel voiced the word in a lilting accent that matched Ezmaunda's. The r's in the middles of the words were rolled lightly, while those at the ends were ignored entirely. The t's and d's at the ends of the words were softened as well so that they were barely more than a light puff of air.

Burying her arm back underneath the cloak, Ezmaunda twisted to face Mel. She narrowed her eyes. Mel had never previously given her a reason to doubt, but this task was different. Ezmaunda was skeptical, cocking one eyebrow at Mel as she continued to question her. "You're certain you're prepared to see this through? You know our orders. And you know Queen won't—"

"I am well aware of Queen's command. And I'm also well aware of the punishment for failure." Mel set her jaw and glared back. Inside, her heart raced, but she kept her eyes locked on Ezmaunda's.

The two stood, studying one another as thunder crackled through the purple-rimmed clouds behind them. At last, Ezmaunda nodded. "Good."

Tucking a stray lock of hair behind her ear, Ezmaunda turned her attention back to the village in front of them. Mel straightened her spine, lifted her chin, and faced the village too.

For several long minutes, the women silently stood there. Mel watched the movements of the villagers, and Ezmaunda shifted to look up at the sky, watching intently as the storm slowly swelled. At last, the clouds sparked with lightning, causing the villagers to leave the square and make their way indoors. Thunder rumbled, long and low, shaking the ground beneath the feet of the two women. Rain droplets fell faster. The wind picked up speed, whistling through the tree branches and tousling the women's hair until it loosened blonde locks from their braid and sent black coils twisting wildly in the air.

The blue and red hoods continued to wait unused on the women's backs as they stood there. When the last village resident finally disappeared from view, the pair resumed walking.

Once the two of them reached the edge of the village, Ezmaunda veered off the path and reached up, over her shoulders to grab hold of her blue hood. With the movement, her dress sleeve shifted. The underside of her bare wrist peeked out, and—even in the dim light—the black, outlined shape of a crown was easily visible on her pale skin. At last, Ezmaunda lifted the blue hood over her head and tucked the braid underneath the dark fabric. For the briefest of moments, the air around her became bright and colorful; it twinkled and danced. Then, as suddenly as it had started, the twinkling stopped, and Ezmaunda vanished without a trace. A moment later, leaves rustled as Ezmaunda's invisible form took off into the forest.

Mel didn't bother to stop and watch the familiar sight. Instead, she continued straight down the path until she came to the edge of the well. She turned and sat back against the cold stones to wait, undisturbed by the pelting rain and bright flashes of lightning that tore through the sky.

As the minutes crept by, Mel absentmindedly ran her fingertips across the image on the underside of her left wrist. It was the outline of a crown, nearly identical to the one on Ezmaunda. The only true difference was that her mark was bright white. And as she stood underneath the gray and purple, cloud-covered sky, the white lines seemed to glow on her dark skin.

Something brushed up against Mel's back. Her breath caught in her throat. In one swift movement, her hand reached under her cloak and flew to the dagger at her hip, pulling it free from its sheath as she spun on her heel.

"Meow."

An orange tabby cat—sopping wet after running through the rain to take shelter underneath the well's small roof—stared up at her.

Mel exhaled heavily and chuckled as she let the dagger slip back into its leather sheath. Normally, she was more aware of her surroundings; normally, she wouldn't feel so on edge. But that night, she had a plan. And whether it succeeded or failed, Mel knew her life would never be the same again.

When Mel slowly pivoted around to sit on the well's edge and reached a hand toward the orange cat, he walked forward, nuzzling his head into her open palm. His short fur was soaked, but he didn't seem overly concerned. She moved her hand across his back and down the length of his tail a few times, listening to him purr softly. Until he decided he'd had enough. Then, he quickly walked to the opposite side of the well and sat down to lick the water off his sides.

With a sigh, Mel twisted to look back over her shoulder, down into the dark opening of the well. She stood. Turning, she slipped one hand underneath her wet cloak, searching for the leather pouch that hung from her belt, hidden within the folds of her dress. At last, she found it. She pulled it open, took out a small, gold coin, then let the pouch fall back to her hip.

Pushing aside the wet hair that now clung desperately to her cheeks, Mel took a deep breath and closed her eyes. She lifted the coin to her lips. And in a voice barely louder than the sound of the pouring rain, she said, "I just want to be free from Queen."

She froze, waiting as she focused on the words, rolling them over and over in her mind. Finally, she flicked the coin. It flew in a tall arc until it turned and came back down, tumbling into the water of the well with a soft, little *plop*. As Mel opened her eyes, a soft tinkling like wind chimes echoed along the structure's stone walls. Colorful, glittering bubbles floated upward, lighting the interior of the well as they rose. They finally made their way out and surrounded her with their multi-colored light as their melodic tinkling crescendoed. They spun around her, then went quiet, and all popped at once in a bright flash of rainbow-colored light. She shivered as she felt their little bursts of magic wash over her.

Then, it was over. The brilliant sparkling from the bubbles was gone, and Mel was left standing by a simple well beneath a dark, rainy, purple-streaked sky.

Opening her eyes, Mel leaned on the well again as she peered toward the forest. Thunder rumbled. She watched as the sky suddenly lit up with a bright flash. Not lightning this time, though; this light was a vivid, unmistakable blue. The glow quickly narrowed. Now, no longer covering the whole sky, it transformed into a thin, tall column of light, spotlighting her target with a distinctive signal that only a chromaveiled could see.

Ezmaunda's part of the task was complete.

Taking a deep breath, Mel stood up and straightened her shoulders. She shoved her drenched hair back, away from her face another time. There was no going back now. She paused for a moment, closing her eyes as she formed an image in her mind.

The rain continued its watery assault on Mel's hair and clothes as it made certain to douse every inch of her. She ignored it.

Mel's eyes abruptly popped open. Grabbing hold of her red hood, she pulled it over her head. The air around her shimmered and churned. Her skin grew wrinkled and saggy as its color faded to a light tan. The tight coils of her wet hair quickly straightened and dried; the tendrils transformed from black to silvery-white. Her eyes faded from deep brown to a pale hazel. The cloudiness of a cataract showed up, marring her right pupil. She shrank several inches, and her back twisted into a thick hunch, making her even shorter still. Her waist thickened slightly, and several of her teeth disappeared.

After the transformations of her body were finished, her simple clothes remained mostly unchanged. No sense in wasting mana on anything that wasn't strictly necessary for the disguise, and her current clothing fit the part quite nicely already. But, her red cloak faded from sight. A moment later, a black, hooded cape cropped up to take its place.

Although only she could tell, the red cloak was still lying there over the top of her clothes, invisible and waiting until she needed its help channeling another spell.

Turning to look at the well one more time, she spotted the tabby cat. He was staring up at her, pupils wide and hair standing on end.

Mel reached out a hand toward him, calling softly to the creature. He lurched backward, hissing as he put distance between the two of them.

Mel stepped back and slid her hand into the small coin pouch again. This time—instead of a coin—she withdrew a small, bronze sphere and pinched it between her fingers. It ruptured, sending out a tiny poof of metallic sparkles that rapidly dissolved into the air. A second later, a magic cloud expanded outward from her fingertips, enveloping the entire village and hanging there for a beat before vanishing. Any nosy onlookers that might have seen her transform herself would now be none the wiser. The cat—overcome by the effects of the very same memory-cleansing spell—blinked a few times. He curled up on the well beside her, closed his eyes, and resumed purring.

Mel gave the cat a few, quick pats before stepping away from the well and making her way over to the side of a nearby building. She grabbed a basket of fruit that had been forgotten there by one of the villagers. A pang of guilt coursed through her at the act. She reminded herself what was at stake that night and shoved the thought to the back of her mind. Tucking her arm through the basket's wicker handle, she hurried off into the forest and toward the blue beacon.

Moving quietly between the trees at a pace that belied her decrepit appearance, Mel glanced down at the basket and its assortment of fresh pears, apples, and peaches. She reached inside her cape and pulled out a small vial. Its green-gray contents swirled violently, changing haphazardly from liquid to gas and back again. Prying the stopper loose, she poured the ever-shifting substance over the basket and watched as it seeped into the skins of the fruits with a soft hissing sound.

The rain continued as she walked, quickly soaking her transformed clothing and hair until she looked like she had just gone for a fully-clothed swim in the river. Mel glanced down at the basket in her hands but didn't bother to shield the fruit. A little water wouldn't be able to make a difference now.

At last, through a narrow gap in the trees, she could see a small, grassy clearing up ahead with a wooden cottage at its center. The blue beacon shone brightly through the thatched rooftop. Her target was inside.

Mel paused, took a deep breath, and mentally steeled herself for what would come next. As she began walking again, she moved slowly, barely picking her feet up off the wet ground. Mud caused her feet to slip and small rocks threatened to send her tumbling to the ground, but still, she tottered slowly along. Her free hand rested against her hip as though the joint ached with every step. Shuffling out from between the trees, she hobbled up to the little house. She took another steadying breath as she stopped. Raising her gnarled, old hand, she rapped her knuckles on the wooden door, then returned her hand to her hip.

The upper half of the door creaked open an inch or so. A young woman peeked out; she was enveloped in the blue aura. All that Mel could see was a dark silhouette surrounded by the bright, rippling azure mist.

"Hello, child." Mel made certain her voice sounded weak and breathy as she slowly croaked out the words. A shiver ran through her. Though the storm's main purpose was to drive the villagers away, the slight chill from the rain added another layer of pitifulness to her disguise. "Would you be a dear and let an old woman warm herself by your fire? This storm hasn't been too kind to these aching joints."

"I shouldn't..." The blue-lit woman in the doorway hesitated, swaying slightly from one foot to the other. She'd been warned not to let strangers into the house. But something was compelling her to help this unknown visitor, though she had no idea that this urge had anything to do with the blue glow she couldn't see. She chewed on her lip, looking this old woman up and down. Finally, the last of her resolve vanished, and she swung the door open wide. "Yes, of course. Please, come in. You must be chilled to the bone."

Mel forced a smile onto her face, and she shambled across the threshold. The door softly clicked shut behind her. As the young woman's footsteps grew close, Mel turned. She sat her basket on the long, wooden table, gesturing toward it with her wrinkled hand. "I haven't much. But I must repay your kindness, child. Take some of my fruit."

"Oh, no, I couldn't—"

"I insist." Mel's heart raced, and the air felt stifling around her. She forced herself to keep her composure. And even though she was here by deceit, her next words were nothing but truth. "I could never forgive myself if you didn't take a bite."

The young woman tilted her head to the side, puzzled by the strange request. For a few long, tense heartbeats, she simply stared. At last, she nodded. She stepped forward, grabbed an apple from the basket, and wiped it with the edge of her white apron.

Mel held her breath.

Bringing the fruit to her lips, the young woman sank her teeth into the crisp, yellow-green skin. She chewed.

Not daring to move, Mel watched, rooted to the spot.

Before the target could swallow her first bite, the apple slipped from her hand. Her wide eyes darted to Mel. Her chest shook as she coughed violently, and she pressed one hand to her chest. The other flew to her throat, desperately clutching at the flesh there as if there were anything she could do to stop what was happening to her.

Reaching up with both hands, Mel grabbed hold of the invisible hood on her head, above the black cape. She pulled it back, then let go. As the transparent fabric fell onto her back, its original red color quickly seeped back into it. All the rainwater that had been dripping from her only seconds ago vanished. Her hair darkened and curled once more. Missing teeth retook their place along her gums. Her spine straightened. As her skin smoothed out and returned to its normal, darker hue, the last drop of red took its place in her long cloak.

The young woman continued gasping and choking. Tears formed in her eyes. Mel moved closer, gently took hold of the woman's elbow, and guided her onto a low bed in the corner. The young woman silently pleaded with her eyes but didn't resist as Mel guided her down onto the mattress.

Closing her eyes, the young woman gradually stopped moving, and the blue light finally faded away; the storm outside rapidly dissipated along with it. Mel stepped back and turned her eyes down toward the woman. She was tall, thin, and a few months past her nineteenth birthday. Her lips were an earthy, dark pink. Her skin was black as raven's wings. And her long, softly curled hair was white as snow.

"I'm sorry." Mel blinked quickly, fighting back the tears that suddenly threatened to fall. Then, without another word, she spun on her heel and swiped a hand through the air in front of herself. A small, circular rift opened. She hurriedly stepped through it. The portal closed behind her, and she was gone from the cottage without a trace.

2

———

"I've got an idea."

"Oh, yeah?" Mel grinned, continuing to look at the art display on the booth in front of her as she spoke.

Stepping up behind Mel and wrapping his arms around her waist, Luke pressed his cheek to hers. "Hey."

With his word tickling her ear, she giggled.

Luke gave her hand a gentle tug, and at last, she twisted around to look at him. He smiled. Pressing one hand to her lower back, Luke brought her in close. With the other, he gently caressed one of the dark coils of her hair and tucked it behind her ear.

Mel felt her cheeks grow warm as she met his dark brown eyes and smiled back. Playfully, she jabbed him in the ribs and watched him squirm. "What's your idea?"

"Our anniversary is coming up. And, well, there's a vendor back that way," Luke paused long enough to tilt his head, gesturing in the direction he was referring to, "that has some really cool, one-of-a-kind, handmade jewelry. We could see if they have any rings you like."

"Luke." Mel's face fell. Her glance darted down toward the crown on the underside of her wrist. The thin lines of the mark burned, but she'd long since grown used to the feeling. She looked back up at him as she pulled down the sleeve of her oversized hoodie, concealing the mark.

When she opened her mouth to speak once more, Mel realized how crowded the sidewalk was and how many people were watching from the corners of their eyes, trying to glean a bit of gossip. So she grabbed Luke by the hand and hurried away from the bustling craft fair. With Luke in tow, Mel hurried across the street and made her way around the corner of a building. She found a metal bench on a nearly abandoned street. It was half-shielded by a small tree and as much privacy as she could expect at the moment. Mel took a seat and pulled Luke down onto the space beside her. "I love you, Luke. And I do want to be with you forever, and I do want to marry you. But we've talked about this. I…"

As Mel's words faded into silence, Luke's expression darkened.

"Right. You can't." Luke slowly pulled his hand from Mel's grip and sighed as he leaned back. Twisting away from her, he quietly stared off toward the bustling crowds.

Mel watched Luke as he sat there. From this angle, she couldn't see the almond shape of his eyes, his wide nose, or his high cheekbones. But she knew him well enough that she could imagine how that handsome face must look as he sat there, deep in thought. The little line that was surely visible between his brows, the slight downturn of his lips, the distant look in his eyes.

Stuffing her hands into her hoodie pocket, Mel leaned back and waited for Luke to say something. She needed something—anything—to break the unbearable silence that hung between them. She couldn't give him the explanation he needed, the explanation that he'd grown more impatient to hear as year after year had passed. So, Mel sat there in tense silence, waiting for Luke to speak instead.

Mel watched him. The blue jeans and pink t-shirt Luke wore were the ones she'd bought for his last birthday, and the fit complemented his muscular physique. His tan skin had grown a shade darker over the summer, making the pale pink fabric seem even brighter than when the shirt was brand new. His shoulder-length hair was pulled into a ponytail at the base of his skull, and she longed to slide the elastic loose and let the straight black tendrils fall free. She'd like to run her fingers across his scalp, slowly massaging the skin there, like she'd always done when he was stressed. She nearly reached out to do just that when she thought better of it. Letting her hand fall into her lap, she slowly leaned back against the bench and chewed the inside of her cheek.

Minutes crept by, each one somehow slower and more painful than the last. When Mel couldn't stand it any longer, she reached out a hand toward his shoulder. She had every intention of pulling him in close and laying a kiss on his cheek, wanting more than anything to reassure him with gestures since words failed her. She loved him; she wanted to marry him. But she knew she couldn't.

Mel's skin brushed across Luke's, and he recoiled from her touch.

Tears suddenly welled up in Mel's eyes. Retracting her hand, she scooted a few inches further away, then pushed up her sleeves. She stared at her wrist, slowly running her thumb across the bright white crown symbol.

Finally, Luke leaned forward, resting his elbows on his knees and burying his face in his hands. After another long sigh, he said, "Just tell me why. At first, I thought you needed more time. But now, I really don't know. You tell me you love me, and you say you want to stay together forever. But then, *why*? Why won't you marry me? I know I shouldn't pressure you into it. Hell, I don't *want* to pressure you into it, but... can't you just help me understand your reasons? Please, Mel."

Mel closed her eyes as she bit her lip. She took a deep breath and looked over at him. "I want to. I promise I do. But I just... I can't."

"Which do you want? You want to marry me and can't? Or you want to tell me why, and you can't?"

She sighed. "Both."

"Give me anything here, Melody! Are you already married? Are you afraid to actually commit? Is there someone else you're seeing? Were you abused by an ex-husband?" Luke's hands waved through the air in front of him as he spoke, punctuating each of his words. He chuckled sarcastically. "Are you a secret government agent who's afraid of being dragged back into a life you thought you had escaped?"

Mel had to bite her tongue to stifle the sudden urge to laugh; the irony of his last question was too much. It was so absurd, yet so close to the truth that it hurt.

Luke clenched his jaw as he saw the look that passed across Mel's face.

Quickly regaining her composure, Mel gently laid a hand on his cheek and gazed into his eyes. "Both. I *want* to marry you, but I can't. And I *want* to explain why, but I can't do that either."

For a moment, Luke's expression softened, and he leaned into her caress. Then, he pulled away as his lips bent downward. "You've only ever said 'I can't.' You won't explain. I need a reason, Melody. Give me something here. Anything."

"I love you so much, Luke." Her eyes filled with tears as she stared at him. She took a deep breath to continue, but the rest of her words came out in a choked whisper. "I swear, I would tell you everything if I could. But I can't."

"Right." Luke stood up. Mel stretched a hand out toward his, but he backed away, out of her reach. He folded his arms across his chest.

"Well, *I can't* keep going with this relationship anymore if you won't open up to me. I don't think that's too much to ask."

They looked at one another. Luke's jaw was set, and even though he was trying his best to look stoic, a faint sheen of tears glimmered in his eyes. Mel's heart ached as she studied him.

"I understand. And I'm truly sorry that I can't give you what you need." Mel stood up as well and swiped the teardrops off her cheeks. She cleared her throat, straightened her shoulders, and forced her voice back to its normal volume. "Just give me a while to grab my things from the apartment, and then I'll be gone."

Luke nodded but didn't look at her as he plopped back onto the bench. Pulling his phone from his jeans pocket, he began scrolling through some random website, making a show of not noticing her continued presence. But it was obvious that he wasn't paying attention to anything on the bright, little screen that rested in his palm.

Mel turned and walked the six blocks back to the apartment. Her mind raced, and even though she didn't walk any faster than normal, it felt as if it was only a matter of seconds until she was stepping out of the elevator on the 11th floor of the apartment building. She unlocked the door, stepped inside, and collapsed onto the couch, sobbing.

Time seemed to grind to a halt while Mel sat there, clutching a pillow to her chest as she wept. As she was beginning to pull herself together and gather the nerve to start packing, she heard the sound of a key twisting in the lock. She leapt up, hurrying across the room to grab a backpack. Mel quickly swiped a hand across her cheeks. Without turning to face him, she called back over her shoulder. "Sorry, I didn't think you'd be back so soon. I'll be done in a minute."

"Hey."

Mel froze. It was definitely Luke's voice that had spoken the word, but something was off. First of all, the calm tone wasn't what she would've expected after the way they had just parted. But beyond that, such a simple greeting under the current circumstances felt unbelievably wrong. The hairs on the back of her neck stood at attention. She wanted to reach for the dagger at her hip, but she'd let her guard down and quit carrying her weapons sometime after she'd arrived on Earth all those years ago.

Taking a deep breath, Mel slowly spun around. When she caught sight of Luke, her eyes went wide, and her jaw dropped. Luke was wrapped in bright blue light and swaying slightly from side to side, looking somewhat dazed.

"Luke?"

He didn't respond.

"Luke!" Mel let the backpack fall to the floor as she walked up to Luke, grabbed him by the shoulders, and shook him roughly. When he still didn't notice, she took hold of his ponytail and yanked. Hard.

At last, Luke blinked a few times before focusing on Mel's face. He opened his mouth as if to speak, but no words came out. His eyebrows drew together, then one rose, soon followed by the other. Tilting his head up a bit, his gaze traveled across the room, twisted back to look at the door, and finally turned to face Mel once more. "What's... How did I..."

"You were..." Mel hesitated. Even if she wanted, she couldn't suddenly drop him into a world of magic spells, curses, and the chromaveiled. He had no idea that any of that existed. In fact, even if she were able to explain it, that would only lead to more questions. There wasn't time for that. She had to get him out of there. "You were drugged."

It wasn't really the truth. But it was as close to the truth as she could give right now.

"What?"

"You were drugged." Mel grabbed Luke's wrist and pulled him into the kitchen, forcing him onto one of the tall, wooden barstools that waited there. Reaching underneath the drawer beside the sink, she slid her hand along the bottom of the wood until her fingertips found what she was searching for. As Mel straightened up, she pulled out two daggers, each with elaborately carved wooden handles and simple leather sheaths. She tucked one into her sock so the handle stuck up above the top of her sneaker. The other, she fastened to her hip.

Hurrying across the room, she went over to a cabinet, grabbed a canvas bag, and began stuffing it with plastic bottles of water. "Do you remember talking to anyone? Seeing anything unusual?"

"I…" Luke's gaze went distant another time.

"Luke!"

"Hmm? Oh." Luke gave his head a vigorous shake, then rubbed the heels of his hands across his eyes. When he at last looked up again, he seemed to truly see her. His expression went sour, but he continued with his story anyway. "I was alone on the bench. And all of a sudden, some woman was there—like she appeared out of thin air—and her hand was brushing across my cheek. She said… something. I don't know what. I just remember thinking her accent sounded a lot like yours."

Mel's heart plummeted. The blue column of light was confirmation enough, but somehow, hearing it put into words made it feel all the more real. She swallowed hard as she faced him. Setting the full canvas bag on the table, Mel dug her fingernails into the palms of her hands and clung to the tiny sliver of hope that told her this wasn't really happening. "Did you notice anything odd about her clothes? Any tattoos? Was anybody else with her?"

"Yeah. She…" Luke narrowed his eyes at Mel, though she could barely tell it through the blue haze that enveloped him. "She was wearing a blue cloak and a dress. Seemed like she was headed to a Ren Faire or something. And some man was standing on the sidewalk, just watching us. He was leaning against the corner of the building at the end of the block. I didn't really pay much attention to him, but I did think it was weird that he had a cloak on also. His was green, though."

"Did the woman have a scar across her cheek?"

Luke's head slowly moved up and down. "You *know* these people?"

"Yes. Babe—"

Luke stiffened as the word slipped past Mel's lips. Realizing her mistake, Mel winced. After so long together, it would take a while to adjust.

Exhaling unsteadily, Mel spoke up. "Luke, I'm really sorry. And I know you're pissed at me and don't want to be around me right now. But please, *please*, just trust me for a little bit longer. Go throw some clothes and your toothbrush in your backpack. We have to go."

Luke folded his arms across his chest and didn't get up.

"Please, Luke!" Mel's eyes darted toward the window. "We have to go. Now!"

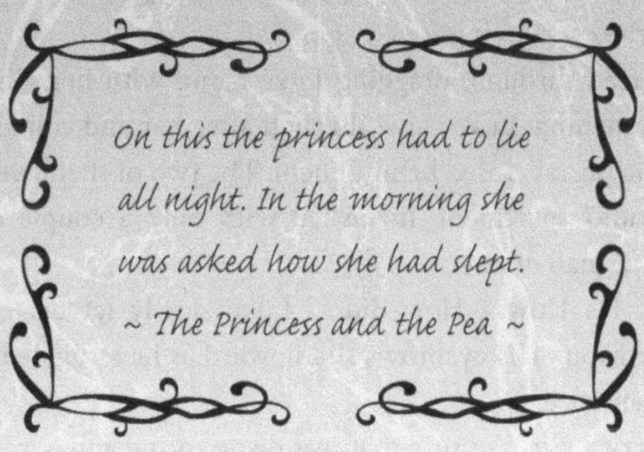

3

"What the hell is going on right now, Melody?!" Luke stood so quickly, his barstool tumbled backward and crashed onto the tiled floor behind him. He winced. Closing his eyes, he drew in a deep breath and exhaled heavily. With a clenched jaw, he stared at her. "How the hell can I trust you now? You cut my heart out, and now, on top of that, I find out that you've been lying to me this whole time? Who are you? Why sh—"

"I promise you can rip me a new one later. But please, Luke, just trust me for one more day. Right now, we have to go."

"No." Luke sighed. "It's time for you to tell—"

"They're here." Mel's wide eyes darted toward the door. She could feel their presence moving closer by the second. They were hurrying up the stairs, leaning their ears against doors, heading down hallways, and then coming back another time. The walls hid the narrow column of blue from the pursuers' view, but with the light extending up through the rooftop, they knew full well that he was somewhere in the building.

"Huh?"

Before Luke could turn around to see where she was looking, Mel grabbed him by the wrist and quickly swiped her other hand through the air. A rift tore in the space in front of her, showing a view of a nearly empty room.

"What the ever-loving f—"

Mel darted through, dragging Luke along with her. She stepped out of the opening. Luke came through after her and collapsed to his knees as the portal closed behind them. The two of them were now in a small studio apartment, furnished with only a couple of folding chairs and a small dresser.

"Wha… I… How… How did…" Luke slowly let his eyes travel around the room. His eyebrows slid upward as he struggled to form a coherent sentence.

"I'm sorry, Luke. I'm sure that was disorienting and confusing, and I can't even imagine all the thoughts that must be running through your head right now." Mel dropped to her knees in front of him and tilted his chin until his eyes met hers. "I swear I will start explaining everything tomorrow. I just can't yet."

"No, Melody!" Luke pushed himself to his feet and walked to one of the chairs. Putting his hands on his head, he shoved his fingertips into his hair and slowly dragged them through the dark locks, loosening the ponytail holder. Luke ignored the elastic as it dropped to the floor, and he lowered himself into one of the waiting chairs.

Letting his hands fall into his lap, he leaned forward, looking down at the floor as his hair shifted to block the view of his face. "No more lies and stalling. Just tell me what the hell is happening."

Mel sighed. Scooting over in front of Luke's chair, she looked up at him but couldn't see his eyes through the layer of hair and the bright blue column that still surrounded him. "I'm… not from here. And I have some very powerful enemies. They've marked you so that they can find me. And if we don't get out of here soon… I don't know what they'll do to you. Or me."

Luke's only response was to let out a low growl.

"I know it's not enough information! I swear I'm trying! I *can't* tell you. Not here."

When Luke didn't acknowledge her comment, Mel grabbed him by the chin and forced him to look at her. "I'm a chro—" The half-formed word died, and her mouth suddenly clamped shut. Her cheeks darkened as blood rushed to them. Tears seeped out, clinging desperately to her lashes as air refused to go into her lungs. She tried to swallow, but it felt like something was lodged in there, something sharp and jagged thoroughly blocking her throat.

"Mel?" Luke half stood, shoving the chair away before dropping onto the floor in front of her. He grabbed her by the shoulders. "What's happening, Mel? What do I need to do?"

Gasping loudly, Mel suddenly drew in a deep breath and started coughing. Luke twisted around until he was seated at her side. He rubbed slow circles along her back. When the coughing fit finally abated, Luke wrapped one arm around her and pulled her in close as he used his other hand to wipe away her tears.

The pair sat in silence for a long while as Mel caught her breath and got her racing heart back under control. Mel tilted her head up toward him. She leaned forward. The scent of his cologne hung in the air.

Luke slid his hand until it cupped the back of her head, and he inched closer, gently pulling her face toward his. His eyes moved toward her lips as he shifted closer.

Without warning, Luke turned away and pushed himself to his feet. "So, when you said you can't tell me..." He glanced at her, cleared his throat, and moved halfway across the room before continuing. "You, uh, really can't tell me what's going on. Like, you literally cannot tell me, can you?"

Standing up, Mel bit her lip and avoided his gaze by pretending to study a small cut on the side of her thumb. "Right. But, Luke, we have to get out of here. It won't be long until they realize... Well, they probably already have realized we aren't in your apartment anymore, and they're most likely already making their way over here."

Luke nodded even though his brows were still furrowed. He folded his arms across his chest. As Luke stood there staring at her, his eyes gradually unfocused. He swayed unsteadily from one foot to the other. Mel moved over and snapped her fingers right in front of his nose.

"What's..." His attention jerked to her and he shook his head rapidly, then cleared his throat. He blinked at her a few times as he found his words. "Shit. I'd ask who is after us and where we are, but I'm sure you can't tell me that either."

"The first one, no. But I can tell you where we are, at least. We're in the building across the street from your apartment."

Luke moved toward the window, reaching out to pull the curtains back and see for himself. But Mel grabbed him by the arm and stopped him.

"Sorry." She quickly pulled her hand away. "It's easy enough for them to figure out which building we're in. If you go sticking your face up to the window, they'll have no trouble figuring out which floor and room too."

"How can they..." Luke shook his head and let out a huff. "Right, you can't tell me. Okay, how about this? How come if you can do... that thing... that teleportation thing, how come you only took us this far instead of, like, I don't know... Egypt or something? That'd have to be better for hiding than the building across the damn street."

Mel turned and stared into the distance, unsure how she could explain without being forcibly silenced again. Finally, she twisted back toward him and blurted out, "How far can you throw a baseball?"

"Hell if I know. Why? What does that have to do with anything?"

"I can't directly answer you, but if you figure it out…"

"Fine." Luke sighed as he looked away, shaking his head. Eventually, he turned back to her once more. "I have no idea. A couple hundred feet?"

"Okay. So why can't you throw it half a mile? Or farther?"

"I don't know. Limits to the laws of physics, I guess? Not enough strength?"

Mel raised her eyebrows and nodded slowly at him. "So, physics and strength limitations mean you'd never be able to throw something all the way from here to Egypt, right?"

"Makes sense, I guess." Luke let out a slight chuckle. "As much as any of this can make sense anyway."

"I know this is a lot, and I know it's all insane and overwhelming. But we need to get moving before they catch up. I swear, I'll explain it all as soon as I can."

"Fine." Luke sighed. "Let's go."

Mel nodded. She swiped a hand through the air. A small circle opened in front of her and they could see an abandoned parking garage. Taking Luke by the hand, she walked through, and he followed with far less resistance than the last time. As he stepped up beside her, she could feel the slight tremble in his hand, but he didn't speak. The portal sealed itself behind them.

Drawing in a deep breath, Mel swiped the air again to form another rift. This time, they stepped through and came out into the disused walk-in freezer of an old, abandoned restaurant. Her heart was pounding, and her hand was beginning to shake as her mana reserves lowered with each spell. She ignored the strange "empty" sensation and opened one more portal. They stepped through into an unoccupied hotel room.

As this last portal closed, Mel's knees gave out, and she collapsed, breathing heavily. Luke dropped down beside her, lifting her chin up so she was facing him. "What's going on? You okay?"

Mel silently bobbed her head up and down. Pushing herself up off the carpet, she managed to drag her body up onto the bed. She met Luke's eyes and lifted her hands to either side of her head.

Finally, she was able to catch her breath. "Don't freak out."

"What are you going to do now that's crazier than..." Luke gestured vaguely toward the center of the room where they'd arrived a moment earlier.

Mel didn't answer. Instead, she grabbed the invisible hood and lowered it to her back. The color slowly seeped back into the cloak's fabric, originating at the center and working its way outward until the blood-red color was fully restored.

"Where the hell did *that* come from?"

"The cloak? I've had it pretty much my whole life. I've just kept it hidden whenever anyone's around."

Luke gaped at her.

"We're staying here tonight." She patted a spot on the bed at her side. "Come over here."

He didn't respond right away. Finally, he snapped out of his stupor. "I don't think that's a good idea, Melody."

"What? Oh." Mel's cheeks warmed. "Oh, good grief. Not *that*. I'll explain tomorrow, along with everything else. But for now, please just trust me. You need to be under this cloak."

"Oh."

It was Luke's turn to blush. He walked over and sank onto the mattress beside her. Mel grabbed a corner of the cloak and extended her arm behind him. Then she waited a moment until the fabric grew large enough to cover them both and laid the end of the red garment around his back. She smiled as the blue glow surrounding him was snuffed out.

"Thank the stars above. That actually worked."

"What worked?"

"The cloak took the mark off you. They can't track you with it now."

Luke's brows knitted together as he watched her from the corner of his eye. "Sure..."

"By the way, um," Mel drew a deep breath before continuing, "my name's not actually Melody."

"What?" Luke's head jerked toward her. He glared. "You lied to me about your name too? You couldn't even tell me your *name*?"

Mel squeezed her eyes closed.

Folding his arms across his chest, Luke said. "I suppose you can't tell me what that is either?"

Looking into his dark eyes, Mel sighed. "Melzia."

"Is that really the truth? If you're stopped from telling me anything, why aren't you prevented from sharing that?"

"That's... not part of what is shielded by the..." Pausing, Mel gestured vaguely at her mouth and throat. "The thing that prevents me from telling. It's just that I've been in hiding. You think I can go around telling everyone my real name and not get caught? It's not exactly a common name here."

"Yeah, but," Luke's shoulders drooped. The anger vanished, this time replaced by deep hurt. "You couldn't even tell *me*? You didn't have to broadcast it to everyone, but... don't you trust me after all these years? Is that why you won't—"

"Luke," Mel cut off his words and reached out to cup his cheek with her hand. When he pulled back, she let her hand fall into her lap. "I do trust you. I swear I do. But if I had told you my name wasn't real, would you have accepted that at face value? Or would that have led to a million other questions I couldn't answer?"

"Hmph."

Mel nodded, then quietly pulled the cloak off of Luke. The fabric slipped from his shoulder and shrank back to its normal size, and for a moment, everything seemed fine. But slowly, steadily, the blue light returned as bright as it ever was. He swayed slightly as the mesmerization retook its hold. Mel's face fell.

Untying the cloak string from around her neck, Mel took it off of her own back. Leaning over, she draped the red cloth across Luke's shoulders alone and tied the string around his neck. The blue light didn't go away this time, and the fabric seemed to unfasten itself and become liquid as it slid down his back, landing in a heap on the bed behind him.

She closed her eyes and sighed. Silently, Mel returned the cloak to her own back and tucked one edge around Luke, the same as she'd done the first time. The light vanished again.

He was looking at her, a broken heart and a million questions evident in his eyes. She was looking at him, wishing things could be different.

It was going to be a very long night.

4

*L*uke tossed and turned throughout the night beneath the shared red fabric, only managing to doze off for several short, unsatisfying naps. During a few of the brief bouts of unconsciousness, his arm had found its way around Mel's waist. But each time, as soon as he awoke, he quickly pulled away.

Mel spent the dark nighttime hours lying on her side, staring at the wall as she tried to force herself to get some sleep. She could feel

Luke's warmth and the way the mattress sank slightly underneath his weight, creating a low valley that fought to pull her closer every time he moved. She could hear his steady breathing. And she could've sworn there was a clock somewhere nearby, slowly ticking away the seconds until dawn and threatening to drive her insane. But the only clock in the room was the digital alarm that sat on the nightstand on Luke's side of the bed.

As the first rays of sunshine peeked through the ridiculously wide gap in the hideous maroon and brown striped curtains, Mel slowly rolled onto her back. She turned her head to look at Luke. His face was already angled toward her, his bloodshot eyes half-open.

"Hey." Luke yawned loudly. "You able to get any sleep?"

"No, not really. You?" Mel longed to reach out and brush the hair off his face and tuck it behind his ear, the same way she did most mornings. Instead, she slid her arms down and tucked her hands into her pockets.

"Couple minutes here and there."

The room lapsed into awkward silence. Luke gently tapped his fingertips against his chest as he turned and let his eyes slowly travel across the room. "So."

"So." Mel pushed herself upright and twisted to face Luke.

"Melody? Er, wait." As he lay there, the little wrinkle between his eyebrows deepened, and his mouth angled down ever so slightly. "What did you say it was?"

"Melzia. But you can keep calling me Melody if you want, though." She grinned at him. "I always liked that name."

Luke's frown deepened into a scowl. He turned his face away.

Quickly blinking the sudden tears away, Mel cleared her throat. "We'd better get going. We'll have to skip breakfast, but at least we have…" She let out a low growl. "Drenkth!"

With his mouth half-open, Luke turned to her and raised an eyebrow.

Mel saw the look from the corner of her eye. "Sorry. I filled that bag with water to take with us and then left it all on the table. I wasn't nearly prepared to leave when they made it into the apartment building, but I thought I could at least do that much."

"Okay, first of all, you had a whole damn escape path planned out. If that was you *unprepared*, I can't imagine what *prepared* looks like." Luke twisted around to get a better look at her, then paused, tilting his head as he rubbed one palm across his jaw. "But that wasn't what surprised me. I've never heard you say a word like that before."

"Hmm? Oh, drenkth? It's a curse word in… one of the languages in the place where I'm originally from."

"And where you're from *isn't* actually Ireland, I'm assuming." Luke turned to look up at the ceiling as he slowly shook his head. Taking a deep breath, he brought his attention back to her. "Anyway, I guessed it was some kind of cuss word from context. I was just shocked. I've never heard you talk like that in the past. Ever."

"Oh." Mel bit her lip. "I guess I don't curse. Not in English, at least. The English counterparts never really felt right to me. And no, I'm not from Ireland. You heard my accent when we met and made an assumption. I just… never denied it."

"Hmm." The corners of his mouth twitched downward slightly before he schooled his features. Sitting up and moving over to the edge of the bed with the cloak still clinging to his back, he stared at the floor. "So, what now?"

"Stand up and grab my hand. I need to test something. Try not to panic."

Standing up simultaneously, the cloak obediently stayed around both their shoulders, in spite of the fact that Luke stood several inches taller than her.

Luke grasped her fingers in his. Reaching up with her free hand, Mel grabbed the hood of the cloak and put it over her head. The air shimmered. Mel looked down at their joined hands, and Luke's gaze followed hers. She sighed in relief even though a faint twinge of pain made itself known behind her forehead.

The skin on Luke's right hand had become neon green. His eyes went wide, and he yelped as he yanked his fingers from her grip. The color of his skin lasted for several seconds more until it finally returned to its normal hue. He gawked at her.

"Right. Well, the cloak alone isn't enough to keep it going, but I can manage it at least. As long as we stay in contact."

"Manage *what*, exactly?"

"To keep you disguised. We've got to get to the border."

"*What?* What border? We're nowhere close to any major borders. And why?" Luke stepped away, shoving the cloak from his shoulders. It quickly shrank back to its normal size as he watched. The blue light quickly blossomed around him."When are you going to actually explain anything?"

Sighing, Mel stepped closer to him, ignoring the annoyed look he was giving her. "It's not a border you've ever seen or heard of. And yes, we are close to it. As for why? Well, firstly, that's where we can get the mark removed from you. Secondly, once we get across the border, that's when I can actually give you real explanations. And please keep the cloak on."

"Fine. Now, can you at least tell me why you said not to freak out with zero warning of what to expect and then went and picked that ungodly, bright freaking green?"

Mel sank her fingernails into her palms in an attempt to subdue her laughter. It took her a couple seconds before she managed to get her amusement under control; when she did, she had to choose her words carefully. "It's a hard color to fake. I figured if I could do that, anything else I did to disguise you would be easy."

"You could've warned me."

"Babe—" She took a deep breath and started anew. "Sorry. Luke, I did warn you. I know it wasn't the most helpful warning, but it's all I could do, considering."

Luke sighed dramatically. "Fine. Now what?"

"We disguise ourselves and walk to the border. You'll have to keep holding my hand the whole time, though. Otherwise, it'll fade away." She paused to look him in the eyes as she fanned the cloak out until it expanded far enough once again to cover both of their backs. "Are you ready? We're both going to look a lot different, but I promise, no green this time."

Nodding, Luke stuck his hand out to his side and let her take it. She pulled the hood up over her head. A moment later, Luke shrunk a few inches in both height and width. His skin darkened by several shades. His hair color and texture stayed the same, but the overall length was reduced to only a few inches.

Mel got taller until she was standing a bit higher than Luke. Her skin lightened until it was practically translucent. Hundreds of little, light brown dots covered her nose and cheeks, painting tiny constellations across her fair skin. Her hair changed into a pale red color and lengthened until it ran midway down her back in delicate waves. The crown emblem on her wrist darkened so that it was still clearly visible on her skin, and since she couldn't do anything to remove the indelible mark, she made sure her sleeve would keep it concealed.

Next came the clothes, but she didn't want to expend much energy on them. The same clothes they were already wearing expanded or contracted as needed until they fit their owners' new bodies, and the fabric colors changed to deep blues and grays. Finally, the red cloak became invisible, and stillness returned to the air.

"Whoa." Luke was staring at the wall mirror, slowly waving, waggling his fingers, and angling his head this way and that, inspecting his new, unfamiliar reflection.

"I know. It's weird the first few times." Mel chuckled as she remembered the feeling she'd had when she'd initially discovered this ability. She forced her thoughts back into the present. "We'd better get going."

Still gaping at his own reflection, Luke nodded.

Mel walked out of the hotel room and into the hallway with Luke behind her, clasping her hand. As the door slowly swung closed behind them, Mel stopped and pinched the bridge of her nose. She could already feel her mana supply dwindling and the tension building between her eyes. She had done hundreds—maybe thousands —of transformations in her lifetime, but this was the first time she'd ever extended that ability to another person. Besides that, it had been years since she'd done a full body transformation. Either or both of those could be the cause for the rapidly lowering supply. In fact, she even wondered if being on Earth might have something to do with it. Whatever the cause, it didn't matter since she couldn't do anything about it.

Straightening her shoulders and doing her best to ignore the increasing pain, Mel set off down the hallway with Luke in tow. Within a matter of minutes, they'd made it down the stairs, across the lobby, and to the front doors.

As they stepped across the threshold and onto the sidewalk, the morning sun met them with full force. Mel winced, squeezing her eyes shut tight. Her feet froze in place, and she leaned precariously to one side.

Luke turned to look at her. "What's wrong?"

Slowly opening one eye and then the other, she looked at his face. "Maintaining this," she tilted her head down, gesturing at their appearances, "is draining my power really fast and giving me an awful headache. I'm not sure how long I can keep it up."

"Here." Luke loosened his hand from her grip. Moving cautiously —making sure his touch never left contact with her—he slid his hand up her arm, over her shoulder, and down to her lower back. He let his arm slide toward the narrow curve at her waist and settled his hand on her hip bone. "Lean on me. Just tell me which way to go."

Mel's knees went weak as she looped her arm around him.

Luke helped her steady herself. "You okay?"

"Yeah." Mel turned away. She hoped he would assume the sudden weakness was due to the strain of the spell rather than the warm caress of his skin on hers. She pointed off to the left. "That way, three blocks, then cross the street in front of the bakery."

Nodding, Luke stepped forward, ready to make their way to the other side of the street.

"No. Don't cross here. We have to go that way first."

With one eyebrow raised, Luke twisted to stare at her.

"Sorry. It's..." She hesitated, unsure of how she could explain. "Well, it's part of how the border stays hidden. You can only get there by following very specific instructions along a certain path. This way, the odds of someone accidentally discovering it are almost non-existent."

Luke glanced up the sidewalk in the direction she indicated, then crinkled his brow, watching her from the corner of his eye.

"Please, Luke, trust me for a little longer. I can't keep this up forever."

He grumbled but turned to walk in the indicated direction. Three blocks later, the duo crossed the street. As they stepped back onto the sidewalk, Luke looked over to ask what to do next. His eyes bulged. The right half of Mel's hair was changing back to its normal black and coily style while one of her irises flickered from green to brown and back over and over.

"Your, um... Your eye and hair..."

"Get us into the alley. I can't keep the disguise going much longer."

They moved quickly around the corner, and Mel let the enchantment disintegrate. The air shimmered for a moment, and Mel's looks quickly returned to normal. Luke's transformation lingered another twenty seconds till it faded away as well.

Mel's heart was pounding. Sweat beaded on her brow, and she felt as if she couldn't quite pull enough air into her lungs. She gestured to a door on the opposite side of the alley, and Luke helped her over.

Raising a fist, she rapped her knuckles on the door in a deliberate, specific cadence. *Dnt-dnt. Dnt-dnt-dnt. Dnt. Dnt-dnt.* The metal door swung open, seemingly of its own accord, and they stepped into the building.

Mel pointed down the hallway. "Elevator up to the fourth floor. Then we'll have to walk down the stairs to the third."

"You've got to be kidding me." Luke scrunched up his face and huffed as he turned toward her.

"I'm sorry!" Her eyebrows shot up toward the top of her forehead.

She shrugged exaggeratedly. "I'm not the one who made up the rules! I don't know what you want me to do about it."

Sighing loudly, Luke turned and helped Mel down the hallway and into the elevator. A minute later, they stepped out onto the fourth floor and took the stairs down one level. Then at Mel's direction, they stepped up to apartment number 302.

"Now what?"

Mel didn't answer. Instead, she simply reached out, twisted the knob, and stepped inside, pulling Luke along with her and letting the door close behind them both.

5

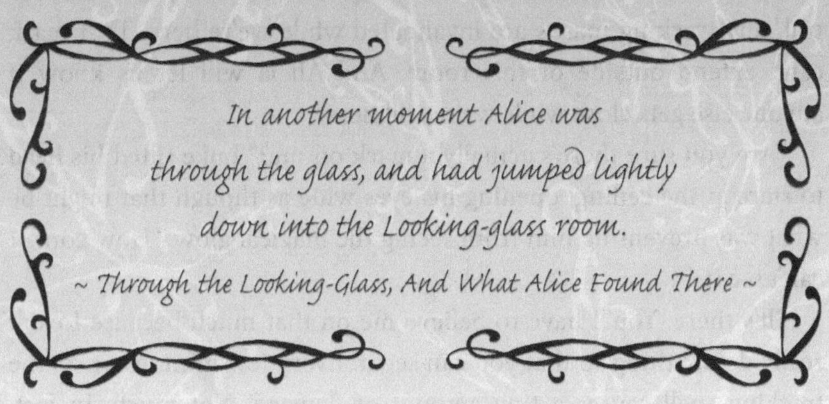

The room was much longer than could actually fit inside this particular building. The right wall was a simple, unadorned white. But the left wall was lined with moving images, almost like television screens, each flicking through different channels. There weren't actually any screens, though; the images simply floated there, only an inch away from the wall's surface. As Luke gawked at all the various people going about their business in the silent images—people walking, talking, dancing, playing, crying—the "screens" all went blank and disappeared; the wall suddenly seemed like any ordinary white wall.

"Luke?"

His eyes found Mel.

"I'll be okay now that I don't have to maintain that spell anymore. Thank you for your help. And we're in a neutral place here. You don't have to stay in the cloak." Mel's grin faltered. "Or keep touching me if you don't want to."

"Oh." Luke hesitated for a moment before slowly sliding his hand away. He stuffed his fists down into his jeans pockets and stood there, awkwardly looking anywhere except at her.

Mel slid the cloak off Luke's shoulders and stepped away. "The mark is still on you, but since transition zones are designated as 'neutral,' any tracking marks are invalidated while we're here. That mark can't extend outside of this room. And Alicia will let us know if anyone else gets close while we're still here."

"Are you sure there's actually a mark on me?" Luke tilted his head to stare at the ceiling, opening his eyes wide as though that might be what was preventing him from seeing the magical glow. "How come I can't see it?"

"It's there. You'll have to believe me on that much because I can't really do anything so that you can see it. Every few minutes or so, the tracking spell causes a tiny amount of damage. Not much. In fact, you'll likely never notice it. And then, before your body has a chance to fully recover, it hurts you a bit more. We chromaveiled can see the damage caused by certain types of magic. Like that tracking spell."

"Ah." Luke was looking at her quizzically, his mouth moving ever so slightly, as if all his questions were bubbling up too rapidly in his mind to choose which one to ask next.

"I'm guessing one of those things you haven't found the words to articulate yet is, 'Why are you suddenly able to tell me this?'"

He nodded.

"Again, neutral zone. The typical curse restrictions don't apply here."

"Sure." He dragged the word out as he squinted at her.

"I know you have a million more questions, but—"

"Yeah, like, how did you know that hotel room would be empty? What if we'd popped into a room with a couple of strangers?"

"Right before I came to Earth, I—"

"Wait, what? 'Before you came to Earth?' What the hell is that supposed to mean? Are you telling me you're an *alien*?"

"No. Well… I mean, I guess technically I am an 'alien' even though I'm human. But, Luke, please just listen to me. I know it's a lot. Prior to coming here, I stole some enchantment vials. One of them was a hiding enchantment. I used it to hide all those places we portaled to."

Luke looked at Mel like she'd started speaking an entirely new language. She sighed another time. "When you use one of those hiding enchantments, no one but the caster can find whatever was concealed by the spell. No one besides me would even know it was there. I used the enchantment as soon as I came here in case I ever needed to make an escape."

One eyebrow slid up Luke's forehead as he stared at her with his jaw hanging open.

"Anyway, like I was saying, I know you've got tons more questions, but they're going to have to wait a little bit longer. I really have to use the bathroom, and that's going to be far easier to do now while you're not stuck sharing my cloak with me. And the sooner we get across the border, the sooner I can put an end to this whole debacle."

"Okay."

"Wait here." Without hanging around for a response, Mel turned and walked off into another section of the apartment. As the bathroom door softly clicked shut behind her, the sound reverberated across the cavernous room.

Exhaling heavily, Mel leaned back against the bathroom door, squeezed her eyes shut, and let her chin sink onto her chest. The skin along her lower back still felt warm and tingly where Luke's arm had been around her. She tried to swallow, but the lump in her throat was making that difficult.

Drawing a long, shaky breath, Mel walked over to the sink and splashed a handful of cold water on her face. She told herself that the most important thing for the moment was making sure Luke was safe. Straightening her shoulders as she took in her appearance in the mirror, she reminded herself there would be time to fall apart later.

Quickly finishing her business, she washed her hands and pulled the door open.

"How is there a door made of water? And what's the point of that one door that's so small your hand couldn't even fit into it? Why is there a rabbit hopping around here wearing a vest?" Luke's eyes were wide, and he was breathing rapidly as the pitch of his voice rose with every question. "And *how* is a tunnel—made of and surrounded by dirt —going down through the tiled floor of a third-freaking-story apartment?!"

Mel blinked rapidly as her feet froze in place. She hadn't expected Luke to be standing there, inches from the bathroom door, ready to bombard her with questions the instant she stepped into view. Reaching out, she placed her cool hands on each side of his face. "Deep breaths. I know this is an insane situation to try to wrap your head around, and the craziness of this is all beginning to catch up with you. I'm going to do my best to answer everything for you. But please, try not to freak out."

Luke stared into her eyes as he slowly got his breathing back under control. Letting his eyelids slide closed, he relaxed slightly, tilting his head to one side and letting his cheek sink into her palm. Eventually, he looked at her once more and nodded. "Thanks. I'm just going to…" Looking over Mel's shoulder, he pointed toward the bathroom.

Scooting aside, Mel let Luke slip past her and watched as he closed the door. She leaned on the wall, trying to gather her thoughts, trying desperately to figure out how to explain everything she'd kept hidden ever since she stepped foot on Earth eight years ago. Her mind was an incoherent mess as she stood there, waiting for him to reemerge. When at last, the door swung open again and Luke stepped out, Mel grabbed his hand and pulled him into a small kitchen. She guided him into a seat at the table and then sat down across from him. Turning toward an empty corner of the room, she called out, "Alicia?"

Luke jumped as a woman suddenly popped into existence next to Mel.

"Hey, Melz!"

Mel beamed. "Hey."

The newcomer leaned over and threw her arms around Mel's neck. Her hair was reddish-blonde and styled into a spiked pixie cut. Her clothing was an eclectic mixture: a t-shirt with white, orange, and green stripes running diagonally across it; a wide, green leather bracelet on each wrist; blue denim shorts; and a pair of lace-up, maroon boots that came up slightly above her knees. Her face was plain, unremarkable. Her unlined peach skin, short stature, high-pitched voice, and odd sense of fashion gave her the appearance of being no more than 14 years old.

"Hey, how are things with you? It's been a minute!" Alicia pulled out of the hug and took a step backward.

"Yeah, it has been. I'm sorry." Mel sighed, "I've been laying low for a while now."

"I know."

For a split second, Mel's eyes slid toward the wall where the moving images had been a few moments ago. Laughing lightly, she brought her focus back to Alicia. "Right. Anyway, Alicia, this is Luke. Luke, Alicia. She's one of the gatekeepers."

"Oh." Luke robotically stuck out his hand toward her.

Grinning, Alicia enthusiastically shook his hand. "It's great to finally meet you in person, Luke. I'd wondered if I'd ever get to."

Luke opened his mouth to respond, but Mel spoke up without giving him the opportunity.

"Hopefully I can come back and catch up with you soon, but we really have to get through and find a way to remove his tracking mark before we're found."

"Ah." Alicia let the word drag out to emphasize her disappointment and then, as if that weren't enough, stuck out her lower lip and widened her eyes at Mel. The look only lasted for a second, though, before she was giggling again. "Alright, I won't hold you up, then."

"Mind if we raid the fridge? We had to get out in a hurry, and I'm starving."

"Help yourselves. I'll be waiting by the gates when you're ready." Before either of them could respond, Alicia disappeared.

"Alicia's one of the gatekeepers. She controls the gateways from Earth to each of the other realms." Mel walked over to the cupboard, grabbed a couple glasses, and filled them with water. After setting them down in front of Luke, she pulled out a couple of spoons and two small containers of yogurt before making her way back over to the table. She plopped down into her seat. "Eat up. Running on no sleep and an empty stomach isn't going to make this whole ordeal any easier."

Luke slowly stretched out his hand and took the food without ever letting his eyes leave Mel's face.

Mel plunged her spoon into the yogurt and scooped out a large bite. Once she swallowed, she continued. "That dirt tunnel and the water door you saw? Along with all the others, those are the gates to the other realms."

Fidgeting in his seat, Luke stared at her. "So, which… Why is… I…"

"I get it. It's going to take a while to organize your thoughts into the questions you want to ask. For now, you just need to know that you were marked because Queen is after me. And since she knows you're important to me, she's decided to come after you. We have to get back to my home world to get the mark removed before they find us."

Luke shoved the spoon into his yogurt and then let go, folding his arms together. "Why mark *me*, though? Why wouldn't they just mark *you*?"

"The cloak prevents it. That's why I was able to at least shield you when we were both wrapped in it." Mel took a long drink of water. "But please, eat. And drink that water, too. We've got a long way to go and no supplies."

Luke obediently downed the entire cup of water in one long swig, then shoved a spoonful of yogurt into his mouth.

"But the cloak is bound to me. So, when I tried to have you wear it all by yourself, it didn't do anything to stop the mark. That's why I had to wear the cloak along with you."

"What are you even talking about when you bring up this 'mark' that's supposedly on me? I can't see—"

"Hey, guys."

Luke jumped and twisted in his seat. Alicia was suddenly standing at the edge of the table, looking at Mel.

"I don't mean to interrupt, but two chromas have entered the path that leads here. They'll be here in a couple minutes. I'll set the gate up to take you to the exit on Lozeriokt."

"Thanks." Mel tossed back the last of her water and stood up. "Come on, Luke. We've got to get across before they get here."

Alicia vanished.

Mel took hold of Luke's hand and guided him out of his chair. Then, spinning around, she hurried out of the kitchen and across the impossibly long room with him trailing behind her.

Already waiting for them next to the gateway, Alicia said, "It was good seeing you again, Melz. Come back as soon as you can, and we'll catch up for real!"

Mel nodded, then gave Alicia a quick hug. As they let go of one another, Alicia moved off to the side. Mel threw one side of the cloak around Luke's shoulders.

Still guiding Luke by the hand, Mel stepped off to the right and stopped in front of an elaborately decorated mirror that was mounted along the wall near the corner. She looked into it to meet the gaze of Luke's reflection. "Are you ready?"

From the corner of her eye, Mel saw Luke beside her speak the words, "For what?"

But his reflection didn't respond the same way. Instead, the reflection's lip curled up in a mischievous grin, and it silently mouthed the words, "Not in the slightest."

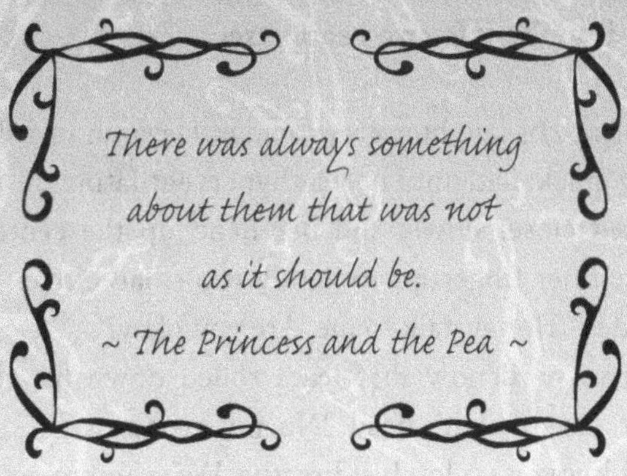

6

Mel stepped out the other side of the mirror and down onto the dirt footpath, still clutching Luke's hand. As he followed her through, she twisted around to watch his expression. His mouth was hanging open. He slowly surveyed their surroundings with wide eyes. Half a dozen deep, horizontal lines formed across his forehead as his eyebrows slid toward his hairline.

Luke slipped his hand out from Mel's and gently patted his chest, his hips, his face, almost as though he couldn't be sure if he were real anymore. He stood quietly, blinking a few times until his gaze finally landed on Mel. "Now we're... Um... We're not on Earth anymore, are we?"

"No. We're actually not even in the same galaxy. We're on Fenglauria; it's the world where I was originally from. Soon, we'll start walking and cross the border into The Westerlands. More specifically, we're headed to the city of Liebrahnt."

Luke slowly nodded as he glanced back at the gateway they had walked through a moment ago. From this side, it didn't look like a mirror. The path they were standing on simply ended beneath a patch of rippling air that looked like waves of heat rising off blacktop on a summer day. Through it, they could only see a blurry green patch, the distorted image of the foliage that grew behind it.

Without warning, Luke burst into laughter, cackling so loudly that a flock of birds took off from a nearby tree.

"Luke?"

No response. His laughter grew louder. He spun in a slow circle as his breathing quickened until he was hyperventilating.

Mel moved close, slowly slid her hand up the center of Luke's back, and used her fingertips to gently rub small circles between his shoulder blades. "Honey, talk to me. Are you okay?"

Laughing so hard now that tears rolled down his cheeks, Luke looked at her and shook his head. "No, not even close."

"Alright. I know it's a lot. Just breathe. We've got to get out of sight before the others come through and catch us here. Alicia's a good friend, and she won't intentionally give us away. But she really won't be able to stall them for very long."

Luke bent down, placing his hands on his knees as he focused on slowly inhaling and exhaling. Gradually, he quieted. As his racing heart finally slowed to normal, he wiped his sweaty palms across his jeans.

With her free hand, Mel swiped her fingers across the air in front of herself. A small portal opened, flickered a bit, and then petered out entirely.

"Drenkth!" Mel stamped her foot in punctuation, then pressed a hand to her forehead as she swayed to one side. Focusing on her balance, she inhaled deeply, making sure she wasn't going to topple over. Then, grabbing Luke by the elbow, she hurried them both off the path and into the nearby bushes. "We've got to get a move on. I'm nearly drained. I definitely don't have enough mana to open a portal, and they'll…"

Mel peeked back over her shoulder at the gateway as it started to shift. The rippling air twisted, writhed, and churned like water on the brink of boiling. Shoving Luke further into the overgrown foliage, she dove in after him and twisted around to steady the leaf-covered branches they had just darted through. Luke opened his mouth, and Mel quickly clamped her hand over it. The cloak was still magically wrapped around them both, keeping them in close proximity and preventing the blue tracking mark from giving away their position. Mel pulled the hood over her head. Doing so used up all but the last few drops of her mana reserves as she rapidly transformed the red of the cloak into a dark, muddy brown.

All of a sudden, two people stepped out of the gateway—a man shrouded in green and a woman wrapped in a blue cloak. It had been almost a decade since Mel had seen Ezmaunda, but the woman looked like she hadn't aged a day.

The gateway air calmed, resuming its delicate rippling. The man turned toward Ezmaunda, and she said something that Mel couldn't quite make out. He shook his head, gesturing somewhere off the trail as he replied.

Ezmaunda slowly turned, letting her eyes scan across the forest that surrounded the gateway. Suddenly, she froze, staring off through the trees. The man turned to see what she was looking at.

Mel stifled a gasp. She had worked with Ezmaunda for years and knew every trick the woman had. Though truth be told, she wasn't overly concerned with Ezmaunda. If it ever came down to a fight between the two women, Mel was more than confident that she would prevail. Even now, with little hope of using magic, Mel knew she was the stronger fighter.

But Ezmaunda's Verdant companion gave her pause. The man in green was Nikolas. Mel only knew him by reputation—one of cruelty and ruthlessness. He'd never had any qualms about carrying out Queen's darkest orders. In fact, the more depraved her command, the more he relished in seeing it through. Even though Mel had never officially met the man, the uncommon combination of dark brown skin and pale gray eyes was unmistakable. And at this moment, those eyes seemed to bore right through the bushes and straight into her soul.

Mel's heart hammered, and her palms grew slick with sweat. She was certain Ezmaunda had spotted them. Luke twisted to try to look at Mel's face. She tightened her grip on him as she glared from the corner of her eye, silently willing him to stay still. Slowly inching her free hand down to her hip, she grabbed the handle of a dagger and quietly slid it free from its leather sheath.

Nikolas stepped off the path, moving closer to the trees where they were hidden.

Speaking up another time, Ezmaunda drew Nikolas's attention away. He nodded. The pair turned and moved briskly down the path.

Mel watched as the two of them disappeared around the bend, and then she waited a full ten seconds longer before finally letting out her breath. As her hand slipped away from Luke's mouth, the muddy brown of her cloak sputtered a few times, then vanished, allowing the red to return in full force. Her eyes rolled backward for a moment. As she slowly tilted to one side, her eyelids fluttered. Taking a deep breath, she laid a hand on Luke's shoulder to steady herself.

Luke wiped his face on the edge of the cloak and then licked his lips. "Can't they sense you being close? Like the way you could tell they were coming into the apartment building? And why isn't there anyone guarding this gateway thing? And where are the other gateways? Shouldn't there be a bunch of gateways, like there was in Alicia's apartment? And wh—"

"Okay, give me a second here. I can't answer a million questions at once." Mel slid the blade back into its sheath, then squeezed her eyes shut and pinched the bridge of her nose. At last, she returned her attention to Luke. "No, thankfully, they can't sense my magic's presence. As far as I know, that's a power exclusive to me. As for why this place isn't guarded, well, these gateways only go in one direction. That over there is an exit. There isn't much point in guarding an exit, is there? The entrances, like the ones we used in Alicia's apartment, are guarded. And—"

"You're telling me that little girl is a *guard*?"

Mel snorted. "Yeah, she's a lot more powerful than she looks. And yes, the entrances are grouped together. But they're in a different kingdom altogether."

Luke slowly bobbed his head up and down, but his gaze was fixed on something a hundred miles away as he was lost deep in thought, already formulating his next barrage of questions.

"I could've sworn she was looking right at us." Mel shook her head. Knowing they needed to get moving before their pursuers realized their error, Mel spoke up once more, heading off Luke's next interrogation. "Now we're going to have to be really careful for a while. My tank is basically dry. I can't do anything big like create a disguise for us again or open any more portals. Not until I get more mana, at least."

"Uh, okay. What exactly is that? And how do you get more?"

"Essentially, it's energy. But it's not..." Mel paused as she tried to find the words to explain this concept she'd always taken for granted and didn't fully understand herself. At last, she continued. "It's not energy for physical activity. It's only used for magical abilities. Although, if it gets drained too low, it starts to cause physical weakness as well. Which is why I keep getting dizzy, I'm overtaxing my mana supply, and my body is trying to rebuild it."

"Alright, I guess that makes sense. But how did you keep the cloak hidden all these years? Why didn't you run out before now?"

"It doesn't take much to keep the fabric invisible, actually. Full body transformations and portals are a different matter."

"Ah. So, what now?"

"As far as getting more?" Mel shrugged. "When your mana is low, you have to wait. It'll build back up slowly over time. Or if you don't want to wait that long, you find a Citrine."

"You, uh, need a gemstone?"

"No, it's… Well, let me back up. There's so much to explain that I don't even know where to start. But we need to get moving. There isn't much daylight left. We've got to get some distance before nightfall."

Mel stood and made her way off into the forest with Luke close behind her. "I'm a chromaveiled."

"A chromaveiled?" Luke shook his head as he tried to process all this new information. "And that queen is after you?"

"Yes. I used to work for her. They," she gestured back over her shoulder, "still work for her. Anyway, I'm one of the chromaveiled. A Crimson, specifically. See?" She lifted one edge of the red cloak and waved it in emphasis.

"Okay…"

"Each color type has its own abilities. Citrines wear yellow-orange cloaks. They're more healing-focused. But besides that, they can also create potions to restore mana. And I think they can probably make a potion that'll take your tracking mark off, too."

Luke stepped over a log, and as the openings between the trees grew a little wider, he moved up to walk beside Mel. "So those two people were, um, chromaveiled too?"

"Yeah. Azures wear blue, and Verdants wear green."

"And what do those colors do?"

"Azures are basically trackers and spies. They can do some basic mesmerism—that's why you were so loopy after you first got marked, by the way. She was able to put a spell on you that sent you hurrying back to me, even though what *you* really wanted was to… um… avoid me."

Mel paused in her speech to push back the pain that came along with the memory of their recently shattered relationship. She swallowed hard and took a moment to regather her thoughts prior to starting again. "Anyway, an Azure's main job is tracking. They can put that blue mark on a target so another chromaveiled can find them. I know you can't see it. As far as I know, only chromas can see that tracking mark. It's basically a pillar of blue light that surrounds the target and stretches up into the sky. That's what Ezmaunda—the Azure—did to you."

"And Mr. Greeny?"

"Verdants are adept at making poisons. Plus, they have a high resistance to the poisons as well." Mel looked into Luke's eyes. "Verdants are primarily assassins."

The color drained from Luke's face. He jammed his hands into his jeans pockets and kept walking.

"There are Amethysts as well. They deal mainly with creating or destroying curses." Mel sighed. "I mean, there are more details to all these, of course. That's only the quick summary. I'm not going to bog you down with every tiny detail."

"Right." For a few minutes, the pair walked on in silence. Finally, Luke said, "So what about the Crimsons? What are you all like?"

"Well, uh…" Mel chuckled. "Like me."

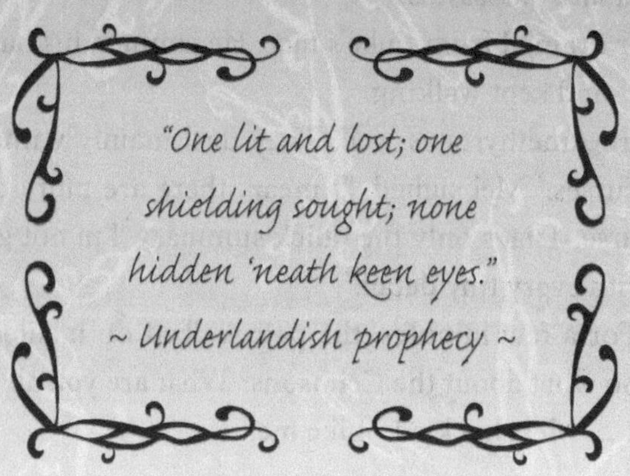

7

Luke rolled his eyes. "Not the time for jokes."

"I mean…" Mel paused, biting her lip and wringing her hands together as she searched for the words. "Sorry. I didn't intend for it to come across like I was making light of things. I'm actually *the* Crimson. There are no more like me. You've already seen a lot of the major things that I can do. Obviously, I can open portals for short-distance travel. I can change my appearance to look like basically anybody I want. And like you saw before, I can usually detect the presence of other mana users and their magic, although it's not foolproof."

"What the hell does that actually mean anyway?" Luke squeezed his eyes shut and rubbed the heels of his hands across his brow. When he finally lowered his hands back to his sides, he again looked at her. "How in the world can you 'sense' them?"

"Yeah, it's… I don't know, it's like…" Mel exhaled heavily and stared off into the distance, trying to find the words to describe the odd sensation. "It's like the air gets thicker and heavier. Denser, I guess. It's like the mana itself is taking up some of the space where the air should be."

"Okay. I have no idea what that means."

"I know. I'm not trying to be evasive. I really don't know how else to describe it."

Luke sighed. "So, what was your job?"

Mel chewed on her lip. "Whatever Queen needed me to be at the time."

Silence took over again as Mel watched Luke from the corner of her eye. It was apparent that he was deep in thought, and his mind still reeled with questions. He just wasn't ready to ask them yet. And she—sleep-deprived, hungry, nearly out of mana, and more stressed than she'd ever been since she'd left this place—wasn't quite sure how many of his questions she was ready to answer.

"You know, I thought this place would look different."

A chuckle slipped out of Mel's mouth. Of all the things Luke could've brought up right then, she didn't expect such a mundane observation. She squeezed between two close trees, then turned to face Luke as he stepped up beside her. Her brow folded together as she peeked at him. "What do you mean?"

"I mean, well… I never thought a place like this, a place with actual magic, would be real. But whenever I used to imagine a magical world, it didn't really look so much like Earth."

As Mel sidestepped a wide puddle, she laughed brightly. "What did you think it would look like? Vivid orange skies and purple striped trees?"

Luke snorted. The sound sent a flurry of butterflies soaring through Mel's stomach. Blood rushed to her cheeks. She tilted her head to watch the ground in front of her feet, grateful that her thick hair currently hid her face from his view.

"No, nothing that crazy. It's just that I thought there'd be, like, *something* that looked so different from Earth that I couldn't deny I was somewhere entirely alien. I mean, look!" He gestured to a tree in front of them. "That's a normal robin in a normal maple tree! And over there is a normal squirrel climbing the trunk of a normal spruce. Tell me this place doesn't look exactly like what you'd see in a forest on Earth."

"Fair point."

Mel's knee suddenly gave out underneath her. Luke twisted, managing to catch her around the waist right before she hit the ground. She gazed up into his eyes as he helped her regain her balance. Her pulse quickened. His eyes met hers for a moment, but as he let go, he turned his head away.

"Thank you." Mel swallowed as she forced herself to look away from him. "I really need to get some rest soon, but I'll be okay for a bit longer."

Luke nodded at her, and the pair resumed walking, slower this time. Soon, they could hear the sound of running water a short distance away.

"This is just…" Luke shook his head. "It's just so much to take in, and it still doesn't feel real."

"I'm sure. And there's so much more you still don't know. You can ask more when you're ready. I'll try my best to answer, but…" Mel let her words trail away without finishing her thought. She shoved her hair away from her face. "There's a creek up ahead. Let's make camp near there. We can at least get some water." Mel laid a hand on her stomach as it gurgled loudly. "Maybe I can forage some food over there too, if we're lucky."

They came out through the bushes at the water's edge. Mel wasted no time in kneeling down and taking a drink.

"Uh, are you sure that's safe? Shouldn't we boil it or something first?"

Mel scooped up another handful and swallowed it before twisting around to look at him with water dripping down her chin. "Yeah, it's safe. We don't have the same pathogens as on Earth. All clear water is safe to drink here. Besides, what other choice do we have? It's not like we have any containers to boil it in."

Luke looked at her from the corner of his narrowed eye. "You sure you don't have some kind of..." He waved his hands in front of himself, looking around as though the word he wanted would pop out of thin air. He once more spun to face her. "An incantation or something to make a cauldron? I'm not great at striking up a fire with a couple of sticks, but I can do it."

Chuckling, Mel lifted one hand. She snapped her fingers, and a tiny ball of fire poofed into existence, hovering directly above her palm. As the dense bundle of flames danced gracefully over her skin, she said, "I don't need sticks to spark up a fire. But I still don't have a spell to create a pot."

When Mel finally swished her hand to douse the small flame, Luke remembered to close his mouth. He twisted back to stare at the water. Eventually, thirst won out. He dropped down beside her to drink. "Holy crap, it's *sweet*! Why is it sweet?"

Mel shrugged. "That's just how it is here." She glanced off into the bushes behind Luke. "Oh, perfect! Blinterberries!"

Pushing herself to her feet, Mel went over and pulled something off the thick bushes near the bank. The cloak stretched another couple of feet to accommodate her movement, keeping both of them covered by the red fabric. It finally reached its limit, though, and began to slide off of Luke's arm. Mel noticed and turned around, coming back with her arms full of fruits that looked exactly like blueberries that had been enlarged to the size of apples.

Returning to Luke's side, Mel shoved two of the berries into his hands and then plopped herself down on the ground next to him. She bit into one of the fruits. Bright pink juice oozed out, trickling down her chin and fingers. She ignored the mess, sighing contentedly as she chewed.

"Go ahead. They're more filling than you'd think. Those'll help tide you over till tomorrow."

Luke peered down at the purplish-blue fruit, then back at the pink juice making its stark contrast with Mel's dark chin. At last, he sank his teeth into the humongous berry. Juice exploded out across his fingers and onto his clothes. He looked down and blinked at the sight, forgetting to chew. This liquid didn't look the same as that covering Mel; this was a deep maroon.

"So, what does yours taste like?"

"Huh?" Luke's head jerked up and his eyes darted to Mel's as he slowly chewed.

"Mine tastes like those little strawberry candies. What about yours?"

"It… What? How is… *What?*"

"They taste different to everybody. It depends on what flavor you like best. I happen to like those little, hard strawberry candies."

"Oh. Uh, pomegranate seeds." Luke swallowed and then looked down at the blinterberry in his hand. "By the way, this is more what I had in mind when I was looking for something that wasn't like Earth."

Mel grinned, but her amusement quickly faded when she saw the slight downturn to Luke's mouth. She finished eating. "You know, I forgot how quiet it is here. I've been on Earth for so long now. There were lots of things I didn't like about this place, but the peacefulness is something I definitely missed."

Luke nodded.

Yawning widely, Mel scooted over to the water and rinsed off her hands and face. As she used the corner of her cloak to wipe her fingers dry, she turned around to look at the horizon through the trees. The first touches of orange and pink and purple were stretching across the sky as the sun sank low. She sat back and watched.

All of a sudden, a giant shadow passed overhead, and the two of them were nearly toppled over by a huge gust of air.

"What the hell was that?"

Mel tilted her head up as the dark shape passed another time, along with a second burst of wind. She smiled broadly. "Hal."

"What?" Luke's voice came out strained and high. He jerked his head toward the sky, gasping.

A dragon was rapidly descending, circling, preparing to land in the water right next to them. Once its feet finally made contact with the ground, its wings stopped beating, and the air gradually went still again, Mel leapt up. She grabbed Luke by the hand and dragged him along as she rushed over to the humongous creature with scales that varied from purple along its head to pale, yellowish-brown near its feet. She threw her arms around the giant beast's thick neck as Luke gawked.

"Hal, I'm so happy to see you're doing okay! It's been ages!" She beamed up into the creature's gold-brown irises with their narrow, cat-like pupils. "Luke, this is Hal."

"Should we be standing this close to a dra—" Luke's words stopped abruptly, and his eyes darted to Mel. "Is he *purring*?"

"Well, yeah. How else would a dragon show he's happy?"

"Of course," Luke said dryly. "How silly of me."

Hal went quiet and leaned his head close to Luke. A small coil of smoke rolled from the creature's nostrils as he stared deeply into Luke's eyes. Luke coughed. Slowly pulling his lips back until his teeth were on full display, a deep rumble escaped Hal's chest. He gave Luke a long sniff. The dragon's pupils grew, rapidly changing from narrow slits to large, black circles.

Luke's breathing quickened, but he stood his ground as he stared back at the enormous creature. At last, Hal nodded, then tilted back away from Luke. The creature's pupils returned to slits. He nuzzled up to Mel and resumed his purring.

"I don't actually know what his name is." Mel lifted a hand to slowly stroke the top of the dragon's large head. "He just seems like a Hal, don't you think?"

Luke crinkled up his nose as he gawked at the dragon, then Mel, and back again. "Doesn't really seem like a name for a giant lizard."

Mel laughed. "Well, I like it anyway, and I think he does too."

As if in confirmation, the dragon purred even louder.

"It's been great to see you again, Hal."

The creature leaned down and gently touched his forehead to Mel's and she threw her arms around his neck once more. Then, Hal stepped away, closed his eyes, and bowed his head toward Luke.

Luke had no idea of the proper etiquette for the *"a dragon just bowed to me"* scenario, so he slowly raised his hand and waved.

Finally, with Hal's farewells complete, he turned away and strolled off. His four large feet made surprisingly shallow footprints in the muddy ground, and even though he was enormous, his footsteps barely made a sound as he moved gracefully down the creek bank.

"Well, that was definitely not like anything on Earth." Luke chuckled as the tip of Hal's tail disappeared around the bend up ahead. "How did you, uh, meet Hal? And how'd you know he wasn't going to eat you?"

"I'd seen him in the sky several times when I was little. Then one day, I was out in the woods all by myself. I was playing, running between the trees, when I fell and twisted my ankle." Mel chuckled softly. "It wasn't anything serious, but of course to an eight-year-old, it seemed like the most awful physical pain I could've ever endured. So, of course, I screamed.

"I really don't know where he came from that day. I hadn't seen his shadow or heard his wingbeats, anyway. But as soon as I cried out, he dove out of the sky. At the time, I was absolutely petrified. I really did think he was going to eat me."

Mel grinned as she stared blindly into the sky, lost in her recollection. "I mean, who wouldn't be petrified with *that* barreling toward you? But he sat down beside me, laid his head on my lap, and simply looked at me. And I don't know, I could tell that all he wanted to do was help me.

"He just sat there with me all afternoon until I nearly forgot what I'd even been crying about in the first place. And well, since that day, he's been a dear friend. He comes to visit me from time to time until he decides to wander off yet again."

"That's... Wow."

"Yeah."

The first stars were speckling the sky, and the crickets were chirping. A gentle breeze fluttered the leaves in the trees overhead.

Luke lowered himself into the grass near the creekbank, lay back, and folded his hands behind his head. "The shapes the stars make look different here."

"Hm?" Mel took a seat beside him and tilted her head upward. "Oh, I hadn't ever really thought about it before now. I guess we do have different constellations here. We are in a different galaxy, after all."

Covering his hand with his mouth, Luke tried in vain to stifle his yawn. Truly contagious, Mel found herself yawning as well. She stretched out beside him.

"We should probably try to get some sleep while we can. We've got quite a journey ahead of us tomorrow."

"Where exactly are we going? I know you mentioned the name of the place. Westlands or something?"

"The Westerlands. I've got a... friend a few miles from here. Fen. He'll be able to help us find someone to get that mark off you."

Luke nodded and let his eyes drift closed. "So, you mentioned some queen is after you. But why? What did you do to piss her off so much that you can't even leave your entire world to get away from her? And once we get this mark removed, what's going to stop her from just sending more people after us?"

Mel rolled onto her side, facing away from Luke. When she spoke next, her voice trembled. "I'm really tired. Can we talk about it tomorrow?"

"I guess." Luke glanced over, but he couldn't see Mel's face from there. He started to reach out, to gently rub his thumb across her cheek and turn her around to face him. But he changed his mind and dropped his hand back to the ground. "Good night."

"Good night."

For a long time, Mel lay there, slowly running her fingertips across the white, crown-shaped emblem that marked the inside of her wrist. It burned more now that she was back in this world. Pushing away the thoughts of the constant pain that lingered there, she forced her attention upward. The stars slowly slid across the sky as she pondered how she would make it through the next few days. Mel didn't dare let herself think about what she'd have to do to keep Luke safe after they removed his mark. But deep down, she already knew.

8

––––––

"So," Luke knelt and picked up a handful of stones from the edge of the creek. "What's the plan for today?"

Stooping down nearby, Mel rinsed the fresh blinterberry juice from her fingertips. Then, scooping up another handful of the cool creek water, she splashed her face to chase away the last of the early morning grogginess. As the water slowly dripped from her skin, she said, "Get to Fen's place without being caught. Hole up there and have him call a Citrine to come and give us a healing potion that will *hopefully* remove your mark. I'm not sure how we'll explain it so that they don't immediately turn around and report me back to Queen, but we'll worry about that when we get there. Maybe Fen will have some ideas."

"Why doesn't everybody just run around with a stockpile of healing potions all the time? Does anybody ever actually get hurt here?"

"They require some specific ingredients that are kind of hard to come by. Once you gather all the materials, only the Citrines can make the potions, and then the process of creating them takes quite a bit of time. Some countries' rulers do try to save up the potions when they can, but asking for too many will draw Queen's attention to them, so they have to be cautious."

Nodding, Luke loosened his grip and let the stones fall back to the ground one at a time until only one remained in his palm. He grasped it between his fingers, pulled his arm back, and then flung it forward, sending it skipping across the surface of the creek. When it finally slowed and sank into the clear water, he turned to face Mel. He stood, swiping the dirt off the back of his jeans. "So after we get those potions, we can quit being cooped up together inside this damn cloak?"

"Yeah." Mel sighed heavily. She stood up and shoved her hands into her jeans pockets. "Let's get going."

"I'm sorry. That came out wrong. I mean..."

Mel started walking without acknowledging his words.

Luke jogged to catch up. He took his place beside Mel and matched her hurried pace. The red cloak rapidly adjusted itself, shrinking as the gap between the two of them closed.

"Sometimes I want some privacy. More than you just looking away while I step behind a tree. And besides that, well... it's just that this is hard, you know? Being forced to stay close like this, under one shared piece of fabric. Especially when we're not... you know... together anymore."

"Mm-hmm."

"Can you tell me your reason now? Just for my own knowledge. Even if you don't want to get back together, please tell me whatever was stopping you from marrying me."

Mel walked faster. She shoved branches aside, barreling her way through the untamed foliage. The babbling of the narrow creek was quickly swallowed up by the forest as it continued into the distance behind them. When she finally answered, her voice was strained. "Let's focus on getting the mark off of you so we can get back to the portals without being seen."

"Mel, please—"

"You know Cali and Fen."

Luke stopped and grabbed Mel's wrist, spinning her around to face him. "What? How could I possibly know them?"

"Well, you don't know them personally." The tension in Mel's shoulders faded slightly as Luke was successfully distracted by the change of topic. "You know *of* them, though. Their first names are Calista and Fenris. Calista means 'most beautiful.' And Fenris means 'great wolf.'"

"Most beautiful and great wolf? Why should that mean anything to me?" Luke's eyebrows scrunched together above the bridge of his nose. He slowly shook his head and shrugged.

"Beauty and the Beast!"

Luke's jaw dropped. "What?"

Turning, Mel resumed walking. With his mouth still hanging open, Luke hurried to follow suit.

Mel shoved a branch forward out of her way, and a twig snapped off, flying out in front of them and crashing into a large tree trunk. She held onto the branch long enough for both of them to clamber through the gap. Letting go, it swished noisily back into place as the two of them kept moving. "Fenglauria is the world where a lot of the European fairy tales originated from. The stories told on Earth are not exactly accurate to what truly happened, but—"

"What do you mean, they're not accurate? They're only stories."

"No, they're not *just* stories."

Luke stared at her in silence.

"Most of those fairy tales are about real, living, breathing people. But by the time their tales make it to Earth, it's been skewed quite a bit. The versions of these stories they tell on Earth are more like 'inspired' by what happens here. Rumors of rumors that get distorted over time with each retelling as they're passed down from one generation to the next."

Luke laughed. But then, catching a glimpse of the serious look on Mel's face, his amusement instantly dissipated. He rubbed the palms of his hands across his face before letting them fall limply back to his sides. Stepping over a jutting tree root, he let out a bemused chuckle. "Fairy tales are real? They're *real*? And they come from here? So that would make this couple, Beauty and Beast, like, what? Hundreds or maybe thousands of years old then, right? That story has been around for ages."

"No, they're in their late twenties, actually. I can't remember exactly. And don't ever dare call them 'Beauty' and 'Beast' in their presence. They hate those names. It's Calista and Fenris. Or Cali and Fen, once they decide they like you enough. They're pretty laid back, as far as royalty goes." Mel glanced back over her shoulder at Luke. "And, before you ask, while Cali is a queen, she is not '*the*' Queen I worked for. There are a lot of different kingdoms on Fenglauria and a lot of different rulers." She sighed, then quietly mumbled, "Though Queen thinks she should be the only one."

"Okay." He shook his head. His eyes were glazed over as he was pulled deep into his thoughts. "Those ages don't make any sense, though. At least not if they're supposed to be the people from the fairy tale. The 'Beauty and the Beast' story is ancient. It's been written down for a couple centuries, at least."

"Yeah, the story is older than they are." The corner of Mel's cloak snagged on the thorns of a large bush. She stopped and reached down to untangle it before continuing their trek. "So, here's the thing. Some of the stories you grew up hearing were wrong because they hadn't actually happened yet when the tale made its way to Earth."

"Oh, well then, okay." Luke made a face. "That totally cleared things right up."

"Beauty and the Beast—at least any version of it that you'd've heard on Earth—was based on a prophecy. There are seers here that can sometimes predict destinies and future events. And sometimes they make those predictions centuries or millennia before they happen. But the problem with prophecies is that a lot of the time, they can't be fully understood until the event occurs. Which means—"

"What the hell? What's the point of a prophecy if no one understands it?"

Mel reached up to pull a leaf from her hair. As she let it fall to the ground, she glanced at him and shrugged. "I really don't know. But the people here aren't going to be convinced to give up their seers and prophecies any time soon."

"Hmph."

Ignoring Luke's skepticism, Mel continued with her explanation. "Anyway, since these prophecies get interpreted before we really know what they're all about, sometimes the story ends up skewed. Well, Earth got a warped version of that 'Beauty and the Beast' story. Which then got retold a bunch of times, so it changed and evolved even more."

"So if the story is older than them, and it's a prediction or prophecy or whatever, how do you know it's about *them*? Couldn't you just assume it's about anyone that it halfway sounds like?"

"The way a 'prophesied' is identified varies from one prophecy to the next. Sometimes, the prophecy will say when and where the child will be born. Sometimes, it'll explain a specific birthmark or a unique ability a child will have. Sometimes it's anyone's guess."

"Hmm. That sounds like a bunch of made-up bullshit then." Luke squeezed his eyes shut, stopped walking, and dragged his fingers through his hair. As he let go, the dark locks tumbled back onto his shoulders, and he sighed. "So, are there other... other, um, fairy tale people here that I've heard of?"

Mel snorted with laughter. She stopped and spun around to face Luke. Then, wordlessly, she reached over her shoulder to grab hold of the red hood of her cloak and lifted it for him to see. She shook the fabric emphatically and then let the hood drop to her back.

Mel and Luke stared at each other in silence. A pair of chipmunks darted between them, then scurried off into the foliage.

"What? I don't..." Luke's words faded, and his jaw dropped. His wide eyes traveled from the top of her thick, black hair down to her sneakers and back up again to meet her eyes. "No way. No effing way. You're Little Red Riding Hood?"

Taking a step backward, Mel dropped into an exaggerated curtsy. Her lips were pinched together as she fought back the urge to smile. Straightening up, she resumed walking.

Luke quickly caught up to her. "Really?"

"After everything you've seen, you're still doubting all this isn't just some dream, aren't you?"

"Okay, yeah." He laughed. "But can you blame me? Less than a week ago, I didn't even know there were other planets with life. Not to mention any kind of magic or anything. It's a lot to process all of a sudden."

Mel's thoughts were pulled backward to that first day she'd set foot on Earth. She'd been alone in the strange land, filled with its own kind of unfathomable magic. The inhabitants on Earth never called it magic, of course. They preferred the term "technology." But in her eyes, cars and airplanes were magic. Movies and television and radio and electricity were magic. Those amazing little rectangles of plastic that everyone carried around in their pockets, allowing them to talk to anyone on the planet at a moment's notice or to look up anything they ever wanted to know. She couldn't believe that cell phones were anything less than magic.

And it had certainly taken her more than a few days to adjust to all those things everyone accepted as perfectly normal on Earth.

Sighing, Mel glanced over at Luke. She pushed aside the thick branches of a bush and stepped over a fallen log. "You know, even if I hadn't been bound by magic that prevented me from telling you about this world, you wouldn't have believed it. I know you wouldn't have. In fact, you'd've probably had me locked in an asylum if I'd told you about my 'delusions' of being a fairy tale character and having powers to make myself look like anyone I wanted."

"You're right. I'm sorry. I mean, I don't think I would've had you locked away for saying you were Red Riding Hood, but I'd have tried to get you to see a doctor. Anyway, I shouldn't—" Luke suddenly stopped in his tracks, gasping loudly.

Mel halted. One hand flew to the dagger at her hip as she spun around. Her eyes darted to the sky, the ground, the leaf-covered tree branches above their heads. But there was no one there, no sign of danger that she could see. Only Luke staring straight ahead with wide eyes as though he'd just seen a ghost.

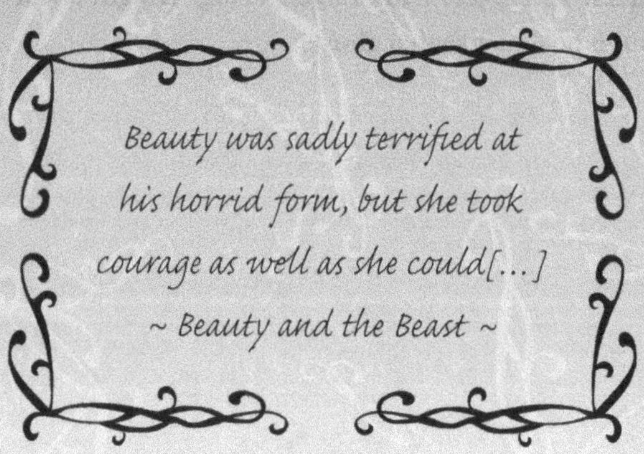

9

"*L*uke?" Mel's heart was racing as she spun around, searching for whatever Luke had seen. "What's wrong? What's going on?"

He slowly angled his head toward her and met her gaze. He blinked a few times before finally finding his voice. "That was Alice, wasn't it? Like, from Wonderland."

"Gleffik," Mel muttered the curse as she relaxed her hold on the dagger's handle. "Don't scare me like that, Luke! I was sure something was about to attack us."

"Sorry."

Mel sighed. "It's alright. Yes, Alicia is 'Alice in Wonderland.' Although, obviously her name is Alicia rather than Alice. And I'm sure you're wondering, but she's not a chromaveiled. The Gatekeepers are a different kind of magic wielder entirely."

"Oh."

"And the land she's from is actually called Underland. Other than the names, though, the version of her story they tell on Earth is fairly accurate since it was based on events that really happened rather than a prophecy."

Luke shot her a look of utter bafflement.

"I know she looks really young, but Alicia isn't a kid. She's something like 600 years old. Close to 630, if I remember right."

"Holy crap. She looks like a teenager. Wait." Luke suddenly took a step closer and peered intently at Mel's face. "How old are *you?*"

"I'm thirty-one, Luke." Mel's lips tilted downward. "I never lied about my age. I never hid anything from you if I didn't have to."

Grabbing Luke by the elbow, Mel forced him to start walking next to her again. The gentle breeze rustled through the treetops and tossed a scent like honeysuckle through the air. A few white, puffy clouds slowly drifted overhead, their large shadows creeping along the ground underneath them.

As the two of them stepped out into a small clearing, a pair of birds sang from the branches of a nearby tree. Luke decided a change of topic was needed to ease the tension that was growing thicker by the second. "Hey."

"Hmm?"

"Why does everyone here speak English?"

"The British colonized here ages ago."

"What? How could... Hold on. You're pulling my leg now, aren't you?"

Mel giggled. "Yeah, I am. I honestly haven't got a clue how we ended up speaking English here. However that happened, it was long before my time. Elves, ogres, and several of the other races also have their own languages, but most everyone knows English."

Luke lightly tapped Mel with his elbow and grinned at her.

"I'm sorry," Mel said, stopping in place and chewing on her lip as she looked at him. "I shouldn't've snapped at you for asking my age. You obviously can't know which things I've lied to you about. I just…"

Luke nodded but didn't speak.

Mel stared down at the aching crown emblem on her wrist and slowly traced the familiar lines that marred her skin. Gradually, she slid her hand over the top of the white mark, covering it as if that would make it easier to speak. "I've always been able to… push back the guilt of the lies because I was cursed so that I couldn't explain on Earth. So, I told myself it couldn't be helped. I literally couldn't do anything about it. And besides, I was trying to keep you safe. If you didn't know about all this, you couldn't get hurt by it, right? Now that the curse isn't stopping me, there are still so many things I should tell you. But what if you hate me after you hear… And I don't even know where to begin. By even having this relationship, I put you in danger. It was selfish. I should've broken it off sooner. Drenkth! I should've never gone out with you in the first place! If we'd never started dating, you wouldn't have that target on your back now! I should've stayed here and—"

"Hey." Luke grabbed hold of Mel and pulled her against his chest, wrapping his arms around her. He slowly rocked back and forth, cradling her against his chest. One hand delicately stroked her coily, black hair as he softly hummed a lullaby. Soon, the front of his shirt was thoroughly tear-soaked and clinging to his chest.

At last, Mel sniffled quietly and wiped the edge of her hoodie sleeve across her eyes and nose. Her mind continued to reel with a million thoughts and worries as she tried to pull herself back together. She pressed her hands to Luke's muscular chest and tried to gently push him back to create a bit of distance between them.

Luke didn't budge, though.

Mel's heart hammered inside her ribcage. She hadn't showered or brushed her teeth in far too long. Moisture continued to leak from her eyes. Her hair and clothes were mud-stained and decorated with stray leaves and twigs. All those thoughts and worries that had filled her head only moments ago suddenly vanished as she saw the way Luke was looking at her.

With his left hand still on her back, Luke brought the right one around and wiped his thumb across the smooth skin of her cheek. He moved the hand slowly downward, caressing her face until he reached her jaw and slid his fingers underneath her chin. With the slightest pressure, Luke tipped Mel's face up until it was angled toward his.

Unable to resist, Mel moved her hands up around the back of Luke's neck, burying her fingers in his dark hair and inching her body closer to his. She licked her lips and waited, barely able to catch her breath. Luke tilted his head down.

Mel was beginning to lower her eyelids and relax into his embrace when a huge shadow zipped over them. She stiffened. Luke felt it and let go of her, stepping back with an apology already forming on his lips. Mel's head jerked up toward the sky. And before Luke could say anything, Mel had grabbed him by the hand, spun around, and pulled them both up against the trunk of a large tree.

"What's—"

Snapping her head toward Luke, Mel silenced him with a look. Her eyes were open wide and the pupils dilated. Her jaw was clenched. And, as if that weren't enough, her hand was squeezing his so tightly Luke was already losing feeling in his fingers.

The pair twisted to peek out from under the tree branches at the spot where they'd been standing a moment ago. The shadow passed across the clearing another time. The silhouette of wide wings, a long neck, and an even longer tail moved more slowly this time.

Luke turned his head toward Mel and mouthed one simple word. "Hal?"

Mel quickly shook her head as her eyes darted back to the clearing. "A wyvern." She held one finger to her lips long enough for Luke to see, then cautiously lowered her hand to the dagger hilt at her hip. The sun shone brightly into the clearing. She held her breath and crouched there, unmoving and silent.

Luke shivered as he slowly craned his neck to look at the clearing once more. The long, unmown grass swayed softly in the breeze. And it was then that Luke realized how strangely quiet it was. No birds chirped from the trees, no squirrels or rabbits ran along the ground. Now, the only sounds were the gentle swishing of the grass and the distant, rhythmic beat of very large wings.

Leaning close and pressing her cheek to Luke's, Mel whispered, "Keep low, step where I step, stay quiet. And if I start to run, keep up."

Without waiting for a response, Mel pivoted in the other direction and crept away from the clearing. She was careful to watch for twigs and dry leaves—anything that might make a sharp noise—and avoided it with each and every cautiously placed footstep. Luke obediently followed her lead, stepping exactly where Mel did.

The two of them had only made it a few yards when the wingbeats got faster and closer, pushing gusts of wind through the trees and flinging their hair across their faces. Mel hurriedly crawled over a large, fallen tree trunk and ducked down behind it. A second later, Luke did the same.

The wingbeats gradually came to a stop, and eventually, so did the brutal wind.

Luke twisted his head to look at Mel, searching for guidance, instructions, reassurance. Anything. But Mel wasn't looking at him.

Removing the second dagger from her shoe so that she now had one in each hand, Mel gradually shifted herself upward, just high enough to peer over the top of the log. The creature's faint, musky odor drifted on the breeze in her direction. As the wyvern moved across the clearing, she caught glimpses of it between the trees. Scaly, blue-gray skin. A frill of horns across the top of its large head. Thick, sharp talons on the ends of its two feet. Another set of talons on the edges of its wings. A long tail, the end of which forked into two spear-like tips.

"Now what?"

Mel didn't take her eyes off the creature as she whispered, "We wait. Hope it only landed to take a nap. Pray it won't notice us when we crawl away."

Luke nodded and leaned against the log.

Keeping an eye on the creature as best she could from their hiding place, Mel watched as it began to walk in tight circles, flattening the grass and weeds under its feet. At last, it stopped. It folded its knees under itself and sank toward the ground.

The gentle breeze suddenly shifted so Mel and Luke were no longer downwind. The wyvern halted, inhaling deeply. Then, its head whipped in Mel's direction. Letting out a loud hiss, it sprang up and charged.

Mel yanked the red cloak off of Luke's shoulder. "Run!"

The blue beacon of light erupted out of Luke and toward the sky as Mel sprang up from her hiding place. Daggers in hand, she leapt over the log to face the wyvern.

Luke turned, then froze as he watched. The enormous creature wove gracefully, effortlessly as it barreled between the trees, hardly making a sound. Luke's eyes went wide. "Fuck."

The wyvern bared its fangs as it got close, galloping on its legs and taloned wingtips.

Mel bolted toward the beast. Her red cloak fanned out behind her. Dropping to her knees, she slid underneath the creature's wing as it swiped at her. She raised one of the daggers overhead, and the blade tore into the skin along the back edge of its wing.

The wyvern let out a shriek. It spun to face Mel again, its forked tail swinging toward her. She ducked below and rolled away as it stabbed into the ground next to her head. Leaping to her feet, Mel lunged to the side.

With a roar, the beast swung a taloned wing at her. Mel dodged behind a tree. Bark and twigs sailed through the air as the wing slammed into the trunk. As it screeched again, specks of spittle flew from its mouth. The faintly green saliva droplets sizzled as they landed on the surrounding foliage.

Spinning around, the creature swung its tail another time, targeting Mel behind the tree. She ducked under it, swinging a dagger overhead as she did, but the blade fell from her hand as it bounced harmlessly off the creature's thick scales.

Before she could retrieve the dagger, the tail swung toward her another time. She bolted out of the way. And as she ran, she saw something that nearly stopped her heart from beating. Luke was still there. He hadn't listened when she'd told him to run. He wasn't even hiding. Her palms grew clammy, and she almost lost her grip on the remaining dagger. Her mind raced, trying to come up with a new plan.

All of a sudden, there was a *thump* behind Mel, then an eardrum-shattering shriek. She stopped and spun around in time to see a trickle of blood dripping from the thin, unscaled flesh beneath the wyvern's eye. Her gaze darted to Luke. He bent and scooped up a large rock and flung this one toward the wyvern as well. At the last moment, the wyvern turned its face away, and the rock clacked off its scales and tumbled to the ground.

Mel didn't waste any time. She threw herself toward the narrow end of the wyvern's tail and leapt on. Before it knew what was happening, she shoved her dagger tip up between the layers of scales near its forked stingers. The beast roared. She dragged the blade through the tender flesh below the scales. The stingers fell to the ground, writhing and convulsing as red blood and green venom spewed from the fresh wound on the tail.

The wyvern roared as it swung its tail hard and sent Mel flying. The back of her head slammed into the trunk of a tree. Her vision went black, and her body went limp.

Screeching in pain and anger, the beast bolted toward the clearing and launched into the air, leaving a trail of sizzling, acidic droplets in its wake.

Mel collapsed in the weeds at the base of a large tree, silent and unmoving.

Luke hurdled over the fallen log and rushed over to Mel. He snatched a handful of leaves off a tree and used those to scoop up her discarded daggers as he went. Keeping an eye on her, he carefully tucked the leaf-wrapped daggers into his belt as the poison slowly spread onto the surface of the leaves.

He stopped beside her. A gash marked one of her cheeks. Her lower lip was split open and rapidly swelling. Aside from that, a thick, green liquid coated the flesh from the middle of her left bicep all the way down to the tips of her fingers, sizzling on her skin and making the air smell like burning meat.

Dropping to his knees beside Mel, Luke had a split second of pure and utter panic. He closed his eyes and took a deep breath. As his heart rate slowed ever so slightly, he reopened his eyes and yanked his shirt off. He wadded up the dirty, pink fabric and used it to scrape off the majority of the venom from Mel's arm. Within seconds, the shirt was sizzling too. A thick droplet of the acid touched the tip of Luke's finger. He dropped the shirt, yanking his hand away and wincing as his entire arm suddenly felt like it were on fire.

Mel's eyelids fluttered, and she groaned softly. Luke didn't want to wake her—surely being awake with those injuries would be agony—but he had no idea where to go, how to find help, or even who to trust.

Slowly scooting close, Luke lifted Mel's head up to rest it on his lap. He reached out and tentatively swept the hair back from Mel's face. Then, grasping her uninjured hand between the both of his, he squeezed it gently. She opened her eyes a fraction, gasping as she tried to push herself up. Tears were already spilling down her cheeks. Her eyes met Luke's for the briefest of moments before rolling back in her head. She slumped back against him.

Luke looked around, unsure of what to do or where to go. But, knowing that any decision was better than just sitting here waiting to be caught, he scooped Mel into his arms and stood up. Then, grabbing one edge of the cloak, he tossed it over his shoulder, unsure if it mattered who used the cloak's powers, as long as the owner was wearing it. He crossed his fingers and hoped that simple action would be enough to hide the tracking mark that he couldn't see.

Up to the point when they'd been attacked by the wyvern, they'd been heading due west. So, Luke turned his back on the sun and ran.

Adrenaline and fear spurred him onward as the minutes and hours passed, and the sun climbed higher in the sky. Luke eventually slowed from a run to a jog, then at last to a walk as his breathing grew labored, but he forced himself onward anyway. Sweat dripped from his forehead and down his bare chest. His hair was plastered to his neck. Mel occasionally groaned but otherwise slept uneasily in his arms.

Every tree and bush looked the same as the last. Luke was starting to wonder if he was going in circles or if there was even an end to this forest.

As Luke stopped and leaned on a tree to catch his breath, he noticed movement ahead. Bending down, he carefully laid Mel on the ground. He pushed the edge of the red cloak from his shoulder as he stood up, slipped the daggers from his waistband, and positioned himself between Mel and whatever was slowly stalking toward them.

Three enormous wolves—one brown, one white, and one gray—stepped out of the shadows with their hackles raised and teeth bared. The gray wolf—the large one at the front of the pack—lowered its head and growled.

Luke's jaw clenched as he raised the daggers, took a deep breath, and braced himself for a fight he was certain he wouldn't win.

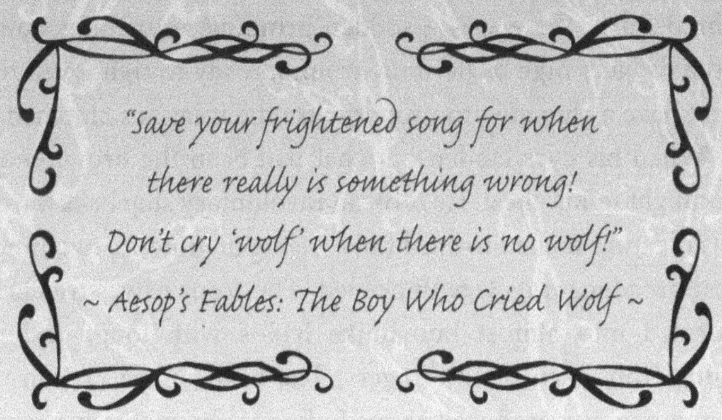

10

Both the brown and white wolves split off. The white one made a wide arc around to Luke's left side while the brown stalked around to his right. Their footsteps were silent as they moved through the tall grass, and their stares never strayed from Luke. A chill ran down his spine as he realized that if his eyes were closed, he wouldn't even know these predators were there.

The gray wolf's hackles were raised. It didn't move from its position as it continued snarling, its yellow eyes locked on Luke's face.

Luke's head twisted back and forth, his eyes darting from one wolf to the next as he tried to keep them all in sight. But soon, the trio of wolves had him surrounded; two of them were waiting now just beyond the edges of his peripheral vision. Since watching them all was no longer an option, he stared at the large, gray one at the front. It took a step closer.

Luke's blood ran cold. His heart pounded, and his knees shook. Every fiber of his being was commanding him to flee. The palms of his hands burned where a few droplets of the poison had seeped around the leaves and onto his skin, but he refused to think about that right now. His thoughts shifted to Mel, lying helpless on the ground. So, he clenched his jaw, tightened his grip on the leaf-wrapped daggers, and planted his feet.

Behind Luke, there was a sudden grinding, crunching noise. He lifted the daggers high as he spun around, ready to fight even though he didn't have a clue how to properly use the weapons clutched in his hands. When his eyes landed on what had been the brown wolf, his breath caught in his chest. He took an involuntary step backward.

This creature inched toward Luke, rising up onto its two hind legs. Its chest broadened; its legs thickened. The front paws stretched and transformed into almost humanlike hands with long, dark claws extending from each of the fingers. The head of the creature grew larger and now towered well above Luke's. Although its fur remained brown, its eyes changed from pale brown to a deep, menacing red as it glowered down at Luke.

Luke's knees went weak, threatening to send him tumbling onto the forest floor, fully at the mercy of these creatures. He took a shaky breath and stood his ground, glaring at the red-eyed werewolf, hoping with all his might that he came across as more intimidating than he felt.

When the grinding, crunching noise sounded once more, this time from the directions of the other two wolves, Luke's heart nearly stopped. His breathing grew increasingly rapid. He stood stock-still as his mind whirled, trying in vain to devise some kind of plan to get out of this. Eventually, the awful, nauseating sounds of mutating bones and shifting tendons ceased. Luke slowly swiveled around to face the large, gray wolf again, mentally preparing himself for another were-wolf to be standing there, leering at him with glowing red eyes.

As he came face to face with a man instead, Luke froze. The man had a short, stocky build and pale skin. The hair on his head was short and gray, while the thick hair on his bare chest and arms was much darker. Brown, leather leggings covered his lower half, although his feet were unshod. His eyes were a bright golden brown, and they bored into Luke unblinkingly.

The man's gaze slid toward Mel's unconscious form for a second before he locked his stare on Luke. "What did you do to her?"

The brown and white werewolves quietly stepped closer. Luke could see one on each side from the corners of his eyes. They waited there, silently staring at Luke, their muscles tensed as though they might attack at any moment.

Luke forced himself to focus on the man that stood before him and ignore the creatures that loomed on each side. Slowly lowering the daggers a few inches, he lifted his chin. "I didn't do anything to her. We were attacked. I'm trying to find someone that can heal her."

The man's golden-brown eyes again moved toward the unrespon-sive Mel, this time lingering far longer. "Why? What attacked you?"

"Some flying monster—kind of a dragon-type thing, but she called it something else. Please, just tell me where I can find help for her, and we'll go."

"A wyvern?"

Luke nodded. "Yeah, I think that's the word she used."

The man inhaled sharply as his eyes darted to the brown werewolf. He wordlessly nodded toward Mel. The brown creature took one large stride over, kneeling down next to her motionless body.

Luke stiffened. He turned, pointing the daggers at the brown werewolf. "No! Leave her alo—"

Reaching out, the white werewolf effortlessly brushed Luke aside, cutting his words short. The brown one scooped Mel into his fur-covered arms as Luke tried to regain his balance and figure out what to do next. But as he stood there, blinking dumbly at the trio, the same grinding-crunching sounded. The strange man's body contorted and twisted until at last, he also transformed into a gray werewolf.

Then, the three towering, fur-covered creatures suddenly whirled around and took off at a jog.

Hurriedly shoving the daggers back into his belt, Luke followed. He had to sprint to keep up with the long legs of the creatures as they tore through the forest, nimbly dodging overhanging branches and leaping over roots and brambles. Meanwhile those very same branches snagged at Luke's hair and clothes while the roots and brambles threatened to catch his ankles with every step.

It didn't take long for Luke to lose sight of the werewolves as they charged into the forest with Mel. He struggled but pushed himself harder, trying in vain to catch up before he lost track of them entirely.

By the time Luke finally made it out of the forest, his bare arms and chest were covered in scrapes while leaves and twigs clung to his hair. Dark green stains marred his jeans. The werewolves were dozens of yards ahead, steadily making their way across an open field, heading toward a sprawling stone castle. Luke stopped. He bent over to place his hands on his knees as he struggled to catch his breath. But as he saw the creatures reach the edge of the castle's long drawbridge, he forced himself back into a run and tore across the field of wildflowers.

Gasping and clutching the stitch in his side while his sweat-drenched hair clung to his face and neck, Luke finally reached the castle's moat and came to a halt. The bridge was already rising; it was more than a foot off the ground. His hammering heart leapt into his throat.

He took a step backward, waving one hand wildly in the air. "Hey!"

The drawbridge continued moving steadily upward.

Luke jerked his head toward the top of the castle wall where a pair of human sentries marched, blatantly ignoring his presence. He tried another round of yelling, waving more fervently all the while, but still, the sentries walked on, and the bridge lifted ever higher. It was now nearly three feet above the ground.

For a moment, Luke contemplated throwing one of the daggers at the wall to try to draw the sentries' attention, but in all likelihood, if it did get their attention, they would consider it an attack and respond in kind. And if the thrown dagger didn't get their attention, it would almost certainly end up lost in the moat.

Looking at the ceaselessly rising drawbridge, Luke took three large steps backward. Then, he charged ahead and leapt, hurling himself at the wooden structure. With a loud *thud*, Luke hit chest first, forcing every last drop of air out of his lungs, but he managed to hook his arms over the top of the planks. His fingers struggled to find purchase, and for a terrifying moment, Luke was certain he was going to fall into the water below and be left to drown. But at last, his fingers found the thick chain. He stretched and clawed his way closer until he managed to curl his fingers around the metal links. He hung there for a moment, breathless and stunned, clinging desperately.

As his lungs finally began to work again, Luke took a deep breath and pulled. He grunted. His biceps ached with the strain. His sweat-slickened fingers threatened to slide off the chains. Tightening his grip, he slowly allowed himself to relax his muscles and took another deep breath. Once more, he pulled with all his might, grunting loudly as he did so. He inched himself over the upper edge and swung his leg until it was hooked over the end of the wood. Using his knee and toe now, he pulled, finally maneuvering the rest of his body over the top.

Looking down at the ground of the courtyard that waited almost a dozen feet below, he let go of the chain and slid down the sloping wood, finally coming to a rest in front of two armed guards as the drawbridge slammed shut and the clanking chains finally went silent.

Luke started to push himself to his feet, but two spear tips jabbed hard into the skin of his throat. He froze. Slowly, he lifted his hands in surrender and tilted his chin up to look at the guards.

He'd been utterly confused ever since that tracking mark had been placed on him, and he'd fallen headlong into a world he couldn't understand. But at least up until now, he'd been able to act, to *do* something, even if he wasn't sure what that something was. Now, though, with two blades threatening to puncture holes in the center of his throat, his thoughts came to a screeching halt.

So, as he lay there, shirtless, dripping sweat, and cornered, he said the only words his brain could come up with in such dire circumstances.

"Uh, hi."

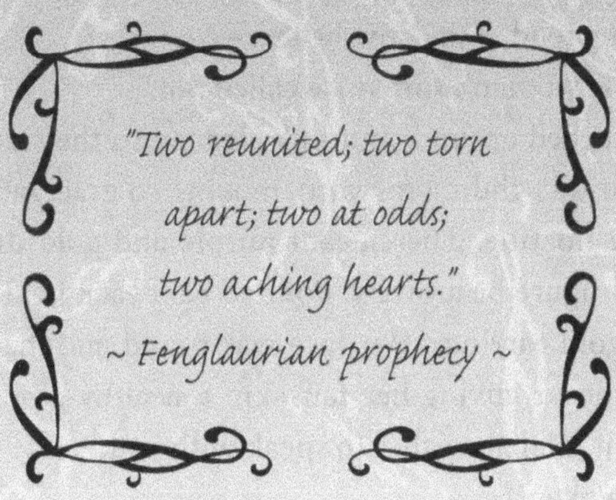

"Who are you?"

The guards withdrew their spears and stepped aside, letting the man who spoke step up between them. It was the same man from the forest. He folded his arms across his chest and scowled down at Luke. "And how do you know Lady Melzia?"

"*Lady* Melzia? How do *you* know her?"

The man responded by letting out a very wolf-like growl from the depths of his chest.

Luke licked his lips. "Sorry. My name is Luke, and she's my, um..." He hesitated, unsure what she was to him now or if he should tell this stranger anything. At last, he decided to go with the simplest answer, even if it wasn't currently the most accurate. "My girlfriend. Where did you take her?"

The man narrowed his gaze and lifted one eyebrow, but he neither insisted on further elaboration nor did he offer any information. "How did you escape a wyvern? And unscathed, at that?"

"Melo... Er, I mean... Melzia fought it. She was able to slice the end of its tail off. That's how she got that acid or poison or whatever it's called all over her arm. Now, what did you do with her? Can I see her yet? I'll answer whatever you want to know, but I need to make sure she's okay."

"She is being tended to. Now, where—"

"Darling?" A woman's soft voice called out.

The man turned around, and Luke leaned to the side to look past him. A woman was gliding forward, moving so gracefully it appeared as if she were floating. The elegant purple and gold dress she wore suited her full figure beautifully. Pointed ears each held a row of tiny emerald and gold earrings. Her face was round and there was a pink tinge to her cheeks, giving her fair skin a healthy glow. "Your questions must wait. Melzia wishes to speak with you."

"She has awoken?"

"Yes," she turned to answer the man, "though I suspect the pain and the effects of the venom will pull her back into darkness soon. Go quickly and speak with her for a moment. I shall continue discussing the situation with our guest as the guards, and I escort him to Lady Melzia's bedside."

The man nodded. He grabbed her hand and lifted it to place a gentle kiss along her knuckles. As he did so, the sleeve of her dress shifted, leaving her wrist visible. The man and the woman each had an identical mark—the simple, black outline of two roses joined by a common stem.

As the man let go of her hand and hurried off to the castle, she directed her green eyes toward Luke. Her expression gave no hint of her emotions as she asked, "Do you know to whom you are speaking?"

Luke shook his head. "No. We didn't exactly have formal introductions. I think I—"

The woman waved her hand to silence him, and for a moment, her rose tattoo was again clearly visible. She interlaced her fingers and let her hands rest just below her waist. "I am Queen Calista. My husband —the man interrogating you a moment ago—is Prince Fenris."

Eyes darting toward the castle to watch as Fenris headed around the corner and out of sight, Luke frowned. The thought in his head tumbled out through his mouth as he muttered to himself, "*Beauty* sure, but Beast is a *werewolf?*"

Squeezing his eyes shut, Luke quickly sucked air through his teeth as if he were trying to pull the words back inside his mouth before anyone could hear them. By the time he cracked his eyelids open once more, both guards had stepped closer.

Calista gave a slight nod to one of the guards, turned, and moved several paces away while he marched after her.

As Luke lay there, the second heavily armored man continued to tower over him. Trying to distract himself from the man's leer, Luke turned to look back over his shoulder. Calista and the first guard were deep in conversation. Luke strained his ears, but the whispered words didn't travel far enough for him to catch anything.

After a long while, the pair returned, and Calista stopped next to Luke. She stood there, her posture ever so slightly more rigid than it had been before. One eyebrow was raised a fraction of an inch. Otherwise, she gave no outward sign of her emotions. She spun away, and as she did, she spoke a single word over her shoulder, "Follow."

Two hands wrapped around each of Luke's arms, and the guards easily lifted him to his feet. As they let him loose, he turned to look at one of them, and that guard already had his spear at the ready once again, jabbing Luke in the side.

Luke hurried to catch up with Calista. "Excuse me, Queen Calista?"

"What is it?"

"I have some kind of tracking mark on me that... Well, I don't know. I can't see it, but Mel said I have it, anyway. It's some kind of, like, light or—"

"Will you soon be arriving at your point?"

"Sorry. One of those blue-cloaked people put a tracking mark on me, and I'm afraid someone hunting us will see it."

Two servants stood on either side of a pair of tall, wooden doors that led into the castle. Each of them dipped their heads as their monarch glided past.

"If you've been marked, how were you not spotted by your pursuers while roaming through the woods of my kingdom?"

"Um, Mel shared her cloak with me." Luke shoved his hands into his pockets as he walked beside the woman down the long hallway built of stone. Light from the afternoon sun shone through the stained glass windows, casting rainbow-colored shadows across the floor.

"I see. Well, as long as you are within the castle grounds, the mark will remain inactive. There is a protective ward over our castle that blocks anything of the sort. Perhaps you were spotted as you approached our territory, but that beacon will not reveal to anyone that you are here."

"What if someone saw me before that? Could they be on their way here already?"

"Perhaps."

Luke sighed heavily. "How can I help Mel? She was in a lot of pain, and I don't know what to do."

"My husband and I have the matter well in hand."

"Hey!" Luke spat the word as he grabbed Calista's arm and spun her to face him. "You and the king—"

One of the guards slammed Luke across the chest with his spear handle, knocking him back into the wall. The guard jammed the weapon against him, not allowing Luke to move.

The entire group stood frozen for a time as Calista and Luke sized one another up. At last, she waved her hand and the guard stepped back, releasing Luke.

Luke rubbed his chest. Straightening up, he closed his eyes and took a deep breath. When he looked at Calista, he spoke much more calmly. "Have I done something to offend you? I'm trying to save Mel's life here and—"

Calista narrowed her eyes at him. "You show up at my castle where you were most decidedly *not* invited. And do not feign that you believed you would be welcomed, as your entrance was made by leaping onto a closing drawbridge. On top of that, you chose to do all this while half-dressed and unclean. You seem not to care that we not only spared your life but also allowed you to enter the castle. As an intruder here, we owe you no such kindness."

The guards stepped back as Calista glided forward, radiating anger.

"You call us 'werewolves,' a name that lost favor centuries ago because of its implications of being a horrific, contagious disease, rather than simply a variation of humans or fae who are capable of transforming into certain wolfish forms. Though, perhaps that slip of the tongue could be excused. Judging by your accent, you are not from these lands, so perhaps that is the term your world uses. However, in the future, you will use the term 'lycanthrope' if you must give a name to our kind.

"On the other hand, you certainly know something of our world. You knew the names given by our prophecy. You called us by those wretched names, 'Beauty' and 'Beast,' as though we haven't rightful names of our own.

"Now, you *dare* to lay a hand on me, ignoring that I am the ruler whose home you intruded into. We have only just met, yet you act as though I owe you favor.

"And while doing all this, you elevate my husband's station to that of 'king' as though *I* were not the rightful ruler here. He is prince consort. You will treat him with the respect he is due; however, he is *not* king of this land. You will not show such disregard toward my birthright again."

Calista's tirade paused long enough for Luke to give a small nod. She continued, "While you disrespect my title, you also question our honor, implying that we would not do all within our power to heal an injured traveler. You ply me with questions, all as you hide behind half-truths when we try to obtain information from you."

She stopped moving as she got within inches of Luke. She was nearly a foot shorter than him, several years his junior, and her voice was never raised, but he quailed as she spoke and filled his veins with ice.

"And as if all that weren't bad enough, the whole of it commenced when my husband and his brothers found you wandering through our lands with a gravely wounded woman in your arms. One that you *claim* to have had no part in harming, though your story seems exceedingly implausible. Wyvern attacks are very rarely survived when the receiver of their aggression is not properly armed and trained. And," she paused as she looked Luke up and down, "I do not believe *you* would be able to manage it.

"Then, after my husband approached you, what did they learn? That it was not any woman in your arms. No! It was his cousin. You use his cousin—the one who has been missing for nearly a decade—as an excuse to gain entry into our castle. Yet, you expect us to welcome you with open arms, putting our full trust in you. Have I overlooked anything?"

Calista turned her head toward the guards. After they shook their heads, she directed her gaze onto Luke once more. "Well, *Luke*, what have you to say?"

Luke's head was tilted down, his eyes unfocused as he shook his head slowly, feeling like a misbehaving child.

"Well?" She gazed at him questioningly.

Slowly, Luke brought his attention back to Calista. He blinked a few times, collecting his thoughts. At last, he found his voice. "They're cousins?"

Calista studied him. "You truly did not know that."

The words did not sound like a question, but Luke shook his head anyway.

"Does her relation to my husband distress you? Perhaps you do not wish to be so closely associated with our kind?"

"No, I swear. I just had no idea she was related to royalty."

Calista tilted her head as she stared intently into his eyes. Luke squared his shoulders, straightened his spine, and refused to look away.

At last, Calista stepped back. "And in that, I believe you speak the truth." She opened her mouth again as if she wanted to elaborate further but stopped. Reclosing her mouth, she chuckled, spun away, and began gliding down the hallway once more.

Luke hurried to catch up, and the guards followed closely behind. "Your Highness?"

"Your *Majesty*." The deep voice came from one of the guards.

"Oh." Clearing his throat, Luke started anew. "Your Majesty?"

"Yes?"

"I'm sorry. Really. You're right. I'm an intruder here. A stranger you don't know and have no reason to trust. I shouldn't have been so rude."

Calista dipped her head in acknowledgment as they descended a wide, spiral staircase. "I accept your apologies. And I expect that your behavior will improve from this point forward."

"Of course." Luke hesitated before finally deciding to continue. "Um, ma'am? Can I ask you a question?"

"You may."

"Like you said, you have no reason to trust me and probably should've kicked me out of the castle, at the very least. So, um, why didn't you?"

"When Lady Melzia awoke, she was in agony and barely able to speak. However, I was able to discern one thing: she believes you are worthy of our trust." Pausing in the middle of the stairwell, Calista glanced at him. "Although, I have not yet decided if she is correct."

The pair looked at each other for a moment. Then, they continued downward and soon entered another hallway. They approached the closest door and stopped in front of it.

"Do not do anything which would justify my initial fears." Calista stared at him as she issued the warning. Finally, she stepped aside and gestured toward the door handle.

Luke pushed the door open and stepped into the room. Mel was lying in a large, four-poster bed, her skin sweat-covered and pale. Her eyes darted back and forth beneath her lids. Walking over, he dropped down to kneel at the bedside. Luke took Mel's uninjured hand and gently stroked her wrist with his thumbs.

Fenris was standing near the window on the opposite side of the bed. As Calista entered the room, she glided over and laid a hand on Fenris's muscular, hair-covered arm. He leaned close and whispered something to her.

"Oh?" Calista's eyes found Luke and studied him momentarily before she brought her focus back to Fenris. A look quickly passed between them.

Luke was so focused on Melzia that he didn't notice the way Calista studied him as she listened to her husband.

Fenris continued with his hushed message, pausing only when Calista interjected with a whispered question. At last, Calista nodded and turned to face Mel. Speaking loud enough now for all to hear, Calista asked Fenris, "Have you summoned Kyahn?"

Silently, Fenris nodded.

"Luke?"

He pressed a kiss to Mel's cheek, then glanced up at Calista when she spoke his name.

"One of the chromaveiled—a Citrine—is on the way. He will be able to help her."

Luke's eyes grew wide. He stood up, gently lowering Mel's hand back onto the mattress. His voice was strained when he spoke. "You didn't let that queen know she's here, did you? Mel doesn't want her to know."

"I suspected as much." Fenris folded his arms across his bare chest as he shook his head. "She'll not hear it from me nor mine."

Luke felt a tap on his shoulder, and he looked over at a maid who had shown up, seemingly out of nowhere. Her arms were outstretched as she handed him a folded bit of fabric. As Luke took the offering from her, she curtsied and whirled away, quickly and quietly scurrying out of the room.

Unfolding the fabric, he realized it was a shirt. His eyes darted over to the shirtless and barefooted prince. Luke opened his mouth to question it, but when he caught a glimpse of Calista's slightly raised eyebrow, he remembered his promise to behave. Besides, they had more important matters to tend to. So, he silently slipped the cream-colored, long-sleeved shirt over his head and tucked the lower hem into his dirty jeans.

"What'll stop this Citrine guy from reporting back to that queen lady as soon as he leaves here?"

"He does not know why he has been summoned. Only that someone in my kingdom has been gravely hurt. We intend to keep it so."

"How can you stop him from seeing her? Also, she needs that magic stuff. Uh, mana? Refilled. And my tracking mark…" Luke's eyes darted over to Calista. "I'm sorry, Your Majesties, I'm not trying to be rude, I swear. It's just that whenever she got hurt, she was already trying to find a Citrine to help me, and I want to make sure she gets that. But I have no idea how anything in this land works. The world I'm from doesn't have anything like this. Please don't leave me in the dark."

"Hmm." Fenris turned, walking over to the wall and leaning his shoulder against the cold stones to look out the window. "That certainly changes matters."

Luke looked at Fenris's back, but no further elaboration was given. So, Luke focused his attention on Calista.

She glanced at her husband, then took a few gliding steps across the wide room toward Luke. "If it were only a matter of healing, it would not be difficult. We would have one of the local children pose as though he were the injured party. No one would question our lending aid to an injured child from our kingdom.

"And—though I am not certain—I believe that a healing potion will also remove the mark that has been placed upon you. I haven't a way of verifying that without raising suspicions. But I would give you some of that potion, and if it did not work, another plan for removing your mark could be formed later, once Melzia was well enough.

"Mana, however…" Calista sighed. "Requesting a potion of mana will draw questions to which we cannot give answers. Kyahn will wish to know the recipient. Few among our lands make use of mana. And even regarding those who do, it is not typically a matter in which we would give such aid."

Luke rubbed a hand across his stubble-covered chin as he thought. "Is there anyone you *would* do that for?"

"Perhaps if an invited guest from another kingdom had such a need. Or an esteemed visitor from another world, should they—"

"That's it!" Luke cringed as he realized what he'd done yet another time. "I'm so sorry, really. We don't have kings and queens in the place I'm from, and I've never hung out with anyone with more political pull than the leader of the local school board, and even that was…"

Luke's sentence trailed off as he noticed Calista waving away his words.

Taking a deep breath and letting it out, Luke went on with his plan. "Dress me up like I'm injured. Maybe a head wound or something. Tell them I'm from another world—shit, I don't know, Underland or whatever—and that I need my mana tank refilled so I can go home."

Calista watched her husband. As Fenris met her eyes, one of his shoulders lifted in a shrug. She returned her focus to Luke. "Are you certain you are up to such a challenge? The chromaveiled are after both of you, and Kyahn might know your appearance. Perhaps he even knows your tracking mark was seen approaching our castle. We cannot be sure what will happen if you are discovered. So, I ask you another time: Are you certain you wish to proceed?"

"Yes."

"Assuming this is successful and we are able to remove the tracking mark from you, they will not cease their search for you or Lady Melzia. You are aware of that, correct?"

"Right. I don't know what Mel plans to do next. She's been very tight-lipped about it, but we'll figure that part out after she's patched up. I know getting rid of the mark and restoring her mana was the next step, so we've got to try."

"Very well. I do not believe this is a *good* plan, but we likely have very little time before Kyahn arrives." Calista sighed as she gazed down at the wound that marked the length of Mel's arm. "We must not delay any further."

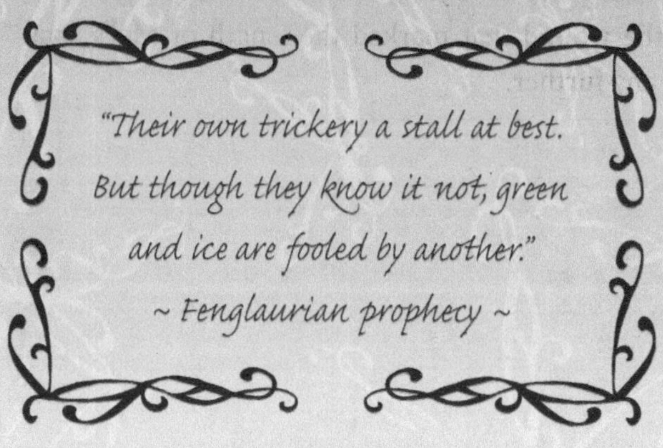

ointedly looking past Luke, Calista commanded one of the guards, "Run to the butcher's shop to retrieve a bucket of pork blood. Be quick. I've a sudden craving for freshly made blood sausages, and Cook does not have the ingredient on hand."

With a bow of his head, the guard backed out of the room, whipped around, and disappeared down the hallway. Calista nodded at the second guard, and he dutifully turned and stepped behind her, ready to follow as needed.

"Come, Luke. If this plan is to have any chance of success, we must do what we can to see that you look the part."

Even while Calista hurried across the room, through the hall, and up the spiral staircase, her movements were smooth and graceful. She looked as though she were lighter than air, floating effortlessly above the floor. Luke lagged behind for a moment, mesmerized by her poise. Even in a situation that required such urgency, such quick thinking and deceit, she was a sight to behold. When Calista was nearly out of view, Luke finally came to his senses. He jogged up the steps after her, the guard close on his heels.

Reaching the top of the steps, Calista went to the third door in the hallway and hurried into the room. As Luke and the guard entered, Calista tugged a bellpull along the wall nearby.

Moving farther from the entryway, Calista gestured first toward a cushioned chair near the fireplace in the corner of the room and then at the polished floor next to where she waited. The guard understood and moved quickly to obey the silent command. He walked across the room and around the large bed, picked up the chair, and placed it in front of a small vanity. Setting it down, he turned the seat to face the large, ornate silver mirror, then moved out of the way.

"You, sit." Calista directed the command at Luke. Then, without pause, she looked at the guard and gestured toward the unlit fireplace. "Take that ash shovel and bring me some of the soot. Be mindful that you do not spill it on your clothing or the floor. We must look our parts at least as well as Luke if we are to succeed."

As the guard nodded, a servant stepped into the doorway. "Ma'am?"

Opening the vanity drawer, Calista reached inside and grabbed something. As she reclosed it, she turned around with a pair of scissors in her hand. Gliding over, she took her place behind Luke's chair. She diverted her glance toward the waiting servant. "I believe that Luke here is similar in build to Sir Ulric. Would you agree?"

"Aye, ma'am. He is perhaps a bit shorter than Sir Ulric, but elsewise very similar indeed."

"Good. Run to Sir Ulric's room and tell him I require an outfit from his wardrobe. Something he might use for hunting or some such. If he demands any explanation, please extend my apologies and tell him I shall provide such information—and recompense as necessary—later this evening. If he is not in his quarters, do not waste time searching for him; simply retrieve a suitable outfit and bring it to me at once. Time is of the essence."

The servant gave a quick bow before dashing out the door, his footsteps echoing rapidly down the hallway as he sprinted away.

Luke twisted around, looking up at Calista as she stood over him with the scissors. "Uh, what are you—"

"This hair must go."

"Hold on a second." He frowned as he stared at the scissors. "Why do I have to—"

"We haven't much time, and we must disguise you as best we can. You cannot grow a beard in a matter of minutes, nor do you have much hair on your face that we could remove. We cannot change your height or weight. The color of your skin and eyes are inalterable as well. Given all this and our current circumstances, I believe shortening your hair and removing the stubble from your face is the best we can do. However, Luke, perhaps you know of something which I do not. Have you any better ideas for a great alteration to your appearance?" She raised an eyebrow, awaiting his response.

Luke clamped his mouth shut. Huffing loudly, he shook his head and turned once more to face the mirror.

Calista paused to watch his face in the mirror. "Perhaps I have spoken too harshly. I do not wish to belittle you. It is simply that we do not have the luxury of time. We must make haste if we have any hope of success."

"Oh. Uh, thanks." Luke shifted awkwardly in the seat. "You're right. There isn't much choice. Go ahead."

"Very well." Calista lifted a lock of Luke's shoulder-length hair. She made the first cut, trimming it down to barely an inch in length. Luke settled back and watched the mirror as the trimmings—and the twigs and leaves still tangled there—tumbled to the floor.

The servant who had been sent to find an outfit for Luke suddenly hurried back into the room. He was slightly winded but held up an outfit for Calista's approval.

"That will do nicely. Thank you, Franklin. Now, quickly, help him change into it." Calista stepped back, letting another thick tuft of Luke's hair fall to the stone floor, watching to make sure it didn't catch on the pristine fabric of her dress. "Go on, Luke. We haven't all day."

Stunned and looking particularly odd with only half his hair shortened, Luke stood and walked over to the waiting servant. With practiced efficiency, the servant soon had Luke dressed in the fine quality—though slightly oversized—clothing. A pair of Sir Ulric's boots were placed beside the bed.

The servant fastened the last of the gleaming silver buttons of Luke's vest. Snatching up Luke's discarded jeans and shoes, he tucked them away inside an empty wardrobe drawer.

"Retake your seat, Luke." When he had settled back into the seat, she hurried to crop the last of the long hair. Soon after, she lathered his face, grabbed a razor, and quickly removed the stubble that had sprouted there over the past few days. Once that was complete, she used a towel to wipe Luke's face and reclaimed the scissors, ready to tidy up the rushed haircut. Without looking away from her task, Calista said, "Bring that soot here. While I finish this, the both of you are to dip your fingers into the soot and use it to discolor his face. Spots and streaks, varying depth of color. He is to look as though he were singed by a dragon. Understood?"

"Aye, ma'am."

"Yes, ma'am."

The guard cautiously made his way over with the scoop of black powder.

Calista resumed cutting as the two men started painting the skin of Luke's face. Once she made the final snip and brushed the last few strands of hair from his clothing, she stepped back to take a better look. She nodded. "The face is sufficiently marked, I believe. Now, the shirt, vest, and coat. His hands as well."

"Ma'am?"

"Do you not understand your instructions?"

The servant and guard glanced at each other. Turning toward Calista, the servant spoke up. "It's not that, ma'am. It's only that... Won't Sir Ulric be displeased?"

"Gentlemen." Calista folded her hands together around the blades of the scissors and directed her eyes toward each of the men in turn. "I understand you do not wish to draw Sir Ulric's ire. However, I ask you to think quite carefully on this."

The two men watched her, waiting nervously.

Calista glided forward and lowered the pitch of her voice a notch. "Would you prefer to draw the ire of Sir Ulric? Or that of your queen?"

The guard cleared his throat as the servant mumbled something that sounded like an apology. Both then set to work staining and ruining the expensive clothing.

Calista nodded. "As I stated previously, recompense will be given to Sir Ulric when all is done."

"Pardon me, ma'am?" A young maid stood in the doorway, waiting for permission to speak. Calista nodded, so the girl raised a pail to show her. "The butcher's boy brought your... um... order of blood, and I... Did you want it, ma'am? I was told to bring it up here, but if that's a mistake I—"

"Yes. Thank you. Please set it beside the door and resume your duties in the kitchens."

The girl's face was utter confusion, but she kept her questions to herself. She sat the pail on the floor, curtsied, then hurried away.

Turning to face Luke, Calista made several small snips in the fabric of the coat and shirt. She looked up at the guard. "Do you see those holes I have created? You are to grab the fabric at those places and tear it. When one of the Dracona attacks, one's clothing would surely become tattered and torn. Though, hopefully our healer will not look too closely. I would like to singe the fabric a bit, but I do not believe we have the time to do so convincingly."

This time, the servant and guard quickly set to work without protest.

Calista walked around Luke as she supervised the destruction of the clothing. "Good. Now, if you'll—"

The woman's words stopped abruptly at the soft buzzing sound coming from behind her. She stiffened. With the wave of her hand, the servant and guard both silently rushed out into the hallway.

She grabbed Luke's hand, pulling him unceremoniously from the chair and dragging him over to the corner of the room. She pointed at the elaborately decorated changing screen that stood there. "Go behind there. Remain hidden and silent until I give you permission to do otherwise. Do you understand me?"

"Y-yeah. Understood." He didn't understand at all, but he was learning not to question her commands. Luke tucked himself behind the screen, out of sight for the most part, but continued peering around the edge as his eyes darted past Calista to search for the source of the buzzing. Noticing a thin gap between the panels of the changing screen, Luke scooted farther out of sight and slowly leaned over to peer through it.

Calista moved swiftly across the room and lowered herself into the chair Luke had vacated only a moment ago. Fanning out her skirt, she covered any trace of the hair littering the floor. She took a deep breath. Then, she lifted both hands in front of the mirror and pushed them out to the sides as though she were parting the curtains at a window.

At first, nothing happened as Calista delicately folded her hands across her lap. Then, the vibrating noise stopped abruptly. The mirror's surface rippled like a pool of water disturbed by the sudden intrusion of a rock. Luke had to stifle a gasp as he watched through the narrow opening.

When the mirror stilled, it no longer showed a reflection of Calista or the room they were in. Instead, it displayed the image of an unfamiliar woman. She had flawless, peach skin and thin, pink lips. Her eyes were an unusual shade of violet. The woman's hair was elaborately braided at the back of her head, but several perfect ringlets draped across her shoulders; the way the color of her hair danced in the candlelight, it seemed as if it were made of gold ore. A purple cloak across her shoulders perfectly complemented the color of her eyes. A silver crown covered in large rubies completed the look. Luke was frozen, entranced by the woman's unique beauty as she sat on the opposite side of the mirror.

"Cali." The gold-haired woman's lips curled up at the edges, but the faint hint of a grin didn't reach her eyes.

Suddenly, the gold-haired woman's eyes darted in his direction. A chill ran down Luke's spine as he wondered if those violet eyes could see him peeking between the panels. He wanted to jump backward, further out of sight, but he was afraid moving quickly would draw even more attention his way. So he sat still, holding his breath and counting the quick beats of his heart.

Calista's left hand twitched ever so slightly at the informal greeting. However, she gave no sign that she noticed the other woman's attention had been drawn away from their exchange. Briefly bowing her head in acknowledgment, Calista replied, "Queen."

Now, the gold-haired woman's smile did reach her eyes as she turned her focus back toward Calista. In fact, the woman positively glowed. She spent a moment basking in it before the emotion faded, and she resumed the conversation.

"I was informed that you've summoned a healer."

"Yes."

There was a long pause where the two women stared at one another. At last, the woman in the mirror broke the silence. "Who was injured? I do so hope it was not your dear husband."

Calista ignored the sarcasm that dripped from the statement. "Thank you for your concern. It was not my husband who was injured. It was a traveler from another realm; this man was ill-equipped to spar with an angry dragon."

If Luke hadn't been so nervous, he would've laughed at Calista's statement. Not a word of it was technically a lie, but the image it painted was certainly not the truth.

"Hmm." The gold-haired woman weighed the words before she pried further. "My Azures were tracking someone who ventured near your lands. The mark vanished as it approached your castle. What do you know of this?"

"Oh?" Calista's voice gave away nothing. "Queen, you know as well as I that only the chromaveiled can perceive such a mark."

Luke lifted an eyebrow, thoroughly impressed by Calista's quick wit and ability to say everything and nothing all at once. He made a mental note to avoid any verbal altercations with Calista.

The woman in the mirror narrowed her eyes at Calista.

Lifting her chin a fraction of an inch, Calista asked, "What would you have me say, Queen?"

Reaching up toward her forehead, the gold-haired woman pretended to brush back a stray lock of her perfectly coiffed hair as she schooled her features. "Well, I suppose your cooperation matters little. I shall dispatch Ezmaunda and Nikolas to find out more. Good day, Cali."

Before Calista could respond, the mirror rippled. It quickly went still, displaying the simple reflection once again.

"Guard!" Calista stood up, spinning around as the guard entered. A pair of servants followed. "Remove this mirror. Cover it and store it away. Have the same done in Melzia's room as well. Quickly."

"Yes, ma'am."

As the mirror was hurried out into the hallway, Calista twisted toward the changing screen. "Come, Luke. We must finish our preparations."

Luke stood and made his way back to the chair. "So… um, was that the woman…"

"That is the woman to whom Melzia is bound."

Calista hurriedly directed one of the servants on how to apply the blood, then wasted no time finishing the gruesome makeover. As she supervised, she said, "That woman tolerates no name beyond 'Queen' and denies the title to anyone else. Even so simple an act as adding her given name to the title and referring to her as 'Queen Victoria' would imply that she is not the only ruler in our world. In her eyes—"

"Ma'am!" A boy rushed into the room, panting. "I'm sorry, ma'am, I don't want to interrupt, but there's a rider approaching the southeastern border. One of the scouts said it was the Citrine and sent me to tell you right away."

"Thank you, child. You may return to your duties."

"Aye, ma'am." He gave a quick bow and ran off, his footsteps echoing down the stone hallway.

"Well, I suppose we must..." Calista's voice trailed away as she watched a maid enter the room, awkwardly carrying a very large painting. "What are you doing with that?"

"Apologies, ma'am. One of the guards said you'd taken down the mirror. He thought it might look suspicious if there wasn't something to cover that stain on the wall where it hung."

"Ah, yes. Thank you. And when you're done here, I hope you will thank the guard for me as well."

"Aye, ma'am."

Calista turned to Luke and gestured toward the painting. He stood and hurried over, taking it from the girl, and he moved over to mount it on the blank patch of wall where the mirror had been a few minutes prior.

"Quickly clean up that hair, please, and be on your way. Do not concern yourself with any blood droplets on the floor."

The girl was confused by the strange orders but curtsied and hurried to obey without question.

"Luke, into the bed. Everyone else, return to your duties. If you are questioned about our guests or what happened, you know nothing. Understood? I shall explain in due time."

The few servants in the room assented and hustled away.

Luke burrowed beneath the thick, down-filled blankets on the bed and sank into the pillows. Slowly congealing pig's blood thickly coated the right side of his head and left streaks down to his jaw. More of the sticky, red substance was splattered across his arms and torso.

Opening his mouth, Luke was ready to apologize for ruining the bedding, but Calista waved him into silence. "If it were a real injury, the bed would not look fresh and clean. It must look the part as much as you. Now…"

The words trailed away. Footsteps echoed rapidly down the hallway. Lowering her voice, Calista leaned close and said, "Speak as little as possible. Do remember, you appear to have a head injury, and it would not be expected for you to make complete sense. If it becomes too much for you to act the part, you may pretend to drift into sleep. I shall tell him that our injured guest has been given something for the pain that causes drowsiness."

The footsteps were close now. Calista straightened up and watched the doorway.

Luke exhaled heavily. He then attempted to look dazed, confused, and exhausted. Which—given the insane, life-altering experiences he'd been through in the last few days—didn't actually require much acting skill.

"Ma'am?" A servant popped into the room and bowed. He gestured toward the hallway. "The Citrine, Kyahn."

Luke had to bite his tongue to keep himself from gasping as this Citrine strode into the room. The exceptionally short newcomer was dressed in a bright, yellow-orange cloak that dragged the ground as he walked. His wispy, pale orange hair brushed the tops of his shoulders, but it was tucked back behind his long, pointed ears. Most jarring of all, though, was the fact that the man's skin was light green. Luke definitely hadn't been prepared to watch a half-goblin-half-human man walk through the door.

"Thank you for coming, Kyahn." Calista greeted the man, drawing his attention before he could process the look on Luke's face. "We would not have asked you to travel all this way if it were not so dire."

"Hmph." The green man tipped his head back so he could look up at Calista, but he didn't bother to extend any kind of greeting. "What happened? And who is he?"

"I am not certain what happened." Calista paused for a moment, distracted by the sight of her husband—now fully clothed—walking through the doorway. She refocused her attention on the Citrine. "Given the state of him, it appears most likely that he crossed the path of an angry dragon. There have been a few dragon and wyvern attacks in the area of late, as I'm sure you are aware."

"Hmm." Kyahn's eyes drifted toward the bed and its blood-covered occupant. "Who is he? Where'd he come from?"

"I have little information on him." Calista deftly sidestepped the first question and moved to the second. "To my ears, his accent sounds foreign. Underlandish, perhaps?"

Kyahn slid his skeptical gaze from Calista to Fenris. Fenris stood with his arms folded across his chest, silently glaring at the healer. The seconds crept awkwardly by until, at last, Kyahn cleared his throat and ended the staring contest by turning around.

"What's your name?"

Everyone was staring at Luke, and he knew he couldn't give his real name. He hadn't prepared for this, hadn't thought through this particular question. His mind raced. He licked his lips. Finally, Luke blurted out his own middle name and prayed that bit of information wasn't something Mel's pursuers would know. "Grayson."

"Grayson?" Squinting, Kyahn tilted his head. He took a step closer to the bed. "Bit of an odd name for an Underlander. Is that where you're from?"

"I'm, uh…"

"Exhaustion and injury have left him rather addled. Perhaps it would be best if we save our questions until he has had time to heal a bit."

"That accent of yours doesn't sound Underlandish to my ears." Ignoring Calista's words, he leaned closer to Luke.

"Kyahn?" Calista glided forward, shooting Luke a stern look. Before the Citrine had fully turned to face her, she softened her features and said, "Such an injury surely causes a great deal of pain. And you have traveled such a long way today. Might you allow our guest to have his healing and mana potions now? After this man has had sufficient time to recover, I am certain he will be able to provide more complete answers for you."

"I don't know." Kyahn looked back over his shoulder, studying Luke intently. "I believe I should examine him bef—"

"This man requires your help." Calista paused long enough to draw Kyahn's attention back to herself. Her tone still perfectly sweet, she asked, "What do you wish to achieve by these delays? Would you have him suffer longer still?"

Calista was already standing quite straight, but as she stared down at Kyahn, she seemed to stand straighter still. Kyahn would never acknowledge Calista as any kind of ruler—he was still governed by the same jealous ruler who held power over Melzia, after all. Nevertheless, Calista was a natural leader, and not easily ignored.

"Fine. Soon as it's worked, I'll have more questions to ask him."

"Might we have a mana potion as well? We cannot in good conscience send him alone to the portals without restoring his mana."

The Citrine opened his mouth to object, but Calista didn't give him the opportunity. She asked, "And do you believe one healing potion will be sufficient? Perhaps we should have a second ready as well."

"I can't offer more than one until I'm allowed to obtain answers to Queen's questions."

"Very well."

Kyahn licked his lips and pulled two vials from a pocket inside his cloak. As he withdrew his hand from the cloak, Luke caught a brief glimpse of a set of brown lines on the underside of the half-goblin's wrist—a set of lines in the shape of a crown that looked astoundingly similar to the mark on Melzia.

Taking advantage of Kyahn's momentary hesitation, Calista turned to a servant near the doorway. Without looking at the half-goblin, Calista delicately loosened his grip from the glass vials as she spoke. "Please take Kyahn upstairs so he might have a respite from his long journey. I am certain he is exhausted. And have the kitchens send up a tray of whatever he might care to have. Make sure he is paid for the potions as well."

"Yes, ma'am."

Kyahn stammered something about mirrors and the orders he had been given prior to arriving here. His words were cut short before he could form a full, coherent sentence.

"I do not believe the guest quarters directly above us have a mirror at the moment. Make certain the room is readied for our newest guest." Calista paused as she met the servant's gaze. She folded her hands together across her waist. "After Kyahn is settled in, please see to it that a mirror is brought to the room. I am sure he wishes to call his Queen."

The servant bowed, and Kyahn was quickly ushered out of the room as he sputtered unintelligibly in an attempt to raise any further objections.

As the footsteps receded down the hallway toward the stairs, Calista leaned close to Fenris and whispered something in his ear. In a blink, he was hurrying down the hallway in the opposite direction.

Spinning around, sending her skirt flaring out around herself, Calista locked eyes with Luke. Pushing the door closed, she moved nearer to the bed and lowered her voice. "I do not believe our disguise was of much use, though I am grateful we were able to stall long enough to obtain the potions. Now come quickly. We must get you away from here."

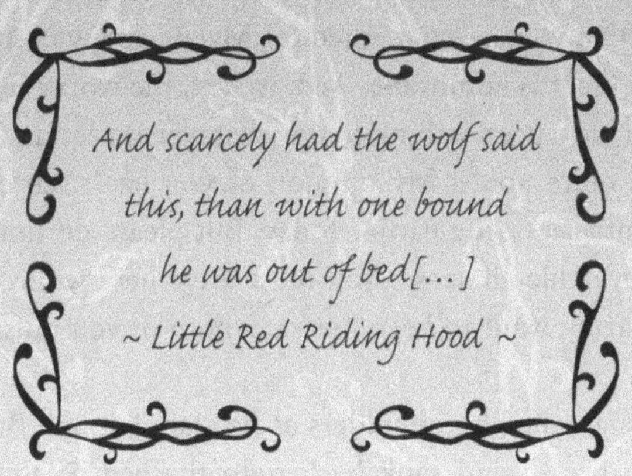

13

"No!" Luke flung the covers off and bolted up out of the bed. "What about Mel? She needs time to heal! I don't know where to go and—"

"I cannot protect Melzia if she is detected here!"

Luke balked at this sudden change in Calista's steadfast composure. At first, he thought it was anger. But as he watched her, he realized it was something else. She was terrified.

Calista took a deep breath and schooled her features. "We have your potions. I agree that it would be best if she had time to rest and let the potions do their work. But now, with a suspicious Kyahn lurking under this very roof, waiting is no longer an option. You both must leave posthaste if you are to avoid being discovered."

"Where the hell am I supposed to go? How can I protect her? How am I supposed to find my way across this continent I've never been to before? Hell, I'm not even good at finding my way around on Earth!" Luke clenched his fists, digging his short fingernails into his palms as he glanced out the window. Eventually, he met Calista's eyes again. "And now you want me to head out on some grand quest? How am I supposed to do this? Especially with Mel's current state! What if she gets worse? How can…" Luke's voice shook as it finally trailed into silence.

"Luke." Calista softened her voice and laid a hand on his cheek. "I understand that you are concerned for Melzia and want that which is best for her. That is admirable. And, in fact, the worry in your voice, the way you have been willing to do whatever is required to help her —that is all quite noble. My opinion of you has risen considerably since our initial meeting earlier today. But please do not allow your passion to overrule all sense. You must leave here while you are still able. If you truly want to keep her safe, both of you must go. Immediately."

Luke straightened his shoulders as he glared at her. But at last, he took a deep breath and sank back onto the bed. Snatching up the boots from beside the bedpost, he shoved his feet into them and stood up, grateful that those at least fit better than the rest of the pilfered outfit. "Fine. Tell me what to do."

"Our servants will have removed the mirror from Kyahn's room prior to allowing him entry. They will be certain to delay the procurement of a new one as well. Beyond that, I swear to you, we shall delay Kyahn as long as we are able. For now, come with me." Calista spun back toward the door as that awful grinding, crunching sound started.

Luke gaped as he watched her transform into one of those tall, humanoid wolf creatures. It had been one thing to see "Beast" change into a creature like that, but Luke hadn't been prepared for this regal woman to do the same. She grew several inches taller, although not nearly as tall as Fenris and the others in their similar form. Her short, nicely trimmed nails grew into long claws. Dark brown fur sprouted all over her body, and when the transformation was nearing its conclusion, her dress, shoes, and jewelry were magicked away. As Calista darted into the hallway, Luke pulled himself together and hurried after her.

Calista led the way, walking quickly, silently until she got halfway down the hall and stopped next to a pair of double doors along one wall. Luke stopped beside her as she raised one fur-covered ear and angled it toward the direction they had just come from. As she lowered her ear again, she glanced at Luke.

Without warning, Calista yanked the double doors open and sprinted through. Luke took off running after her. His footsteps pounded, the sound reverberating off the stone walls. Calista's footfalls were far quieter, barely making a sound as she went. And even in this form, her movements were graceful and almost hypnotic. But as Luke struggled to keep up with her, he could barely spare a passing thought for any of those observations.

The pair raced down one corridor and then the next, through doorways and a few elaborately decorated rooms before finally bursting out into the courtyard. Lanterns were set at regular intervals. None had yet been lit for the evening, letting the shadows stretch long across the ground as the sun sank toward the horizon.

At last, Calista came to a stop in front of the stables. She transformed back into her human shape—her clothes and hair reappearing and leaving her looking as majestic and composed as ever while she stood there, waiting for Luke to catch up.

Skidding to a halt in front of Calista, Luke doubled over, fighting to pull air into his aching lungs.

Calista took Luke's hand and shoved one of the vials into it. The contents swirled with a glittery, red liquid. "Only drink a drop or two.

The rest is for Melzia. Keep her cloak about your shoulders until she is healed, if you can. When she awakens, she can help you determine whether the mark has been removed."

Luke nodded as he straightened up. Pulling the cork from the top of the vial, he carefully tipped it up until a tiny bit fell onto his tongue. He made a face as the bitter liquid slithered down his throat, burning the whole way until it finally reached his stomach.

As soon as Luke jammed the stopper back into place, Calista shoved the second vial into his hand. The liquid in this one was bright blue, and it bubbled incessantly as though it were boiling. He stared down at it.

"Based on what I have learned of you in these past few hours, you are quite brave. From what little my husband has told me so far, he has seen the same. Your actions are foolish and impulsive, perhaps, but brave nonetheless. Do not forget that."

"Brave?" Luke rolled his eyes. "You didn't see me freaking out when I found out about this world. Or when I about pissed myself because a dragon dropped down in front of us. Or me quaking in my boots when your husband found me in the woods."

"If you had not been 'quaking in your boots,' you would have simply been a fool acting with reckless disregard for his own life. You were afraid, as well you should have been. Regardless, you were prepared to fight to protect what you loved."

"Like I could've done anything if they'd wanted to kill us."

"You would have tried. There is no dishonor in that."

Looking entirely unconvinced, Luke gave a small nod and turned his eyes away.

"I see that the fates have chosen well for Melzia."

Luke's head snapped toward Calista. "What do you—"

"When next we meet," Calista continued, ignoring Luke's half-formed question, "we would be honored to consider you a friend."

As her words rolled through his mind, Luke stared, unseeing, at the vials in his hands.

"Luke?"

He jumped at the sound of his own name. When he looked up, Calista was watching him intently. Fenris towered behind her, Melzia held in his fur-covered arms. An exceptionally large, saddled horse stood waiting patiently at the prince consort's side.

With a nod, Fenris gestured toward the waiting animal, and Luke took the hint and felt the tiniest bit of relief. For once, it was something he knew how to do in this world. As he climbed into the saddle, he silently thanked his late mother for ignoring his youthful protests and insisting on those horseback riding lessons when he was a kid.

As soon as Luke was seated, Fenris placed Melzia on the horse in front of him.

Luke glanced down at Melzia's mangled arm and the tear trails on her cheeks. A lump formed in his throat. He brushed the hair back from her face and blinked away the tears that suddenly threatened to spill from his own eyes. Vowing to himself he'd be strong, he straightened his spine. He pulled his eyes away from her face. Wrapping one arm around Melzia's back and lifting her cloak over one of his shoulders, he took hold of the horse's reins.

With that same loud crunching and grinding, Fenris shrank back into his human form and moved over to stand beside his wife.

Still breathing heavily, still trying to maintain control over his emotions, Luke looked down toward Calista and blurted out the only word he could find. "Why?"

Calista sighed as she glided a step closer to him. "There are not many whom I fear. Nor are there many from whom I would brook such blatant disrespect toward my title, but that woman chills my blood to ice. For the safety of my kingdom, I bite my tongue and do my best to play by her rules."

"Thank you, Queen Calista and *Prince* Fenris. I don't know what I would have done without your help."

Calista grinned as Luke put the extra emphasis on the title. "No more titles and formalities. Please call me Cali."

"Cali." A brief smile crossed Luke's face. As it faded, his eyes darted toward Fenris and then back to Calista. "Why would you stick your neck out for us? Wouldn't your whole kingdom have been safer if you'd just given us over to her?"

"Perhaps you are right, Luke. I love Melzia and would never wish harm upon her. But perhaps, for the safety of my kingdom, I should have surrendered her to that wretched woman. I could not, though. I believe Melzia is the only one who can unseat her and end her reign of terror. And you are the one who must help her do it."

"What do you mean?" Luke's eyes darted down toward Mel's unconscious face. "How can I—"

"We have no more time." Fenris interrupted Luke's words. "Go west until you reach the coast, then south. It will likely take you several days of riding to reach the portals."

"Give Melzia the healing potion as soon as you are beyond sight of the castle." Calista glanced back over her shoulder and returned her attention to Luke. "My husband and I must go back before our absence is noted. As he stated, we do not have time for more questions. Take Melzia and go, lest you find yourself trapped."

Luke looked at the pair of them, then swallowed hard. "Thank you, Cali and Fen."

"You are welcome, Luke." Calista moved away from the horse, and Fenris wrapped an arm around her. She grinned sadly up at Luke. "I truly hope our next meeting will be under more pleasant circumstances."

"Me too."

Pulling the reins, Luke turned the horse around and tapped his heels against the horse's sides. The creature readily bolted across the drawbridge. Riding hard toward the lowering sun, Luke pulled Melzia tight to his chest.

Melzia whimpered softly but didn't open her eyes.

As the castle shrank in the distance behind them, Luke hoped with every fiber of his being that this was the right choice.

14

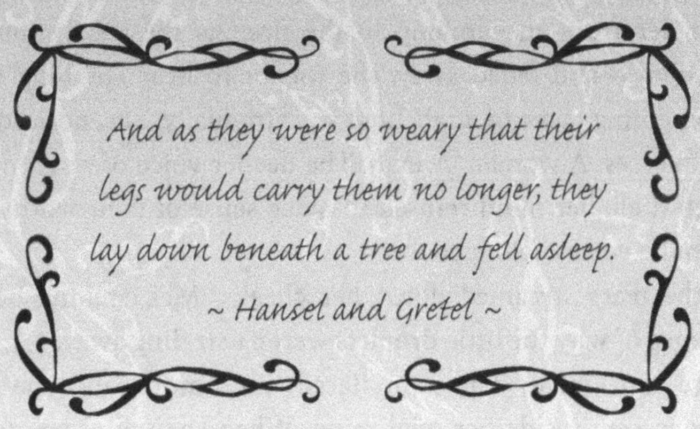

Mel's body was roasting from the inside.

When she had first been attacked, the blaze had started inside her arm, but slowly—*slowly*—the flames had worked their way over her shoulder, along her torso, and down her limbs, scorching every last bit of her. She couldn't speak or think. She could barely even breathe.

Every inhale charred her lungs more thoroughly.

Every exhale stoked the flames.

An eternity passed, or maybe mere seconds—time held no meaning for her now in this all-consuming inferno. But then something changed. She was no longer still. Something lifted her up into the air and clutched her tightly. The pain doubled, and inside her head, she screamed. Tears rolled down her cheeks as her mind played images of bright orange flames lapping at her skin, making it darker and darker until pieces of it fell off as flecks of ash.

She was being moved. She could hear something beyond the roar of the fire inside her. Mel struggled to place the sound, but forcing her mind to focus on the faint, steady rhythm that came from somewhere nearby, the pain was pushed back the tiniest bit. She focused hard, fighting, struggling to latch onto anything that wasn't agony. At last, her mind recognized it. Quick, quiet footsteps echoing off stone walls.

Mel grabbed hold of that knowledge as if it were the only thing keeping her from succumbing to the fire. As the steady thumping finally slowed and faded away, she fought to hear anything else, to find something new to grab hold of. Gradually, she noticed other sounds. Voices. A woman. A man. The deeper voice of a second man. Through it all, her mind refused to make sense of their words or tell her who the voices belonged to.

As the tears streamed down her cheeks, Mel couldn't begin to make sense of why the little droplets weren't sizzling away.

More movement. The pain flared once more, and she loosed another scream inside her own mind. When she found her sense of hearing again, she caught a new thumping rhythm. Faster than it had been a few moments ago. Heavier, too. And no longer only two feet.

Mel tried to focus. To keep hold of that sound, to count the beats and pull herself away from the blaze. But it was too much for her now. Every thump jostled her poisoned arm and added fuel to that inner fire.

The inferno engulfed her once more.

This time, it was the sudden stop to the thumping sound that pulled Mel's attention enough to dim the pain. She struggled to hold that feeling and drag herself away from this hellfire.

More jostling movement, more internal screaming before her world grew still another time. Someone lifted her head and held something to her lower lip. A fiery, bitter liquid made its way into her throat.

Mel tried to twist, to pull away, to close her lips tight. But whoever held her wouldn't let her go. The liquid kept seeping downward, doubling, tripling, the flames that already burned inside her. She thrashed. Her throat threatened to close up, and her chest shook as she coughed. The thing pressed to her lower lip was lifted away. But still, her captor wouldn't let her go.

As the coughing finally subsided, the pressure on Mel's lip returned. She lifted her uninjured arm and tried to push the thing away from her face, but it was no use. The liquid again made its way into her mouth and down her throat. But this time, she noticed something different. The liquid continued to burn all the way down to her belly, but her hands and legs were barely warm now; the blaze inside them diminished to a few smoldering embers.

Reaching up again, she now tried to pull it closer. The visions in her head of skin and flesh burning to ash slowly faded away, and conscious thought seeped back into her mind. The blaze receded until it was contained within her torso and the injury in her arm. It was all still warmer than she'd like, but at least it was no longer unbearable. For the first time in what felt like eons, she believed she might make it to the other side of this.

The last droplets of the liquid made their way into her stomach, and the slight pressure on her mouth went away.

For a long time, Mel lay there silently. When she finally dared to open her eyes, the thin sliver of a moon peeked down at her. Stars glittered against their black backdrop. She inhaled deeply and savored the feeling of the cool grass tickling the backs of her arms and neck.

"Mel?"

She turned toward the voice. In the darkness, she could just make out the worry lines that creased Luke's forehead as he looked down at her.

"Hmm?" Mel's voice came out hoarse and weak. She winced at the unexpected ache and lifted a hand to her throat.

"Thank the stars above." Luke sighed heavily. "I thought I'd lost you."

"No, I—" Mel croaked out the words but stopped abruptly as Luke wrapped his arms around her. His weight pressed on her injured flesh, and she gasped loudly.

"Sorry!" Luke let go and pulled back. "Are you okay?"

Clenching her eyes tight, Mel focused on drawing air in through her nose, then pushing it back out through her mouth as she waited for the fiery pain to subside again. The flames inside her had been nearly extinguished, but the physical damage had barely begun to heal.

When the burst of pain finally abated, Mel looked up at Luke. She nodded weakly, unconvincingly. "Yeah, I'm…" Tears stung at her eyes as her vocal cords forced the sounds out. She again laid her palm on her throat. "I guess I shouldn't have screamed so much, huh?"

"What?" Luke reached a hand out to touch her face. But then, as if he were afraid of hurting her again, he stopped. He refolded his arms across his chest. "You didn't scream. Whimpered a little bit, but no screaming."

At that, Mel couldn't hold back the tears. Somehow, knowing that the screaming had only been inside her mind made the whole ordeal that much more horrifying. And then, even if it had been something only she knew was happening, it still took its physical toll on her.

"Hey." Luke reached out hesitantly. He gently lifted up the hand of her uninjured arm and delicately caressed it. "I can't imagine what you felt. I ended up with a few little drops of that venom on my finger and felt like my whole arm was going to burn away. Considering how much you had on your arm…"

Mel nodded but didn't try to speak. Her chest shook with silent sobs.

"How are you feeling now? Is there anything I can do?"

Sniffling loudly, Mel managed to croak out a single word. "Water?"

"I don't have any supplies." Luke glanced back over his shoulder at the horse they'd ridden here on. The creature waited patiently at the side of a tree, drinking from a narrow puddle at his feet. And no one had pointed this out before they'd left, but there was a large set of saddlebags resting on the horse's back. "Oh, hold on."

Gently lowering Mel's hand to the ground, Luke stood, walked over to the horse, paused momentarily to give him a scratch between the ears, and moved over to open one of the bags. Luke lifted up the leather flap and stuck his hand inside. His fingertips found a glass bottle, and he pulled it out. Removing the cork, he took a tentative sniff of the contents and sighed in relief. Water.

Another quick foray into the bag and he found two firm parcels, each wrapped in cloth. He grabbed them both and returned to Mel's side.

"Here." Setting the cloth-wrapped packages on the ground, Luke slid a hand underneath Mel's head and tilted her up. Holding the bottle against her lips, he slowly leaned the bottom up and let her drink the cool liquid. His own lips were dry and cracked, but he waited.

After a while, he pulled the bottle away. She tried to grab it and continue to drink, but he set it aside and lowered Mel's head back to the ground. "Give it a minute. I don't want to make you sick from guzzling too much all at once."

Mel let her hand sink down onto her chest.

Picking the container up again, Luke took a mouthful of the cool liquid, then stuck the cork back in the opening. He reached for the parcels, pulled them into his lap, and unwrapped them. It was hard to see, but as the cloths were pulled away, the unmistakable aromas of cheddar cheese and rye bread filled the air. Luke's stomach rumbled loudly in response.

Tearing a large chunk of bread from the end of the loaf, Luke shoved the piece into his mouth. As he chewed, he pulled off a smaller section and lifted Mel's head to feed it to her. When the tiny bit of bread was gone, he allowed them both another drink.

Luke was ready to tear off another piece of bread to give to Mel, but she reached over to lay her hand on his. She shook her head.

"They packed cheese too. Do you want that instead?" Luke grabbed the other package, tore off a chunk, and jammed the piece in his mouth.

Mel shook her head. "Just water. There's still a fire burning in my stomach, and I don't think the food will help right now."

Quickly shoving the food away, Luke grabbed the water and held it up for Mel. When she had finished, he used the last of the water to clean up his face and hands before setting the empty container on the ground nearby.

"So," Luke shoved a small morsel of bread in his mouth. "How are you feeling now? Any better at all?"

Mel nodded weakly. "A bit."

"Do you need me to do anything? I can check to see if there's more water. Surely they gave us more than one bottle. Or I can check to see if there's any other food, or I can get the blanket from under the saddle, or maybe—"

"No." Her word came out a notch above a whisper. "I need rest. Just…"

"Just what?"

"Keep me company until I fall asleep."

"Alright." Luke's head turned toward the horse. "Let me take the saddle off him and double-check that he's hobbled. I'll be right back."

Mel tried to push herself upright, wincing as the movement jostled her battered body. She groaned as she slumped back against the ground. " He won't go anywhere. He's trained that he's on duty as long as he's still wearing his saddle. If you remove it, he'll fly off toward home."

"Oh." Luke glanced over at the creature. Finally twisting back around, he leaned against a nearby tree and nodded. He took hold of Mel's hand. "What did it feel like when you were unconscious? You said you screamed."

Mel drew a long, shaky breath and released it. "Hell."

Luke waited a while, rubbing his thumb across the back of Mel's hand, but she didn't elaborate further. He let the subject drop, and the pair sat in silence.

At last, Mel glanced over at the horse. "How'd you convince Fen and Cali to let you borrow him anyway?" She brought her attention back to Luke, finally noticing his appearance. "Wait. What happened to your hair? And when did you get a chance to shave? How'd you get rid of your tracking mark? Whose clothes are those, and why are you covered in blood?!"

"It's okay, it's not mine. I'm not hurt. The tracking mark is really gone, though, right? I wasn't sure."

Mel nodded.

"Really? How…" Luke chuckled. "Never mind, I'm not even going to ask how that works."

"It's not that complicated." Mel tried to grin at him, but her tired and aching body morphed the expression into a grimace. "Remember how I told you the tracking mark works by doing a little bit of damage? We've always been taught that the mark can only be removed by whoever cast it. But I thought maybe if you had a healing potion, it could heal you before the tracking mark had time to damage you further. Then, if it did, maybe the mark would quit working. Well, considering it's gone now, I guess I was right."

"Huh." Luke's voice held a mixture of equal parts amazement and confusion. He scooted closer. "So, can I ask you something? I know you're feeling kind of shitty and all, but I tried to ask earlier, and you were too tired."

"Sure."

"Why'd you leave this place? I know it had something to do with that Queen I saw in the mirror."

Mel's eyes widened. "You saw her? She didn't see you, did she?"

"No. I'll tell you about it later." Luke waited a moment, but when Mel didn't continue, he asked again, "Why'd you leave?"

Mel turned her face away. Her already weak voice lowered into a whisper. "Queen ordered me to do something that I… couldn't do."

Luke leaned in close to hear but didn't dare speak as he waited for her to say more.

Eventually, Mel drew a shaky breath and continued. "She tried to make me kill someone. I couldn't. I-I…"

"Oh, Melody."

Luke reached out a hand to wipe the tears from her face, but she jerked away from his touch. As the long seconds crept by, the only sounds were the horse chewing grass and Mel's sniffling.

At last, Mel wiped her face with the edge of her cloak and looked toward Luke again. "Can we talk about something else? Ask me whatever you want, but not that. Not yet, anyway."

"Yeah." Luke lay down on the grass beside Mel, propping himself up on his elbow so he could look at her. "So, I'm sure you want to hear about everything that happened while you were out of commission. What do you remember?"

"I cut off…" Mel tried to clear her throat and start anew, but her aching larynx simply refused to allow much more than a whisper. "I cut off the wyvern's stingers. That ticked it off, it hit me with its tail, and everything went dark. Then, I mostly remember the flames. I could hear distant voices sometimes, but I couldn't really catch the words."

"That fight was the most impressive thing I've ever seen anyone do, by the way. I always knew you were a badass."

Mel shrugged.

"I'm serious! I mean, don't get me wrong. I hope you never have to do anything like that again. But it was damn impressive watching you fight like that."

"Thanks." Mel felt her cheeks go warm. She squeezed his hand and asked, "What happened after that? I know I woke up a few times to talk to Cali and Fen, but I don't remember much else."

"Well." Luke sighed heavily. "It's been an eventful day."

Settling back against the tree's rough bark, Luke recounted everything that had happened since Mel was knocked unconscious.

Pressing a hand to her mouth to stifle a yawn, Mel watched Luke's face as he finished his explanation. When the feeling finally passed, she lowered her hand. "You actually called Cali a werewolf? Like, to her face?"

"That's the part you focus on from all that?" Luke tried to glare at her, but his grin couldn't be contained. "Yeah. I definitely stuck my foot in my mouth with that one."

"It's a wonder you—" Mel paused, unable to suppress her yawn a second time, then laughed. "It's a wonder you still have your head."

"I know. It was dicey there for a while. So, um…"

"Hmm?"

"If Fenris is your cousin, does that mean you're also a… a… um…"

"A shifter?" She grinned at him as she lifted an eyebrow. "A werewolf?"

Luke shrugged. "Yeah."

"Yes, I'm part lycanthrope." Mel exhaled heavily. "Although it's only from my mother's side, not both. So, I can't hold the transformation as long as Fen and Cali can. And I can't convincingly pull off the wolf form, only the lycan."

"Holy shit, Mel."

"I know. There's a lot I still haven't told you yet."

"No, it's not that you didn't tell me. I mean, don't get me wrong, that is absolutely nuts." Luke leaned back on the tree and sighed. "It's just that, a few days ago, I wouldn't have even believed that creature existed. I'm not sure when you would've been able to tell me that you were one of them. If you'd tried to tell me that back home before all this… I mean, I know I said a while ago that I wouldn't have had you committed to an asylum, but, uh… that changes things. If you'd told me you could change into a wolf or an eight-foot-tall wolf-person at will, I probably would've tried to have you committed."

"What is it then?"

"It's just… it's a damn big piece of information to learn about you all of a sudden. I don't know how I feel about that or, well, any of this, really."

Mel squeezed his hand as she nodded. Then, rubbing a hand across her eyes, she yawned another time. "So, where are we?"

"Not certain. They sent me off in such a rush, I didn't really have time to get much info. Fenris told me to go south to the shore and then west. Or west and then south, I can't remember. Southwest, anyway, so that's what I've been doing."

As her eyelids slowly drifted closed, Mel nodded. "Did he say—" Another yawn cut off her words. Something about his directions bothered her. When she made another attempt to finish her question, the urge to sleep was far too strong for her to resist any longer, and all she could manage was a string of incoherent syllables.

"Go ahead and get some rest while you can." Luke lay on the ground beside Mel, still gently clasping her hand. "We probably ought to head out at first light. I'm sure those people are still going to be after us."

Mel's head bobbed up and down the tiniest bit. Within moments, her breathing had deepened and slowed as sleep overtook her.

Luke lay there for a while, watching Mel drift off into slumber, but it didn't take long until his own exhaustion caught up with him too and pulled him into dream.

15

"Hey." Luke set his hand on Mel's shoulder and shook her lightly. "Sun's not all the way up yet, but we should probably get a move on. I'm sure they've noticed we're gone by now. That Citrine guy was pretty skeptical, so I don't know how long they'll be able to keep him occupied."

Mel grumbled loudly as she squeezed her eyes shut tighter.

"I know, I'm exhausted too. But I don't think those goons that are after us care about letting us get our rest."

"Mm-hmm." Mel rolled onto her back but still didn't open her eyes.

"I think I heard a stream nearby. I'm going to go see if I can clean up a bit more and fill up our empty bottle. I think there's one more full bottle in the saddle bags, but I'd rather stay topped up if we can. See if you can eat something. I'll be right back, and then we can get going."

"Hmm."

The breeze swept past, rustling the leaves overhead. As the sound of Luke's footsteps receded into the distance, he called back over his shoulder, "Don't fall asleep again!"

Mel's eyelids were still too heavy to open. Her mind swirled with images: a horde of wyverns circling her before morphing into blue-cloaked Azures, who leered at her with Nikolas's gray eyes. She jerked her head from one side to the other as the dream grew stronger, but sleep wasn't ready to let go of her yet. Rolling onto her side, she suddenly woke with a wince as pain tore through her mangled arm. Pressing it to her chest, she used her good arm to push herself upright.

After wiping the sleep from her eyes, Mel reached down and gingerly pulled the edge of the cloak away from the wounds. The red fabric clung angrily to the tattered and bloody skin, breaking loose several large scabs as she cautiously peeled it backward. The fire that had been lightly smoldering within from her bicep to her fingertips only moments ago was suddenly reignited, and her stomach rolled in response. She swallowed back the bile that was rising in her throat, forcing herself to finish the task.

As the last of the fabric was pulled away, Mel gasped loudly, finally managing to pull air into her lungs again. She squeezed her eyes shut and sat there, clenching her jaw and focusing on her breathing. The flames inside her arm eventually died back to smoldering embers.

Mel opened her eyes and slowly tilted her head down to inspect the damage. Blood had thoroughly soaked the edge of her cloak as she'd slept, leaving it now with a layer of crusty brown. Her arm was coated in scabs and blisters, but fresh blood oozed out where she had pulled the cloak free from the tattered skin. Deep craters pocked the length of her forearm and hand, exposing bits of the inner flesh.

For the first time, Mel noticed someone had removed her hoodie, leaving her in her dingy, maroon t-shirt. The hoodie sleeves had been destroyed in the wyvern attack, and whatever remained of the ripped fabric would have been in the way of anyone trying to tend to her injuries. She sighed, disappointed to have lost one of her most comfortable pieces of clothing. But there were more important matters to worry about.

She carefully raised her arm and tried to squeeze her hand into a fist. Sucking air through her teeth and doing her best to ignore the pain, she focused on her goal. The muscles wouldn't cooperate; she could barely curl the fingers before her strength gave out entirely.

The crown emblem on the underside of her wrist caught her eye. As she realized that the mark had made it through the attack unscathed by the venom, a sour taste grew in her mouth. That white crown still burned against her skin. Forcing her eyes away, she dragged her thoughts back into the present.

Mel's maimed arm shook as she lowered it into her lap. While the healing potion had staved off the worst of the poison's internal damage, it hadn't done much for the external part so far. If she'd had access to it sooner, maybe the poison wouldn't have had as much time to work its way into her system, and a single vial would have been sufficient. Now, she'd love to have one or two more doses to heal the rest. But, of course, that wasn't an option. She'd have to finish healing the slow, non-magical way.

Standing up, Mel walked over to the horse and rubbed the velvety skin at the end of his muzzle. He nickered in response, nuzzling into her open palm. Gradually moving around to the horse's side, she lifted the flap on one of the saddlebags and laughed with relief as she saw the vial that waited in there. She lifted the glass container out, watching the blue liquid twist and writhe as though it were trying to escape the confines of its glass prison.

Since one of her hands was virtually useless, she tried to push the cork free with her other thumb, but it wouldn't budge.

She stepped back and glanced around. Luke was nowhere to be seen. Staring off into the trees where he'd gone, she listened to the sounds of the forest and wondered what could possibly be taking him so long if he was simply cleaning up and filling a bottle with water. So, with a shake of her head, she brought her attention back to the glass container. She lifted the vial up to her mouth and clenched the cork between her teeth, slowly twisting and pulling.

When the cork at last popped free, Mel's hand jerked forward. The vial tipped, and the blue potion sloshed toward the rim, threatening to spill over onto the ground, never to be seen again. Mel gasped loudly.

Spitting the cork out, Mel hurriedly brought the glass container up to her lips before she had another close call. She tipped it back. The bubbling liquid slid down her throat. Unlike the other potion, this one felt colder than ice, making goosebumps break out across her skin as the elixir worked its way down. She shivered. The bubbles made her stomach gurgle noisily. She stood there for a while with her teeth chattering as both the chill in her body and the commotion in her belly finally faded.

She already felt better. Not that the blue potion did anything directly for her health; it only brought back a portion of her mana. But now—since her body didn't have to split its energy between restoration of mana and restoration of health—significantly more of its resources could focus on healing alone.

Mel retrieved the fallen cork, jammed it back in the opening, and then placed the empty vial back into the saddlebag.

Once it was tucked safely away, Mel began riffling through the bag. Near the top was a loaf of bread wrapped in a strip of white cloth.

She pulled the cloth free, shaking the breadcrumbs loose as she did. When the bit of white fabric was as clean as it could be in the current circumstances, she draped it across the most badly damaged section of her forearm and—with the use of her good hand and her teeth—tied a simple knot to keep the fabric from moving too much.

She looked at the crudely bandaged arm as she lowered it to her side. The pain increased drastically—whether due to the straightening of the muscles or gravity pulling blood toward the injury, she wasn't sure. Lifting her arm, she placed it diagonally across her chest and exhaled heavily as the pain ebbed another time.

Standing there beside the horse, Mel looked down at herself. Specks of dirt, leaves, and a few small feathers clung to her cloak. She shook the fabric, sending the debris fluttering to the ground as she walked away. When the worst of the mess had been dealt with, she grabbed the lower corner of her cloak and tossed it up across her injured arm and over her shoulder. Then with one hand, she tried to tie the corner to the hood, hoping to form a sort of makeshift sling. The red fabric refused to cooperate with her fingers, though.

As the corner of the cloak slipped from her grasp for what felt like the millionth time, Mel stomped her foot.

"Gleffik!"

The horse lifted his head to look over at her but quickly decided it wasn't anything to be concerned about, and he resumed nibbling at the grass.

Turning around, Mel glared off through the trees. "Where did you go, Luke?"

The only response was the horse snorting behind her.

Mel sighed. She'd only just begun to get her mana back—now her supply was a bit shy of half full—and she was loath to use any of it so soon. But not seeing any other choice, she used her one good hand to pull the red hood up over her head.

The change this time was simple; she didn't bother to transform her hair or skin or clothes like she'd done previously. The only real difference now was that a white sling manifested across her arm, keeping the injured limb strapped diagonally across her chest. She could've used the spell to make her arm look normal; she could've disguised the blood and scabs, the black char marks that lined the deep, acid-formed divots in her dark skin. But since the wounds would've still been there, simply hidden beneath the spell's glamour, it wasn't worth the extra mana cost. Besides, the sling would keep the worst of the damage concealed.

However, she did change the cloak's appearance, making it invisible. No sense attracting attention to its noticeable hue as she and Luke tried to evade their pursuers.

"Where is he?" The words slipped quietly out as Mel stared off into the trees again.

With a sigh, Mel turned back to the saddlebag. She pulled out a loaf of bread and a strip of jerky, setting them on the ground at her side.

She reached again inside the bag and paused as her fingertips brushed across a familiar shape. Mel gasped and jerked her hand back. Mentally chiding herself, she stepped closer to the horse so that she could peer inside the deep, leather pouch.

She could see the dark handles of her daggers at the bottom of the bag, their blades sheathed and hastily wrapped in leaves and strips of cloth. Dried streaks of green wyvern poison left intricate designs on the handles, but there didn't seem to be any damage to the weapons themselves. And at the moment, it didn't appear to be damaging the cloth or anything else either.

Mel had no idea if the dried venom had become inert or if it only caused a reaction with living tissue. She wasn't going to willingly test it out, either.

Carefully draping the cloth over the handles of the daggers, she took out a glass bottle of water and stepped away. She grabbed the food from the ground and then moved over to the base of a nearby tree, sinking down to enjoy the first substantial meal she'd had since the chromas had located her on Earth.

Mel sat the bread on her lap as she tore a bite from the jerky, chewing slowly as she savored its saltiness. She chased the first bite down with a swig of water. Her stomach growled in response, demanding more in the way of sustenance. She gladly obliged as she sat, studying her surroundings and appreciating the fact that the pain in her throat had nearly gone away.

This portion of the Lozeriokt continent was not a place she was familiar with. She'd been to certain parts of the Westerlands hundreds of times. She was certainly no stranger to its capital, Liebrahnt, having visited the castle there regularly since she was old enough to remember. She'd been to the northern coast and to several of the small towns and tiny, nameless villages. But this area to the southwest of the castle was somewhere she'd never been.

Ripping off a large chunk of bread and popping it into her mouth, Mel looked out at her surroundings as the sun climbed higher. She was encircled by massive trees. Dense tufts of weeds and wild bushes covered the ground. The area immediately around her where they had spent the night was the only relatively clear spot in view. All the rest of the land had been thoroughly claimed by nature.

As Mel swallowed her last bite of jerky, she pulled off another large bite of bread and tucked the remainder into a pocket that lined the inside of her currently-invisible cloak. When the fabric folded up around it, the food seemed to vanish into thin air.

Shaking the crumbs from her clothes, Mel stood up. Off to one side, she could see a narrow gap in the dense greenery. She walked over to get a better look. A short distance away, the trees and grass petered out, giving way to vast swaths of thick, intertwining briar bushes, their three-inch-long thorns jutting out in every direction.

Mel's heart suddenly hammered. She stepped backward and then slowly pivoted in place as her breathing quickened.

Trees, grass, weeds, bushes as far as the eye could see. But there should be some sign of where Luke had gone. There had to be a patch of grass that was trampled down, a footprint in the dirt, broken branches on a bush where he'd had to force his way through—*some-*

thing. But there was nothing. It was as if he'd never been there in the first place.

Mel took a deep breath, trying in vain to calm the racing of her heart. She knew exactly where she was.

And suddenly, she felt someone's eyes on her.

16

Draining the last of the water, Mel stuck the cork back into the opening. As she replaced the water bottle in the saddlebag, a noise somewhere off to her left drew her attention. Her hand habitually moved to her hip, searching for the handle of her dagger before Mel remembered she wasn't carrying it. Keeping her eyes on the bushes, she slowly lowered herself toward the ground and grabbed a large rock.

Standing back up, Mel crept forward. The hair on the back of her neck stood at attention. She spotted a flicker of movement ahead, so she charged forward with the rock held high and burst through the bushes. A small, purple bird on the ground squawked loudly and then took off, disappearing up into the dense canopy of leaves overhead.

Mel let the rock fall to the ground. She twisted around to see the horse shuffling his feet as if he were suddenly anxious to be on their way.

"Yeah." Mel patted the side of the horse's face as she looked off into the trees. "We need to get moving."

Unhobbling the horse and picking up the reins, Mel stood there, looking around the clearing one more time. Still seeing no signs of Luke, she picked the direction her instincts told her was correct, and she started walking.

Mel and the horse had only gone a few steps when the clearing vanished and they were swallowed up by the forest entirely. She stopped, looking backward at the place she'd just come from. Just like when Luke took off, there was no sign that she'd been back there only a moment ago. Even the thick and winding briar patch was no longer visible through the narrow gaps between the trees.

Lost in her thoughts, she stood there for a minute, chewing on her lip. She knew where she was, but still, a niggling voice of denial in her mind compelled her to make sure.

Mel looked at the horse. He was tightly surrounded by trees; he wouldn't be able to turn around here. She could simply let go of the reins and step away; she wouldn't have to go far to see if she was correct. If she was wrong, she'd make her way back to the horse, find a way to return to the clearing, and give Luke a bit longer. If she was right, then stepping out of sight of the horse would make the whole situation that much worse.

Taking the reins, Mel tied them to the branch of a nearby oak tree and coaxed the horse forward until he stood with his muzzle only a few inches from the trunk. A young pine tree stood at his left, a cluster of rocks piled at its base.

"You wait here. I'll be right back."

The horse pawed at the ground.

Mel pulled the loaf of bread from her cloak pocket, tore off a large chunk, and let the piece fall to the ground at her feet.

Tipping his head down, the horse sniffed at the piece of fallen bread.

"No!"

At Mel's sudden outburst, the horse jerked his head back and tried to back away, tugging at the reins that held him near the tree.

Mel softened her voice and laid a hand on the horse's side. "Sorry. I didn't mean to scare you. Just don't eat that bread. Okay?"

He looked at her sideways but eventually calmed down enough that Mel pulled her hand away and stepped backward. She watched the horse for a few moments to make sure he wouldn't approach the bread again. He turned his head away.

Knowing this was the closest she would get to a true agreement with the equine, Mel tore off another piece of bread. She took a step backward. The horse didn't try to mess with it, so she repeated the process a few times, slowly moving farther away.

Eventually, she only had two small pieces of bread left in her hand. She kept hold of one and let the other fall. As it hit the ground, Mel tilted her head so the horse was no longer in her view, focusing entirely on the bread. Then, taking a deep breath, she lifted her head. The horse was gone.

She groaned. "Drenkth."

Taking a deep breath, Mel reminded herself that the horse was *not* gone. Not really, anyway.

"Luke!" She shouted the name and waited. No response.

By veering south from the castle, Luke had unknowingly led them into The Pathless Greenwood. The witches that lived here had cast a curse over this place more than two centuries ago. Stay with your group, keep within each other's sight and it's hardly different than any other forest. But this place would trick and tempt you, make you see things that weren't there, make you smell food when your stomach rumbled, make you hear the babbling of a brook when you were thirsty. One way or another, the forest would lure you, one at a time, to the witches' cottage. Then, the pair would happily, greedily drain your life to lengthen their own.

Few ever willingly stepped foot into The Pathless Greenwood. Fewer still made it out the other side.

Mel looked off into the distance, peering through the gaps in the trees as worry gripped her heart. She had to hurry; she had to find Luke soon, hopefully before the witches did.

She inhaled deeply, reminding herself that worry wouldn't help. That, of course, didn't do anything to assuage the growing fears. But she exhaled slowly and set to work anyway.

Lifting her hand, she looked at the piece of bread she'd kept clutched there. Bending down, Mel picked up the bit of bread that waited near her foot and took a step forward. She scanned the ground for the next piece. Her heart leapt up into her throat when she couldn't see it.

Her thoughts whirled. The bread pieces were all part of one loaf— as long as she kept one within sight and the rest weren't too far away, the curse wouldn't make them go away. She hoped. Maybe she'd been wrong, and the trail of breadcrumbs couldn't lead her back. Maybe she'd made a huge mistake by letting the horse out of her sight. Maybe she was now completely alone without any supplies and lost in this cursed forest.

But then she spotted the bread at last. A relieved chuckle slipped out. She walked forward, picking it up and then moving ahead to find the next one and the next until she was finally back on the side of the tree where she'd left the horse. She reached out, swiping her hand slowly through the air until it collided with something warm and furry. Suddenly, the horse was back in front of her. He jerked back a step, startled by Mel's abrupt reemergence.

The young pine that had been at the horse's left was now directly behind him and the pile of rocks had been scattered across the ground. The tree she'd tied the horse to—the tall oak—was now a sprawling redbud.

Mel didn't have a choice now; she had to keep going. She shivered as she untied the horse from the tree. Straightening her shoulders, she stuck the broken pieces of bread back in her pocket, took the reins in hand, and stepped deeper into the forest.

She didn't have any idea where she was going, but she knew the forest would only let her go where it wanted.

Everything around Mel was eerily silent. The breeze grew stronger, tousling her hair and the leaves in the trees, but it didn't make a sound. She could see the birds visible in the branches squawking their warnings at her, but no sound reached her ears. She was encased in silence. If it weren't for the quiet breathing of the horse near her shoulder, Mel would think she'd gone deaf.

"Luke!" Mel shouted the name, but her voice came out soft and muffled as the air around her swallowed the sound.

Mel's heart pounded as she wound back and forth between the trees, sometimes clambering through bushes when there wasn't a big enough gap between tree trunks for the horse to fit through. Several times, the horse could barely fit beneath the lower hanging branches. The eerie sounds, the denseness of the plants, the ever-shifting scenery—really the entire place—set Mel's teeth on edge. Fortunately, the horse didn't seem to mind the strangeness of the forest.

Right as Mel began untangling her thick hair from the spindly branches of a bush, she froze. The forest sounds had suddenly come back in full force. The cacophony restarted the racing of her heart.

No longer trying to be gentle, she clutched the lock of hair and yanked, breaking off a half dozen twigs in the process. The cracking it made sounded like a shotgun, but the squawking birds that screamed down at her from the treetops only grew louder and more insistent. The wind howled, tossing her hair into her face and forcing the tree branches to bend and flail wildly.

She was close now, and they would be waiting.

Reaching up overhead, Mel took hold of the invisible cloak hood and adjusted it. The movement was subtle. Not enough to create a full reset this time—her magicked sling still kept her injured arm fastened across her chest, and the color didn't seep back into the cloak fabric. As she let her arm fall back to her side, a one-handed sword formed in her grip. Then, a metal shield formed over the sling's white fabric, anchoring itself to her arm. It wasn't comfortable to have the extra weight strapped across the injury, but if she couldn't use that arm to fight, she figured she might as well use it to defend.

Feeling her mana reserves depleting faster, she hoped she could maintain the spell long enough to find Luke, escape the forest, and get to the gateway.

Giving a tug on the reins, Mel and the horse moved forward once more. The trees grew closer, leaned in, darkened the sky with their dense canopy of leaves. Shadows deepened and seemed to dance at the corners of Mel's vision. The horse started to grow anxious, tugging at the reins, nearly pulling them from her hand that gripped the sword as well. She clung tighter as she led the way, weaving through the trees until she could finally see a clearing through the gaps.

Suddenly, the air around her felt thick. The witches were close.

She took a deep breath, bracing herself for the fight that was to come.

Mel stopped behind a tree at the edge of the clearing, studying the scene that lay in front of her. Everything inside was telling her to run, to get out of this forest while she could. But she held herself back, the horse shuffling his feet restlessly at her side.

In the clearing, the sun shone brightly. Though the wind continued to plague the forest around her, the air inside the clearing was calm.

The right half of the open space had a garden with an astonishing assortment of fruits and vegetables. Strawberries beside ginguen fruits, green beans next to orange bhalya beans, zucchinis and cauliflowers alongside pinfalbs. The sight made Mel's mouth water and her stomach grumble loudly. Scattered haphazardly amongst the various foods, bright flowers in every color and shape stood tall, basking in the sunshine.

The left half of the clearing held a small, cheerful cottage. Bright yellow-green curtains hung in the windows, and more flowers and vines decorated the wooden walls.

Unlike the way the garden called to her, the sight of the simple building made a shiver run down her spine.

"Hello!"

Mel's eyes darted in the direction of the high-pitched voice. A little, blond boy—he looked like he was no more than six years old—stood near the back edge of the cottage, smiling at her. She glanced around the clearing once, searching for a sign of anyone else before returning her focus to him. "Where's Luke?"

The little boy's smile dimmed. He tilted his head, keeping his light blue eyes fixed on her. "I don't know anyone named Luke. Are you lost?"

As Mel let go of the reins, the horse wasted no time bolting forward, out of the tightening grip of the trees. Mel rebalanced the hilt of the sword in her hand, took a deep breath, and stepped out into the bright sunshine.

The sounds from the forest—the fierce wind, the squawking birds, and the creaking tree limbs—vanished. The clearing was serene.

"What's your name? Why do you have a shield? Are you a knight?" As the boy's words came out, his eyes lit up, and his smile returned in full force. He took a step closer to Mel.

"Stay there." Mel pointed the tip of the sword at the boy. She kept her voice calm as she glared. "Where is he?"

The boy took another step. "Who? I haven't seen anybody all day. Except my sister."

As if summoned by the mention of her, a young girl stepped out from behind the cottage and walked up to stand beside the boy. She was several inches taller than him and maybe a couple years older. Her hair was pale brown and styled into two braids, one draped across each of her shoulders. Her eyes were a deeper shade of blue than her brother's, but her face sported an exact copy of his smile.

Mel stepped backward, not daring to take her eyes off the boy. "Don't lie to me, Hans."

The children stopped in their tracks, any trace of happiness erased from their faces. Clenching his jaw, Hans narrowed his eyes at Mel; Greta's nose crinkled as she glowered.

"Just tell me where he is, and we'll leave without a fight. I'm not leaving without him." Mel's eyes bored into Hans's. "Where. Is. He?"

"What makes you think you can leave?"

For the first time, Mel's focus was drawn to Greta and those deep blue eyes. She tightened her grip on the sword and set her shoulders as she faced the girl.

All of a sudden, a shrill, eardrum-shattering shriek tore through the air. Mel winced. She jumped back, jerking her head toward Hans as he continued to scream. At the same time, Greta charged off to the side, moving faster than humanly possible. Mel moved quickly backward, away from them both as she focused on the blurred shape that was Greta.

By the time Greta came to a stop, she was no longer a little girl with brown pigtails. Now, she was much taller and hunched over. Sagging, wrinkled skin covered her body. Her hair had become pure white, lying in a tangled mess down her back.

It took a moment for Mel to realize the screeching sound had stopped. What she heard now was the ringing of her ears, mimicking that horrific noise. Mel twisted her head back toward Hans. His form had changed too. He had grown taller, but his shoulders were drooping with age. Deep wrinkles and dark spots marred his skin. Most of his hair was long gone, though what remained of it hung down to his shoulders in thin, wispy, unwashed locks.

Mel's ears continued to ring loudly, blocking out any other sounds. And as she stood there, her gaze flitted between the two hags—though Hans was a man, he and his sister were both equally deserving of the derogatory title—and Mel waited for one of them to make the first move.

Greta leapt off the ground and flew at her.

Simultaneously, Mel saw a bright flash from the corner of her eye. She spun toward Hans to see an orb made of purple-blue shadow sailing toward her. Mel rolled to the side, ducking beneath the spell, and jumped back onto her feet to face Greta. Bringing the sword up, she dodged out of the way. She swung the blade, making a deep gouge in the witch's arm. As Greta landed on the ground, she screamed, doubling the volume of the ringing in Mel's ears.

Hans's head was tilted toward the sky, and his arms were raised. His lips were moving, rapidly uttering an incantation in some ancient language that Mel wouldn't have understood even if her ears were working. She prepared to charge toward him, but movement off to the left drew her attention. Ducking her head and twisting just in time, Mel positioned the shield between herself and Greta, jerking her body in that direction as the two collided. The witch bounced off the metal plate, and Mel staggered backward, wincing from the force of the impact.

Greta darted away and started to speak another spell alongside her brother.

Tears stung at Mel's eyes. She gritted her teeth but didn't have time to think about the pain in her arm. Fireballs rained down on all sides of her. They pelted the ground, singeing her hair and scorching her exposed skin as they crashed around her. Smoke swirled in the air and seeped into her lungs. She held her breath.

Wishing right now that the sling wasn't there keeping her arm and shield fastened tightly across her chest, Mel lifted her sword over-head. Pivoting, weaving, and dodging, she finally made it outside the circle of fire-rain.

Greedily gulping the fresh air, Mel looked around. She was surrounded. Dozens of copies of both Greta and Hans filled the clearing. The majority glared at her silently from the sidelines, waiting for their chance; others stood, reciting their dark enchantments up toward the sky. The rest charged at her.

Mel spun, swinging the sword at one after another. As the blade sliced through each one, they turned to vapor, quickly disintegrating into the air. The ones who made it past, though, used their long, jagged fingernails and rotting teeth to tear at her skin and clothes. Painful, bloody tracks marked her skin.

She was losing strength quickly as trails of blood oozed down her arm. Her mana was nearly depleted as well. She wasn't sure how much longer she could last through this. The summoned attackers were relentless. She had to find the real one. The air was thicker to the right. Her head jerked up. She locked eyes with the one standing there. The lifelike apparitions on all sides were hurtling toward Mel, but none of the figures had bloody gouges in their arms.

Except for one.

Raising her sword high, Mel rounded on that one and bolted forward. The ghosts around her kept clawing and snatching as she cut them down one after another. She ignored the ones her sword couldn't reach.

Greta—the real one—spoke faster, refusing to stop the spell-casting even as Mel charged at her. More apparitions formed and attacked. More were cut away to dissipate into the air.

At last, nothing more stood between Mel and her target. She shouted and swung the sword. Greta's eyes grew wide, and her mouth finally quit moving. Terror filled the witch's face as Mel's sword connected with the woman's throat, slicing a gaping hole across it. Blood sprayed out as Greta fell to her knees. All the copies vanished at once and the intense ringing in Mel's ears finally went silent as well.

Greta gasped for breath one last time, the air gurgling through the deep wound. She slumped to the ground, her eyes fixed in place as she went silent.

"No!"

To one side, Mel saw Hans flying toward her. She spun. Using the flat of the blade, she knocked him from the air. He slammed hard into the ground. The air left his lungs, and he lay there, stunned and gasping for breath.

"Where is he?" Mel panted heavily. She pointed the tip of her sword at the center of his throat as she moved closer. "If you care about your life at all, tell me where he is!"

Hans roared. He leapt up and hurled himself at Mel. She thrust the sword forward, driving the blade through his chest. As the blood seeped out around the blade, his knees went weak, and he sank into the grass. Mel pulled the sword out, watching him fall.

"What makes you…" His voice was weak now. What little color the man had in his face drained away. With a loud moan, he sucked in an unsteady breath. "Think you can leave this place?"

Hans collapsed into the grass with one last rattling exhale.

A moment later, both Hans and Greta turned to dust that was lifted up and carried away on the wind.

Mel backed away, dropping the sword and it vanished before it could hit the ground. Reaching up and pulling the hood off her head, she turned and hurried toward the cottage. The shield and sling disappeared as the hood came to a rest on her back. The red of the cloak returned as she sank into the dirt at the edge of the garden, dripping with sweat and blood.

"Hello? Is anyone there?" The voice was weak and slurred, as though he had recently woken up from anesthesia.

Mel twisted around to face Luke. He was standing in the sunshine, covered in scrapes and bruises, leaves and twigs in his hair, mud on his too-large, pilfered clothes. Half the buttons were missing from his vest, and the pig's blood stains were still plainly visible on the torn clothing. But Mel's pounding heart raced ever faster at the sight of him.

Luke turned her way, and Mel smiled. Then, as though he had stepped out of a dense fog, the spell that lingered over him dispersed. He smiled back, running toward her across the clearing.

Forcing herself to stand, Mel opened her arms wide, ignoring the pain that flared up beneath her injuries. Luke crashed into her, wrapping his arms around her waist and lifting her off her feet to spin her around. Both of them were laughing.

Coming to a stop at last, their laughter faded away as Luke leaned back, and they stared into each other's eyes. He lowered Mel back to the ground, then buried his fingers in her hair. Her arms wrapped around his back, her fingertips trailing up his spine until her hands flattened out across his shoulder blades.

"I thought I'd lost you." Mel's eyes filled with tears as she looked up at Luke.

Luke nodded. When he finally spoke, his voice shook. "Now you know how I've felt over and over and over these last few days."

Before Mel could form a response, Luke's lips found hers. He pressed his body close, and she found herself melting in the warmth of his strong embrace.

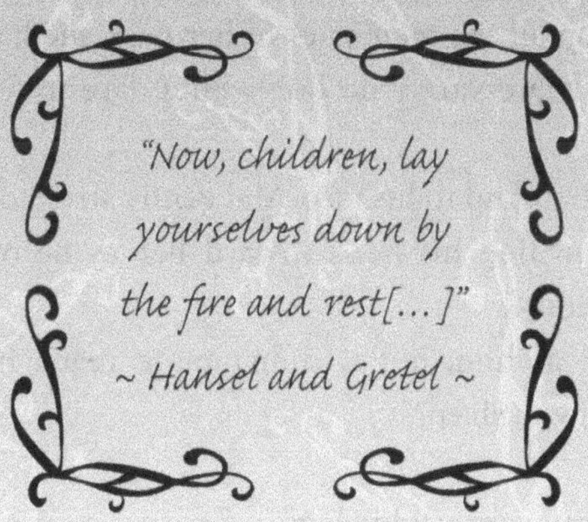

17

Mel's eyes fluttered open. She was lying on her side with her cheek resting on Luke's bare chest. And even though he was still snoring softly, his arm was curled around her shoulders, keeping her close to his side. Twisting slightly, she looked up at the sky. The thick clouds growing along the northwestern horizon glowed with gold along their edges as the dawning sun's rays reflected off them. Overhead, the last of the stars were fading away for the day.

The couple had fallen asleep in the tall grass behind the cottage, her cloak draped across them both like a blanket. The horse had found his way back into the clearing sometime during the night and was now lying near a small pond by the edge of the trees.

Lifting her wounded arm, Mel reached up and used her fingertips to slowly trace a path down the center of Luke's chest, feeling the thin line of coarse hair until she reached the top edge of the red cloak draped across his belly. Sliding her hand back up again, she held it lightly against his pec so she could feel the steady beating of his heart.

She wanted to forget about curses and the chromaveiled. She wanted to lay together like this forever. But soon Luke would wake up and she couldn't keep avoiding his questions. As much as it would hurt to dredge up all the memories of her past, she had to do it. Here —in this place where surely no one would dare to follow—they had time.

Moving her hand up to his face, Mel gently stroked Luke's cheek.

He sighed, turning his head toward her as he opened his eyes. "Morning, gorgeous."

Mel grinned at him, but it didn't quite reach her eyes. "Good morning. How'd you sleep?"

"Like a log."

"More like you were sawing logs."

He laughed, then squeezed her close and kissed her forehead. "What about you? You get much rest?"

"Mm-hmm."

A few moments passed in silence. At last, Luke glanced down at Mel's arm with all its scabs and half-healed gore. "Is that feeling any better? It's, uh… it's not looking great."

She shrugged. "It feels about as good as it looks. But at least it's getting easier to use it now. I can wiggle my fingers without agony, so…"

As her words trailed away, silence returned between them. Luke's brow crinkled as he looked at her.

Tilting her head down, facing away from Luke, Mel chewed on her lip. She wasn't sure how to strike up the conversation that she knew they needed to have.

"Hey." Sliding his finger underneath Mel's chin, Luke tipped her head up toward his. "What's wrong?"

"We need to talk." Mel paused, shaking her head. She went on, "Well, *I* need to talk. I need to start answering the questions I haven't answered yet."

"Oh. Okay."

They lay in awkward silence for a while, not looking at one another, before Mel finally reached across Luke and grabbed his discarded trousers. She silently placed them on his chest, shoved the cloak aside, and hurriedly threw on her clothes.

"Are you hungry?" Mel leapt up without waiting for an answer. She started walking around the side of the cottage, talking rapidly as she went. "You've got to be starving. I know I am."

"Mel." Luke stood up and went after her.

"Come on, there's a bunch of stuff in that garden. It'll all be enchanted to grow here all the time, but I'm sure it's safe, at least. You'll like the ginguen fruit. The bhalya beans would be good if we had some butter and garlic salt for them, but I don't know if I'd trust anything like that from inside the house. I'm not sure—"

Luke laid a hand on Mel's shoulder and spun her around to face him. "Mel! Just tell me what's going on with you."

She opened her mouth, closed it, and opened it yet again. But no words came out. Mel was still working up the first syllable when a soft noise came from behind her. She and Luke both looked toward the garden to see a pair of opossums walk out between the rows of strawberries.

"Whoa. This place has opossums?"

The sudden, unexpected arrival of the creatures and the absolute disbelief apparent in Luke's voice made Mel laugh. "Since we've been here, you've met a dragon, saw me fight a wyvern, and learned that some people have the ability to shift into wolves. But *that's* the thing that surprises you? Opossums?"

"You're able to make friends with a dragon and face down a wyvern with only a couple of knives, but you can't just talk to me?"

As quickly as it had shown up, the laughter vanished from Mel's face. She blinked back the sudden tears that formed in her eyes. "Of course I can face a dragon and a wyvern! Of course I can run from an assassin and take on a pair of witches! None of that is as terrifying as the idea that you'll think less of me."

Luke tilted his head and sighed. He stretched a hand toward her, but Mel stepped out of his reach.

Spinning on her heel, Mel marched over to the garden, scaring off the opossums in the process. She snatched a strawberry off the stem, shoved the whole thing into her mouth, and chewed aggressively as she plopped onto the ground.

Walking over, Luke sat in the grass beside her and waited. Somewhere far off in the distance, the low rumble of thunder sounded.

When Mel finally swallowed, she stuck out her left arm with all its half-healed wounds plainly visible. She took a deep breath and flipped her arm over so her palm was facing up. "See that mark?"

"What? Your tattoo?"

"It's not a tattoo."

Luke leaned over, peering closer at the crown-shaped insignia on Mel's wrist. He sat back. "What is it? I saw that Citrine guy had something similar."

"Queen would take in orphans. The ones she thought had some sort of power, anyway. The ones who didn't have any magical proficiency she'd..." Mel paused, focusing on stifling the nausea that rose up as she began her story. When she continued to talk, her voice was soft, shaky. "If they were lucky, she would kill them."

"If they were *lucky*?" Luke gaped at her.

Mel nodded. "If they weren't, she wouldn't hesitate to change them into monsters and set them loose near the places she'd taken them from. Then she didn't need to kill them. The frightened villagers would do it for her." Mel sniffled loudly and squeezed her eyes shut. She softly added, "And I'll never forget the smile she wore as she watched."

Those words lingered in the still air as they both sat there, lost in their own thoughts.

After a long time, Mel took a deep breath and slowly released it. These long-ignored memories were ones that she could only handle for a few minutes at a time. Now that she'd allowed the words to come out and successfully wrestled the overwhelming despair back into its prison inside her mind, she felt like she could breathe again.

Popping another strawberry into her mouth, she stared at the white lines on her inner wrist as she chewed. "The ones she deemed worthy, she'd have them branded with this, the crown symbol. All the chromas under her power end up with this mark." Mel paused momentarily. "By the way, I don't mean 'branded' like you're thinking of. It's not like she took a hot piece of metal and seared the flesh. I mean, she cursed the orphans, binding them to her permanently, obedient to her."

"So, you—"

"Please, Luke. Just let me get through this." Mel laid her hand on his, but she wouldn't look at his face.

"Sorry."

"After she claimed the orphans, she'd have them trained. Not only to use those powers, but to work for her. That's how she built her chromaveiled army. She slowly took children who had no one to protect them or love them. She tricked or coerced them into being soldiers.

"But it got worse. Over time, she felt like her army wasn't growing fast enough. So she'd send her most loyal chromas out to *find* more suitable orphans... by whatever means necessary."

"What the fuck?"

Mel ignored the interruption and continued. "When she first started all this, she wasn't a queen. She called herself that, but she wasn't any sort of royalty at the time; she only wanted to be. And she managed to keep all this—creating and gathering the orphans, training them, cursing them—a secret. Some combination of threats and curses kept word from getting out to anyone who could have stopped her.

"So, she was building this army in secret. I was only a little kid at the time, so I don't really know all the details. But, she…" Mel's throat closed up. She sniffled loudly and buried her face in her hands.

Luke laid an arm around Mel's shoulder, silently waiting.

Drawing a shaky breath, Mel lifted her head again and wiped her sleeve across her face. "My mother died when I was really little. I don't remember her at all. So it was always just my dad. Until Queen came along. Introduced herself as 'Victoria' and used some kind of magic to convince my father to marry her."

Sliding his hand across her back, Luke began to gently massage the back of Mel's neck. Leaning close, he asked, "So this evil woman became your stepmother?"

Mel nodded. "That's also how she became Queen."

Luke's brow furrowed as he tilted his head to one side. Licking his lips, he tried to sort out his thoughts well enough to respond.

"My father was the king of Losmehdyos!"

"What? So you… You're a…"

"Yes, that makes me a princess! My father was the king, so I'm a princess! I've only been called 'Lady' because Queen stripped me of my actual title when I left."

"Oh." Luke blinked at her. "Okay. I mean, holy crap, that's a big thing, and it's going to take me a while to wrap my head around it. But it's not *bad* that you're a princess. Is that what you were so worried about telling me? Because that's really—"

"No." Mel closed her eyes as she massaged her forehead. The deep acid wounds and the various cuts and scrapes were still obvious on the skin of her arm, but at least most of its functionality had come back. She rested the arm back on her lap, carefully avoiding bumping the injuries as she did so. Finally taking a deep breath, she said,

"Things seemed okay at first. Don't get me wrong, she was a monster doing horrible things to those other children, but at the time, I had no idea. I didn't know about any of that until later. As far as I knew, she was a decent person. As good of a stepmother as I could've expected.

"Anyway, a few months after they were married, my father suddenly went missing without a trace. Queen cursed or blackmailed everyone into agreeing that he'd died, even though she had no body to show for it. Anyone who she couldn't control, well, she simply killed them. It didn't take long until eventually, no one asked anymore. But if I ever get a chance to put my dagger against her flesh, I *will* find out what she did to him."

Having no idea how to respond, Luke sat in silence as he watched Mel work her jaw.

She was completely absorbed in the idea of destroying the woman. At last, she sighed loudly before continuing her story. "Then she took over as ruler. Marked me with this." Mel paused to hold out her arm and display the white crown once more.

Luke reached out and lightly traced the emblem with his fingertips. "Did it hurt when she marked you?"

"Yes. It's also how she would let you know that either your services were required or she was displeased with you. When your wrist started to burn, you knew it was either time to go do her bidding or come back to face her punishment. It still hurts, in fact. It's been hurting for years now. But I learned to live with that a long time ago." Slowly pulling her arm away from Luke's touch, Mel covered the emblem with her other hand. "Anyway, I, um… I would have been the next ruler if I had been old enough when my father went missing. But since I wasn't, she was supposed to hold the throne for me until I came of age."

Mel stopped and buried her face in her hands. Her breathing was becoming ragged, and her throat was tight. She took a few minutes to rein in her emotions. Finally sitting up again, she cleared her throat.

"She'd never willingly give up her power. She wouldn't have allowed me to stake my claim, but she wasn't worried. I was cursed already. She never believed I'd be able to disobey her. The problem was that… Well, as the years passed, there was someone else who began asking questions. Someone who also had a claim to the throne. Queen wanted her gone. What better way to prove that I would never betray Queen than to have *me* be the one who had to kill her?

"So, Queen gave the command." Mel wiped a tear streak off her cheek. "She ordered me to kill my own little sister, Yvette."

"Oh, Melody…"

Mel sniffled loudly. "I couldn't, though. But I couldn't outright refuse, either. If I did, Queen would've had us both killed. She would've sent Nikolas or one of the other Verdants after the both of us.

"Yvette had already run away and gone into hiding. Ezmaunda was sent to track her down. I was supposed to come along after and, well… The only thing I could think of was to trick everyone. Make it seem like Yvette had died, then get out before anyone realized. So I did. I cursed my own sister. I'm the one who tricked Snow White into eating the poisoned fruit.

"That was Queen's mistake, though. She would've kept control over me if she hadn't gotten rid of my father and sister. Threats against them would've kept me here under her thumb forever. But with them gone, what's a little pain? Physical pain was nothing compared to losing them. What more could she take from me besides my freedom? So I took my chance and fled to Earth."

"What the… Wow." Luke blew out a big puff of air, shaking his head. As he sat staring off into the distance, he finally said, "Shit, that's horrible."

"I know! That's why I didn't want you to find out!" Mel slapped the ground at her side.

"What?"

"You're right! It is horrible! That's why I didn't want to tell you."

"I heard what you said." Luke scooted closer and slid his hand around Mel's shoulder. "But how was any of that supposed to make me think less of you?"

Mel twisted around to glare at Luke with tears spilling down her cheeks. "Weren't you listening? I poisoned my own sister and abandoned her here! I don't even know if she's okay!"

"Yeah, I was listening. But you know what I heard?" Mel tried to pull away again, but Luke wouldn't let her this time. Leaning over, he rested his cheek on the top of her head. "You were put in a shit situation, and you didn't let it defeat you. Yeah, you poisoned your sister. In any other situation, that would've been a horrible thing to do. But you did it to *save* her. Then you gave up everything. Your home, your friends, your inheritance, *everything* just so you could escape that woman's hold over you. You didn't let her win."

Raising her hands up to push against Luke's chest, Mel forced him to move back far enough that she could look at his face. "So me doing that to her didn't change your opinion of me?"

Luke brushed a stray coil of hair back from Mel's face and tucked it behind her ear. "Of course it did. A couple weeks ago, I thought I couldn't have been any more amazed by you. I was wrong."

Mel's lips curved upward at the same time a loud sob worked its way out. She quickly buried her face in Luke's chest. For a long time, they sat there together. He gently stroked her hair and rocked her from side to side, whispering that everything would be alright.

Eventually, when the worst of the emotional storm had finally passed, Mel sat up and wiped her face. Tilting her head down, she looked at her hands in silence.

"I'm sorry I didn't have a better reaction at the end of your story. It's just, you know, my whole world has been flipped on its head the last few days. In less than a week, I've found out that magic not only exists, but that you can wield it. There is life on other planets. Werewolf-Lycan-whatevers are real, and you are one of them! Now, I learn you're a princess on top of everything else? Oh, not to mention that your sister—a person I didn't even know existed until just a few minutes ago—is freaking Snow White! It's... I mean..."

"Yeah." Mel chuckled. "I guess it is a lot all at once, huh?"

"Well, that's the understatement of the century."

Luke reached into the garden next to them and pulled off a few strawberries. He handed a couple to Mel and then took a bite of his own. "So, was that why you wouldn't marry me? The guilt?"

"No." Mel held out her arm, displaying the white crown. "This is why. As long as I'm bound to her, I can't take a vow that binds my life to another. You know how the curse kept me from telling you anything as we were leaving Earth? How it nearly choked me when I tried to form the words?"

He nodded.

"If I ever tried to speak the marriage vows, it would do the same thing. As long as she has this hold over me, I can't get married."

Luke's eyes lit up as he looked at her. "So, that's the only thing stopping you? And you... *would* marry me if you could?"

Reaching out and clasping Luke's hand in hers, Mel grinned sadly at him. "Yes."

Laying a kiss on the back of her hand, Luke sat there for a moment, letting his mind process everything he'd just learned. Eventually, he let go and settled back to continue his questions. "I guess that's why Kyahn has that same symbol. I noticed it when he came to the castle."

"Mm-hmm."

Luke nodded as he reached out to trace the white lines on Mel's wrist. "Why are Cali and Fen marked? Theirs was something different, but it was in that same place."

"A pair of intertwined roses." Mel sighed. "Theirs isn't because of a curse. When someone here finds their perfect soul match, an identical symbol shows up on each of them. Something that holds meaning to them as a couple."

"Oh. So, um... if you can't be marked, does that mean you can't know who your soul match is?"

Mel faced Luke. She took his face in her hands and pulled him nearer. Leaning in, she closed her eyes and brought her lips to his. When Mel finally pulled away and looked at him, she slid her hand around to the back of Luke's neck to slowly run her fingers through his recently shortened hair. She smiled at him. "I don't need a mark to tell me who I belong with."

Color seeped into Luke's cheeks, and he could barely keep the grin off his face as he pulled Mel back into his side.

"So how come you don't sound like Cali and Fen? I mean, your accent is kind of similar, but you don't speak as formally as them. Er, well, Cali, at least. Fen didn't really seem to talk much."

Mel laughed. "Yeah, Fen isn't exactly what you'd call 'verbose.' I used to talk a lot more like them, but nothing will make you stand out more in a strange, new world than talking all prim and proper like Cali does. When I arrived on Earth, I had to learn to fit in real quick."

"Makes sense, I guess." Luke scooted away and twisted to look around the clearing. "So. Now what?"

"We probably can't stay here too much longer. I'm sure the curse over the forest would've kept the other chromas away, but I don't know how long it may be until they figure out that the witches are dead. Their curse would've died along with them." She looked up at the sky. Overhead was still bright and clear, but the clouds on the horizon were still slowly growing. "And I'd like to head out and beat that storm anyway."

"So…" Luke lifted his eyebrows in question.

"Well, first, we're going to sit here for a few minutes and eat our fill. Then I guess we ought to see what we can find in that cottage. A couple of centuries-old, evil, hermit-witches ought to have something worthwhile in there, right?"

"Alright, but, uh…" Luke glanced down at the dirt and blood that stained his clothing. "How about we go over to that pond and get cleaned up first?"

"Okay. It's about time you had a bath." Grinning, Mel pushed herself to her feet.

Luke stood up. "Oh, it wasn't me I was worried about." Smirking, he took a moment to watch Mel's exaggerated look of indignance, and he pulled her in for a kiss.

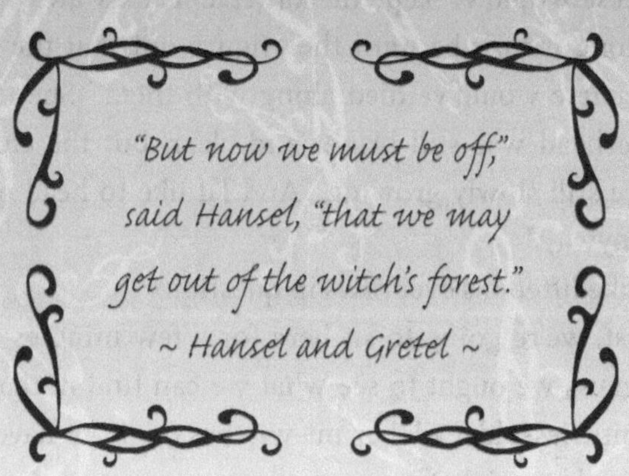

18

"**W**atch where you're walking. And don't touch anything without running it by me first." Mel glanced over her shoulder as she pulled the cottage door open.

Luke scrunched up his face at the command. His clothing was still damp and the shirt was clinging to the muscles of his biceps and chest.

Brushing a wet strand of hair away from her face, Mel forced herself to stay focused. "Sorry, I really don't know how to teach you what to watch out for in the next thirty seconds. There might be some world-ending curse sitting around in here for all we know."

"Ugh. Fine, if you insist." Luke sighed dramatically, folding his arms across his chest and sticking out his lower lip. He couldn't quite hide the corners of his smile, though, and the exaggerated pout faltered.

Rolling her eyes and laughing, Mel stepped into the house and turned to hold the door open for Luke. "You are such a dork."

"But you love me anyway." Luke grinned as he waltzed through the doorway.

Near the far corner of the single room, two narrow beds sat beside one another, separated by a faded brown curtain. Matching wooden chests sat near the foot of each bed. Small bouquets of fresh flowers sat in each window, offsetting the dreariness of the slowly darkening sky. Everything inside the room was tidy and organized. Even the fireplace in the center of one wall looked like it had been recently scrubbed clean.

As Mel let the door swing closed behind Luke, he stopped and looked around the room. He said, "So, that was a joke, right? There aren't actually curses just sitting around waiting to be picked up? Like, they're not physical things, are they? And besides, wouldn't the spells have died with those, um... witches? Was he a warlock? Or would he be a witch, too? I don't—"

"Yes, he was a witch as well. Now, slow down and give me a minute to answer." Mel laid a hand on his arm and gave it a light squeeze. She walked past him and lifted the lid to one of the wooden chests. "Yes, spells can be bottled, so yeah, there might be curses sitting around in here somewhere. No, they wouldn't have died with the people who created them."

"But didn't you tell me before that—"

"Right. Give me a minute. Yeah, the curse over the forest broke when they died. A spell that has been cast will end with the death of the caster. Well, usually. There are some exceptions where the spell will last beyond death. Anyway, it normally dies with the caster. If the spell was bottled, then Hans or Greta may have *created* it, but they wouldn't be the caster. Whoever released the spell would be the caster."

"Okay, so if I knocked a spell bottle off a shelf…"

"Well." Mel shifted some blankets aside in the chest to look underneath them. Finding nothing of interest, she closed the lid and stood up to move over to the next one.

"Some spells are set off by breaking the containers or setting the liquid on fire or reciting specific words over them. Really a million different ways, depending on the spell. Anyway, *if* breaking the container is the way that particular spell gets initiated, and you break the container, then the spell would generally last until you die. So please don't break anything."

"Noted." Luke took a step away from the table. He folded his arms together, tucking his fingers against his sides, far away from anything breakable.

Mel knelt in front of the second chest and lifted the lid. The hinges squealed as she forced them to loosen their grip. Finally letting the lid come to rest on the end of the mattress, she leaned forward, peered inside, and grinned.

"What'd you find?"

"Ambrosia."

"Huh?"

Luke stepped forward to look into the chest. Before he could get close enough, Mel reached in and grabbed hold of something. Beaming, she stood up and lifted two vials—the contents of each one swirling with a familiar, glittery red liquid—as she turned to face him. Without waiting for a response, Mel raised the bottles to her mouth and jerked one of the corks free with her teeth. She let the stopper fall to the floor and lifted the potion to drink.

"Wait!"

Raising her eyebrows, Mel turned to look at Luke. "What?"

"How can you be sure that's going to heal you? What if it's a curse or something?"

Chuckling, Mel shrugged. "Well, if I change into a toad, I guess you'd better see if you can find your way back to Fen." She raised the container and tipped the liquid into her mouth, wincing as the fiery potion made its way down to her stomach.

Luke darted over. "Mel? Are you okay? What's going on?"

Mel coughed, pressing a hand to her chest as the burning sensation finally faded. "I'm fine. It's just a healing potion."

"Are you sure?" Luke reached out and laid his palm on Mel's forehead as he leaned closer to examine her eyes. "What if it was one of those curses you were talking about? How can—"

Reaching up, Mel grabbed his hand from her forehead and laced her fingers through his. "I'm alright, I promise. I was teasing you. I am absolutely, positively, one hundred percent certain it was only a healing potion. See?"

Backing up a step, Mel lifted her arm in front of Luke. The skin was beginning to knit itself back together, leaving only a faint, narrow line of scar tissue up the center of her forearm.

Luke was still looking at her through narrowed eyes so she walked over and cupped his face with her hands. "I know this world is all crazy and unfamiliar to you, but please trust me on this. I grew up here. I know what to watch out for."

Finally, he nodded. She guzzled the second vial and placed the empty containers on the table. With that, she stood on her tiptoes, placed a kiss on his forehead, and moved a pace backward. "Now, help me look around."

"Uh." Luke's eyes darted around the room. "Are you sure? You told me not to. What if I set off a curse? And how would I know what to look for anyway?"

"It'll be okay. I can't sense any big spells in here. But be careful not to break anything, just in case." Mel started to turn away but then spun back to face Luke again, her red cloak billowing out as she spun. "Oh, and don't eat or drink anything you find in here."

Luke's jaw fell open. "I shouldn't eat or drink anything? What? After you just—"

"That was different!" Mel moved back to the bed and knelt down to peer underneath it. Seeing nothing, she stood back up.

"If you say so," Luke muttered. Shaking his head, he walked over to a cupboard at the far end of the room and pulled it open. "Well, damn it. What the hell am I supposed to be looking for anyway?"

"I don't know. Anything that'll distract you enough to take your mind off worrying about me drinking a healing potion."

Luke snorted, and the corners of his lips curled upward, but he dutifully rummaged through the various cabinets and furniture.

A few quiet minutes passed as each of them wordlessly riffled through things in the cottage. At last, Mel cleared her throat. Luke turned to see her setting her findings on the table. He grabbed a couple of items from the cabinet he was looking inside, closed the door, and walked over to stand across from her.

"Another healing potion and a few mana potions!" Mel grinned up at Luke, triumphant. Pulling her hood over her head, she magicked her hair and clothing dry.

"Aw," Luke groaned.

"Hmm?" Mel looked down at herself. As she realized Luke had been ogling her clingy clothes the same way she'd been admiring his, heat filled her cheeks. He'd seen her in all states of undress prior to now, including a little while ago at the pond. But even after all these years, it never failed. Every time she noticed how he watched her, a flurry of butterflies took flight inside her. She lowered the hood and drank one of the mana potions, focusing on the cold liquid until the blushing finally subsided. At last, she turned her attention back to Luke. "You find anything interesting?"

Luke shrugged and then laid his findings on the table. "A couple of pots that might be handy if we have to cook anything while we're traveling. And, there's a satchel in that wardrobe over there. I think it's enchanted or something. It looked... weird."

"Weird?" Mel laughed. "What makes you say that?"

"I don't know. Something about it just looked weird."

"You mentioned that." Going around the table, Mel made her way over to the wardrobe and pulled it open. Inside, hanging from a hook situated on the wardrobe's back wall, a white leather bag hung. Silvery flecks rose from the fabric and danced in the air. She lifted it up, watching the enchantment swirl around as her eyebrows rose. Turning back around, she looked at Luke again. "How'd you know? Can you see that magic?"

Luke's head slowly bobbed up and down. "Yeah. Should I *not* be able to see that floating glittery stuff? I mean, it's kind of hard to miss."

"No. That's really strange."

"Told you it was weird."

Mel didn't acknowledge Luke's comment. Instead, she looked from him to the bag and back again. It wasn't the fact that the bag was enchanted that she found odd, just the fact that Luke could tell that it was. Finally setting the bag on the table, she shook her head. "Good find, anyway. This'll be handy. The bag looks like it's got a capacity enchantment."

"And that means what exactly?"

"It can hold more than it should. See how it's only a few inches thick and maybe a foot wide? Watch." Mel picked up the satchel and carried it to one of the beds. She grabbed both fluffy pillows off the mattress and stuffed them inside the bag. Once they were out of sight, the leather flattened out, leaving the leather piece looking as empty as when it was first found.

"Oh! Is that why Alicia's apartment was so big?"

Mel chuckled. "I don't know if it's the exact same enchantment, but it's likely it was something similar."

Luke reached out to take the bag from her. He opened the flap and stared at the pillows as they sat inside the cavernous interior. "So we can carry everything in there now?"

Mel tipped her head from side to side as she looked across the room, trying to figure out a way to explain. "Sort of. There are a couple limitations. First of all, you need to be able to fit the majority of the item inside so the enchantment can take effect. I probably couldn't hide an elephant in there because I wouldn't be able to fit enough of it through the opening."

"I can't carry my pet elephant with us? Damn."

"I know. Such a bummer." Grinning, Mel rolled her eyes. "Anyway, the second major limitation is that even if I could somehow fit an elephant through there, I wouldn't be able to lift the bag. It may have more room than you'd expect, but it doesn't make anything inside there any lighter."

"The elephant still weighs as much as an elephant. Got it." Luke jammed his hands into his pockets and rocked back on his heels. "Now what? You said you didn't want to stay here long, right?"

"Mm-hmm. We need to get to the portals."

"What are we going to do when we get back through to Earth? Aren't they going to track us down again? It sounds like this Queen woman really wants to get you back under her thumb. I don't think she's going to give up easily."

"Let's just worry about packing up and getting to the portals for now." The room lit up as the sky flashed. Mel avoided Luke's gaze and walked over to stare out the window. After a long pause, there was a low rumble of thunder. "We'll talk about the rest later."

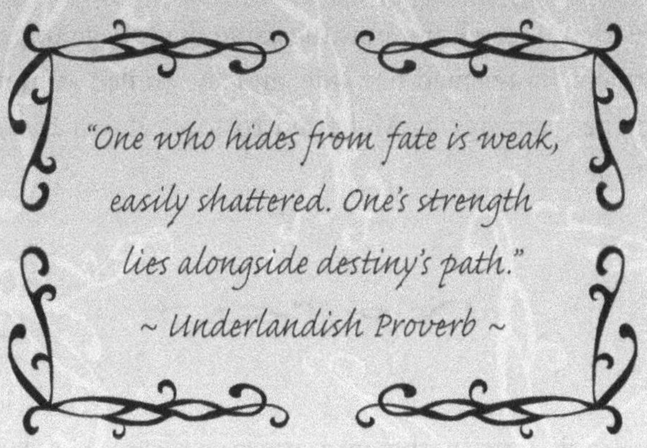

19

With the strap of the enchanted satchel looped diagonally across her torso, Mel grabbed the horse's reins and looked up at the sky. It was still an hour or so until noon, but they needed to get moving if they were going to make it out of the forest before dusk.

Suddenly, goosebumps broke out across Mel's skin. She twisted around, certain that someone was watching her. It felt as though the air had grown ever so slightly thicker as well, though she couldn't be certain. Her free hand slid to her hip where her dagger used to reside, and—finding nothing but empty air in its place—she dug her fingernails into the palm of her hand. Turning her back toward the horse, she slowly scanned the trees surrounding the clearing. Not seeing anyone, she moved to the opposite side of the animal and did the same thing. Still, no one except Luke was in sight. And even he wasn't looking at her.

Mel squeezed her eyes shut and took a deep breath. When she reopened her eyes, she met Luke's gaze and he smiled at her, causing her heart to skip a beat. She pushed back her worried thoughts, telling herself it was simply the stress of the journey and the uncertainty of what came next that was making her paranoid. Grinning back at Luke, she gestured for him to walk beside her as she made her way toward the trees.

Luke hurried to catch up, pushing aside the foliage to get closer to Mel. Eventually, he reached her side, and she smiled at him. They set off toward the gateways as Mel tried to force down the uneasiness growing inside her.

As the sun sank low in the mid-afternoon sky, Mel led the way underneath the cover of a large tree, grabbed three ginguen fruits from the saddlebags, and tossed one to Luke. She gave a fruit to the horse before settling down on the ground to have the last one herself. The storm continued behind them, its deep gray clouds rimmed with purple. But at least now, the storm no longer stalked them. It hung over the center of the forest, far behind them.

Dropping down beside her, Luke looked at the large fruit in his hand, slowly tracing his thumb across the purple and green stripes that covered its outer peel. "So, what's this thing going to taste like?"

Mel quickly swallowed her bite of fruit and used the back of her hand to brush a stray droplet of juice from her chin. "It's sort of like if you crossed an apple with a peach."

"Huh." Lifting the fruit up, Luke sank his teeth into it, pulling off a large bite. He nodded. "Yeah, it kind of is."

Leaning forward, Mel looked between the trees at the sky. Behind them, it was becoming increasingly dark. The sounds of rain and thunder were growing closer with each passing minute. Quickly finishing off the fruit and tossing the pit into the grass, Mel stood just as a gigantic shadow passed overhead. She looked upward through the gaps in the trees, but whatever it was had already vanished. Mel shivered. "Let's go."

Luke was staring up, trying to find the source of the shadow as well when Mel's words caught his attention. He stood, brushing dirt from the back of his trousers as they resumed their trek, weaving their way between the densely packed trees. With one hand, Luke reached out to lace his fingers through hers. "What happens when we get to the gateway?"

Mel tensed, sucking air through her teeth. Turning her face away, she bit her lip.

"Shit! I'm sorry! I forgot that you only started to heal up a little bit ago. That's got to be tender." Luke pulled his hand back and shoved it into his pocket.

"Oh." She glanced down at the thin scar that now decorated the length of her forearm and spiderwebbed out across the back of her hand. She cleared her throat. "Um, yeah. I guess it is a bit sore." Shifting her cloak to hide the scar, she sped up her pace and kept her attention focused upward, trying to peak through the canopy overhead in case the creature came back.

Luke looked at her sideways, puzzled by her tone. Reaching out, he tried to lay his hand on Mel's back, but she stiffened as his fingertips brushed across her.

They walked on in silence for a time. Mel finally sighed. She reached out of the cloak, extending her hand toward Luke. "I'm sorry."

"It's alright." He laced his fingers through hers. "We can talk about it when we get—"

"Did you hear that?"

Luke opened his mouth, ready to question her, but before he could form the words, Mel darted over toward a weeping willow. She yanked on the reins, and the horse obediently trailed after her; they disappeared beneath the overhanging leaves. Luke hesitated a moment and then followed.

Mel reached out and parted the leaves that hung down in front of her. She leaned forward, peering upward through the gap in the greenery.

"Hear what?" Luke mimicked her movements as he tried to look at the sky through the thick canopy of leaves that surrounded them.

"Wingbeats. I think it's coming back."

Luke waited, listening intently until the sound came again, closer this time. His head jerked toward Mel. "You think it's another wyvern?"

Still searching the skies through the narrow gap, Mel shrugged. She kept the expression from her face, but the color drained from her skin as she stared at the clouds. After a few minutes of tense silence, she took a deep breath, let the curtain of leaves fall back into place, and looked away. "Gleffik. We need to keep moving. Stick close to the trees. Hopefully, whatever's flying around up there won't notice us."

Turning, Luke glanced over his shoulder. Mel followed his gaze to the horse standing there. Luke asked, "How are we supposed to keep him hidden?"

She sighed as she brought her attention back to Luke. "I honestly don't know."

"Couldn't you use your cloak on him? Maybe you could make him invisible or something."

"No. For a creature that big, I don't think I could maintain a disguise long enough to do us any good."

"A portal then?"

"It's really hard to open a portal to a place you're not familiar with.

You have to have some idea of what it looks like first. And I'm not too familiar with this area we're in right now."

Mel took a moment to look around at the dense forest that still surrounded them on all sides. As she turned back, she ran her hand across the horse's neck, brushing away a bit of soft, down-like fluff as she did. "I'd go ahead and send him back now, but I'm worried he wouldn't be able to make it back from here. I want to wait until we're out of the woods first."

"Hmm. Then no, I don't have any better ideas."

Mel nodded and tugged on the horse's reins. "Alright. Let's go then."

For a long time, they walked in silence, darting from the cover of one tree to the next, pausing to peek up at the sky when the sound grew closer, or a large shadow passed across the ground near them.

As they waited beneath another large tree, Mel scanned the sky, and Luke moved over to pull a bottle of water from the horse's bags. He took a drink and handed the container to Mel. "So, is this place ever safe to walk around in?"

"Hmm?" She swallowed the water and twisted toward him, returning the bottle to the saddlebag and pulling out the last of the cheese as she did. She bit into it and asked, "What do you mean?"

"We can't walk half a mile without running into something that wants to kill us! That can't be normal!"

"It was *one* wyvern."

"Which was more than enough, by the way. Plus, whatever the hell is flying around above us right now."

Mel chuckled. "Are you telling me Earth's forests don't have bears and rattlesnakes and mountain lions and wolves and—"

"Okay, okay." Luke held up his hands in surrender. "I get your point. But don't forget the assassins that are still following us. And those psycho witches who lured us to their house to kill us. Oh, and Queen."

"Yeah, we've got a lot of people looking for us right now. As far as that thing in the sky, though? A lot of Fenglauria is unadulterated wilderness. There are going to be wild beasts here. Truth be told, we're lucky this area doesn't have much in the way of large wildlife. Most of that is over on the eastern half of the continent." She sighed, pausing as the shadow passed by another time. When it finally receded from view, she continued. "Anyway, I'm getting off topic here. We don't know if that thing flying around up there even cares that we're here. It might not. But…" Mel continued walking again, letting her words fade into silence.

"But, what?"

"Well, it was strange coming across that wyvern where we did. They tend to stay away from human populations. And they don't usually live out this way since there isn't much big game for them." Mel ate the last bite of cheese and then paused to wipe her hands off with a cluster of wide, pinkish-gray leaves. "I'm not sure what's above us right now. I'm certain it's not a harpy; it's too large for that. I'm guessing a gryphon or dragon, but it could be another wyvern. I really haven't been able to get a good look at it."

Luke hurried ahead of Mel, stepping over a half-rotted log as he grabbed the branches of a tall bush and pushed them aside. A little way up ahead, they could finally see the outer edge of the forest opening up into a wide field. The forest continued on along the west side of the clearing, but off toward the east, mountains stretched across the land. Luke took a moment to stare, his eyes tracing the jagged silhouettes upward until their peaks were obscured behind a thick layer of clouds. He leaned back, letting Mel and the horse squeeze through the opening before he followed.

As Mel stepped into that field, she suddenly felt that same, familiar "watched" sensation. But there was something else too. She could feel the air thickening around her. Someone—some magic wielder—was close. Shoving the reins into Luke's hands, she grabbed the hood of her cloak and whispered, "Take him and get behind those trees. Stay out of sight. You hear me?"

Luke turned toward Mel, ready to question her, but the look on her face had him quailed. "Mm-hmm."

"But if that thing in the sky sees you, you come running. Alright?"

Nodding, Luke clamped his mouth shut and hurried away to do as instructed.

As she spun around, her hand still clutching the hood of her cloak, she scanned the trees for any sign of whoever was following them. All was calm. Not even the wind dared to move. She couldn't see anything unusual, but the air felt heaviest off to her left.

The huge, winged shadow came back, passing over them yet again. It was slowing down, its distant wingbeats moving closer to the ground. Mel couldn't concern herself with it right now. One problem at a time.

Pulling her hood over her head, she crept backward, away from the source of that dense feeling. The air shimmered around her, and her red cloak vanished. In her hand, a shortbow formed. At the same time, a quiver manifested on her back, only two arrows held within it. She reached back, grabbed one of the arrows, and nocked it. Turning, she looked at a spot just to the side of where the presence felt strongest. She inhaled and drew the arrow back, aiming as she rested the bowstring and her curled fingers against her cheek. Then, holding her breath, a *twang* sounded through the still air as she released her hold.

A moment later, the arrowhead embedded itself into the trunk of a tree. There was a flash of blue and an abrupt rustling of leaves. Just as quickly, the color vanished. The leaves behind Mel rustled, and the dense air shifted that way as well.

Mel grabbed the second arrow as the first one vanished from its spot in the tree and popped back into the quiver, ready to be loosed all over again. In one fluid movement, she nocked the arrow in her hand, spun around, and sent it flying. This one sank deep into another trunk. There was a loud gasp next to it.

A blonde woman came into view there with a blue cloak around her shoulders and a bloody gash across the side of her neck. The hood of the cloak was fastened to the tree by the arrow only briefly before the arrow vanished and rematerialized inside the quiver.

Clapping one hand to the fresh wound, Ezmaunda used the other to pull her hood over her head and vanished once more into thin air.

Twisting slowly, Mel tried to gauge where the air was thickening, where her target would pop up next.

Suddenly, she felt it. She tried to spin. Ezmaunda's arm was around Mel's throat. She said something next to Mel's ear, but Mel wasn't listening.

Mel slammed an elbow into Ezmaunda's belly, then threw her head backward into the woman's nose. There was a loud crunch. Ezmaunda's hold slipped, and she stumbled backward.

"Gleffik, túls effylz!"

"Same to you, Ez." Mel spun around, nocking an arrow as she faced the other woman. She pulled the bowstring back halfway and pointed the arrow at Ezmaunda. "I can't let you mark him again. And we need to settle this before the creature in the sky decides to come down here and settle it himself."

"I had no intention of marking him another time." Ezmaunda's words were muffled and hard to make out behind the hand that was clutching her broken nose.

"Sure you didn't. Now, where's Nikolas?" Mel dared to take a quick glance around. She looked at Ezmaunda. "Or did you get partnered up with someone else this time?"

"No. I'm here alone."

Mel pulled the string back a bit further. "Don't lie to me."

"It's not a lie." Ezmaunda turned to cough, spraying blood across the ground as she did. At last, she wiped a sleeve across her bloodied mouth and looked back toward Mel. "There once was a time when you could sense it if a chroma were nearby. I assume you've not lost that ability?"

Mel rolled her eyes but realized Ezmaunda was telling the truth—at least about being alone. She couldn't feel the presence of any other magic users in the vicinity. Mel narrowed her gaze. "Why should I believe you weren't going to mark him? What else would you be doing out here? I've felt you following me since we entered the cursed part of the forest."

"Melzia, I'm here to help you."

"Yeah. Sure. That mark you put on Luke was only—"

"Melody!"

Mel moved to one side, twisting slightly so she could keep Ezmaunda and Luke both in sight as he came jogging into the clearing. "What are you doing?"

"It's Hal."

"What?"

Mel's arm relaxed as her eyes darted over to a wide gap between the trees. The leaves rustled momentarily before a huge, purple-scaled head poked through the greenery. The only sound after that was the gentle swishing of the tall grass as Hal's feet carried him out into the clearing. Relieved that one of the potential disasters was averted, Mel turned back to the Azure in front of her.

Ezmaunda's jaw hung low as blood continued to pour from the broken nose and ooze from the slice on her neck. Her green eyes slowly slid from the dragon to Mel. "You are on a first-name basis with a dragon? What sort of deal did you strike to form an alliance with a dragon?"

"That isn't up for discussion right now, Ez. Right now," Mel paused to let her words hang in the air as she pulled the bowstring back halfway once more. "Right now, you're going to tell us why you're following us."

Hal moved closer until his head was inches from Mel's shoulder.

"I told you already, Melzia." Ezmaunda's eyes met the dragon's and she swallowed hard as she forced herself to look back at Mel. "I'm done working for her. I'm here to help you."

"Unless you can somehow prove to me that you've defected, I don't see how we can ever trust you." Adjusting her stance, Mel pulled the bowstring back all the way. "Take off your cloak and get over to that tree. I'm going to tie you up until Luke and I can figure out—"

Mel's words came to an abrupt halt as a yellowish talon was gently laid on her arrow, forcing her to loosen her grip and lower the bow to her side. She looked up into Hal's eyes. He shook his head slowly, and Mel's eyebrows bunched together as she watched.

"I can't just let her go!"

Hal shook his head again, more forcefully this time. Then he laid down, slowly and carefully resting his chin in Ezmaunda's lap as she waited in stunned silence.

Mel watched for a long time and then finally exhaled heavily. She turned back to Ezmaunda and spoke through clenched teeth. "Well. I guess you're part of this alliance now too. Whether I want you to be or not."

20

Shoving her hood backward, the bow and arrows vanished. She aimed her glare at Hal and shook her finger at him as she spoke. "If you're wrong about her…"

Hal lifted his head from Ezmaunda's lap until it was at eye level with Mel. He glared back, leaning closer and closer to her until, at last, she was forced to take a step backward. She broke eye contact as her foot caught on a rock. Hal repositioned his head onto the ground at

Ezmaunda's side and curled up beside her, though his eyes were still fixed on Mel.

"Hmm." Ezmaunda leaned back, eyeing Hal as she did. "I suppose I should be grateful that I've been endorsed by your pet dragon."

Raising his head off the ground and turning his eye toward her, Hal snorted, sending a plume of smoke spiraling up from his nostrils.

"I don't think he's too happy being called my 'pet.'"

"Hmph." Ezmaunda glanced over at Mel, then turned to face him. She leaned over into an exaggerated bow. "Please accept my utmost apologies, sir."

Hal rolled his eyes and turned away.

Ezmaunda let go of her shattered nose and reached toward the side of her blue cloak. Seeing Mel stiffen, she froze momentarily. At last, she moved again, slowly bringing her empty palms into view until Mel's shoulders relaxed.

Never letting her eyes leave Mel's, Ezmaunda felt around inside a hidden pocket before pulling a vial of red liquid into view. She pulled the cork free and tossed the liquid down her throat. As it worked its magic, she grimaced. The gouge in her neck sealed itself shut. After a few seconds of a sickening grinding sound, the shattered pieces of her nose slid back into place, and the cascade of blood slowed to a stop.

Mel fought back the urge to respond to Ezmaunda with an equal measure of sarcasm. Instead, she put her hands on her hips and glowered. She growled, "You stay here. I'll deal with you in a minute." Without waiting for a response, Mel stormed off across the field toward Luke and the horse.

Luke glanced up as Mel got close. He opened his mouth to speak up, but seeing the fire in Mel's eyes, he chose instead to wait for her to say her piece first.

"She's lying." Mel folded her arms across her chest as she halted in front of Luke. She ground her teeth together and rocked back and forth from her toes to her heels. Her gaze went distant as she fell deep into her own thoughts. Unfolding her arms, she moved her hands to her hips and rapidly drummed her fingers on her hipbones.

"She's still loyal to Queen. I know she is. Ezmaunda would never defect."

"How do you know?"

Mel's eyes shot toward Luke's, and she went still. "I know her."

"Okay, I get it, Melody. I promise I get it." Luke reached out, laying his hands on Mel's shoulders. "I understand you are skeptical of her intentions. That's good. She needs to prove herself. But how do you *know* she's lying?"

"Well." Mel twisted, looking back at Ezmaunda briefly before turning around once more. "I just know her, okay? She was my partner for years. I know how she thinks. I know how loyal she always was. How she never questioned Queen's commands or did anything to stop her."

"Right, but…" Luke hesitated, taking a deep breath and then letting it go. He hooked a finger under Mel's chin and tilted her face toward his. "Based on what you told me earlier, wouldn't she say the same thing about you? That you were loyal? That you never questioned any of your orders? That you never stopped her?"

Mel's eyes brimmed with tears. Her lip quivered, but she didn't respond.

He stopped long enough to pull her against his chest and wrap his arms around her. "Baby, I'm sorry. I'm not saying that to hurt you. You did what was necessary to survive. You were a scared kid who was forced into an unimaginable situation. All I'm saying is that, well, maybe she was too."

Squeezing her eyes shut tight, Mel relaxed into Luke's embrace and returned the hug briefly before pushing him away. She blinked rapidly, refusing to let the tears fall. "Fine. I'll hear her out. But if I don't like what she says, she's not coming with us."

"Alright. Let's go listen to what she has to say then."

Side by side, the two of them marched back across the field and came to a halt in front of Ezmaunda. Still sitting in the same place Mel had left her, she was twiddling her thumbs and watching Hal as he paced slowly near the trees.

Ezmaunda laced her fingers together in her lap and looked at Mel. "So, what have you decided to do with me?"

"For now, we're going to listen. Anything beyond that depends on whether I like what you have to say."

"Very well. What do you want to know?"

"Why should we believe you left her service after all these years?"

"Truly? That is what you would ask?" Ezmaunda tipped her head to one side and eyed Mel. "I've already told you I left her service, and you didn't believe it. Is there some mystical answer I might give you that will prove anything and end your doubts? Of course not, so let's not waste our time."

Mel's jaw clenched. She leaned forward, pointing a finger at Ezmaunda. Opening her mouth to give a retort, she stopped as Luke's hand landed on her shoulder. She twisted around and scowled at him.

Luke gave Mel a look as he stepped forward, placing himself halfway between the two women. "Okay, you're right. As nice as it would be if you could just whip out a copy of your letter of resignation, I'm sure that's not how it works. So, maybe start with telling us *when* you decided you weren't working for what's-her-name anymore."

One of Ezmaunda's eyebrows slowly climbed upward as she moved her gaze from Mel to Luke. She eyed him up and down before leaning to one side to see around him and refocus on Mel. She smirked. "My, my. You require your companion to speak for you these days? Your time on Earth really did soften you."

From the corner of his eye, Luke could see Mel's hand clench into a fist. She took a breath. Luke cut her off, commanding, "Knock it off. Both of you." He heard Mel's sharp intake of breath behind him, but he didn't acknowledge it. He moved forward and knelt in front of Ezmaunda. "Look. If you really want to help, quit the snark and answer our questions. I mean, honestly, if you can't even offer that much, I don't know why I should stop Mel from putting you down here and now."

"Very well. But I speak to Melzia."

Luke stood and backed out of the way.

Ezmaunda's glare was aimed at Mel. "You carried out your task. The next day, when we saw that you had left, that was when I came to realize I had to find a way to escape as well."

"Why? From what I can remember, you had no issue working for her prior to that."

"True. Though there was a time when I would have said the same of you."

Mel shot a look toward Luke. He decided the safest move at the moment was to keep his attention fixed on the Azure in front of them.

Ezmaunda turned to stare off into the trees. "When the task had first been given to us, you swore to me that you would see it through. There were no tears, no pleading. If you were so resolved when the target was your own flesh and blood, who was I to question it?"

Mel stiffened. Swallowing the lump in her throat, she waited.

Ezmaunda swiped a loose strand of hair from her face as she twisted back to face Melzia. "When I discovered you had fled this realm, it was as if I had suddenly awoken from a long, feverish dream. Of course at the time, I hadn't yet learned that you had disobeyed. I thought you had fled due to guilt after killing your own sister. But that—realizing how that act must have tormented you—was enough to sow the first seeds of doubt.

"In those early days, Queen didn't care that you were gone. I found that odd. Not because she had ever shown any affection toward you; I knew she never felt you were her family. It was more that you were her most prized possession. And Queen does not give up the things she feels belong to her. That, too, raised my suspicions. Why would she not care that you—her most unique and versatile chroma—were gone?

"It wasn't until later that I realized if you were gone, you were not a threat to her or her crown. And if your leaving was of your own free will, it would not likely stir the other kingdoms to action. If she had a more direct hand in your disappearance, perhaps they might make a more active response."

The two women stared at one another in silence. At last, Luke chimed in, "Go on."

For a moment, Ezmaunda's glare was directed at him. She finally looked away as she resumed her story. "The day after you left, Yvette's body was retrieved and taken to Queen's castle at Malkidahn.

"Queen then chose not to inter your sister in the family mausoleum. She told us all that it was her manner of grieving, that she could not bear to part with your beautiful sister, especially after what she said you had done. Through her tears, she told the kingdom, 'I lost one daughter when Melzia allowed such evil to consume her heart. Do not now ask me to part with my darling Yvette!' I am well aware that her words were simply for show, but there were many who accepted them for truth."

"So what did she do with my sister?"

"Instead of putting her in the resting place of your ancestors, Queen declared it was more appropriate to have the body on display. She had it placed in an enchanted glass case in the throne room, watching with barely hidden glee as mourners came from across the realms."

"Is Yvette's body still there now?"

Ezmaunda jerked her head toward Mel. "You've not heard?"

Narrowing her eyes at Ezmaunda, Mel stepped past Luke and leaned forward. She growled out, "Apparently not. I wouldn't be asking if I had."

Luke laid a hand on Mel's shoulder. She didn't acknowledge him but bit back whatever else she had been about to say.

"Yvette was on display for a bit more than a year. One day, the royal family of The Whitnalls came. Prince Zachoriun was, of course, among the visitors. When he arrived and stepped forward to view your sister within the glass case, identical marks formed on each of their wrists. That was the moment he realized she was cursed, not dead. If she were dead, the mark would not have formed."

Mel's voice cracked as she asked, "She's his soul match?"

"Obviously."

Mel ground her teeth together. "Keep talking."

"Once he was aware that she was only cursed, he demanded she be removed from the enchanted case so the curse could be removed. Queen tried to deny his request, citing again her supposed grief and stating that Yvette was far beyond saving. Prince Zachoriun became King Zachoriun soon after, and he began hinting at war. As ruthless as Queen is, she does not do battle unless she is certain she can win. So, she allowed him to take your sister's lifeless body back to his castle. Within days, your sister's curse was removed."

Mel let out a loud, shaky exhale. Her hands trembled. "So she's... Yvette's okay then?"

"Aye."

"What did he do? How did he break it?"

At Mel's side, Luke muttered, "A kiss."

Both women turned to stare at him, utterly baffled at his sudden, random comment.

"Huh?" Mel tilted her head as she looked at him.

At the same time, Ezmaunda asked, "What is that supposed to mean?"

Luke's eyes went back and forth between the two women. "Th-th-that's how the curse gets broken, isn't it? The prince just kisses her, and she wakes up? Right?"

Ezmaunda pushed herself to her feet and folded her arms together. "You believe that a prince of Fenglauria would kiss an unconscious woman with whom he is barely acquainted? Or perhaps it is that you believe a prince of Fenglauria would choose to kiss a corpse? Please, do tell."

"No! I didn't mean—"

Mel, suddenly understanding what Luke was referring to, raised a hand to signal that he should stop talking. She took over. "Calm down, Ezmaunda. In the world he's from, they believe that's part of the prophecy. She is cursed, and she can only be awoken by the kiss of her true love."

"Hmm."

"Shut up, Ez." Mel rubbed her temples and took a deep breath. As she exhaled, she put her hands on her hips. "And sit back down, or else I'm going to *make* you sit."

Ezmaunda glared but slowly lowered herself back onto the grass as instructed.

"So, keep going. What did he do?"

"It is my understanding that he summoned several of the elven healers. I am not aware of the specifics, but I gather that they were able to work together to perform some sort of ritual to remove the curse."

"I..." Mel hesitated as she tried to collect her thoughts. "I didn't realize that the elves could remove curses they themselves hadn't cast. I thought I would have to find a way to remove it."

"I do not believe Queen did either. I'm certain she would have fought harder to keep Yvette in her own castle if she had. Queen had been angered when she learned that you had only cursed your sister into a deathlike slumber. But whether she were truly dead or only cursed into such a state, Yvette was no more threat to Queen's rule. When Queen learned that the curse was broken, her anger became a rage unlike any I have ever seen."

"That's when she first went looking for me, wasn't it?"

"Aye. Though, she began within our own world." Ezmaunda leaned back onto her elbows, stretching her legs out in the grass. "She spent two years searching, burning down villages, and torturing anyone who she thought might have information on you. At last, one of the gatekeepers came forward, hoping to prevent further bloodshed."

"No." Mel's knees shook.

Luke hurried forward and wrapped an arm around Mel's waist, pulling her close.

"I wouldn't have left if I'd known." The world went fuzzy around Mel as her breathing started to come in quick, shallow gasps. Panic was written across her face. "I didn't mean for that... It's my fault those people died. How can..."

Moving so that he could grab Mel by the arms, he turned her so that they were facing one another. He leaned down, his face close to hers, and waited until she met his gaze. "It is *not* your fault for the things that monster chose to do. Her craziness is her own fault. *She* hurt and killed them, not you. *She* is the one who needs to answer for what she's done. Do you hear me?"

"But I—"

"No!" Luke shook her slightly. "Listen to me. You are *not* responsible for *her* actions."

Tears streamed down Mel's cheeks, and Luke wrapped his arms around her and gently rocked her from side to side.

"Ahem."

Luke looked over at Ezmaunda as he continued swaying with Mel. "What?"

"This," Ezmaunda paused, waving a hand in the general direction of the couple, "Is sickeningly sweet, but it's time for the two of you to decide whether you will trust me to join you or not. I will be leaving this area shortly. I can accompany you to help, or I can make my way alone. But I'll not be staying here much longer either way."

At those words, Mel finally stepped back from Luke and wiped her face. She took a deep breath as she looked at the other woman. "What do you mean?"

"Have you lost all intelligence in your time away? Have you gone blind? Have you forgotten the things that Queen can do? You are still being pursued, whether you choose to believe that or not. Either I leave here with you, or I leave here alone. I'll not sit here and wait for her to find me."

Mel crossed her arms but didn't reply.

Ezmaunda gestured over her shoulder, pointing toward the sky above the forest where they had come from. "That storm back there is not of nature. It is one of hers, Melzia. I convinced her that you were near the northern edge of the forest and had not yet made it to the witches' cottage. The storm was meant to force you there so Hans and Greta could hold you captive until you were retrieved by one of the chromas. She has not yet learned that you killed them. How much longer do you believe it will be until she discovers that you succeeded in defeating the witches? How long until she knows I have not obeyed her command to retrieve you?"

"I still don't see what reason we have to trust you."

"Use your logic, Melzia! If I had truly wanted you captured or dead, I'd have sent Nikolas after you the moment we stepped through the portal into Fenglauria. Instead, while the pair of you hid behind the trees, I turned him away from you."

"You knew?"

"Of course I knew! You spent years watching me use my abilities. Do you truly believe my tracking skills have declined so greatly since you left?"

Mel huffed and twisted to look at Luke. At the slight nod of his head, she turned toward Ezmaunda with a sigh. "Fine. Let's go."

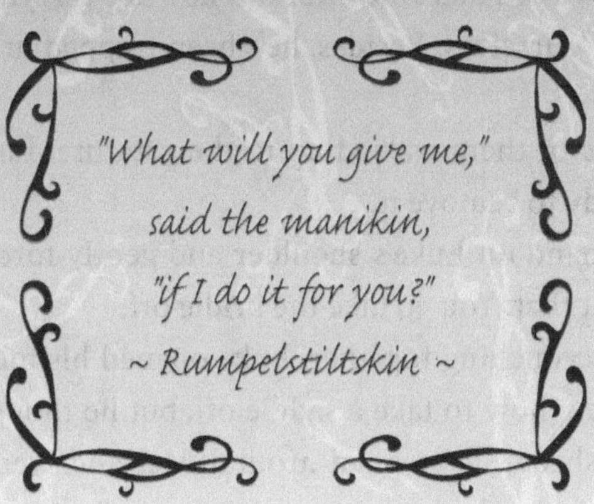

21

Mel took Luke's hand and started to turn around, but as she did, she saw movement from the corner of her eye. Ezmaunda was pushing herself to her feet, moving as though she intended to follow right behind the couple. Mel shook her head as she twisted back to the blue-cloaked woman. "Hm-mm. Not yet. You go wait over there by Hal until I say otherwise."

Rolling her eyes, Ezmaunda stalked over to Hal's side, crossed her arms, and repeatedly tapped her toe against a fallen tree branch.

"If she's coming with us, you know you won't always be able to keep your distance from her, right? At some point, we're going to have to give her a real chance."

Glancing back over her shoulder as they continued to walk across the field, Mel loudly groaned. At last, she called back, "Fine! Come on!"

Ezmaunda rolled her eyes yet again but quickly caught up with the others.

"Alright," Luke spoke up as Ezmaunda got within earshot. "What are we doing now?"

"Letting him go home." Mel pointed toward the horse as he stood at the edge of the field, chewing on what looked like an oversized, white onion. "We can't all ride him, and he's not carrying anything we can't just carry ourselves. Besides, he's been trapped in that saddle for days."

As the three of them walked up to the creature, Luke reached for the saddle, ready to remove it.

Mel laid a hand on Luke's shoulder and gently forced him to face her. "Let me get that. You go take the bridle off."

Eyebrows scrunching together, Luke opened his mouth to remind her that he knew how to take a saddle off, but he thought better of it. With a slight shrug, he stepped around Mel and went over to deal with the bridle instead.

"Make yourself useful."

"You just…" Luke went silent as he looked up and realized Mel wasn't addressing him. Her eyes were locked on Ezmaunda.

"Come get ready to pull the blanket off as soon as I lift the saddle."

The furrowing of Luke's brow deepened. He stood there, staring as Ezmaunda silently moved around to the other side of the horse. Eventually, he forced his attention back to the bridle and mumbled to himself under his breath. As he slid it free, he looked up. Mel was standing there with both hands clasping the unfastened saddle.

Ezmaunda was on the opposite side, gripping the front edge of the blanket. Both women were staring at him.

"What?" Luke's eyes darted between Mel and Ezmaunda.

"Go over by the trees."

"Why would I—"

"As soon as we pull these off him, he's going to take off. You don't want to be in his path when he does."

Luke growled as he turned and trudged over to the forest's edge, fiddling with the bridle as he went. When he was just out of earshot, he muttered, "I know how to act around horses. Good lord, you make it sound like I've never been around one before."

Stopping next to a large oak tree, Luke spun around, folding his arms across his chest. He leaned his shoulder on the thick trunk and waited.

Mel nodded once and faced Ezmaunda. For a moment, the two stood frozen, watching one another. Suddenly, Mel yanked the saddle off and flung it into the clearing. Simultaneously, Ezmaunda tore the blanket free and hurled it toward the woods. Then, as if the two women had rehearsed and synchronized this strange routine, they both dove to the ground.

The horse reared back on his hind legs with a loud neigh. As soon as his front hooves touched the ground again, he bolted forward, and a pair of enormous wings unfurled from his sides. The force of the air coming off the flapping wings nearly bowled Luke over as the creature galloped past. A moment later, he was up in the air, flying back in the direction they had come from.

Abandoning the saddle entirely, Mel and Ezmaunda stood up, gathered their bags, and walked over to the wide-eyed, open-mouthed Luke. Hal was slowly making his way up behind them.

"Hey." Mel reached out and laid a hand on Luke's arm. "We need to go."

Luke slowly tore his gaze away from the sky as the bridle fell to the ground. He focused on Mel with wide eyes. In a soft monotone, he said, "You didn't tell me he was a Pegasus."

"Uh…" Mel looked at Ezmaunda, lifting her eyebrows in question. When Ezmaunda shrugged, Mel asked, "What's a Pegasus?"

Luke's eyes managed to open wider still. He pointed up toward the sky. "That!"

"Is that Earth's word for a winged horse?"

Luke nodded.

"Ah. Here, *that* is called a pferdvolar."

"Well then why the hell did you call it a horse? And why couldn't we have just flown here on it?!"

Mel looked at him skeptically. "When did I ever call it a horse?"

"When… Well, it was…" Luke huffed. "Okay, fine. I guess maybe you didn't actually call it a horse. But you also didn't call it a… whatever that word was."

"Pferdvolar. They can't fly very well with someone on their backs, so when we use them for transportation, they're basically treated like really big horses." Mel paused. "I assumed Fen or Cali would've told you what he was when they brought him out for you."

"Well, they didn't!"

"No wonder you didn't know not to take the saddle off." Mel chuckled and squeezed his hand as she stepped closer. "I'm sorry. I honestly thought you knew. But I wish you'd trust me a little bit more when I'm telling you something to do in this world. This place isn't like Earth, and there's a lot you still don't know."

Letting out a long sigh, Luke's face finally relaxed. He inched forward and leaned so that his forehead rested against Mel's. "It's alright, I just really wasn't prepared for that. As long as we're giving suggestions, though, maybe you could explain a little better when I don't understand."

"You're right. I'll work on that." Mel stepped back, grinning mischievously. "Bet you're glad I made you move out of the way now, huh?"

Chuckling, he nodded another time as his gaze landed on Mel's lips. Lifting one hand, he gently tilted her chin up, and he leaned forward.

"Ahem."

Luke froze, a slight blush creeping into his cheeks.

Mel sighed. "Yes?"

"We *are* still being pursued by a power-hungry queen who would very much like to imprison, torture, and kill the lot of us. Perhaps the two of you can keep your hands off one another until the situation is a teensy bit less dire?"

Twisting back to Luke, Mel placed her hand on his cheek. "I hate to admit it, but she's right. We need to get moving." Mel slid her hand down into Luke's, then pivoted around to veer southward and continue their journey.

They'd only gone a few steps when Luke laughed. He said, "You know, I never expected to see a Pegasus here. Unicorns, of course, but not a Pegasus."

"Hmm?" Mel stopped and faced him. "What was the thing you said you expected?"

"Would you two be silent?"

"Shut up, Ez! Luke, what did you say you expected?"

"A unicorn."

Mel frowned as her eyes met Ezmaunda's. "What does that word mean?"

Luke laughed. Tugging her hand, he tried to start walking, but Mel stayed rooted to the spot.

"No, really." Mel tilted her head to one side as she waited. "What is that word?"

"A unicorn? You've never heard of a unicorn?"

Both women shook their heads.

"Oh, come on! A unicorn!" Luke's face fell and his glance went from Ezmaunda to Mel and even to Hal in hopes that someone would know what he was talking about. "The horse with the long, twisty horn in the middle of its forehead!"

"A horse with a horn?" Ezmaunda burst into laughter. "Don't be absurd!"

Mel's lips twitched, but she was able to subdue her own laughter into a passable cough.

Before Luke could figure out what else to say, the trio was suddenly buffeted with a huge burst of wind that had them stumbling forward. By the time they found their footing again and turned to see what was happening, Hal was darting into the sky in quick pursuit of three other gigantic, winged figures.

"Hey, Ez, could you tell what those were? I didn't get a good look."

"Not particularly. But I suspect they might've been wygon younglings." Ezmaunda kept searching the skies for another glimpse of the creatures, but they were well out of sight by now. "I believe there's a wygon pack that resides not far from here. From what I understand, that pack has gotten quite restless of late."

"Ah. Well, I'd rather not stick around and find out if that's what it was. Let's get moving. They'll be coming back soon." Somber now, Mel set off with the others in tow.

"Uh, wygons?" Luke glanced up into the sky, but the creatures were already long gone.

"It's a cross between a dragon and a wyvern." Mel stepped over a jutting root. "You think that wyvern we came across was big and mean? That's nothing compared to a full-grown wygon. Some breathe fire, others ice. They have an acid stinger kind of like the wyverns, too. Oh, and as if that weren't bad enough, they also travel in packs."

"Ah. That, uh… doesn't sound fun to deal with."

Mel exhaled a huff of air through her nose. "Yeah."

For the better part of an hour after that, the three of them trekked along in silence, moving as quickly as the wild terrain would allow. As the sun sank behind the trees, Ezmaunda suddenly halted. "We need to stop for the night."

"What?" Mel looked at her, pulling Luke to a stop at her side. "Why here? We need to get farther from that wygon pack and find somewhere with some cover. This is way too exposed."

"No. We'd best stay here. You know the wygons roost at night. They'll not be out hunting now." Ezmaunda plopped onto the ground, sliding the leather bag from her shoulder and setting it in the grass beside her. "Beyond that, have you forgotten about the pixies?"

Squeezing her eyes shut, Mel groaned loudly. When she finally opened them, she sighed. "Yeah. As a matter of fact, I had forgotten about the pixies down this way."

"Um, pixies?" Luke looked from one woman to the other. "Are they dangerous?"

Mel shook her head. "Not really. As long as you don't react to them, they're more of a nuisance than anything. They'll try to trick travelers or split up their group or delay them. They're probably already coming out for the evening, so she thinks it's best to stay put until morning since it'll lower our chances of getting harassed by them."

"Oh, by all means, you two continue without me if you'd prefer. My specialty is tracking, after all." Ezmaunda smirked at Mel. "I'm sure it won't take me more than half a day to reunite the two of you after the pixies have their fun with you. We only have to hope there won't be enough time for Queen to send someone else after us all."

Fighting back the urge to roll her eyes, Mel slowly pulled in a deep breath. "Have you become more insufferable since I last saw you? Or did I somehow forget this attitude of yours in all these years I've spent away from you?"

Grinning, Ezmaunda simply shrugged.

Mel dropped the saddlebag on the ground and sat down beside it. "Fine. We'll stay here for the night."

"Good." Ezmaunda leaned back in the grass, stretching her legs out in front of herself. "Now you can explain to me what your plan is."

"I don't think so." Mel stared daggers at the other woman. "I'm still not sure I should trust you."

"Melody."

Twisting around to face Luke as he knelt in the grass beside her, Mel narrowed her eyes at him. "What?"

Luke tilted his head and lifted an eyebrow at her.

Glaring back at first, Mel finally caved. She lay down and rolled away. "We'll discuss it in the morning while we walk. Right now, I'm going to sleep."

Sighing, Luke settled into the grass beside Mel and wrapped his arm around her waist. He was about to close his eyes when he suddenly asked, "Uh, what's that?"

Mel twisted around to face him. "What's what?"

"That." He extended his arm, pointing toward the sky.

Mel turned. She could see a few stars scattered across the growing darkness along with the semi-circular orb of the moon. The only other thing she could make out was a faint, distant beam of blue light —a tracking mark somewhere far off in the distance. Mel glanced over at Ezmaunda, but she looked as baffled as Mel.

"Never mind."

Mel lay down, wiggling until she managed to find a semi-comfortable position on the ground. "What did you see?"

"I'm not sure. I think it was my eyes playing tricks on me." Settling back into the grass, he closed his eyes again. "I probably just need to get some sleep."

Ezmaunda and Mel shared one last, confused look. Mel's eyes lingered for a moment longer, even as Ezmaunda rolled away. Slowly, Mel grabbed the corner of her red cloak and waited for the fabric to stretch out until she was able to cover Luke with it as well. Finally, exhausted and knowing they were as protected as they could be given their current circumstances, she nestled into the grass and let sleep overtake her.

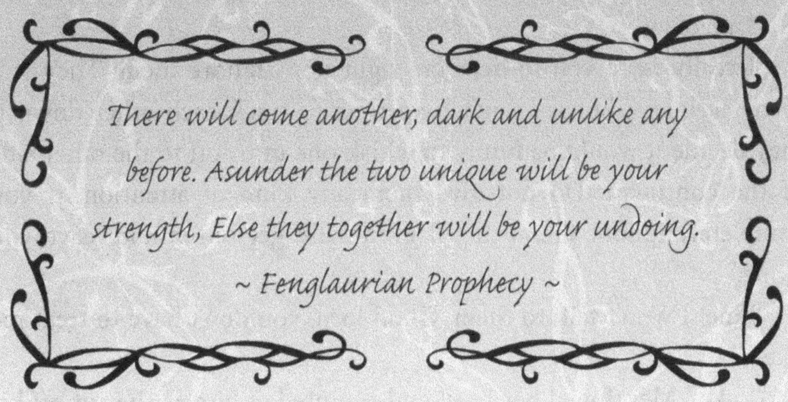

Using the tip of her shoe, Mel nudged Ezmaunda's shoulder. "Get up."

Ezmaunda groaned, rolling over onto her back and yawning. She slowly opened her eyes. "The sun's not yet up."

"I know. We're leaving. If you're coming with us, get up."

"Gleffik, woman!" Ezmaunda sat up, rubbing her hand across her eyes. "What's your rush? The pixies'll still be flitting about!"

"Yeah, they'll still be out for maybe another hour. But the wygons won't be. I want some distance between us and them before those ravenous, giant, winged lizards start their day and decide to have us for breakfast. Oh, and in case you haven't noticed, that magicked storm seems to be gone, which means she's probably figured out you're not bringing us back."

Groaning, Ezmaunda pushed herself upright. "Fine. Let's go."

Mel twisted around and nodded. At the sign, Luke grabbed their bags and made his way over, taking a bite out of a piece of fruit as he did. Stepping up beside the women, he produced a couple more pieces of food from the enchanted satchel and passed some to each of them.

As Mel held out her hand, she stared hard into Luke's eyes. "Pixies might approach you as we walk. Do not interact with them. Do not acknowledge them at all. I don't care if they only say 'hello,' you do *not* respond. Okay?"

"Um, okay."

"I really need you to hear me right now. Ignore them. They will seem harmless, but we don't have time to track each other down if they decide it would be funny to whisk one of us off to the other side of the continent. Do not give them any kind of attention. If you completely ignore them, they'll eventually get bored and leave you alone."

"Fine! I won't talk to them. Good lord, you don't have to treat me like—"

"Luke." Mel tipped her head and squinted at him as she cut off his words. "Yesterday, you said you needed more guidance when I told you something about this world. That's what I'm trying to do now. I'm intentionally being very explicit with these instructions and explaining exactly why you need to listen."

Closing his eyes, Luke exhaled slowly. His shoulders sank as he looked at her again. "You're right. That is what you need to do. I just hate feeling like a confused toddler in a world where everything is new to me and nothing makes sense."

"I know it's hard. I remember feeling the same way when I first came to Earth." Mel took his hand in hers and gave it a squeeze. "I'm sorry. I promise I don't mean to make you feel bad. We'll be at the portals soon and—"

"Aye. He's clueless, you're a know-it-all, and the both of you are deeply remorseful. Perhaps we can recommence our journey before those wygons awaken for the day? Remember those 'giant lizards' you were terrified of a few moments ago when you were so rudely demanding I wake up?" Shaking the dirt and bits of grass from her blue cloak, Ezmaunda chomped into the piece of fruit and started walking southward without waiting for a response.

Sighing, Mel gave Luke a kiss on the cheek and let go of his hand as she twisted away. "Come on, we do need to get moving."

Luke followed.

They'd only gone a few dozen steps when a trio of the little, humanesque pixies arrived out of nowhere. Two hurried over to Luke, making themselves at home on his shoulders. The third flew to Mel. As this one grabbed hold of Mel's curly hair, it settled its feet against her neck and slowly climbed its way up the side of her face.

Showing no reaction to the creature's antics, Mel turned to peek back at Luke and silently mouthed the words, "Ignore them."

By now, one of the pixies had burrowed into Luke's hair and begun pulling out individual strands, one at a time. Luke winced slightly as the other tiny troublemaker started gnawing on his earlobe, giggling in a high-pitched voice as it did. His eyelid twitched as he quickly grew frustrated with the creatures, but he nodded his understanding at Mel.

As she faced forward once more, she asked, "Would you please hang back a bit? I think it's time that Ez and I talked."

"Um, sure." Luke slowed his pace. Then, he jammed his hands into his pockets, fighting the urge to swat the pixie that had decided to fly directly in front of his face to tug on his eyelashes.

The second little nuisance was now shouting questions directly into Luke's ear. *Who are you? Where are you going? Why don't you want to be our friend?* And—as if that weren't enough—the pixie that had been pestering Mel had already lost interest in her and came flying back to join its companions in tormenting Luke.

Mel hurried forward until she caught up to Ezmaunda. She glanced back over her shoulder to make sure Luke was out of earshot. Seeing that he was a fair distance away and seemed to be thoroughly concentrating on ignoring the pixies that swarmed around him, she turned to Ezmaunda. "You and I need to talk."

"Aye, we do. No more stalling. What is this plan of yours into which I've been pulled? I believe I already know, though I'd like to hear it from you." She leaned closer to Mel. "And why have you not told your beau? Do you believe he's such a dolt that he can't figure out what you have in mind?"

"He's not…" Mel's voice came out louder than she intended. She stopped herself and tried again, hissing now, "He's not a dolt! Don't call him that. He's overwhelmed with this place, but he's not stupid. And who says I haven't told him, anyway?"

"Oh? Have you? Well, I'm sure you won't mind if I call him up here to join this hushed conversation then."

Ezmaunda twisted around, opening her mouth to call out to Luke, but Mel's hand landed on the woman's arm. As Mel's fingernails dug into her pale skin, Ezmaunda turned toward the front.

"Okay, fine," Mel hissed. "I haven't told him. Not all of it, anyway."

"What, precisely, have you told him then?"

"Well, first of all, I want it to be known that I still don't trust you." Mel folded her arms together and let the red fabric of her cloak close up around her. She watched Ezmaunda from the corner of her eye as they walked.

Laughing, Ezmaunda shook her head but didn't comment.

"Anyway, I, uh… told him that we're going to the portals."

Ezmaunda stepped around a small patch of mud as she finally glanced over at Mel. "You told him, 'We are going to the portals.' But you neglected to mention that only he is going through. I thought as much. You plan to surrender yourself to Queen."

It wasn't a question, but Mel nodded anyway. "I don't have a choice. If I don't turn myself in, both Luke and I will always be in danger. At least by giving myself up, he can be safe."

Ezmaunda scoffed, "You truly see no other way?"

"Look. I really don't know what to think of you or your motivations right now. You were always so loyal, so desperate to do anything that Queen wished that I have a hard time believing you've changed. But please, please let me send him back to Earth before you take me to her."

"I'll not deny that once upon a time, I was loyal to her. As were you, Melzia. That time is long passed, for the both of us."

The two women stopped walking to stare at one another.

After several long seconds, Ezmaunda said, "If you're hoping to be given to Queen, it'll not be my doing."

Mel opened her mouth to respond, but hearing Luke say something from somewhere far behind her, she stopped. She couldn't make out the words he'd said, but it was his voice, nonetheless. She spun on her heel, ready to ask if he'd forgotten about ignoring the pixies, ready to go find him if they'd magicked him away. The pixies had already been chased away by the sunlight that was growing brighter with every passing minute. Luke was standing there, his eyes fixed on something in the sky.

Both women moved closer to him, their heads tilting upward to see where he was looking.

Ezmaunda was the first to speak. "What precisely did you see last night?"

"There was a really faint blue light. After I stared at it for a while, I couldn't see it anymore. I thought maybe my eyes were playing tricks on me. But it's back. It's a little farther to the west than yesterday, and I can see it better now, but I'm pretty sure it's the same thing."

Grabbing Mel by the arm, Ezmaunda growled at Luke, "You stay here."

As Mel tried to pull her arm free, Ezmaunda cast her spell, and the two women vanished. Half a heartbeat later, they reemerged in the foothills of the mountains with Luke nowhere in sight.

Jerking her arm away, Mel rounded on Ezmaunda. "How dare you! I can't just abandon him back there in the forest where Queen is hunting us!"

"Did you not see what he was looking at?"

"Of course I saw what he was…" Mel's words faded as her anger melted into confusion. Her brow furrowed. "How could he see that tracking mark if he's not a chromaveiled?"

"What other signs have there been? Any inexplicable spells around him? Have you sensed his growing mana?"

"No, nothing like that. And he definitely couldn't see the tracking mark when it was on him." Mel chewed on her lip for a moment as she thought. Finally, she said, "But when we found that bag at the cottage, he could see it was enchanted."

"You're certain you can't sense any mana within him?"

"No, I can't. He's never had any mana. How could he suddenly have any? How is he suddenly showing any signs of powers?"

"He mustn't have much mana then if you're unable to feel it. As far as showing any powers, perhaps this place unlocked something latent inside him?"

"I guess so." Mel tapped her toe on the rock-covered ground. "Still doesn't explain how he could've started building up a mana supply if he never had any to begin with. It can't develop out of nowhere."

"He only showed these signs after the mark was removed, aye? How did you remove that anyway?"

Mel's eyes grew wide. "The healing potion that removed the mark. He must've drank more than he needed, and it initiated his mana supply as well."

"You are certain that's all you did? Hmm." Ezmaunda stared off in the direction they had teleported from. The blue light in the distance shone clearly above the tops of the forest canopy. Whoever it was marking, they likely had no idea they were a target of Queen's ire. Crossing her arms, Ezmaunda continued. "I do not believe that a healing potion alone could do such a thing. But that is neither here nor there. Regardless of whether the potion is what removed the mark and ignited his abilities, I believe it's time he was given his own cloak."

"What?" Mel's jaw dropped. "No way. That's way too dangerous. I just need to get him back to Earth and give myself up. She won't care about him anymore as long she can punish me."

"I do not think so." Turning back toward Mel, Ezmaunda slowly rubbed the back of her own neck. "There is something I believe you need to know, Melzia."

Mel narrowed her eyes, peering sideways at the Azure.

"Shortly prior to Queen deciding that you must be found, there was a prophecy. I do not know the full extent of it, and the portion I had heard made little sense previously."

"Go on."

Ezmaunda sighed. "Something regarding 'two unique ones' who will be her downfall."

"And you think…"

"You are the only Crimson. And whatever the cloak chooses for him, I believe he will be as one-of-a-kind as you."

Luke yelped, spinning toward the two women as they suddenly popped up next to him. He rushed forward and flung his arms around Mel, turning his narrowed eyes on Ezmaunda. "What did you do? Where did you take her?"

Ezmaunda gave no indication she noticed Luke's glare or his words. She strode forward and commanded, "Close your eyes, imagine a roaring fire, and snap your fingers."

"What? I don't understand." Luke's eyes slid toward Mel.

"Just try it, please."

Luke slowly lifted his hand out in front of himself, palm up, and did as instructed. Nothing happened. So he tried again. And again.

And *again*. Still, nothing. He finally peeked down at his hand, shrugging as he faced Mel once more.

Mel walked up and placed her palm on his cheek. "Try it another time. Really concentrate."

Luke huffed. He closed his eyes and breathed out slowly as he let an image of fire grow in his mind. He thought about the heat that radiated from it, the sparks that flew off and crackled as they rose into the sky. Once more, he lifted his hand and snapped. A tiny, orange flame burst into life there, bouncing erratically in the air above his fingertips. The little fire was unsteady, flickering and sparking as though it would peter out at any moment.

Feeling the warmth that suddenly erupted there, Luke opened his eyes. A moment later, when the flame brushed across his palm, he gasped and jerked his hand back with a yelp. The flame vanished, leaving only a tiny puff of smoke. "What the hell?"

Still giving no acknowledgment that he'd spoken, Ezmaunda planted a hand on her hip as she reached toward Luke with the other. "We're going to see the goblin."

"What? What goblin? Why?" Luke jerked his arm away before Ezmaunda's fingers could close around his wrist.

Stepping away, Mel planted herself between the other two. Standing there with her red cloak billowing in the light wind as she stared at Ezmaunda, she suddenly felt as though she were a bullfighter, taunting the Azure to attack. She tried to push the mental image aside as she turned her focus back to Luke. "Don't listen to her. We're going to the portals."

"Oh?" Ezmaunda's right eyebrow slid upward until it nearly met her hairline. As she crossed her arms, she looked at Mel. "Perhaps you'd like to tell him the rest of your plan?"

"What's she talking about?"

The color drained from Mel's face as she peeked in his direction, unwilling to meet his eyes.

Luke glanced at Ezmaunda. When he finally brought his focus

back toward Mel, the hurt was already apparent on his face. "You're planning on making me go back to Earth alone, aren't you?"

Mel's head tipped in the slightest of nods.

"No!" Luke buried his fingers in his hair. "Either we both go back, or we both stay here."

"You might be a bit of a dunce—"

"Ezmaunda!"

Ignoring Mel's admonishment, Ezmaunda came over to stand beside Luke. She continued, "But I agree. Sending you back is not an option. Which is precisely why we are taking you to see the goblin."

"Gah!" Mel stomped her foot. "I said no! It. Is. Too. Dangerous!"

"Which is the same damn reason why I'm not abandoning you, and I'm not letting you turn yourself in!" Luke walked up and grabbed Mel's hands. "You think that someone who creates orphans to enslave them into her army is going to just let me go back to my life and let you go unpunished?"

"Precisely." Ezmaunda crossed her arms. Turning toward Mel, she said, "In this regard, he and I are in agreement. You only have two options. The two of you can run away and disappear forever, though you'll be eternally watching over your shoulder, wondering if you are about to be found. Or, you can stay here and try to put an end to her ill-begotten reign. Which is it going to be?"

Mel's shoulders slumped.

"What does this goblin do? Why should we go there?"

Seeing that Mel would not answer the question, Ezmaunda intended to address Luke directly for once. "Rumpelstiltskin is the cloak maker. It's time you had one of your own."

"*Rumpelstiltskin?* You're dragging me to go see *Rumpelstiltskin?*" Luke's brow furrowed as he slowly twisted to look at Mel. "Wait, scratch that. That's the least weird thing to happen to me since I've been here. Why the hell would I need… Nope, never mind. *How* the hell could I get a cloak if I'm not a chro—"

"You *are* a chromaveiled," Ezmaunda responded before Mel had a chance. But while she did, she rolled her eyes and sighed, as if explaining anything with more than two words were the most grueling task anyone had ever asked of her. "Or rather, you have shown signs that you are capable of becoming one. I haven't a clue when your powers were unlocked, nor did we have any reason to believe you had any such latent abilities."

"Powers? What the hell are you talking about? I don't have any powers."

"I suppose that flame you conjured was only our collective imagination."

"Well... That, um..."

Ezmaunda raised an eyebrow at him and plowed ahead. "If you are seeing the tracking beacons and enchantments on items—and now sparking fires with only your hand and a bit of thought—there is no doubt they were unlocked. So now that we have this information, you need a cloak. It will prevent you from being tracked, and it will help you control these new, burgeoning abilities."

"Melody?" Luke's voice came out barely louder than a whisper as his heart raced.

"It's true. I just... I didn't realize it was happening until you saw the blue light in the sky this morning." Mel drew in a deep breath and slowly released it. Suddenly, she gasped. She hurried over to Ezmaunda's side. "Give me your hand. We need to test something."

Scowling, Ezmaunda held out her hand. As Mel took hold of it, she lifted the red hood over her own head. An instant later, Mel stood there hunched over as her body switched into that of an old man. Ezmaunda's figure shifted just as quickly, changing her form into that of an elf. Her skin and hair grew several shades darker, her eyes transformed to purple, and her ears stretched until they were long and pointed.

The old man looked around momentarily and said, "I don't feel anything."

A look passed between Ezmaunda and Luke, but since neither of them knew what Mel was talking about, neither one offered a response.

As Mel dropped Ezmaunda's hand, the Azure's appearance immediately returned to normal. Mel reached up and lowered her hood, reverting back to her usual form. She walked over to Luke, silently grabbed his hand, and pulled the red hood up once more. She was almost instantly reverted back into the old man. Luke transformed into that same elven woman that Ezmaunda had been only a few moments ago.

Mel winced, pressing a palm to her forehead. "There's that headache again."

Letting go of Luke's hand, Mel stepped back and watched him. For thirty full seconds, his glamoured form didn't falter. But then, at last, it slowly reverted back to normal. Mel lowered her invisible hood and allowed herself to change back as well.

Sporting a look that seemed to exist halfway between delighted and terrified, Mel looked over at Ezmaunda. "When we were leaving Earth, I changed our appearances to hide from you. That must've been what unlocked his abilities."

"*What?*" Luke looked between the two women as they ignored his question.

Ezmaunda—who had been quietly gaping at Luke as the experiment unfolded—gave herself a shake and schooled her features. "Aye. Well, now that that mystery has been solved, it's time we resumed our travels. No doubt we'll be found if we stay here too long. So, if you'd prefer not to be captured and tortured, let's retrieve that cloak."

"No!"

"Mel, I don't care what you say. I am *not* going back alone!"

Marching over to where Luke and Mel were staring at one another, Ezmaunda grabbed them each by the hand and teleported them all away before the others realized what was happening. As they reappeared by the side of a lake, she let go of them and pressed her thumbs hard into her temples in an attempt to rub away the pain that had erupted there. She squinted at Luke. "Gleffik, you truly do leech one's mana."

Neither Luke nor Mel was paying any attention to her. They were both focused on the burned remains of the village in front of them. Sitting there alongside the ruins of homes and buildings was a massive pile of charred, human bones. The acrid scent of smoke wafted into the air as their shoes stirred up the ashes that covered the ground.

"What happened?" Mel's voice cracked as she stared at the destruction in front of her.

"Queen had each of the villagers tortured. When they could not or would not reveal your whereabouts…" Ezmaunda clenched her teeth as her words trailed away, and she stared at the destroyed village. "Lindenbracht is not the first village she's razed. Nor has it been the last."

Mel slowly turned her widened eyes toward Ezmaunda. "Didn't your girlfriend live here?"

"Yes. Rhéya didn't deserve this." As she stared at the ashes that stirred in the slight breeze, Ezmaunda blinked rapidly, clearing the moisture from her eyes. She said, "I told you I no longer serve Queen. Do you now believe I speak the truth?"

"Yeah." Tightening her shaking fingers into fists, Mel growled, "We're going to see Rumpelstiltskin."

23

"Come on." Mel looked away from the destruction and swiped her hand through the air, opening a portal in front of herself. She grabbed hands with the others and pulled them along through the rift. "I can't keep looking at this place."

As they stepped out into the foothills of the mountains—the exact same location she and Ezmaunda had gone to earlier in the day—she released her hold on them. To Ezmaunda, she said, "I'll disguise the two of us. You teleport us up there—"

"What? That pain from the previous one has not yet fully abated. You, however, don't seem to be bothered by the portal you so recently manifested. Why would it not cause you the same pain?" Ezmaunda glared at her as she continued. "Regardless, why should I let him drain more from my reserves? Let him draw from yours."

"Yeah, I know it's weird. I guess since the spell isn't on him directly, it doesn't cause the mana draw. *But,*" Mel paused a moment to let the word hang in the air, "I know maintaining a disguise for both Luke and me will drain my mana particularly fast. I need all I can get if we're going to get through this ordeal without getting ourselves caught. Speaking of which…"

Mel turned around and opened the enchanted satchel Luke was carrying over his shoulder. She stuck her hand in to feel around inside the small bag. Not finding anything after a few moments, she leaned forward and reached in farther until her whole arm and head disappeared into the bag. At last, she pulled herself free and stood up, two vials of swirling blue liquid clutched in her hand. She took a sip. As she held out the partial container, Luke reached for it, but Ezmaunda snatched it away.

Tossing back a small swallow as well, Ezmaunda replaced the stopper and tucked the half-empty bottle into a pocket inside her blue cloak.

"Shouldn't I have some?" Luke held out his hand expectantly as he looked back and forth between the two of them. "I can't believe I'm even entertaining this idea, but maybe I won't drain your mana so fast if I'm topped off."

Ezmaunda answered, "No. You don't have need of it. However, I might need it in order to get us out of there. Aside from that, I'd much prefer the one who has no notion of how to control his powers *not* have access to a full mana supply." Folding her arms across her chest, she raised an eyebrow as if daring Luke to challenge her.

Mel laid her hand on Luke's forearm, gently moving it down to his side. "For once, I agree with Ez. It's probably best if you held off."

Luke slowly nodded in resignation.

"Alright, I'll change the two of us into kids, and Ez will take us up there and get us each a cloak. We've got to make him believe we belong there, so we're simply a pair of orphans who are being recruited by Queen. Do not let go of my hand. Stay behind me as much as you can. You're a shy mute who won't look at or talk to anyone while we're there. Got it?"

Clamping his lips together, Luke lifted one hand and mimed locking his mouth and throwing away the key. Then he gave her a quick, double thumbs up while grinning goofily. Mel chuckled and poked him in the ribs.

"If the two of you are quite finished…"

The smile faded from Mel's face as she twisted around to face Ezmaunda. "Can you get us the rest of the way there in one go?"

"Two." Ezmaunda walked over and grabbed each of them by the elbow. "I'll take us halfway. You'll make your transformation, then we'll traverse the rest. Ready?"

Mel's head had barely dipped down in a nod, and the trio were already popping out halfway up the mountain. White flakes of snow swirled rapidly around them. Sharp, frigid wind whipped past as it tugged at their clothes and hair. Mel hurriedly pulled her red hood up, transforming herself and Luke into a pair of dark-haired children. The color of Mel's cloak faded into invisibility as Ezmaunda brought them another stretch closer to the summit.

Now, the snow filled the air so densely, they could barely see more than a few inches past their own noses. The whipping wind now howled in a high, deafening pitch as if the wind itself were somehow in agonizing pain. It tore at them, setting their teeth chattering as goosebumps broke out across their skin. Tiny droplets of ice pelted them. Stumbling forward, struggling against the force of the wind, Ezmaunda led the way up the incline, with Mel and Luke following close behind.

Right as Luke opened his mouth to ask how much more of this they would have to endure, they suddenly broke through the edge of the raging storm. They were no longer surrounded by ice, and the sudden change in temperature made the air around them seem hot and stifling. A thick layer of lush grass covered the ground. Each green blade looked as though it had been meticulously measured and trimmed; there was no sign of weeds or rocks in this well-maintained mountaintop landscape. In the center of the massive lawn sat a very skinny, very tall, very lopsided house.

Luke paused and twisted to look behind them at the wall of swirling white, the storm seemingly held at bay on all sides by an invisible forcefield. He couldn't help but feel like they were traipsing through some sort of reverse snow globe.

"Let's go," Mel whispered the words at Ezmaunda, all the while feigning that she was chewing her fingernails so she could hide her mouth from any prying eyes. "I can't hold this transformation forever."

Ezmaunda dipped her chin in acknowledgment. Grabbing Mel's arm, she started walking and yanked the little girl forward. The young boy that was Luke followed closely behind. As Ezmaunda quickly led the way forward, she loudly exclaimed over her shoulder, "You'd best do as you're told. Queen won't tolerate disobedience!"

Tears formed in Mel's eyes and streamed down her pale, freckled cheeks. She yanked against the arm that held her, but Ezmaunda's grip didn't loosen.

First, Luke looked at Ezmaunda. Now that he was staring up at her from a child's vantage point, listening to her threaten a little girl as she dragged them both closer to danger, a chill ran down his spine.

His gaze then darted over toward Mel. Deep down, he *knew* it was only an act, but her performance—the tears, the trembling lip, the way her fingers clawed at the hand that clutched her arm—set his heart racing. He wanted to remember that this was all for show, that this was how things were supposed to play out. Instead, he allowed the illusion to overtake him. He was expected to play the part of a frightened child, so he would do precisely that.

"Rumpelstiltskin!"

Luke's feet froze in place and Mel's grip nearly pulled him over as she continued after Ezmaunda. He jerked his head toward the Azure, gaping at her.

Noticing his surprise, Mel shot him a look. He blinked rapidly. Both of them managed to get their expression back under control just as a loud *pop* sounded, and a cloud of silvery white cropped up in front of them. A moment later, the cloud quickly dissipated, and in its place stood a dark-green-skinned goblin, barely more than two-and-a-half feet tall. Perhaps a dozen strands of long, white hair were scattered across the top of his otherwise bald head. Very slowly, his large, brown eyes scanned across the group before finally coming to rest as he looked up at Ezmaunda's face. He scowled. "What you doin' here? Queenie didn't tell me you was coming."

"Aw. You seem displeased to see me." Ezmaunda stuck her lip out.

The goblin huffed and crossed his arms.

Ezmaunda only held the pouting look for a few moments before she let her lips slide upward into a lopsided grin.

Reaching out, she lightly brushed the tip of one finger down the length of Rumpelstiltskin's cheek. As a blush crept up the goblin's neck and face, making his green skin an almost purplish-black, Ezmaunda giggled and straightened up. "Queen is unaware that I came here."

"Aye?"

"I found this pair, and I believe Queen would be delighted to have them under her rule." Ezmaunda paused to brush a stray lock of blonde hair from her face and tuck it behind her ear. "She is quite overwhelmed with her search for the Crimson. I did not see a need to bother her with such trivialities as I'm certain she'll have them sent to you for cloaks soon enough."

As the color of his cheeks slowly faded back to its normal toadish resemblance, the goblin turned his stare on the two children. He moved closer to them, bringing his attention to Luke. The boy stood half-concealed by Mel, but the goblin didn't seem to notice. He leaned forward, his eyes scrutinizing the boy's face.

After several tense seconds of staring, he finally stepped back, sniffing noisily as he did. Tilting his chin up toward Ezmaunda, he said, "Does seem as if this one's got a bit of power to 'im. Not much, but might be enough for Queenie to keep 'im alive."

Luke inhaled sharply. It had been shocking enough when Mel and Ezmaunda had suggested he held some degree of magical inclination. But now the words somehow felt real to him in a way they hadn't up to this point.

"As I suspected." Ezmaunda nodded, a mischievous grin spreading across her face.

Without warning, Rumpelstiltskin suddenly shoved Melzia aside. She gasped as her hand slipped from Luke's fingers, and she went tumbling to the ground.

Wide-eyed, Luke darted forward, his hand outstretched toward Mel, but he was stopped. The goblin's grip on Luke's arm was surprisingly strong, considering his small stature. Luke squeezed his eyes shut, focusing every last ounce of his energy on holding the spell that was keeping him disguised. He had no idea what he was doing, no idea if his concentration would help anything, but not seeing any other choice, he had to try.

Yanking Mel back to her feet and grabbing her by the shoulders, Ezmaunda quickly pushed her to the goblin's side. Her voice was steady as she asked, "And the girl?"

During the momentary pause as Rumpelstiltskin looked up at Ezmaunda, Mel rushed over and laced her fingers tightly through Luke's. At the same time, both children exhaled heavily.

The goblin turned back and scooted over in front of Mel. His round eyes met hers, and as he stared, his forehead slowly crinkled. He reached out and snatched up Mel's wrist, yanking her closer. "How old are you, girl?"

The tears slid even faster down Mel's face. She swallowed hard, looking at Ezmaunda. When she finally tore her gaze back to Rumpelstiltskin, she squeaked out, "Nine."

He leaned closer until his long nose was nearly touching Mel's. Reaching out, he pinched her chin between his thumb and forefinger, keeping her from looking away. "Are you now? You've got more power than I've seen in such a young one."

Ezmaunda suddenly clapped her hands together, smiling from ear to ear as she bounced on her toes. All eyes slid back to her.

"What you so 'appy about?"

"Queen will be delighted I've found such a powerful one!"

"Aye, I believe so." He nodded. Letting go of Mel's chin, he said, "You lot wait 'ere. I'll fetch your cloaks."

Stepping close, Ezmaunda leaned down, laid the palm of her hand on Rumpelstiltskin's cheek, and batted her eyes at him. "Once I've turned these two in, I'll see that Queen rewards you handsomely for this."

The blush crept back up the goblin's skin. There was a *pop*, a small cloud of silvery white, and he was gone.

"Shit, that was intense."

Though she didn't verbally respond, Ezmaunda looked at Mel, raised her eyebrows, and gave a slight nod.

"Something's not right." Mel twisted around to face the others. "I knew this was too dangerous. We need to go. Now."

Luke glanced at the door to the house as he leaned in. He said in a hushed voice, "But he bought it. Why would we run off before we get the cloak?"

"He didn't buy it! I've been through this process before, remember? I've joined others during this as well. He didn't bring us inside or ask where we were found or..." Mel let her words trail away. She looked up at Ezmaunda. "Look, if you don't believe me, that's fine. But we don't have time to stand here and argue. Please go in there and keep an eye on him. Make sure he's really getting the cloaks."

"What else do you believe he would be doing?"

Mel's jaw clenched, and she let out a low growl of frustration. Pulling Luke behind her, she stomped toward the house and stormed inside.

Ezmaunda, having no choice but to follow after them and play along, hurried to catch up and resume her performance as captor. As the door swung closed behind them, she called out, "Rumpelstiltskin? Did you wish to…"

The three of them froze as they caught sight of the goblin on the other side of the long, sparsely furnished room. At his side was a large spinning wheel with a tall stack of white, glittering fabric crumpled on the floor beside it. He was standing in front of a simple mirror that wasn't showing his reflection; instead, it held the image of a woman in a silver crown and purple cloak.

Queen's violet eyes bore into Mel's. Then, suddenly, her attention shifted, and her gaze locked on Ezmaunda. As she rose from her seat, she snarled, "Betrayer!" She whispered words to some incantation, shifting the hood of her cloak as she did. In the next moment, the image of Queen split into two nearly identical bodies. The first was solid and stayed there inside the mirror, glowering at them; the second one was nearly transparent, a ghostly copy of Queen.

The ghost strode forward. When it reached the mirror, it laid a hand against the glass and pressed on it. At first, nothing happened. But then, the glass shimmered and rippled, changing to liquid. The ghost stepped through into Rumpelstiltskin's house, its evil glare fixed on Ezmaunda.

Mel spun back toward the door, pulling Luke along behind her yet again. She grabbed the door handle and suddenly realized Ezmaunda still stood rooted to the spot—rigid and unblinking—as the ghost slid closer. Its face contorted into a snarl. It moved forward slowly, lifting one arm out in front of itself and sending yellowy-brown, glowing tendrils of magic toward Ezmaunda. They snaked their way around her body, dragging Ezmaunda closer.

Mel's eyes darted toward Luke.

Not giving her a chance to protest, Luke jerked his hand from Mel's grasp. "Save her so we can get the hell out of here!"

She hesitated. As Luke started to revert to his own body, he laid his hand on the door handle and yanked it open. Mel spun around, shifting the hood of her cloak as she did. Her body reverted back to normal, a spear appeared in her hands, and she charged forward.

The ghost's head jerked toward Mel. It raised its other arm in her direction, sending out those same swirling tendrils at her now, but these weren't slow and slithering like those that trapped Ezmaunda. These tore through the room like lightning. Mel spun to the side, sucking air through her teeth as the spell grazed the side of her bicep and tore a jagged streak across her flesh.

Something moved past the corner of Mel's vision. The goblin's voice shouted, but she couldn't risk taking her focus off this fight.

She lunged forward with the spear aimed at the ghost's translucent face. It leaned backward, and the speartip narrowly missed the target. The spell holding Ezmaunda faltered.

Mel let out a yell, pulling the spear back and thrusting. The ghost's new spell was cut short when steel connected with ghostly flesh. The weapon punctured a hole through the phantom's shoulder and burst out its back. It opened its mouth as if to scream, but the agonized screech that came out was emanating from the other side of the mirror.

Mel pulled back again, tearing the speartip free from the ghost's body and sending translucent droplets of blood spraying across the wooden floor. She swung the weapon downward, tearing through the now tenuous yellow-brown spell that held Ezmaunda captive.

The magical cords gave way, and Ezmaunda stumbled backward.

"Go!" Mel screamed the word.

For once, Ezmaunda obeyed.

Mel risked glancing back at the mirror long enough to see Queen standing there, fury etched across her face as she held one hand against her shoulder and blood oozed from between her fingers. For a moment, their eyes met.

The ghost flickered as Queen screamed her fury.

Spinning around, her red cloak fanning out around her as she did, Mel bolted out the door. She stepped into the grass, turned back to the doorway, pulled her arm back, and launched the spear at the ghost. As the weapon flew through the air, the ghost reached out and caught it when the tip was mere inches from its face. The spear—now having lost the influence of Mel's cloaking spell—vanished.

Locking eyes with Queen through the mirror, Mel glared at her. The ghost fizzled out of existence. Queen began muttering to herself another time, and the sky above Mel quickly went dark. She glanced up as the first thick black and purple cloud formed overhead, crackling with lightning.

She ran. Ezmaunda and Luke were at her sides as more clouds formed above them and swirled together, creating a growing funnel at their center. Wind and thunder shook the air above them. The bright glow of the sun was swallowed up by the growing storm until the only light was from the purple glow around the clouds.

Between heaving breaths, Luke shouted, "Portal... us... out!"

"I can't!" Mel screamed back. "We have to get past... the boundary!"

A bolt of purple lightning struck the ground in front of Mel and she yelped, pivoting on one foot, barely avoiding the blast. A second landed directly behind them. The wind whipped faster as the funnel grew closer. Chunks of ice pelted down, denting the ground and leaving deep bruises on their skin.

Ezmaunda reached the boundary first and darted through without looking back. Mel grabbed Luke by the hand and pulled him faster. They finally burst through the magical barrier, leaving behind Queen's storm but stepping back into the frigid, blinding white blizzard of the mountaintop.

Snagging them both by the wrist, Ezmaunda teleported once, then once more. When, at last, she let them go at the base of the mountain, each one of the trio collapsed onto the grass, breathless and exhausted.

Mel rolled onto her side, pressing a palm to her chest where her heart hammered violently. She looked at Ezmaunda. "I told you... it was too... dangerous."

24

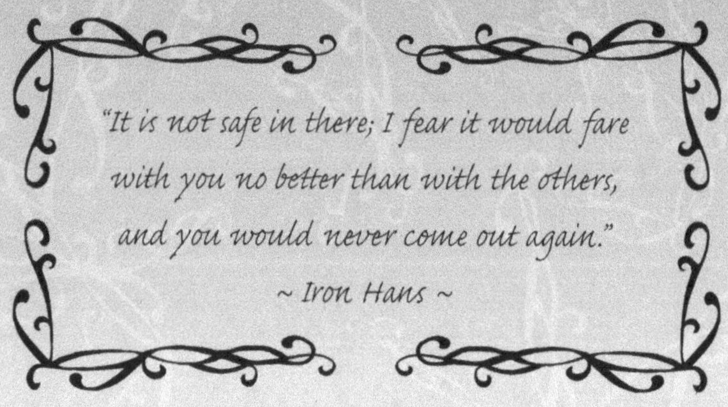

"That was entirely useless and far too risky!" Mel slowly pushed herself to her feet and leaned on a tree to take a deep breath. "We won't try anything like that again. We've got to go. She'll have someone here searching for us within the hour."

Luke interjected, "Hey, I—"

"We require that cloak if we're to have any chance against her! He is not the prophesied one if he does not have that." Ezmaunda stood and shoved Luke out of her way. She turned long enough to glance up at the mountaintop where the storm continued to rage. "She'll soon realize we made it off the mountain, cease her spell, and send her lackeys to find us. We'll make our way back up there while they are preoccupied down here."

"Hey!" Luke's voice fell once more on deaf ears.

"No!" Mel glared at Ezmaunda. "I just saved your life back there. Don't try to tell me what we need to do now! We are not going back!"

Ezmaunda shoved a hand into her cloak, searching for the remnants of that mana potion, but when she pulled her hand back, it dripped with the swirling blue liquid. At some point in the scuffle, the glass container had been shattered. She grumbled while she wiped her hand clean on the inside of her cloak. As she opened her mouth to retort, Luke pushed his way in between the women, holding up a bundle of white fabric. Sparkles of magic steadily rose from it and dissipated as they drifted off into the air. He looked from one stunned woman to the other. "This is what we were after, right?"

Mel slowly nodded. "When did you get that?"

Luke shrugged. "When you two were busy dealing with Miss Psycho-Sorceress."

"I watched you go outside!"

"No, you didn't. You watched me open the door. As soon as you were distracted, I tried to figure out if I could help. When I saw the pile of magic cloth, I thought that had to be what we needed, so I ran back there to grab one."

Mel gaped at him. "How did you get it from him?"

Luke shrugged. "As I was going back there, the goblin saw me. I guess he tried to cast some spell, so I just walked up and punched him in his ugly mouth. He was out like a light. So I snagged one of these, shoved it in the bag, and ran back outside right when you broke that spell."

"You *hit* Rumpelstiltskin?" Ezmaunda's jaw hung wide, but her eyes shone with amusement.

"Nice!" Mel laughed and walked up to Luke, one hand raised. "I always wanted to do that. Little punk deserved it."

Giving her a high five, Luke grinned. "Yeah, can't say I feel bad about it."

"Well, that certainly raises my opinion of your beau considerably."

"You know I'm standing here next to you, right?"

Mel gently laid a hand on Luke's forearm and said, "Alright, Ez, do you have enough mana left to get us out of here?"

"No. Why can't you do it? And where are we to go?"

"For now, just away from here. And I'm not familiar with this area, so I can't portal us. Your teleportation isn't quite so restrictive." Mel pushed back a stray lock of hair and tucked it behind her ear. She reached into the satchel at Luke's side, fishing around for a moment until she found what she was looking for. With a quiet word to Luke, he wadded up the white fabric and slid it into the enchanted bag with everything else.

At last, Mel turned back to Ezmaunda and offered a vial of blue liquid. "Here."

Ezmaunda took the mana potion. She didn't hesitate to pull the stopper and take a large drink. Ignoring Mel's outstretched hand, she reclosed the bottle and shoved it into a pocket on the inside of her cloak. "Where to?"

Mel lowered her outstretched hand with a sigh. "I think it's time we went to my sister."

"Aye." Ezmaunda grabbed their wrists, and they were suddenly in a new location. The mountains were still at their backs, but now their feet sank into the muddy ground as they stood in the marshes. Two rivers converged in front of them.

A moment later, the scenery changed again. They were once more on solid ground, surrounded on all sides by tall trees. Though they couldn't see the river, they could hear it rushing by somewhere to the west of them.

"I recognize this place." Mel stepped away from the others as Ezmaunda released her wrist.

"Ah." Ezmaunda rolled her eyes. "Whatever became of 'I'm not familiar with this area, so I can't portal us?' Hmm?"

"Well, this is the one place on this side of the continent that I *am* familiar with. And you knew that."

Luke stepped forward and laid a hand on the middle of Mel's back. "What's special about this place? Where are we?"

"She brought us back to Eldévas Woods?" Mel folded her arms across her chest, tears stinging her eyes as she glared at Ezmaunda. "We're closer to Queen's castle than we have been since leaving the gateway. And on top of that, this is where my sister was hiding when I... When..."

"It's alright." Luke pulled Mel close and rocked her side to side. When she had calmed slightly, he turned his angry stare on Ezmaunda. "Why the hell did you bring us here, of all places? Are you trying to hurt her? Are you trying to get us caught? What's wrong with you?"

Ezmaunda leaned back against a moss-covered boulder. Reaching inside her cloak, she pulled out the vial, poured the remainder of the mana potion into her mouth, and tossed the empty container into the tall grass. "We require somewhere to hide while you accustom yourself to the cloak. I thought perhaps somewhere shielded by trees to limit the risk of being spotted by chromas or spies or wygons or eavesdropping villagers. This forest is near our destination as well. And while it is true that we are nearer to Queen's castle, do you really believe she will expect us to willingly venture so close?"

"You could've picked anywhere else."

Mel took a step back and laid a hand on Luke's chest. "It's okay. She's right."

"What? Are you sure?"

She nodded.

Luke tilted his head down until his forehead was leaned against Mel's. He brought one hand up to her face, gently cupping her cheek and wiping away a stray tear with his thumb. As Luke tilted her chin toward his, she licked her lips and leaned closer, pressing into his chest.

From somewhere a few feet away, Ezmaunda groaned. Loudly.

Mel scrunched up her face and took a step backward. "Right. Well, let's get you cloaked."

Moving to the side, Mel reached into Luke's satchel. The entirety of her arm and shoulder quickly disappeared into the bag. It took a few moments of feeling around inside until she finally located the cloak. She pulled it out and let the white fabric unfurl in the breeze.

"Is my cloak going to be white?"

"No. It will change when it determines your skill set. If Ez is right, you'll end up with some color that no other chroma has had previously, and I guess that'll confirm that the prophecy really is about us."

"Do you think she's right?"

Shaking her head, Mel sighed. "No idea."

The two stood there, quietly staring at the fabric clutched in Mel's hands. Finally, Luke took a deep breath and broke the silence. "So, how's this going to work? Am I suddenly going to know all this magic stuff as soon as I put this thing on?"

Mel chuckled. "No. It's going to take a lot of practice. And I imagine it'll be even harder on you since you weren't raised here. I can teach you some things to get you going, though."

"Oh yeah? You're going to have me put on a special outfit and teach me some things?" Luke grinned as he waggled his eyebrows at her. He stepped close to her. Slowly trailing one fingertip down her arm, he touched his cheek to hers and whispered, "Is that a promise?"

"Drenkth!" Ezmaunda stomped off into the forest, muttering a long string of elvish insults and expletives as she stormed away.

As the couple burst into laughter, Mel stepped back. "If I'd known it was that easy to get rid of her, I would've told you to whisper naughty things in my ear yesterday!"

"Okay, her reaction definitely killed the mood, but damn, was that worth it!" Luke turned his back on Mel, still grinning as he wiped a tear from his eye. "Let's do this."

"It might feel odd when the cloak first binds itself to you."

"Odd?"

"Every cloak color is different, so I don't know what exactly you should expect. Mine grew really warm, like I was standing a bit too close to a fire. From what I understand, the Citrine cloaks feel like they're becoming liquid as they change. There's no telling what yours will do."

"So." Luke paused to look down at his wrist. Am I going to end up with one of those marks like you and Ezmaunda have?"

"No. That's a separate spell, performed by Queen herself. And it's a spell I don't intend to give her the opportunity to use on you."

"Alright. Cloak me up."

Mel reached up and draped the cloak across his shoulders. She then walked around to the front, tied the string across his collarbone, and stepped away to watch. It simply sat there, fluttering lightly in the slow breeze as its little, gold flecks of magic continued to drift off into the sky.

"Can you see anything yet? I think I can feel it changing."

"Not yet." Mel slowly walked in a circle around him, looking over every inch of the cloak. As she stopped in front of him once more, she asked, "What does it feel like?"

"It's kind of like…" He paused, looking down at the cloak as he tried to think of the right words to describe the strange sensation. He raised his arm for Mel to see the hairs standing on end, and he continued. "Static electricity. And all the tiny, annoying little zaps that come along with it."

Reaching out, Mel touched a finger to his arm. As a small spark shot from his arm to her fingertip, she jerked her hand back and shook away the quick, little jolt of pain as she laughed. She stepped back. The hairs on Luke's head splayed out as the static grew. Hundreds of little sparks danced along his skin, crackling as they raced a few inches from their starting points and vanished.

"How about now?"

Luke shook his head. "It's a little weird. Okay, it feels *a lot* weird, truth be told. But it doesn't exactly hurt."

"That's good. It seems…" Mel's half-formed thought was carried off on the wind. She bent down to stare at the fabric near Luke's feet. "Look."

The bottom hem was darkening. Its color wasn't yet apparent—maybe a blue or gray or purple. Regardless, it was no longer a simple, sparkly white. Thin, shadowy, zigzagging trails spread upward, slowly branching out across the fabric. As the two of them silently fixated on the changing cloak, they didn't notice that the dancing electricity on Luke's skin had finally stopped.

The dark lines kept creeping and made their way up Luke's back, onto the hood, and across the shoulders. Then suddenly, the trails seeped outward as if they were watercolor paints spreading out across a canvas. But unlike paints, as these lines bled across the cloth, the color didn't get paler. Eventually, the shadows melded together and deepened until the cloak was transformed into a black so deep it swallowed any shadows that tried to mark its folds.

"Obsidian." Mel grinned as she looked at the black cloth.

Luke turned his attention toward Mel. "Now what?"

"Try the flame spell another time."

Taking a deep breath, he held out his hand, closed his eyes, and envisioned a roaring fire. Then he snapped his fingers. A quick flash of warmth zipped across his palm, but nothing more. He tried again, and this time, he felt the heat on his hand and looked down to see a tiny but strong flame, dancing hypnotically just above his skin. Luke stared in awe.

"Fantastic!" Mel beamed at him. "Now, keep your palm flat and pull your hand back quickly, and it'll snuff out."

He did as instructed. Though Luke's movement was clumsy and unpracticed, the flame sputtered out, leaving behind only a wispy trail of smoke.

"That was awesome!" Luke bounced on his toes as he rubbed his palms together. "What's next?"

Chuckling, Mel replied, "What's next is that you keep practicing until you can do that spell in your sleep."

Luke's face fell. "What? I don't get to practice making portals? Or learn fighting moves or, I don't know. Something actually useful? I don't think that's going to be much use in a fight versus some evil queen. If all I am is a living lighter in a black piece of cloth, you've got to admit that's pretty lame."

"Oh, I don't know." Mel stepped closer. She reached out to slowly stroke her fingertips up the length of Luke's arm. Inching forward, she looked up at him. "I think stuff being magically lit on fire is pretty... *hot*."

Groaning loudly, Luke rolled his eyes. But—in spite of himself—his lips curled up slightly at the edges. "Okay, ha ha. I'm being serious, though. How is that going to help beat her?"

"I know that spell feels very basic and unimportant. But it doesn't take a lot of mana, and it's the simplest one to practice by yourself over and over and over. Striking up a tiny fire in the palm of your hand is useful, of course. But yeah, in most fights, it's not going to help you all that much.

"Here's the thing, though. I'd say roughly ninety-nine percent of our spells start with the ability to focus. We chromaveiled need to concentrate to the point that we believe our spell is already real in order for it to manifest. If we don't, if there's any doubt, it just doesn't happen. Having the cloak helps channel the spell, but it's still up to the caster to have the mental focus to get it going.

"So, you need to practice that concentration. In the midst of battle, you're not going to have a nice, calm, quiet moment to gather your thoughts; there won't be a do-over or a timeout. You need to get to the point that you can watch what's going on around you, dodge or hide without a second thought, think of the right spell to respond with, and bring that spell to life so quick there isn't an opportunity for your concentration to break."

"Ugh. Fine." Luke sighed and pressed a quick kiss to Mel's lips before gently pushing her off to the side. "Now make room, gorgeous.

I need to practice casting a billion of these. I'm about to make this human-lighter spell my bitch."

"Alright, you do that." Mel laughed as she spun around. She walked toward the trees and called back over her shoulder, "I'm going to see if I can find Ez. Be back in a minute."

Mel moved further into the forest as the sound of snapping fingers —and intermittent cursing—faded into the background behind her. At first, her path was aimless as she zigzagged back and forth in a solo game of "hot or cold." Eventually, she felt the slight thickening of the air off to the east. Not certain whether she was about to find Ezmaunda or someone else entirely, Mel grabbed hold of her cloak and shifted it so the vivid red transformed into the deep green of the forest. She pulled the edges of the cloth tight around herself until all but her eyes and nose were hidden beneath the forest-colored fabric.

As she began making her way toward the source of the sensation, Mel's training took over. She moved slowly, carefully stepping over fallen twigs, gently moving through the leafy greenery. Her movements barely made a sound.

Eventually, Mel crept out from beneath the cover of a large tree with magnolia-like flowers; the petals were deep purple, though if you looked closely, faint yellow swirls could be seen as well. She stopped. A few small tufts of grass looked trampled, as if someone had walked through recently. A little bit further, a patch of grass was squashed flat to the ground like something heavy had recently been resting on it. Mel squinted at it. Grabbing hold of her hood, she slowly lowered it. The green receded into red as she said, "Hi, Ez."

There was a sudden gasp, and the flat patch of grass shifted slightly. A split second later, Ezmaunda appeared there, lowering her blue hood with one hand as the other pressed against her hammering heart. "Ostrenia zindt!" Ezmaunda stood up and brushed a few stray bits of dirt from her cloak. "Rather reckless, don't you think? How were you to know who you would find here?"

Mel hadn't known for certain who was sitting there, but she'd taken a calculated risk in assuming it was Ezmaunda. She'd kept her cloak at the ready in case she were wrong and needed to fight. Now that it was clear that wasn't a concern, she finally let loose of the red fabric. Ezmaunda was staring, waiting for an answer. But Mel simply smirked and lifted one shoulder.

Folding her arms across her chest, Ezmaunda walked over beside Mel and turned so they were both facing the same direction. "The village lies not far beyond those trees. I ventured over and mesmerized one of the villagers and asked all he knew of any chromaveiled in the area. When he gave nothing, I located and questioned another. His answers were much the same."

"Good. Hopefully, that means they haven't been down this way, and maybe we'll be safe here for at least a night or two."

"Aye."

They went quiet—each lost in their own thoughts—as they stared off toward the village. After a long while, Ezmaunda broke the silence. "He's not so terrible, I suppose."

Mel arched an eyebrow as she glanced over. "I'm surprised to hear you say that. You didn't seem to care for Luke."

The corner of Ezmaunda's lip twitched upward. "You say that as if I care for anyone."

"True. Someone being 'not terrible' is high praise coming from you." Mel laughed. "So, what changed your mind?" "Do you recall the boy you were so enamored with? What was his name? Jasper, perhaps? Jack? I don't remember now. The thin one with the dark hair. You were convinced he was your soul match."

"Jayse?"

"Aye. That's the one."

"I'd nearly forgotten about Jayse. I haven't seen him since I was eighteen. I thought you hated Jayse."

"I loathed Jayse. I *detested* Jayse." Ezmaunda turned to look Mel in the eye. "Admittedly, though, it was simply because I believed he was not good enough for you. This Luke seems to be a far better match."

Mel grinned. "I think he is, too."

Ezmaunda pulled her cloak tighter around herself and turned away.

"We'd better head back." Mel pivoted around and started walking. "I don't want to leave Luke alone for too long."

Ezmaunda raised an eyebrow as she stared at Mel's back. "The pair of you seemed rather *enthusiastic* when I left. Have you both quite finished with your..." There was the faintest hint of laughter in her voice, but she curled her lip in disgust as she let the words trail away into silence.

Not slowing her pace, Mel responded with nothing more than another shrug. She could practically feel Ezmaunda's eyes rolling, and the thought had Mel biting her lip to keep herself from laughing out loud.

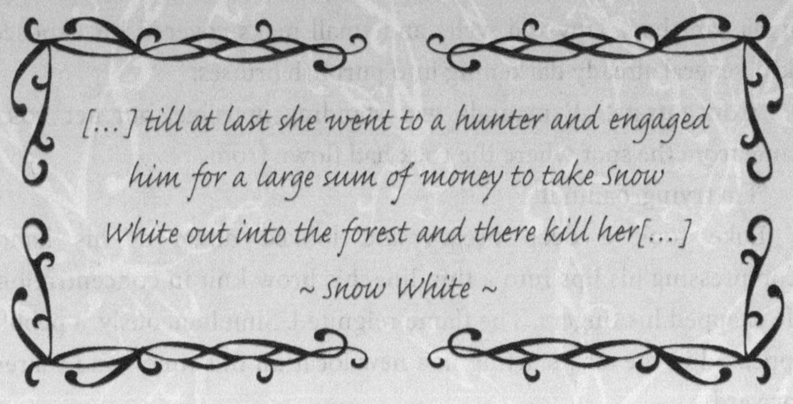

25

Early the next morning, Mel woke, her hip aching from sleeping on the hard ground yet again. She slowly pushed herself upright, shivering as the fabric of the cloak slipped off her arm. Pulling the cloak tightly around herself to ward off the unseasonable chill, she turned to look around. Her heart began to pound inside her ribs.

She was alone.

Bolting up off the ground, Mel reached for her hood. She flicked the red fabric and her bow and arrow materialized in her hands as she heard a noise a little way off through the trees. It was quiet, indistinct at first as she made her way toward the source. Though at the same time, the sound was steady, repetitive. After a few steps, she paused. She could feel the thicker air ahead. Two magic wielders; one mana source was strong, the other fainter. She listened closely. Suddenly, she realized what the sound was. Snapping. Chuckling softly, she let the bow and arrow fall to the ground to fade from existence.

Moving a bit faster now, Mel popped out from between the trees to see Luke standing there, staring intently at his hand. He snapped his fingers, and a little ball of flame burst into life. At the same time, a pebble suddenly appeared in the air and flew toward him, smacking him in the collarbone. As he winced, he jerked his hand back, and the flame vanished. Tiny red welts and small nicks covered his exposed skin, several already darkening into purplish bruises.

"Concentrate!" Ezmaunda was standing invisible, but her voice came from the spot where the rock had flown from.

"I'm trying, damn it!"

Luke took a deep breath and looked down at his hand. Compressing his lips into a thin line, his brow knit in concentration. He snapped his fingers. The flame reignited. Simultaneously, a pebble appeared in the air—starting in a new location this time—and soared forward.

Mel reached out and swatted the little projectile away as it sailed straight toward Luke's eye. "That's enough, Ez!"

"Spoilsport." Ezmaunda let herself become visible once more.

As Luke's head jerked up, the flame sputtered out all over again. He stood there, blinking at Mel. "Where'd you come from?"

Ignoring the remark, Mel kept her attention on Luke. "I've been standing here in plain sight for a couple minutes, watching you get pelted with stones. Interesting training technique." Her narrowed eyes slid toward Ezmaunda.

"He must learn to counter attacks while he's using his abilities. Have you a better idea for achieving this?"

"Uh, yes! Anything that doesn't involve hurling rocks at his eyeballs!"

Ezmaunda shrugged, setting her blue cloak flapping as one side slipped off her shoulder.

From off to the side, Luke laughed. "Who wants to play it safe? Danger is part of the motivation!"

Mel pinched the bridge of her nose. When she finally looked up at the other woman again, she said, "I'm taking over this training. Go do something else, Ezmaunda."

"I haven't all the spells and weapon skills of yours. What would you have me do?"

"Not this!" Mel paused and breathed in deeply. Her jaw was clenched as she spoke, but her voice was steady. "Go scout the area or something."

Without another word, Ezmaunda adjusted her hood and became invisible another time. A quiet swishing of leaves and the muffled sounds of footsteps through tall grass indicated the Azure was making her way to the north.

When at last they were alone, Mel turned to Luke. She chuckled as she poked him in the chest. "I can't believe you were just standing there letting her do that."

Luke smirked at her. "No worse than the wild crap my friends and I would get up to as kids."

Mel rolled her eyes as she suppressed a laugh. Then, grinning, she moved closer and stood on her tiptoes to kiss his cheek. When she moved away, Luke reached out and wrapped his arms around her back, pulling her against his chest. He leaned down, nuzzling into the curve of her neck and slowly kissing his way up toward her ear.

Sliding her hands up Luke's chest, she gently pushed him away. "As much as I'd like to let you keep going with that, we need to focus on your training."

Luke frowned. "Well, damn. In that case, I agree with Ezmaunda."

"What?" Mel's forehead scrunched as she looked at him. "What are you talking about?"

"You *are* a spoilsport."

Mel bit back a grin. "Fine. I'm a spoilsport. Now show me your progress."

Taking a step backward, Luke lifted one hand out in front of himself and looked at it. He thought for a beat and then snapped his fingers. A little ball of flame burst into life. Pulling his hand back, the flame snuffed out. Another snap had it quickly springing up again; another movement and it was extinguished.

"Good. You're getting faster at it. But you do need to be able to do these spells while distracted. You won't always have a chance to stop and stare at your hand and give it your full attention. So—"

"So now *you're* going to chuck stones at me?" He grinned.

"I will if you don't behave." Mel reached out and poked Luke in the ribs. "No, I'm not going to throw anything at you. You're going to talk to me while you cast this spell."

"Uh, about what?"

"Babe. Your entire life has been completely upended over the last however many days. Don't tell me you've processed all this already."

"Well, this is all insane, and I'm not—"

"Practice."

Luke growled. He dutifully lifted his hand and snapped his fingers as he continued to talk. "I'm not saying it hasn't—" *Snap!* "—had an impact on me." *Snap!* "But it's the path my life has taken and —" *Snap!* "—like it or not, it's what I have to deal with. No use whining about it. I just have to suck it up and make my way through it."

"Yeah, life threw this at you, and you're right. You don't have much choice but to see it through." *Snap!* As Mel finished speaking, a flame sprang to life in her hand. She slowly wiggled her fingers and the red-orange ball of fire became bright blue and grew as she said, "Doesn't mean you can't have feelings about all this craziness."

"It's a lot, but—" *Snap!* "—most of it, I just have to get used to it.

There's no other option." *Snap!* A tiny spark erupted but vanished as quickly as it had appeared.

Mel shifted her hand, and the fire hovering above her skin returned to its original red-orange hue. But it split into five separate fires, and each slid out in a different direction to dance above the tips of her fingers. "Right. For *most* of it, you've got to adjust. But there's something else, isn't there?"

His glance flitted to her momentarily.

"Luke, you have to—"

"You lied to me." *Snap!* Luke exhaled heavily as another spark popped up, but it didn't last. "For years." *Snap!* "That hurt. Well, still hurts, but I understand it at least." *Snap!* "But what I don't understand —" *Snap!* "—is why the hell—" *Snap!* "—you were going to trick me into leaving—" *Snap!* "—and just abandon me!"

Luke froze, his chest heaving as he stared at Mel. It took him a moment to realize she wasn't looking at his face. Her gaze was locked on his outstretched hand. He looked down. A brilliant orange ball of flame danced above his palm, sending shadows flickering wildly over the ground. As the truth sank in, the conflicting emotions flitted across Luke's face. Hurt and betrayal over his situation warred with happiness and pride at what he'd accomplished with this spell. After a long stretch of silence where he tried to sort out all these over-whelming emotions, he pulled his hand back and let the flame die away.

"Oh, Luke." Hurrying forward, Mel threw her arms around him. "I thought it was the only way you'd be safe. I couldn't bear the thought of you getting hurt because of me, so I—"

"So you thought you'd hurt me instead?"

Mel clenched her eyes shut as the tears started to sting.

"We're supposed to be a team. You and me. That means you don't get to make unilateral decisions, even if they are supposed to keep me safe." Luke sighed. He grabbed Mel by the shoulders and moved her back a step so he could look into her eyes. "What if I'd done that to you? Decided what I would do to keep you safe, regardless of whether it was what you wanted or not. And then, I'd refused to tell you that was the plan. I was going to keep you in the dark until the last second when I abandoned you, never to see or talk to you again."

Reaching up, Mel placed the palm of her hand against Luke's neck and lightly stroked her thumb across the dark stubble that lined his jaw. She nodded. "You're right. I shouldn't have tried to force you to leave, and I shouldn't have kept you in the dark. I am so sorry, Luke."

Luke tilted his forehead down until it was settled against hers. He wrapped his arms around her and the two of them slowly rocked back and forth while the only sound around them was the quiet rustling of the breeze making its way through the leaves overhead.

At last, Mel slowly—begrudgingly—opened her eyes. "Can you forgive me?"

Lifting his hand, Luke tilted Mel's chin up. He inched closer until her chest was nestled tightly up to his. He leaned down. Their lips met, and as they did, Luke's every negative thought faded into nothingness. Eventually, he pulled back and gently brushed a stray lock of hair away from her face to tuck it behind her ear. "Always."

Mel gave him another hug. As she finally broke away from the embrace, she wiped away the tears that had spilled onto her cheeks and cleared her throat.

Holding his hand out in front of himself once more, Luke looked at Mel. "I guess I better get back to practicing."

For the next few hours, Luke practiced performing this spell as the two talked; fortunately the conversation had eventually switched to more lighthearted topics. The first night they'd met and how he couldn't stop smiling at her. Their first date to that ridiculously awful movie that neither one could now remember the name of. How nervous he'd felt the first time he'd dared to kiss her. The first night that she was brave enough to say "I love you" and picked out that pale yellow dress specifically for the occasion; the red wine stain that had made an unexpected appearance on the dress that same evening had somehow only made the night that much more memorable.

As the sun approached the center of the sky, Mel laid a hand on

Luke's outstretched arm and motioned for him to be quiet. She stared off through the trees. Her eyes widened. She slowly leaned over to Luke, pressed her face close to his ear, and whispered, "Someone is close."

Luke turned to her and silently mouthed the name, "Ezmaunda?"

Shaking her head, Mel reached for her hood. "Two people to the west, and I'm afraid Nikolas might be one of them. There might be a third person a little way to the north. Keep close." She adjusted the hood of the cloak and the fabric transformed from red to a leaf pattern in multiple shades of green and brown. As she lowered her hands, a sword and shield materialized in them.

Mel crept to the southeast, away from the sources of the dense air, but she didn't dare turn her back toward the possible pursuers. The magic wielders that had been moving due east a moment ago now changed directions, veering southeast and picking up their pace. Still hoping for coincidence, Mel changed course to go west. Once more, the magic wielders turned in the same direction and sped up even further. Mel stopped. She ducked down in the greenery and kept her eyes locked in the direction of their pursuers.

Dropping down next to her and leaning close, Luke whispered, "Why don't you summon a gun instead? They wouldn't stand a chance if you had one."

"I'm going to open a portal. Go through it and be ready to run. I'll be—"

There was a blur of movement. Something tiny and reflective zipped toward them, whistling through the air as it flew. Shoving Luke to the side, Mel threw herself backward. *Thunk!* The throwing star embedded itself deep into the bark of a nearby tree. The weapon was dripping with a bright orange substance. It quickly seeped into the tree, making the trunk turn black as coal.

Mel's heart leapt into her throat as she realized that the neon poison was not the only thing dripping from the multi-sided blade. One side of it dripped red.

Time slowed to a crawl. Mel turned. The sword and shield slipped from her hands, disintegrating into thin air as they fell. A soft, rain-like sound started as chunks of bark came loose around the throwing star and fell into the grass. Mel's gaze found Luke's. His eyes were wide, and sweat was beading on his brow.

Her glance traveled down. Luke's right hand was clutching his left bicep. Only a tiny trickle of blood was visible across his flesh. It was only a small nick, not much worse than a paper cut, but the skin around it was already beginning to darken, and thin rivulets of black were eagerly snaking their way out from the wound.

A second projectile—a dagger, no sign of poison on its blade—made a narrow arc over Mel's head and broke through her stupor. She swished her hand through the air. A portal opened.

Dodging out of the way as another orange-dripping throwing star sailed toward them, Mel grabbed Luke and forced him to his feet. She groaned under the strain. Mustering all of her strength, she dragged him forward. The two tumbled through the portal, falling to the hard ground on the other side. A throwing star followed them through, soaring only inches over their heads as they fell. Mel forced the portal to close so that nothing else could follow.

"Why'd you…" Luke's words were slurred together and difficult to hear above the gentle sounds of the forest. He took a deep, shaky breath and tried again. "Why here? Go farther."

"I don't know this area well, and I can't portal very far away. There's only so many places I could take us." They were back where they'd slept the previous night. Their enchanted bag with all their supplies was still lying there in the grass. Mel grabbed it. As she settled the strap across her torso, she stood up and pulled Luke to his feet as well. "Can you walk? It won't take them long to find us. We have to get you help—"

A flash of blue popped up as Ezmaunda teleported into view. Before Mel could react, Ezmaunda wordlessly grabbed the others. She teleported the entire trio away from the spot, depositing them within view of a distant castle. Then, still silent, Ezmaunda's knees buckled, and she toppled onto her side.

Mel lowered Luke to sit on the ground. She rushed over to the Azure. Something protruded beneath the cloak, so Mel gently peeled the blue fabric back. Nikolas's throwing star was sticking out from Ezmaunda's flesh, just below the collarbone, dripping with that same orange poison. Around the wound, the skin was already fully black. From there, the poison was spreading rapidly up her neck, across her chest, and down her arm. Thick lines of blood oozed from the injury and left chaotic trails down the front of her clothes.

Tears stung Mel's eyes. She reached out and took Ezmaunda's hand as their gazes met. "Hang in there. We can fix this. I still have a potion."

Ezmaunda shook her head weakly. "It's too far gone. My life is beyond saving."

"You can't give up." Mel paused as she heard a heavy *thud* behind her and then the sound of something moving. She turned to see Luke crawling toward her. Reaching out with her other hand, she laced her fingers through Luke's and brought her focus back to Ezmaunda.

"Even as my life leaves me," Ezmaunda took a deep breath and grinned, "you two still refuse to keep your hands off one another."

Mel laughed at the playful jab, but the tears streamed ever faster down her face.

"There is still hope for him. There is still hope that you will fulfill the prophecy. Now, leave me, or else you'll be found. I'm on my way to see Rhéya." Ezmaunda suddenly lifted her arm and looked down at the crown emblem that had marred her wrist for so many years. Its color was fading as her impending death removed the hold that Queen had had all this time. Her smile grew. Slowly lowering her wrist onto her chest, she said, "At last, I am free."

Ezmaunda's eyelids slowly fluttered closed. She let out one last shaky exhale as her spirit left the world.

Drawing a deep breath, Mel let loose of Ezmaunda's hand, stood, and turned toward Luke. She was about to ask if he could run, but the way his breathing was already labored was answer enough.

Grabbing the enchanted bag, she pulled out the last of the health potions. Bringing it to Luke's mouth, she made him drink every last drop of it. The poison racing through his body stopped, and the black lines quit expanding. She sighed, thankful that the damage was no longer getting worse.

It wasn't getting better either, though. Swallowing the lump in her throat, she steeled herself for making the transformation she hadn't done in years. The one transformation that she could do without the help of the cloak.

Mel could feel the pain of her bones shifting and reshaping as that cracking-grinding-crunching noise filled the air. She clenched her teeth tightly, fighting back the urge to scream. When the long, agonizing seconds of the transformation finally passed, she stood there in her lycan form with dark gray fur covering her from head to toe. Her red cloak expanded to cover her now broad shoulders. She reached out, scooped Luke into her arms, and sprinted toward the distant castle.

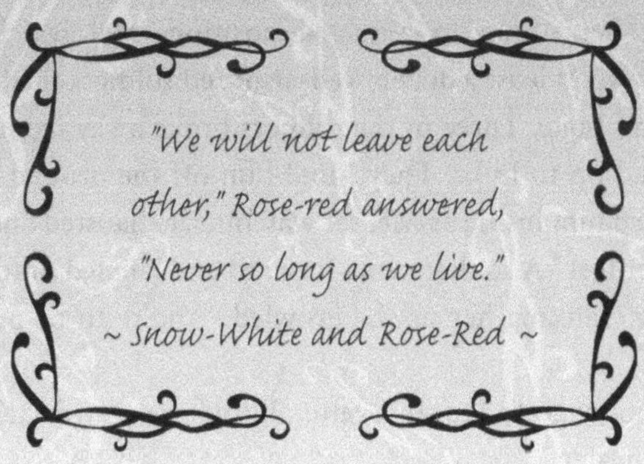

26

As she bolted down the hill, wind whipped across her thick fur. Even though her lycan form was able to run much faster than she normally could, she still felt as though the castle were a million miles away and only getting further.

Her thoughts ate at her. She wasn't sure she could hold the lycan form long enough to get Luke to the castle. She couldn't possibly carry him when the transformation inevitably wore out. She had no idea if anyone at the castle would be willing to help them. She was heading straight toward the home of the sister she had betrayed. And even if those at the castle were willing to help, she wasn't certain there was still enough time to counteract the poison that worked its way through Luke's body. Mel forced the dark thoughts away, not allowing the morbid questions to take root.

Looking down, Mel realized with horror that the black poison lines were beginning to slowly spread once more. Holding him close, she forced her thoughts toward the castle in the distance.

Mel's strength began to falter shortly before she reached the castle walls. She stopped and knelt down, setting Luke on the ground. Then she stepped away to let her body shift back to its human form. Again, those awful pains racked through her. She barely managed to avoid crying out as bone, tendon, and skin reverted to its former state. As her body finally reverted to normal, she fell to the ground.

Pushing herself up to a seated position, Mel watched as the portcullis rose. At least a dozen well-armored soldiers filed out, encircling her and Luke. Three of the soldiers broke away from the others and marched up to Luke. They lifted him off the ground and wordlessly hurried him inside as Mel sat watching, exhausted and helpless.

"On your feet." A soldier came forward and latched onto Mel's arm as he spoke. Yanking her up, he growled, "You're to be presented to the queen."

"I'll willingly go to Queen Yvette. But where are you taking Luke? He needs a healer."

"He's off to the dungeon. You're welcome to ask Queen Yvette to send a healer, but I'd not get my hopes up if I were you." His grip tightened painfully around her bicep. "She doesn't owe any favors to the little red-cloaked wolf who tried to kill her."

A second soldier came up and latched onto Mel's other arm. The two then forced her to walk as the remaining soldiers followed along after them. She clamped her lips together, fighting the urge to talk back as she complied with their orders. They marched her across the courtyard, into the castle, through several ornately decorated rooms and hallways, finally entering the throne room. Unceremoniously, the two soldiers tossed Mel to the floor directly in front of the throne and stepped back to watch.

"Melzia."

The voice—the one she had so recently thought she might never hear again—sent a shiver down her spine. Mel pushed herself to her knees. A whirlwind of emotions stormed inside her as she slowly tilted her head to look up at the woman seated in front of her. She never knew before that someone could feel such guilt, relief, terror, and joy all at once. Her voice gave out as she tried to speak and only a notch above a whisper, she replied, "Yvette."

The woman sat rigidly on the throne, her white hair glimmering in the light beneath her gold and opal crown. Slowly folding her hands together in her lap, Yvette leaned forward slightly. Gold rings sparkled brightly around the dark skin of her fingers. "The familiarity we shared as children is no longer a privilege you are allowed. I am the queen of this realm. You would do well to remember that."

Mel nodded. "You're right, Queen Yvette. I'm sorry."

"Sorry for what?"

Though her voice was not raised, Yvette's words carried easily throughout the entire room. The nobles, soldiers, and servants who stood watching the event dared not make a sound.

As Mel did not immediately respond, Yvette continued. "Perhaps you regret that you neglected my title? Or perhaps you are sorry that even though you are my sister—the only family I had left—you vanished without a trace for nigh on a decade? Perhaps it's the attempt on my life you regret? Or," Yvette stood and slowly walked down the steps that led from the throne to the stone floor where Melzia waited. "Perhaps you regret that your attempt on my life failed?"

"No!" Mel's voice came out far louder than she had intended, setting a flurry of whispers out across the onlookers.

"No? To which?"

"Of course I'm not sorry it failed! I never wanted to hurt you. Please, let me explain!"

"In time, perhaps. At present, I wish for you to be removed from my sight. Guards?"

"Do whatever you want with me, but please send a healer to Luke! Please, I'm begging you! He had no part in anything I did to you. He doesn't deserve to die because of me."

"And I *did* deserve death?!" The shout echoed across the room. Yvette's hands were clenched into fists. She took a deep breath and unfurled her fingers as she spun around and returned to the throne. "Remove her cloak, and take her to the dungeon. My husband and I shall deal with her in due time."

With that, one of the guards marched over to Mel and tugged the string that held her cloak in place. It refused to budge for him. He laid one hand on her shoulder to keep her in place and pulled harder on the string. The cloak was bound to her soul, though, and would not allow anyone else to remove it from her.

The guard reached for his dagger—whether to threaten Mel or to attempt to forcibly remove the magical attire from her, she wasn't sure. Before he could free the blade from its sheath, Mel swallowed hard and reached up toward the string. With the slightest movement of her fingers, it slipped loose and tumbled to the floor.

The guard sneered at her. He snatched the cloak off the floor and stuffed the hood into his leather belt. A second guard came forward. Mel was forced up and dragged away, her pleas for Luke's life falling on deaf ears. She lost track of all the twists and turns the guards made as they brought her down further and further through the castle. Finally, they stopped at a room with no windows and no fire. Only the tiniest bit of light came in through the hole in the wooden door that sat at the foot of the spiral stairs. In that dark room of unknown size, they turned and went through another door. The two soldiers dropped her onto the cold, stone floor and walked back out, locking her cell door behind them. A moment later, there was a squeaking of a hinge and another sound of a key twisting against metal as they locked the main door as well. The guards' footsteps quickly pounded up the stairs, and she was left in silence.

The air around her smelled of must and mold. Occasionally, her footstep landed on something not quite solid, sending the faint odor of animal droppings wafting up from the floor. Mel stretched out her arms, her fingertips easily reaching the walls on opposite sides of the tiny cell.

Not knowing what else to do, she sank down and curled into a ball. Ezmaunda was gone. She had no idea where Luke was or if he was even alive. Yvette had been brought out of that deathlike curse but despised Mel. Even her ever-present cloak was gone, making her feel like she'd suddenly lost a part of herself. She was locked away in a dark, tiny box with no one to help her. Burying her face in her hands, she burrowed her fingers into her black hair. Despair threatened to pull her into a dark, bottomless pit and never let her go.

She dug her fingernails into the skin of her scalp, forcing herself to focus on the here and now, nothing else. As her heart slowed its racing, she climbed back to her feet. Holding her hand out in front of herself, she snapped her fingers, bringing a ball of fire to life above her palm. It sparked and crackled as it shifted around erratically above her hand. She paid it no mind as she slowly spun around. The walls were plain stone, and a simple wooden door sat in the center of one wall. Nothing else. Not a bench, not a bucket, not a pile of straw.

A pit formed in her stomach. Doing her best to ignore it, she moved over to the door. There was a small gap at the bottom, so she knelt down and held the fire up to the lower edge. It licked at the wood and wrapped around it but refused to catch. She wasn't surprised that the door had been enchanted to prevent such things. After all, she wasn't the first caster to have been imprisoned here.

Standing back up, Mel brought the flame toward the upper part of the door where there was a small, barred opening. She stuck her hand through along with the ball of fire, but all it did was blind her to the darkness in the room beyond. So, snuffing out the spell, she stood staring out the opening as she waited for her eyes to adapt.

A rat skittered past her foot, but she was focused so intently on the darkened room in front of her, she hardly noticed. It was no use, though. Even once her eyes fully adjusted, the light was so dim she couldn't see the opposite side of the outer room.

Mel stepped back to lean against the wall while she gathered her thoughts. If she had her cloak, she might be able to summon a mallet or a crowbar to get the door open, or at the very least, a weapon for when someone returned. She knew what would happen but decided she had to try anyway. Closing her eyes, she fixed her thoughts on a dagger. A moment later, a small blade manifested in her hand. She looked down at it with eyes that hadn't yet readjusted to the darkness, but she could already feel the blade flickering, threatening to puff out of existence as it quickly depleted her mana supply. She needed that cloak if she wanted to maintain a spell like that for long.

With that idea thoroughly squashed, her next thought was reverting back to lycan form to brute force the door off her cell. She dismissed that idea as quickly as it arrived. For one, if the door was enchanted against flames, there was every reason to believe it was also magically strengthened. Besides that, she'd used up the last of her lycansia in transforming to bring Luke here—one of the drawbacks of being only half-blooded lycanthrope.

She sighed, announcing her frustration to the darkness. Propping herself against the cold wall and closing her eyes, Mel concentrated on the room outside her small cell. There was that familiar density to the air. A mana user was nearby. She pulled a shaky breath and tentatively called out, "Luke?"

Silence.

She tried again, a bit louder this time. "Luke?"

A deep voice groaned. It was coming from the direction she could feel the presence, but she still couldn't tell who it was. She silently begged, pleaded, hoped it was him. But she couldn't be certain.

Chewing on her thumbnail as she tried to think, Mel froze at the distant sound of echoing footsteps. As the noise gradually grew closer, she realized it was more than one person. Four, maybe five sets of feet were quickly descending the spiral staircase outside the main room of the dungeon. Mel peered out the small opening in the door of her cell.

The footsteps came to a halt. There was the clanking of metal as a ring full of keys was shifted this way and that until someone found the one they were looking for. After that was a short scrape and a click as the key fulfilled its purpose. The outer door swung open, and as it did, the room was suddenly filled with light from multiple torches. Mel winced and threw a hand over her eyes.

By the time she carefully looked out again, the jangling keys had found their way into her cell door. The key turned, and the silhouette on the other side stepped back to let someone else move forward. Mel's eyes still stung, and she couldn't tell who was in the room.

Her cell door slowly opened outward. The sudden emergence of more people and the bright light sent a pair of rats scurrying from the cell, squeaking loudly as they disappeared from view. Mel looked at the silhouette standing before her, waiting for them to do something.

"You will kneel before me, *sister*." Yvette's voice was cold, but the last word was ice.

A shiver ran down Mel's spine. She slowly lowered her knees to the hard floor and bowed her head, dropping her eyes toward Yvette's feet. Licking her lips, Mel hesitated, unsure what was expected of her now.

Mel's mind raced, wondering whether it would be safer to speak or hold her tongue.

Yvette, at last, broke the tense silence. "Leave us."

Mel's head jerked up. It took her a moment to realize that Yvette had turned, her words directed toward the soldiers. They, too, seemed taken off guard, glancing between one another as they stayed rooted to the spot.

"Ma'am?" He leaned forward and lowered his voice, though it still traveled easily across the cavernous room. "Are you certain?"

"I wish to speak to the prisoner. She must answer for her crimes."

"Begging your pardon, ma'am," his eyes flitted over to Mel, and he sneered before bringing his attention back to Yvette, "but seeing as how she already tried to kill you once, I'd not put it past her to make another attempt."

"Thank you for your concern. My husband will remain here and ensure my safety."

A tall, lean man stepped forward. Mel hadn't recognized him at first—after all, she hadn't seen him since they were children. And in the last few moments, she'd been so focused on her sister that she'd hardly noticed the others. King Zachoriun was tall and lean with pointed ears that were half-hidden behind his long, brown hair. He nodded his agreement.

The soldier opened his mouth once more, thought better of it, pressed his lips together, and gave a small bow. He deposited his torch into a holder by the doorway. Then, with a signal to the other two soldiers, they all turned and made their way into the stairwell, their boots clunking against the stone steps.

"You know your crimes." Yvette looked at Mel as the sound of footsteps resumed. "What have you to say?"

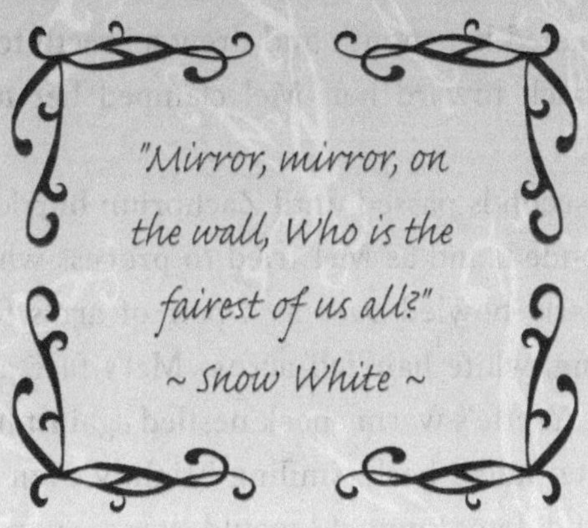

27

Mel's eyes slid from Yvette to Zachoriun as she tried to decipher the look he was giving her. It was impossible, though, as his light brown skin was cloaked in shadow. Yvette's expression was nearly as unreadable, but Mel could feel the frigidity in her sister's stare.

Regret filled Mel's chest with a deep ache and pushed aside any fears she might've had for her own life. She knew she deserved whatever they chose to do with her, and she would willingly accept that. But first, she had to find a way to help Luke.

"I am so sorry, Yvette. I—"

"You will not address her as a familiar!" Zachoriun's deep voice rang out, laced with fire as it reverberated from the thick stone walls.

The distant echoes of footsteps on the stairs paused as the soldiers debated whether they should return. Mel ignored it, trying to find her words. She licked her lips and whispered, "Queen Yvette, I am sorry."

"I am not seeking apologies! Explain yourself. Tell me why you dared betray me!"

Zachoriun's eyes darted toward the dungeon's main door as he laid a hand on Yvette's shoulder, cutting off her words and drawing her attention to the door as well. With silent footsteps, he rushed out into the stairwell.

Mel leaned forward, looking from Yvette to the door and back again. As she opened her mouth and drew a breath to speak, Yvette's head whipped back toward her. Mel clamped her mouth shut and waited.

A few tense seconds passed until Zachoriun hurried back into the dungeon. He nodded, and as Mel tried to process what was happening, she was nearly bowled over as a pair of arms found their way around her. Long, white hair fell across Mel's face as she sat wide-eyed and frozen. Yvette's warm cheek nestled against her neck.

Finally, Yvette pulled back, smiling brightly even as tears flowed down her face. "I did not know if I would ever see you again!"

"Y-you aren't... I mean, why aren't..." Mel paused as her fingers clenched together. This couldn't be real. Not after all she'd done. When she couldn't find any more words, she held her breath and waited.

"Melzia." Yvette lifted her hands to cup Mel's face. "I've missed you."

"I..." The lone syllable came out before Mel went back to quietly staring.

Yvette sighed, then said, "When the curse was first lifted, words cannot begin to convey the anger I held toward you. I couldn't fathom that my own sister would betray me the way you did. It did not matter to me whose idea it had been. You and you alone held all blame. I swore that you would pay for that treachery."

Mel hung her head. Yvette tucked a finger under Mel's chin and gently lifted it, forcing Mel to meet her eyes once again.

"Over time, Zachoriun and Cali softened that anger. Eventually, I was able to see that, had you wanted me dead, I would be. You were given no choice, yet you still chose to save me. Even knowing the kinds of torture that Queen would dole out when she caught you."

Chest shaking as though her lungs had forgotten how to work, Mel slowly pulled in a deep breath. She whispered, "You don't hate me? You don't want to give me over to Queen?"

"Have you forgotten your promise? The one you made to me as a young girl, shortly after father went missing?"

Mel's mouth opened, but words failed her.

"You told me, 'We will not leave each other. Never so long as we live.' And now, I intend to hold you to that promise." Yvette reached out to clasp Mel's hands in her own.

This time, it was Mel's turn to tackle Yvette. Mel threw herself forward, wrapping her arms around her sister and burying her face in her sister's shoulder. Tears now flowed freely for them both. They sat on the cold floor for a long time, holding one another as they slowly rocked side to side.

When Mel finally pulled back and wiped her eyes, she questioned, "If you aren't angry with me, why did you throw me down here?"

"Oh, Melzia, I am so sorry. I hope you can forgive me." Guilt had the recently dried tears reforming in Yvette's eyes. "When I still carried so much anger toward you, Queen offered a deal. If I were to find you first, I would have my chance at revenge, and she would not interfere."

Yvette sighed. "I am not naive, however. She does not wish to face your powers and my army at the same time. She hoped that either you or I would defeat the other, and she could fight only whosoever remains. So, I did not accept her offer at first. As time progressed and my anger waned, I did not let her know my feelings had shifted. Eventually, I told her I accepted."

Mel laughed, though there was no amusement behind it. "You can't possibly think that my abilities are as much of a threat to her as your entire army is! Especially if you can convince any of the other kingdoms to support you."

"No, of course not. No matter how great your powers are, you cannot match the strength of an entire army." Yvette took both of Mel's hands in hers. "But it matters not what I think. It only matters that *she does* believe it. And she also believes, at least for the time being, that I am on her side."

"So, this was all for show?"

Sniffling loudly, Yvette nodded. "I have a feeling there are those amongst my court who will inform our dear stepmother of today's events. As long as that woman is under the assumption that I am leading you to a slow and painful demise, you are safe."

Mel sat there chewing on her lip, her eyes vacant as a flurry of mixed emotions overwhelmed her.

"So." Yvette broke the silence. "Can you forgive me?"

Her eyes coming back into focus, Mel smiled softly at her sister. "If you can move past what I did to you, how could I not forgive you, too?"

Yvette squeezed Mel's hand and smiled back. "I cannot wait for the children to meet you!"

Mel's breath caught in her throat. "I didn't even think to ask. I'm so sorry."

With a wave of her hand, Yvette dismissed the apology and said, "The oldest, Harry, already looks so much like his namesake."

"You gave him father's name?" Mel beamed at her.

"Of course! The twins, Anya and Katrín, are not yet walking. Though I think it will happen any day now."

Pressing her hands to her cheeks, Mel watched her sister. "So you have a good life then?"

"Yes. And it will only become better now that you have returned home."

Mel leaned forward and embraced Yvette another time. Yvette smiled and used the edge of her sleeve to dab at the tears that spilled down her own face.

Suddenly gasping, Mel's eyes darted toward the cell door. "Where is Luke? He needs help. Please, he's been poisoned. I can't just let him die. He's—"

"Zachoriun is with him." Yvette interrupted, pushed herself to her feet, and helped Mel stand as well. "Come. I shall take you to him."

The two hurried out into the main area of the dungeon as the torches sent shadows dancing across the walls. They made their way over to another cell on the far side of the room, its open doorway lit by a faint blue glow. Stepping inside, Mel's eyes found Luke lying on the floor, still wrapped in his black cloak. He was stretched out on the floor of a cell twice the size of the one she'd just come from, his chest moving shakily as his body struggled to draw breath. Zachoriun was kneeling next to him, quietly chanting something in Elvish as thin tendrils of blue light flowed out from his hands to encircle Luke.

Mel rushed over and dropped down on Luke's other side. She clasped Luke's hand in hers and squeezed. When there was no response, a lump formed in her throat, and she turned toward Zachoriun.

Yvette gently sat her hand on Mel's shoulder. She softly said, "Don't interrupt him."

The words flowed faster from Zachoriun. His head rocked side to side, and the blue light swirled more quickly as green and purple tendrils braided themselves in. The brilliant streaks of light were now tightening around Luke and seeping into his skin.

The glow grew brighter and brighter until Mel was squinting. Through her dark eyelashes, she could barely make out Luke's shape behind the blinding glow. She refused to tear her eyes away, though, squeezing his hand tighter as she watched with bated breath. Yvette knelt at Mel's side and pressed her hand to Mel's back. Mel still kept her attention on Luke, but the simple touch filled her with warmth, and she leaned into it.

Eventually, Zachoriun's voice faded away. The last of the colorful light disappeared into Luke, and the room was plunged into a pitch-black hush.

Mel searched for Zachoriun's silhouette, her eyes struggling to make sense of the shadows as she adjusted to the return of the overwhelming darkness. She opened her mouth to question him, to demand he keep going, but something held her back. The silence felt important. So she squeezed his hand tighter and chewed on her lip, waiting as her heart hammered against her ribs.

A dull flicker of light brushed across the wall. Mel twisted around to see where it was coming from. She hadn't noticed Zachoriun sneaking away in the darkness, but now he returned with a torch. He used its flame to spark up a second one and placed them each into holders that waited along the wall. Nodding at Yvette, he took her by the hand, helped her to her feet, and wordlessly led her out of the cell.

Now alone with the unmoving Luke, Mel looked down and touched a hand to his cheek. Sweat clung to his cold skin. The black tinge from the poison still marked his arm, but the color was slowly receding until it was little more than a thin line along his bicep. At last, unable to bear it any longer, Mel leaned close to Luke's ear and whispered his name.

He groaned in response.

Mel clamped a hand over her mouth, fighting back the sob that tried to escape. She swallowed the lump in her throat, took a deep breath, and lowered her hand to cup his cheek. As she slid her hand upward and slowly ran it through the short hair on top of his head, she said his name once more.

Another groan, louder this time. His eyes remained tightly closed. A moment later, Luke mumbled, "Why didn't…" Luke's voice continued, but the rest of the words fell out in a tangled, nonsensical mess.

"Luke?" Mel leaned close, her ear tilted toward his mouth. "Baby, speak up. I can't tell what you're saying. Are you alright? What's going on?"

"Why didn't you," Luke shakily pulled in a lungful of air. Turning his head toward Mel, he lifted his eyelids and looked at her. He finally finished his question, "Summon a gun?"

Mel's mouth dropped open as she sat there, unsure whether to laugh, cry, or roll her eyes. When Luke's lips curved up at the corners, she decided to do all three. At the same time, she collapsed onto him, flinging her arms around his neck.

After several seconds spent planting kisses all over Luke's forehead, cheeks, and neck, Mel finally pushed herself up and wiped her eyes. "Seriously, are you okay?"

"Well, I feel like I could sleep for a week." Luke—winded after forcing himself through an entire sentence—inhaled deeply. "And my body aches like crazy. But at least I don't have boiling acid in my bloodstream anymore."

"Is there anything I can do to help?"

"Yeah." Luke squeezed her hand. "Answer my question!"

Mel laughed. Seeing the look in Luke's eyes, though, her amusement quickly dissipated. "Wait. Are you serious right now?"

"Yes. I need time for my body to finish healing. So, for now, I just want a distraction."

"Alright, fine." Mel sighed and stretched out next to Luke on the cold floor, propping herself on one elbow. "A sword is a big stabby piece of metal. An arrow is a stabby bit of metal on a stick. Easy enough to picture, right? Well, I don't know all the little intricacies of a pistol or a shotgun, which makes them pretty difficult to conjure into existence. Besides that, even if I could summon a gun, it's not exactly a subtle weapon. Everyone for miles around would know where I was as soon as I fired off a shot."

"Guess that makes sense. So, how the hell did you get us here? Actually, where is 'here' anyway? And where's Ezmaunda?"

"You don't remember?"

Luke shook his head.

"She was injured by one of those poisoned weapons too. But she got a lot more than a small scratch. I tried to give her a potion, but it spread too fast. She didn't…" Mel swallowed hard, unable to finish the statement.

Pulling Mel into his arms, Luke stroked back her hair and kissed her forehead. As the sound of footsteps drew their attention to the cell door, Mel shot to her feet, weaponless and uncloaked but prepared to fight. Yvette's face showed up in the doorway, and Mel relaxed.

"My apologies for interrupting."

Mel sank back onto the floor beside Luke and waved away Yvette's words. "No apology necessary."

Dipping her head in acknowledgment, Yvette continued, "I don't think it would be wise to allow you into the upper levels of the castle just yet. We do not, at present, have anywhere that you can remain hidden, and it would arouse far too many questions when you are seen. I cannot, however, allow you to sleep in quite such wretched conditions. I hope this will suffice until we can find a way to bring you upstairs."

For the first time, Mel noticed the enchanted bag hanging from Yvette's shoulder. Mel took it from her sister just as Zachoriun arrived in the doorway. She looked up to see him holding a rolled-up, thin mattress tucked beneath his arm.

Spreading the mattress out on the floor, Zachoriun then made his way over and helped Luke slide up onto it. He then gave Luke a small bow of his head and turned toward Mel. "The guards have been given orders to remain at the top of the stairs, at the far end of the hall. Additionally, no one—aside from Yvette or me—is to be allowed down here."

"Your guards didn't ask about the bedding?" Luke glanced from Yvette to Zachoriun, a bemused look plastered across his face.

"I would not normally condone such a thing," Zachoriun said, "but I felt a brief sleeping spell would be prudent in this instance. By the time we next interact, they'll have awoken and will not remember our previous encounter."

Mel nodded in understanding. "Thank you."

"Get some rest, if you are able." Yvette knelt down, giving Mel a quick hug. "We shall return in the morning."

Zachoriun bowed his head toward Mel. Taking Yvette by the hand, they turned and walked out of the cell and headed up the stairs.

Once her sister and brother-in-law had gone out of sight, Mel looked down at the bag in her hands. It was the same one she and Luke had found in Hans and Greta's cottage. She opened it up to find the contents of the saddlebags, along with several blankets and two pillows. Pulling on the corner of one of the blankets sent the entirety of the bedding spilling out across the mattress next to Luke.

From the center of the mess, a deep red piece of cloth tumbled out. Mel grabbed it and fitted the cloak back around herself, relaxing her shoulders as she tied it in place. If there had been any lingering doubts about Yvette's trust in her, they were now thoroughly banished. She settled onto the mattress next to Luke and spread out the blankets to cover them. Tears—*again*—stung at her eyes.

"What's going on?"

"Nothing." Mel sniffled and wiped the trail of moisture from her cheek. "It's been a roller coaster of emotions today."

"Want to talk about it?"

"You need to heal up! I can't ask you to listen to me whine right now!"

Luke pulled Mel closer until she was cradled against his chest. "It's not 'whining' to confide in me when something traumatic happens. And I want distractions. Remember? Besides, we're a team. Just because I was hurt doesn't mean you're not hurting too. So talk to me."

"Alright." Mel nodded. She moved closer, snuggling up to his side. "Let's talk."

2 8

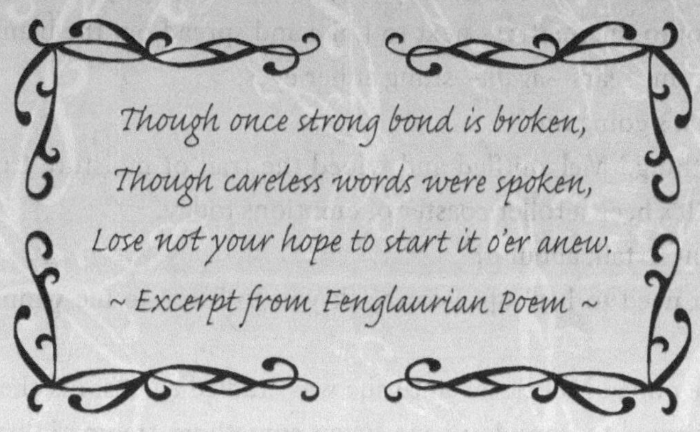

In the depths of the musty dungeon, Mel awoke feeling so light she was half-surprised she wasn't floating above the hard floor. Her sister didn't hate her. Or at least, Yvette didn't hate her *anymore*. Either way, Mel was glad. On top of that, she'd never felt more connected with Luke. He knew of the darkness in her past and hadn't hated her for it. And as much as she might want him to be far away from here and safe from Queen's wrath, his presence gave her strength.

Lying there in the dark room, she tried to keep her thoughts focused on the fact that the people she loved most in the world also loved her. They hadn't abandoned her, even though she'd spent years imagining them both doing exactly that.

But that comfort was quickly seeping away. Flashbacks of the Verdants who had attacked them in the forest eked into her mind. Along with that came the memory of their poisoned blades, Luke collapsing as the toxin found its way into his bloodstream, Ezmaunda dying in front of them. More than that, the worries of the future were creeping in. She wasn't sure if she had enough time to train Luke properly. And she certainly didn't know how to win a battle against the soulless dictator who now ruled the kingdom where Mel had grown up.

Footsteps echoed down the stairwell and broke through her thoughts. Mel pushed herself upright. Luke stirred beside her. She helped him sit up as the doorway flickered with torchlight that was steadily becoming brighter.

Yvette stepped into the room and used her torch to reignite one of the others that waited along the wall.

A moment later, Zachoriun followed. Stopping beside his wife, he eyed Luke's damaged arm. "It is good to see you are well enough to sit up. How are you feeling?"

"I'm exhausted. And my arm feels like I decided to do about five million one-armed push-ups yesterday, but other than that, I feel great."

"Good." Zachoriun knelt down to take a closer look at Luke's wound. "You are lucky it was no more than a scratch and that you arrived here so soon after. The 'weeping widow' poison is quite aptly named."

"So he'll be okay then?"

Zachoriun stood. "Yes, I believe so. It seems to have been neutralized. However, it will likely leave a scar."

"That's alright. It'll just make me look more badass." Luke winked at Mel, then returned his attention to Zachoriun. "Anyway, thank you for healing me, um..." His eyes slid to Mel.

"Right, sorry. I forgot you two haven't actually met. Luke, this is my brother-in-law, Zachoriun. King Zachoriun, actually. Though he was still a prince the last time I'd seen him. And, of course, this is my sister, Queen Yvette. Zachoriun, Yvette, this is Luke." Mel watched him for a moment and smiled. "My betrothed."

Luke's heart skipped a beat as he took in her words. Not noticing Zachoriun and Yvette as they bowed their heads to him in greeting, he smiled. Leaning forward, he kissed Mel's neck, drawing a giggle from her as his stubble tickled her skin. Sitting up once more, he pushed the hair back from Mel's face. It took a while for him to tear his eyes away from her. When he finally did, he turned around and said, "Thank you, Zachoriun. I wouldn't be here without your help."

"I am relieved to find that my skills were sufficient. You're lucky you had a potion, or else my abilities likely would not have been enough." Zachoriun reached into an inner pocket of his jacket and pulled out a small package wrapped in a white cloth. A second search produced a small bottle of water. He handed each to Luke. "Here. I apologize that it is not more substantial. I'm sure you're famished after your travels."

Stomach grumbling loudly as the scents of bread and ham filled the room, Luke broke off a chunk, sighing as he sank his teeth into the warm food. Mel pulled off a handful as well and popped it into her mouth.

"Melzia?"

Mel's eyes slid toward her sister, and as she chewed, she lifted her eyebrows. "Hmm?"

"I believe you should go upstairs with Zachoriun."

Quickly swallowing the food, Mel glanced over at Luke. "Um, I think I should really work on training Luke. He's only had the cloak a couple days and we need to prepare for this grand fight everyone expects us to have with Queen. I can't imagine we have much time till she finds out you're on our side and forces our hand."

"Please, Melzia." Yvette moved closer and laid a hand on Mel's shoulder. "I shall remain here and work with him."

"But…"

"Melzia. How many hours did I watch you and the other chromaveiled train? How many times did I try to mimic your abilities? Though I am not nearly so proficient with magic as you are, I believe I am quite capable of training your beau in the basics."

"I guess you might be able to, but why would—"

"You and I," Zachoriun interjected, "are going to strategize for this 'grand fight.' We are to convene with the war council this morning."

"You think your war council is going to listen to me? Why would…" Mel grinned. She turned toward Yvette. "Ah, okay."

"What's happening?" Luke questioned no one in particular as his eyes darted between them all, and he slowly moved another morsel of food to his mouth.

Standing up to face Yvette, Mel carefully looked her over from head to toe, slowly circling so she could see her from all angles. After a second pass, Mel stopped and grabbed the hood that rested on her back. "I finally get to try my hand at being monarch."

She lifted the red fabric over her head, and its color quickly became transparent. Her skin went several shades darker. Rings and a necklace coalesced from nothing and her clothing transformed into a pale teal and silver gown. At the same time, Mel's hair lengthened, the curls became looser and softer, and the dark color became a bright, snowy white. Within a matter of seconds, Yvette and a near-perfect clone of her were standing side by side.

"Alright." Mel clapped her hands together and stepped toward the doorway. "Let's get this show on the road."

Zachoriun grimaced but quickly forced himself back into a neutral expression. "Um, Melzia?"

"What?"

"Your form is now a good likeness to that of your sister. And the voice is a good match as well, now that your spell has been completed. However..." Zachoriun hesitated as he looked toward Yvette—the real one—for assistance.

"Oh, just spit it out already!"

Yvette held out her hand, palm up, gesturing toward Mel. "That is precisely where my husband's hesitation comes from. You seem to have acquired some idioms and unique manners of speech from your time in Luke's realm. That, combined with your softened accent from your years living abroad, will rouse suspicion. If you are to stand in my place at this meeting and speak on my behalf, you must sound like me as well."

"Ah. Good point."

"Come. You and I shall go practice for a time." Yvette linked her arm through Mel's and escorted her outside the small cell. "You and I used to sound much the same. I am certain you will have relearned my manner of speaking in no time."

After the two women walked out of sight, Luke looked around awkwardly. "So. I guess you're going to be my brother-in-law, huh?"

"It appears so." Zachoriun bowed his head in greeting once again. "I wish we were meeting under more favorable circumstances, but I am pleased to meet you, nevertheless."

Luke laughed. "Likewise."

Silence reclaimed the room.

"So, um..." Luke spoke up when he could no longer stand the uncomfortable quiet. Wiping the grease from his fingertips on the cloth the food had come in, he said, "We were with someone else. An Azure. She got a larger dose of the poison than I did, and she didn't make it."

"I am sorry for your loss. Her body has been recovered and is being prepared for burial nearby."

"That's good. I didn't want to just abandon her body there. But won't that seem suspicious? I mean, isn't that being nice to the person who was helping us?"

"I do not believe so. It is well known that we would not leave our worst enemy to be found by scavengers. If we were to do so now simply because of who she was, it would draw all the more attention from Queen."

Luke's shoulders relaxed as he repackaged the remaining food. "Do you think she could be buried near Lindenbracht?"

Zachoriun tilted his head. "I suppose so. What is the significance of Lindenbracht?"

"I didn't know her real well, and I don't know anything about her final wishes, but someone she loved was there, and I think maybe she'd want to be there too."

"Ah. Yes, I believe that can be arranged."

"Thank you."

Zachoriun nodded, and the pair lapsed into an easy silence. The muffled sound of the women's voices drifted across the dungeon, but the words were unclear.

After a long while, Luke said, "Do you—" His question was cut short by the sound of approaching footsteps.

Both men looked toward the doorway as two identical Yvettes stepped through, one immediately following the other. In sync, the women each gave a small curtsy. As they straightened, the first one said, "Have you a guess as to which of us is which?" The second followed up with, "I am certain that if you choose correctly, it will be naught more than luck."

"Okay, that's downright creepy." Luke laughed, turned to Zachoriun, and shrugged.

Zachoriun moved closer, inspecting each woman as he searched for any discrepancies. At last, he stepped back. "Perhaps if we were to have a lengthy conversation. As of yet, though, I haven't any idea. Well done, both of you."

The Yvettes bowed their heads in a nearly identical motion. Then, the one nearest the door stepped toward Zachoriun. "Well, *husband*." She made sure to emphasize the word as she settled her palm into the crook of his arm. "Shall we meet with the council?"

"I knew it!" Luke punched the air.

Breaking character even as she kept her arm tucked into Zachoriun's, Mel laughed and turned toward Luke to stick her tongue out at him. "Oh, you so did not. Now, wish us luck."

"Good luck. Here, I saved some of this for you." Luke reached over to pass the food to her.

Zachoriun shook his head. "That is for you. Yvette and I are expected for breakfast prior to the meeting. Once more, I apologize. I swear I shall find a way to procure a better meal for you later in the day."

Luke waved away the apologies. "I'll be fine."

With that, Mel took a deep breath. Then she and Zachoriun walked out of the dungeon.

Zachoriun escorted Mel up the stairs and down the long hallway, the clack of their heels echoing loudly off the stone walls. Periodically, they walked by a bowing servant, and Mel kept her face impassive, merely nodding in polite recognition as she continued on her way.

Eventually, they slowed near an open doorway. Zachoriun leaned closer to her ear and whispered, "Marvelous job thus far, though we've not been truly tested as yet. So, keep up this charade, and don't let your nerves get the better of you now."

Mel's head jerked toward Zachoriun as her eyebrows shot upward. She hissed back, "Since when has 'the worst is yet to come' and 'don't be nervous' ever helped anyone not be nervous?"

Pinching his lips together, Zachoriun averted his gaze. Deciding that he'd learned from his mistake and that the matter wasn't worth dwelling on, Mel gave his arm a tug. "Come on. Let's get this started."

Straightening his shoulders, Zachoriun entered the room with Mel next to him. Inside the massive room sat a long table draped with a white tablecloth. The edges of the fabric were covered in intricate embroidery in various shades of pink and gold. Resting on top of the table were dozens of platters of fruits, cheeses, and meats. A variety of breads sat alongside the other foods, surrounded by jellies and jams in every color imaginable. It was more than enough to feed a small army. Fortunately, at the end of the meal, anything not finished by the king and queen would be shared amongst the servants.

Mel's stomach growled loudly as the mixture of sweet and savory aromas washed over her. Off to one side, a servant giggled in response to the sound. The man quickly composed himself at the dark look he received from Zachoriun.

Gesturing with his free hand, Zachoriun steered Mel toward a chair. After pushing the seat in for her, he sat beside her at the head of the table. Half a dozen servants came forward and filled each of Zachoriun's and Mel's plates before returning to their stations along the edges of the room.

As Zachoriun picked up his fork and knife, he waved his free hand and said to the room at large, "My wife and I would like to dine in solitude this morning."

The servants—apparently familiar with that particular command—quietly filed out around the long dining table. Zachoriun leaned close to Mel as they were left alone and said, "Keep your voice low. Never assume they are not listening at the door."

Mel dipped her head slightly in acknowledgment. Picking up one of the silver forks from the table, she speared a small slice of cheese and took a bite. As hungry as she was, she would've preferred to shovel half the contents of her plate into her mouth all at once, but well aware that she might be seen at any moment, she was careful to keep up the ruse.

"The meeting is set to commence..." Zachoriun glanced at the timekeeping device on the opposite side of the room. Fourteen dots formed a circle near the perimeter. Four thin metal strips spun at the center, each one moving at a different speed. "A bit over half an hour from now. So, if you have questions, now is your chance."

"Who is to be in attendance at this meeting?

"Let's see. General Braithe is the leader of the army. Tall man, softer spoken than one might expect for a man of his stature. Do not let that fool you, however. He knows what he is doing and uses his apparent 'meekness' to his advantage. He will likely bring a few of his higher-ranking soldiers, though I am not certain who that will be." Zachoriun paused to think for a moment. "Lady Gwendella will attend as well. She leads the Coalition of Mages. Loud and quite self-assured. Fortunately, she is willing to listen to others when something lies outside her area of expertise. She, too, might bring along one of her more advanced mages."

"Any others?"

"A few of the high lords and ladies have seats on the council. They or their representatives will likely be in attendance. I doubt they will do much besides listen and nod."

"I see. Will any of the other kingdoms be involved?"

"Cali and Fen plan to participate via mirror."

Mel looked at him sideways.

"The council is aware that they had recently harbored Melzia and Luke. We made certain the council also knew Cali and Fen had every intention of surrendering them to us if they had not escaped. There is no ill will between our kingdom and theirs."

Footsteps sounded in the hallway. Not wanting to be overheard, Zachoriun and Mel both focused on their food until silence returned.

"What of the others?"

"As far as the other kingdoms' rulers, I am not certain who among them can be trusted, so they have not been asked to attend."

Mel nodded, savored the last bite of her meal, and sat the fork and knife down on her plate. "And how will I be expected to behave during these proceedings?"

"What do you mean?"

Mel lowered her voice another notch and leaned closer. "I haven't seen my sister in years, and that was long before the two of you got married. Does she sit meekly in the corner at these meetings? Does she run the show?"

"Ah." Zachoriun nodded. "I will take charge. She does not speak often during such meetings, so when she does speak up, those in the room will stop and listen."

"Very good. So, will your council believe that we are suddenly rebelling against Queen? Why would we not have attacked before now?"

"They are under the impression that a truce had been struck. Melzia would be offered to us so that we might mete out justice. Though, as you can clearly see, Queen had no intention of honoring that, given that her Verdants nearly put an end to you both in our woods." Picking up a cloth napkin, Zachoriun dabbed at his mouth, then placed it back on the table next to his plate. "Now that Melzia and Luke have arrived here, her end of the bargain has been fulfilled. There is no reason to believe she will not invade our territory soon. In fact, I believe the only thing holding her back is that she is not certain if this 'justice' has yet been doled out. She does not wish to attack while 'the unique ones' from the prophecy might continue to threaten her reign."

Mel sat quietly for a bit. Zachoriun caught her eye and asked if she had any more questions.

She closed her eyes and inhaled deeply, trying to slow the sudden racing of her heart. "Do you truly believe we can convince this council of what needs to be done? Do you truly have that much faith in me?"

"Of course." Zachoriun stood up, pulled her chair out for her, and offered her his arm.

Settling her hand in the crook of his elbow, she rose. Together, they walked out of the room. Mel gave his arm a slight squeeze, leaned close to his ear, and whispered, "Thank you."

29

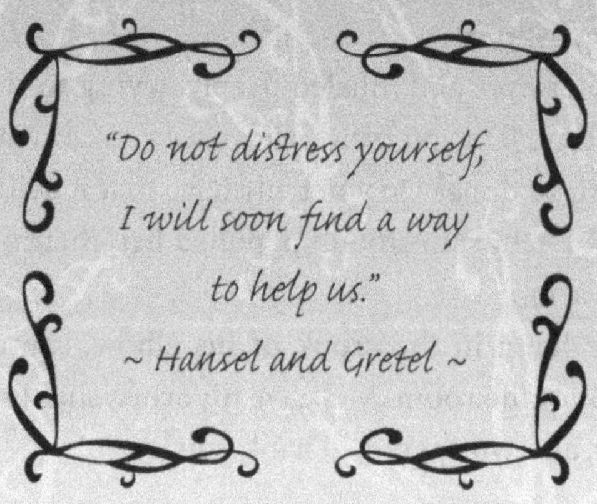

Zachoriun and Mel-disguised-as-Yvette made their way down the steps at the front of the castle and into the courtyard. A shiver ran down Mel's spine as she looked up at the dark, overcast sky. The wind whipped against her dress and threatened to loosen her hair from its ties. There was no purple edge to these clouds; they were nothing more than the beginnings of a light, summer storm. Nevertheless, she shivered slightly at the memory of Queen's spells and her rage on the mountaintop.

Movement in the sky caught Mel's attention. She turned to see a massive purple and yellow shape fly past. All the doubts and insecurities from a moment ago fluttered away. She gasped, "Hal."

"Hmm?" Zachoriun turned to see what Mel was looking at. Misunderstanding her reaction, he placed a hand over hers. "Don't be frightened. He has lived nearby for years and regularly flies over the castle. He has never given any reason to fear him."

"I know!" Mel laughed. "I mean, I am familiar with him as well. He has come to my aid a few times when I was injured or in trouble. I named him Hal."

Zachoriun grinned. "That was your father's nickname, correct?"

"Yes. I don't know precisely what it is, but something about the dragon has always reminded me of my father." Mel blinked rapidly and took a deep breath. "I'm sure King Harold would have thought it quite an honor to have a grandson named after him. And he would have found it rather hilarious for a dragon to be named in his honor as well."

"I do not have much memory of your father since I only met him a few times when I was a young boy. But I do recall he was always laughing or reciting a joke. Oftentimes both at once."

"That was him." Mel smiled. She was on the brink of saying more about her long-lost father, but as she and Zachoriun re-entered the far section of the castle and halted outside a room at the end of the long hall, she bit her tongue. Reminiscing would have to wait.

The wide double doors stood open, so she and Zachoriun entered side by side to face the already crowded room. The entire gathering rose, filling the space with the sounds of chair legs scraping across the hard floor. Bows, curtsies, and nods came from the various members of the assemblage.

Mel studied the room as she was led toward the oval-shaped table at its center. A dozen chairs were filled with the most important of the council members, while several of the lower-ranking attendees sat in seats that lined the walls. The only two windows in here had already been shuttered, as much due to the incoming storm as it was to prevent any unwanted listeners.

Behind them, a servant quickly backed through the doorway, giving a brief greeting to the king and queen before exiting into the hall and pulling the doors closed. The room was full; all eyes were on them. Mel's palms grew sweaty, and she wondered if her pounding heart could be heard across the room. Taking a seat at the table, Mel folded her hands together and waited.

Mel let her enchantment fade away, her form reverting to normal as she stepped back into the dungeon.

Luke was seated on the mattress, leaning against one of the stone walls, half-asleep with his arms folded across his chest. But at the sound of Mel's footsteps on the floor, he slowly opened his eyes. He yawned and stretched. "Hey."

"Hey."

"There's a mana potion by the door for you. Your sister said you'd need it after being disguised all day. She also said she should be able to find enough to last a few more days. She's working on tracking down more for when that supply runs out, but you may have to cut some of your meetings short if this drags on for too long."

"Well, let's hope she finds more soon." Quickly drinking the potion and settling onto the floor, Mel scooted up close and kissed Luke on the cheek. "How'd your magic lessons go?"

"Good. Really..." Luke's words trailed into another yawn. "Really good, I think. Yvette's an impressively good teacher."

Mel waited a moment, but Luke gave no further explanation as his eyes drifted closed again. She smiled. She remembered those first days of training and how exhausted she'd been at the end of them. Even after taking the restorative potions, it always took a person's body a while to adjust to the prolonged use of their newfound abilities. Gently pulling him closer, she waited for him to rest his head on her shoulder. Once he was comfortably situated, she leaned back and slowly slid her fingers through his short hair.

"How was the council?" Luke mumbled.

Mel chuckled. "Terrifying. I've never had a total roomful of delegates and leaders looking to me to make a decision on behalf of an entire kingdom. Never mind having to do that while I was disguised as someone else because they most likely hate the real me."

Not knowing how to respond, Luke pressed a kiss to Mel's collarbone, wrapped his arm around her waist, and waited for her to continue.

"But at the same time, it felt right. Like it was where I was meant to be."

At the words, Luke opened his eyes and craned his neck to look at her. "Is that what you'd want? I mean, assuming that horrible woman had never seized power. If you had grown up with your father like you should have, would you want to take over his kingdom?"

"When I was little, I never gave it much thought. It's just what was going to happen, so I simply accepted it. As I got a bit older, I did start to plan for it. I'd have daydreams about what I'd do as queen. Of course, all that went out the window when I gave Yvette the apple." Mel sighed. "Coming back here now, I just want to fix this place. I don't know if that means eventually leading it in some way or fighting for it or what. But whatever it is, I can't run from this place anymore."

Luke laced his fingers through hers and pulled her hand forward. He planted a kiss directly below the white crown emblem on the back of her wrist before laying his head in her lap. "Well, what happened in there? Any important decisions made?"

"Decisions? Ha! At this rate, this council won't make a decision in a month. Unless you count deciding who's going to speak first. It was mostly a roomful of people giving reports about what's going on around the continent."

Trying unsuccessfully to stifle his wide yawn, Luke asked, "Do we have a month?"

"I doubt it. But we did need to get through today. No sense making any decisions if we don't know what's happening. I'll do what I can to speed things along tomorrow. On the bright side, the longer this takes, the more time you have to train."

They sat quietly, listening to the sounds of a pair of rats scampering across the floor.

Mel said, "It went—"

Luke jumped at the sound of her voice. She looked down at him, grinning. "You falling asleep on me already?"

"Sorry. I'm just so worn out. I didn't realize how damn tiring magic would be."

"Want me to be quiet so you can sleep?"

Luke shook his head. "I like listening to the sound of your voice while I doze off. Who was at this meeting?"

"Cali and Fen weren't physically present, but they joined through the mirror. I guess Zachoriun had already told the council that you and I had been there a few days ago. But he let the council believe that Cali had intended to surrender us to my sister prior to our escape. There were also a few representatives from the goblin clans. They had a lot to report, but there really wasn't much substance to any of it. I'm pretty sure they all just wanted to feel important. Several representatives from the fae and elves were there too, but they were mostly quiet throughout the meeting."

"Wait." Luke twisted to look at her. "Fae *and* elves? Those are the same thing, aren't they?"

"Same race, vastly different cultures." Mel laughed. "Cali is fae, and Zachoriun is elf."

"Ah." Luke settled back again to let Mel continue.

"A few of the higher-ups from Zachoriun's military were there too. They didn't have a whole lot to report, but they did mention hearing some unidentified roaring and screeching coming from the cave system near Queen's castle. They think she's got several large creatures trapped there. They weren't able to get close enough yet to find out how many. In fact, they couldn't even decide *what* the creatures were. There was some speculation that it could be gryphons, but no one has any idea why she would be capturing gryphons, of all things.

"Um, what else?" Mel paused, chewing on her thumbnail as she thought back to the meeting. "Oh, there was a mermaid delegate there."

"In a tub?" Luke's words were starting to slur together as sleep crept nearer.

Mel grinned. "No, they didn't have her in a bathtub full of water. She was in human form. In all honesty, I wouldn't have recognized her as a mermaid if it weren't for the tiny, blue freckles all over her pale skin. Oh, there was a pair of harpy mages there as well. They didn't really have anything to report, but I think they'll be a big help with the planning. From what I gather, they are both incredibly intelligent and both truly accomplished spellcasters, so I'm grateful we have them on our side. It should…"

Her voice grew quiet as Mel realized Luke had begun softly snoring. Carefully sliding her legs out from beneath Luke's head, she stretched out beside him on the mattress, laid her arm across his chest, and closed her eyes. Her thoughts tried to race, but the exhaustion in her body soon pulled her into a deep sleep.

The next few weeks went much the same way. First thing in the morning, Mel would disguise herself as Yvette and go to the meeting while Luke stayed behind with the real Yvette to train. When the meeting finally adjourned, she would return to the dungeon, where Luke would fall fast asleep at her side a few minutes later.

With the third week drawing to a close, Mel and Zachoriun headed upstairs as usual, leaving Yvette and Luke to their training.

Just past midday, Mel rushed back into the dungeon. Zachoriun followed close behind.

"What's wrong?" Luke let go of his black hood, putting an end to whatever spell he'd been in the middle of practicing.

"We're out of time." Mel quickly adjusted her own hood and let her disguise fade away. "We have to go now."

Yvette stepped around Luke. "What has happened?"

"Today was the first time Cali and Fen didn't mirror into the meeting. We hoped we'd hear from them at some point. Instead, Alicia barged into the room a few minutes ago, demanding an audience. I'm not sure how Cali got word to her, but she found a way. Liebrahnt is under attack."

"What?" Luke's eyes went wide. "That's where Cali's castle is, right? Why would she attack that instead of here?"

"To draw us out into the open. If she attacks here, she has to contend with the castle walls. If we go help Cali and Fen—which, she knows we will because we won't abandon them—then we have to mobilize the entire army immediately and fight out in the open."

"No more delaying then."

Everyone in the group spun toward the unexpected newcomer entering the dungeon. The harpy woman folded her wings to fit through the doorway, her large, yellow eyes quickly sliding across each member of the group. The feathers that covered her head, wings, and tail were a deep mahogany color that looked nearly brown in the dim light of the dungeon.

"Lady Gwendella?" Yvette stepped around her husband to move closer to the harpy. "Why are you—"

"No disrespect meant, Your Majesty, but we must go to The Westerlands."

Mel's jaw dropped as she realized the woman wasn't addressing Yvette or Zachoriun. "I'm not..."

"I know well enough that Queen Yvette and King Zachoriun rule The Whitnalls. And that is as it should be. But I'll not recognize that cruel, horrible, vile, loathsome... *woman*... who calls herself Queen of

Losmehdyos. That title belongs to you, Your Majesty. And I believe you'll find you've more support across the kingdoms than you yet realize."

"Th-Thank you." The words fell out of Mel's mouth quietly and more question-like than she'd intended.

Gwendella gave a slight curtsy. "Now, we haven't time to wait for that useless council to form a consensus. Nigh on half think it best if we simply step aside, naively believing that horrible excuse for a queen will let us live in peace if she's allowed to continue her reign. The rest of the council knows that we must fight, though they cannot come to an agreement on the correct way to make our stand. As I said, no more delays. We must go if we're to help your cousin. Delthan?"

At the spoken name, a man stepped into the doorway. He was also a harpy, though he looked far more humanlike than his female counterpart. Rather than true wings, he had arms that were covered in bright red-orange feathers. More of the feathers lined the top of his head and trailed down his back, disappearing beneath the fabric of his shirt. His deep green eyes darted toward Gwendella. He gave a nod, then stepped up, grabbing the wrists of Yvette and Luke. A quick, muttered incantation from him, and the three seemed to blend together in a vivid swirl of color before they melted into thin air.

"Gleffik! Where did he take them?"

Gwendella wrapped her wings around Zachoriun and Mel. She, too, spoke a handful of words and magicked them all far away from the castle.

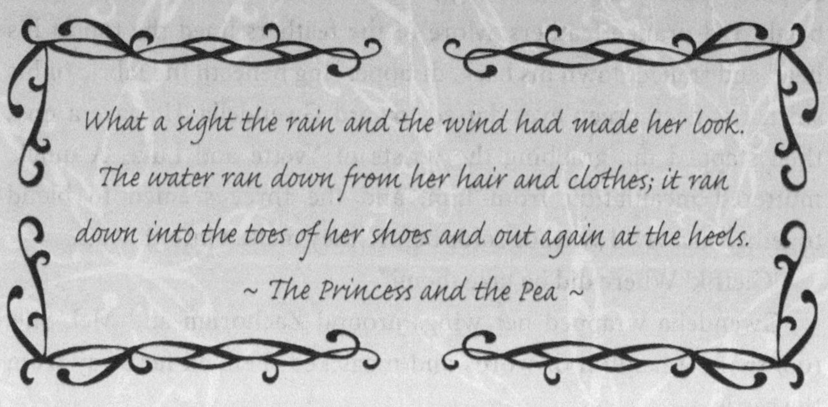

30

Everything around Mel swirled into a kaleidoscope of color. She closed her eyes as the spiraling wind yanked at her hair and cloak. Her stomach spun—or maybe it stayed in place while the rest of her spun—and she swallowed back the sick feeling that was steadily building inside her.

When the spinning abruptly stopped, Mel fell to the ground, opening her eyes as she breathed deeply. She'd been teleported in the past, and she'd obviously been through portals, but this method of travel the mages used was something entirely new to her. Fortunately, the nausea and dizziness passed quickly. Gwendella reached out with one of her wing talons, took Mel's hand, and helped her to her feet.

Screams, roars, and the sounds of weapons colliding tore through the air around them. In the distance near the castle, a group of lycans fought a contingent of soldiers. Flashes of color brightened the battlefield where other chromaveiled had joined the fighting. Mel was surprised to see how many of them were working in opposition to Queen's forces. Spells sparked through the air, weaving their way past the soldiers to explode against the lycans instead. Mel hoped that Calista and Fenris were nowhere near the thick of that battle, but she knew that's exactly where they would be.

Zachoriun slowly pushed himself to his feet at Mel's side. Thunder rumbled as dark, purple-lined clouds grew in the center of an otherwise bright blue sky.

Gwendella let Mel go. As she stepped back, her eyes darted toward the lycan group. "Your Yvette disguise was remarkable. Even Delthan and I did not suspect at first. Though if you choose to perform that particular disguise again, do not forget the small scar on your sister's chin." The harpy unfurled her wings. She shot up into the sky and flew toward the lycans' fight, a crackling ball of electricity forming in front of herself as she took aim at Queen's soldiers below.

"Yvette!" Zachoriun's voice was swallowed by the sounds of battle just a short distance away. He spun on his heel, frantically searching for any sign of her.

Mel twisted around, too, until she spotted her sister behind a small cluster of trees. "Over there!"

The two rushed over. Zachoriun pulled Yvette tight against his chest, wrapping his arms around her. Luke clasped Mel's hand and touched his forehead to hers.

"King Zachoriun, I've left weapons for you. Watch out for one another. I will return soon."

Mel hadn't realized Delthan was still there. "Where are you going?"

"To gather reinforcements." He spoke his spell, there was a momentary cyclone of red-orange, and then he was gone.

"What the hell are we supposed to do now?"

"Luke, you are to come with Zachoriun and me. We three must find a way to divert Queen's attention so Melzia has a chance to get close. She is the one who must end this."

"What? No!" Thunder cracked the air as if emphasizing her words for her. "We're in the middle of a war. I'm not letting Luke out of my sight."

Luke placed a finger beneath Mel's chin and gently tilted her head to face him. "Do you have a better idea?"

"We need to face her together! The prophecy said we had to be united."

"We *are* united. But we can't both run at her head-on."

"Melzia, I do not wish to part either. You and I have spent far too many years as enemies, controlled and separated by that woman's wiles. But if we don't stop her now, we will not be given another chance." Yvette's voice cracked as she said, "Death would likely become the least of our concerns."

Tears stung at Mel's eyes. Her hands trembled, and the dizziness from a few minutes ago began to return. Squaring her shoulders as she took a deep breath, Mel planted her hands on her hips and turned to Luke. "Fine, I don't have a better plan. But you better not die. You still have to marry me after this."

One of Luke's hands cupped the back of Mel's head, his fingers buried in her thick hair. The other was held against her lower back, bringing her up against him. Her palms caressed his biceps as he lowered his face, pressing his lips onto hers. In that moment, Mel's fears dwindled until they were nearly extinguished.

She knew she could do this.

She knew she *had to* do this.

Eventually, Luke stepped back. Mel bit her lip and sighed as she stood there, wishing the moment didn't have to end. Slipping a hand into Mel's, Luke interlaced their fingers. His other hand went to his hood and shifted the black fabric.

A sharp pain filled Mel's head. She squeezed her eyes shut and sucked air through her teeth. Then, as suddenly as the pain had cropped up, it was gone. Mel opened her mouth to ask what he was doing, and as she did, a massive shriek rent the air. Clapping her hands over her ears, she looked up as four massive creatures flew overhead. Finally dropping her hands, her ears rang, leaving the sounds of the battle muffled as the fighting raged on.

"Wygons?" Mel could barely hear her own shocked voice. "*That's* what she had trapped in the caves? *She's* the queen they follow?"

Zachoriun stood, transfixed on the monsters heading toward the thick of the battle and the rapidly growing purple-black clouds. He held two swords in one hand, a bow and quiver in the other. Breaking his attention from the terror overhead, he passed the bow and arrows to Yvette. He shifted his grip on the swords, settling the hilts into the palms of his hands he said, "We must go, Luke."

"We shall distract her," Yvette nocked an arrow as she hurried away. "Now go, and put an end to this!"

Luke gave Mel one last quick embrace, and he sprinted off after Zachoriun and Yvette. Mel—now left alone on the outskirts of the battlefield—watched as they headed toward the castle, moving to the east around the main battle.

The first wygon in the pack arrived at the edge of the fight and exhaled a white column of ice at the lycan combatants below, freezing dozens of them mid-attack. Queen's soldiers charged forward as the wygon passed, hacking and slashing each of the ice statues. Broken crystals of ice were flung from their weapons.

As Mel's hearing finally returned to normal, a loud peal of thunder shook her from her stupor. She took a deep breath. Her instincts told her to run toward the main battle, to help them, to fight—and likely die— alongside the other lycans and her family. But that wouldn't help, and she knew it. Even from this distance, the odor of blood-soaked dirt drifted through the air; even from here, she could hear the anguished screams of pain and fury. At one time, long ago, Mel had been sickened at the hint of those things. Now, it only hardened her resolve to see this through.

Forming a vision in her mind and shifting the hood of her cloak, Mel summoned a sword and shield into her hands. Her cloak transformed from red to a deep, forest green. She headed off into the trees. Mel's movements were quick as she tried to move westward around the fighting and closer to her target without drawing attention to herself.

Overhead, the sun disappeared behind the thickening clouds. Crickets chirped all around her as the light of early afternoon was swallowed up by the storm. Dark purple shadows covered the ground. Powerful gusts of wind suddenly tore at the trees around her, sending branches whipping from side to side and smaller twigs and leaves flying across the ground.

Fat raindrops started to fall, quickly soaking through Mel's clothes and plastering her hair onto her head. Using the hilt of her sword, she shoved back the hairs that tried to flatten out across her eyes and block her vision. The temperature plummeted. Goosebumps broke out across Mel's skin, and her breath formed a white cloud in front of her. She ignored the shiver that passed through her body and quickened her pace.

A blinding flash off to the right caused Mel to stop. She turned, blinking rapidly to clear her vision as thunder boomed overhead. A giant, blackened crater sat steaming in the middle of the battlefield where the lightning bolt had struck; charred bodies from both sides of the fight were strewn across the ground. Wounded cried out or moaned as they tried to drag themselves out of the fray.

Between Mel and the battle emerged a huge, colorful swirl. The pigments were exceedingly bright against the backdrop of false night, and Mel squinted, unable to tear her eyes away. As the various hues straightened out and separated into individual shapes, it became apparent that Delthan had returned, exactly as he'd promised. Hundreds more harpies—winged females and wingless males—

popped into existence all around. And not only that, but each of them had transported multiple soldiers from Zachoriun's army as well.

The reinforcements rushed toward the battle. Those who could fly did so, struggling somewhat against the raging wind but preferring to attack from the air for as long as possible. A group of the female harpies took off toward the group of wygons, charging up their spells as they flew upward and tore across the sky after the scaled monsters. The newly arrived soldiers broke into two divisions as they ran into the battle, each group heading in a different direction to surround the enemy.

Mel pulled her attention away and resumed running. As she came out the far end of the forest, she slowed momentarily. Traveling across the open field and straight toward the castle would be less painful, but heading into the thick mess of thorns and briars would make her approach somewhat less obvious. A quick shift of her hood had her drenched shoes transforming into knee-high leather boots and the cloak itself changing to a more brownish shade of green as she darted into the wild brambles.

The cold rain droplets transformed into pellets of ice, stinging and leaving small welts as they pummeled her skin. The little chunks of ice quickly became increasingly larger. As the projectiles became hail-stones, Mel raised her shield overhead and plowed onward.

All of a sudden, Mel spun to the side. Something flew at her through the darkness. She dodged just in time to avoid the arrow that nearly collided with her shoulder. A thorny vine tangled its way around her boot. She was sent sprawling to the ground. She barely managed to slam the shield down in front of herself, smashing the spiky plants and blocking the tangled mass from sinking into her arms and face. A few long thorns of the plants snuck below the shield to tear into her hip and thigh. She winced.

Another arrow had Mel leaping to her feet. The embedded thorns dragged across her flesh, sending thin sprays of blood out across the ground. A large hailstone slammed into the bone along the side of her wrist. Her fingers reflexively loosened around the sword hilt. The weapon tumbled to the ground, and it vanished. Mel clenched her teeth and ducked as a throwing star flew over her head.

Weaponless, surrounded, and bombarded from above, Mel's heart raced. She couldn't see her attackers through the darkness. They didn't seem to have any difficulty spotting her, though.

Another arrow flew. She dodged out of its way with her shield still held overhead and pivoted to the direction the arrow had flown from. Waiting half a heartbeat, she took a breath, brought the shield down, and swung it forward with all her strength. The metal collided with a hailstone, the sound echoing across the landscape like a gunshot. The apple-sized hunk of ice flew forward. A fraction of a second later, there was the distinct sound of something colliding hard with flesh and bone. There was a brief, gurgling groan as the unknown Verdant crumpled.

One down.

Mel whipped to one side as a pair of throwing stars flew at her. She was able to dodge the first entirely, but the second sliced a thick lock of hair as it went by. The cut hairs tumbled to the ground, sizzling as the bright orange poison seeped into their sheared ends. The shortened lock on her head sizzled too. She ignored it, hoping the poison up there would peter out before it worked its way to her skin.

Another throwing star. She pivoted. Thorny plants caught at her again, sending her down to one knee. She found her balance on the way down and swung the shield forward. A resounding crack sent a new hailstone flying toward the origin of the last poisoned weapon. A moment later, Mel gasped as she dodged another throwing star, this time coming at her from somewhere off to her right. Her trick with the hailstone wasn't going to work again.

Springing to her feet, Mel took off, trying not to lose her footing in the thick brambles or the large hailstones that littered the ground. She had to put distance between herself and her attacker; she had to think. As the raised shield continued to deflect the hail from above, her back was left unprotected. She grabbed her hood, shifting it. The fabric transformed into chain mail, clinking against her back as its added weight slowed her even further.

No sooner than the transformation was complete, something slammed into her shoulder blade. She flinched at the impact, but the metal cloak served its purpose and deflected the weapon. As the throwing star *thunked* to the ground, Mel spun around and snatched it up. She flung it, wincing as it left her hand and missed Nikolas by an embarrassingly wide gap. Her wrist—swollen and deeply bruised by the hailstone—suddenly made its injuries known with a sharp jolt of pain.

Though Nikolas was barely more than a silhouette in the darkness, his pale eyes practically glowed now. They thinned to slits, crinkling up at the corners as he laughed.

Clutching her damaged wrist to her chest and keeping the shield aloft with her other hand, Mel sprinted away. She did her best to dodge the hail and thick thorns on the ground as she moved, wishing in vain that she had whatever protective ward that allowed Nikolas to run through this storm without being battered by the falling ice.

Mel ran ahead, at last coming to a hill. She ducked behind it, pulling on her hood. Her body and everything on her person lost color and texture, becoming invisible. As that transformation finished, she took a deep breath and started another, more painful one. Her bones cracked and shifted, muscles realigned themselves, fur and claws sprouted from her skin. The sounds of her change echoed across the land as Nikolas drew close.

Finally, it was done. Ducking back against the hill, trying to protect herself from the hailstones, Mel let the shield evaporate into nothingness and waited.

"Our game has been remarkably enjoyable, Crimson. Few of my victims prove such worthy adversaries." Nikolas called from the other side of the hill as the sound of his footsteps slowly drew closer. "But you well know I've got the upper hand now. Give yourself up, and perhaps I'll make your death swift."

Mel knew better than to respond. She only needed a moment, but he had to move closer. She waited, breathing slowly, concentrating hard to maintain both transformations at the same time.

A footstep.

Another.

At last, Nikolas stepped around the edge of the hill, and Mel sprang forward. His eyes shifted toward the sound of her sudden movement. She swung her massive, invisible claws at him.

Nikolas's eyes widened as four wide gashes formed across his throat. Clasping a throwing star with one hand, he swung wildly in front of himself. His other hand clutched at his bleeding throat. The red liquid gushed between his fingers in time with the slowing beat of his heart.

The noises of Mel shifting back into human form were interspersed with the gurgles and choking of the Verdant. Mel became visible again and reconjured her shield. She knelt next to Nikolas. He made one last, pathetic attempt at slicing her with his poisoned weapon, which she easily avoided. Eyes rolling back in his head, the throwing star slipped from his hand, and he went still.

Mel stood for a few seconds, catching her breath and watching in silence as the hailstones finally began to slam into him.

With her head starting to pound, Mel turned her attention to the castle again and broke into a jog. Soon, she was out of the tangled mess of thorny vines and entering the clearing that surrounded the castle. Now that she could run without so many obstacles, she picked up her pace, but Mel had only made it a few dozen steps when she skidded to a halt and squeezed her eyes shut. She had broken through the outer wall of the magicked storm, and suddenly, the sun was bearing down on her in its full brightness.

Turning, Mel squinted back at the area she had just come from. The magicked storm continued to rage there, still wrapping everything below it in darkness and howling winds. Off in the distance, the battle showed no signs of slowing.

Mel blinked a few times, transferred her shield to her injured arm, and summoned a sword into her good hand as she took off toward the castle. Moments later, she was darting across the drawbridge, alert and ready to defend herself. But the courtyard was empty. Silent. She warily continued forward and into the castle.

Then, at last, she could feel it: that familiar thickening of the air. She rushed toward it, making her way into a tower and darting up the stairs. Bursting through the door and out onto the flat section of roof atop the castle, she saw her. That violet-eyed woman who had ruined so many lives. Queen.

Charging forward with her sword held high, Mel aimed for the woman's cold heart. Queen was barely fazed, simply shifting her cloak and waving a hand through the air to send a burst of wind at Mel. Mel was flung backward, crashing hard into the stone parapet. The air rapidly left her lungs, and the world went fuzzy around her.

As Mel sat there, dazed and trying to clear her vision, Queen took a step forward. "I thought I already killed you, my darling Melzia."

Mel's heart plummeted. She whispered, "What?"

"Quite clever of you, really." With one hand, she nonchalantly gestured toward a spot along the outer parapet wall where a streak of blood slowly dripped.

Dragging herself to her feet, Mel moved over to the bloody wall and peered down at the lower roof. She saw a copy of herself, red cloak and all, though the glamour began to flicker. A moment later, she watched as "herself" transformed into a barely-breathing Luke.

Mel twisted around, teeth clenched as she glared into those violet eyes.

"I must say, I believe this is truly for the best." Queen smirked. "I would so like to teach you a proper lesson prior to your end."

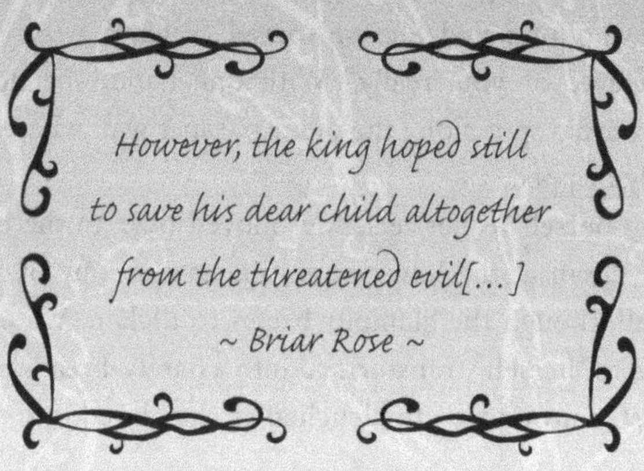

Queen inched closer, an arrogant grin plastered across her face. "You dared turn your back on me? I cannot allow such—"

Leaping up, Mel hurled herself toward Queen. She screamed as she raised her sword overhead.

Gripping the edges of her cloak, Queen slammed her hands together, sending out a thunderclap that shook the very castle itself and set Mel's ears ringing loudly. Pulling her hands apart and pushing them forward, a lightning bolt shot out toward Mel.

Mel spun away, launching her sword at Queen as she did and haphazardly tossing the metal shield in front of herself. The lightning veered away from Mel. It slammed into the shield with a loud *crackle*, the metal circle instantly becoming black and brittle immediately prior to vanishing into nothingness. At the same time, the sword flew at Queen's face, but the woman waved her hand, forcing a gust of wind to brush the blade aside. It, too, vanished before it could clatter onto the stones beneath her feet.

As Queen lifted a cloaked arm out in front of herself and aimed it toward Mel, half a dozen yellowy-brown tendrils of magic shot out. Mel tried to dodge, but the magic was too fast, wrapping itself around her and lifting her into the air. She struggled against its hold. It tightened around her, squishing her arms to her body and squeezing hard on her ribs. Breathing was becoming difficult.

Gritting her teeth, Mel yanked her arm up and out of the magical bindings, grabbed her hood, and transformed. Her body shrank, and she fell out of the Queen's hold. She crashed to the stone floor, wincing as her knee connected with stone. The pain behind her eyes intensified, and she let the transformation vanish.

A peal of cold laughter rang out across the rooftop.

Reaching over her head, Mel pulled the hood of her cloak to conjure a new weapon. Nothing happened except a sharp pain that shot through the inside of her skull. She squeezed her eyes shut. She had to get up, run, hide. *Anything* was better than sitting here, waiting to be annihilated.

Forcing herself to her feet, Mel pried her eyes open. A gust of wind hit her, knocking her back to her knees. Mel jerked her head up and shoved her hair back from her face. There, in the air above her, was Hal.

On the far side of the roof, Queen picked herself up and leered at the dragon overhead. He roared. She tried to slam her hands together again, but before they could connect, Hal exhaled a plume of blue and white fire at the woman.

The towering wall of flames blocked Mel's view of Queen. Now that the woman was occupied, Mel jumped over the parapet and down to the lower roof. She ran over to Luke. He was still breathing. Slowly and shakily, but it was something. His clothes were tattered, and there were scorch marks and welts all over him. A thin trail of blood oozed from the back of his head. Mel wanted to cradle him, to comfort him, to find some way to heal him. Guilt and fear threatened to overwhelm her. But she had to end this first, or else she and Luke were both done for.

Dropping down at Luke's side, she searched his pockets for weapons. She desperately hoped that maybe Yvette had given him a knife to tuck in his shoe or a slingshot to carry in his pocket. Not finding anything weapon-worthy, Mel pulled his black cloak back. A strap was lying diagonally across his chest. She leaned forward to see where it went, sliding back the other side of the cloak as she did. It was the enchanted satchel they'd found at Hans and Greta's house.

She dragged the satchel closer and opened it. Her eyes lit up as she spotted the weapons that waited there. She briefly hesitated, her body screaming at her not to touch them. Taking a deep breath, Mel scooped them out, set the bag back at Luke's side, and exhaled slowly.

Standing up, Mel rushed over and lifted herself back up over the low wall that separated this roof from the higher one. Her injured wrist howled at her, but she managed to make it over anyway. The fire still raged on the other end of the structure, but it writhed and twisted wildly as it tried to get closer to Queen. She was forcing it back with winds that whorled violently out from her on all sides. Hal had landed and between bouts of rebuilding the flames, he was striking at the woman with his claws and teeth. Bursts of hail and bolts of lightning periodically broke through the whipping winds, forcing the dragon backward.

Mel hurried over to the far side of the roof. She ignored the slight burning in her palms as she took her place behind Queen and the great wall of flames surrounding the woman. Mel crouched, unsure how to break through the fire or the howling winds to do anything.

Suddenly, there was a deafening shriek from the sky, and a pair of wygons emerged at the top of the wall. Hal twisted around with a roar and launched himself at the gargantuan monsters as the first wygon exhaled a river of ice, quickly dousing the flames that encircled Queen. Then, all three of the massive, winged beasts met in the sky. The wygons spewed more ice and tried to puncture Hal's wings with their tail stingers while Hal ripped at them with teeth and talons.

Now that the flames were gone, Queen let her stormy protections dissipate. She stepped forward, set her eyes on Hal, and prepared another spell.

Mel charged forward, ignoring the aching of her wrist and the slight burning in her palms where they were wrapped around the weapons. Her heart raced as she raised the blades high. She yelled and brought both wyvern-poison-encrusted daggers down into Queen's back.

Queen screeched. The spell she had been working up fizzled out as she spun around, one hand reaching back in an attempt to pry the blades loose from her flesh. Setting her sights on Mel, she whipped her hand to one side, sending Mel tumbling backward on another gust of wind. Queen's knees trembled, and her steps became shaky as she crept forward. Blood trailed down her back, darkening as it mixed with the wyvern poison and dripped behind her as she moved.

She went to slam her hands together right as Hal came crashing onto the roof between the two women. He pivoted toward Queen and swung one of his enormous, battle-torn wings, slamming her onto her back and driving the blades deeper into her body. She screamed.

Astoundingly, the woman found a way to push herself upright. Sweat poured from her, and her hands trembled as she shoved one inside her cloak and used the other in an attempt to conjure a new spell. Before it could fully form, her eyes rolled back, and she slumped to one side, trembling violently.

Though two of the wygons were still entangled in the battle, one lay mortally wounded at the foot of the castle after Hal had been able to drive one of his talons through the beast's eye. The fourth wygon showed up and landed on top of the castle. Hal growled. He stepped forward, but the wygon wasn't paying attention to him. Instead, its focus was on the incapacitated woman. The creature walked over and sniffed her. Lifting its head toward the sky, it let out a long shriek. The other two remaining wygons in the distance responded in kind. Then, it unfurled its wings and took off. The others turned away from their fight and followed their new leader into the woods.

Mel stood and walked up to Hal. One of his wings was badly torn, and several of his talons were broken or bent at unnatural angles. Patches of scales were missing along his face and neck, and his blood seeped out from those spots, boiling due to his internal fire and slowly self-cauterizing the injuries. Moving forward, careful to avoid the blood and wounds, Mel threw her arms around Hal's neck and buried her face in his shoulder. In response, he let out a low, rumbling purr.

There was a commotion nearby, and Mel stepped back. Gwendella and Delthan had materialized on the roof, bringing with them Yvette and Zachoriun. Each of them sported a variety of scrapes, cuts, burns, and rapidly darkening bruises. Gwendella had the worst of the damage, though; one wing was broken at the center, and both were missing vast sections of feathers where the hail and wind had taken their toll on her.

Yvette removed her quiver, tossed her bow aside, and hurried over to wrap her arms around Mel. The two of them stayed like that for a while as the others made their way over.

"How severely are you injured?" Zachoriun approached them to look Mel over.

Mel shook her head. "My wyvern-poisoned hands can wait. Luke is in really bad shape."

"I'll do what I can to help him, though I'm not certain it will be sufficient."

"Wait. Give me a moment." Gwendella walked over to the dying woman. Kneeling just outside the growing pool of blood, she folded back the edges of the purple cloak and reached into the pockets hidden there. She pulled out a vial of red liquid, stood, and returned to the group. Gwendella held it out to Mel. "She never would have joined this fight without such a potion. We're lucky the poison worked quickly enough that she couldn't access it in time."

"But your wing. I—"

"No." Forcing the vial into Mel's hand, Gwendella said, "My broken wing, too, can wait."

Mel turned and jogged off, calling over her shoulder, "All of you keep an eye on her. Don't you dare let her sneak away!"

Without awaiting a response, Mel ran off, with Zachoriun following close behind.

Delthan called out, "You do realize that she can't possibly escape if we end her life immediately?"

"After all the pain and death by her command," Gwendella's voice carried easily across the rooftop, "why would anyone wish for so swift an end to her torment?"

Hal crept closer to the group and settled down again, one eye fixed on the dying woman. Her silver crown had fallen too and lay several paces away, shattered into small, glistening bits of metal and gemstones.

Mel dropped down to the lower roof and sat down beside Luke. His chest movements were now shallow and jerky. Sliding a hand beneath his head, she lifted it to rest on her knee. Luke groaned. Pulling her hand away, she looked down to see her palm was sticky with his half-dried blood. She wiped her hand as best she could on the edge of her cloak. Tears formed in the corners of her eyes. Uncorking the vial of red potion, she brought it up to his lips.

When the last of the glittery, red liquid had disappeared down Luke's throat, Mel sat the vial aside and moved back, anxiously fiddling with the hem of her cloak.

Zachoriun took her place, chanting words over Luke like he had done previously. His magic wrapped itself around Luke, slowly helping to heal him. After only a few moments, though, the tendrils of magic abruptly stopped. Zachoriun clutched his head and took a deep breath. As he moved back to sit beside Mel, he put a hand on her shoulder and said, "I'm sorry I cannot do more."

Mel nodded. She chewed her thumbnail as they sat there and waited.

And waited.

Just when she was about to lose control to her emotions, Luke loudly gasped and began coughing. Mel helped him sit up. The wound on the back of his head knitted itself closed as the welts and bruises and burns on his skin quickly faded away. Reaching out with the edge of her cloak, Mel gently wiped away the blood from Luke's head. Most of it came away on the fabric. The only remaining evidence that he'd ever been hurt were the dark patches where the blood had already dried.

Exhaling shakily, Mel pulled Luke close, leaned her forehead against his, and smiled.

"Don't scare me like that, you jerk."

Luke laughed. Taking Mel's face in his hands, he leaned forward and kissed her deeply. She leaned into him, melting into his arms.

Reluctantly scooting back an inch, Mel slowly brushed a hand across Luke's cheek. "So, you can transform too?"

"Not exactly." Luke grinned. "I can copy powers and use them for a short time. Oh, and as a side effect, I apparently steal some mana too."

Mel sat up straight, her eyes wide. "That's why I kept getting the headaches and going through my mana supply so fast when I'd transform with you!"

"Right. And that's also why when you shifted me, I stayed in that form longer than Ezmaunda did. That was my power, channeling the same spell that you'd done to me. But that's not all. I can transfer the powers I copy to someone else, and they can use them for a while."

"What? Are you serious?"

Luke nodded. Mel leaned closer, giggling as she touched their foreheads together. She slowly ran her fingertips up Luke's bicep. At the sound of someone clearing their throat, Mel's cheeks went warm. She pulled back to see Zachoriun waiting near the parapet wall.

Pushing herself to her feet, Mel then helped Luke stand as well. The three of them made their way onto the upper roof to join the others.

"So, what happened? Did we win?"

"Almost." Mel gestured toward the woman on the ground as she thrashed against the poison raging inside her and working its way toward her heart.

Giving Mel's hand a gentle squeeze, Luke asked, "Were you able to find out what she did to your father?"

Mel shook her head. Luke stepped closer and quietly pulled her into a hug.

Zachoriun suddenly exclaimed, "The storm is gone!"

The group all turned to look out at the battle. The storm that had continued throughout the fight was now nothing more than an awful memory. With both the storm and the wygons no longer there, Zachoriun's army and the lycanthropes quickly won the battle. The remnants of the invading army surrendered or ran. The victors let out a cheer that echoed all the way up to the rooftop of the castle.

Mel looked around to look at the dying woman just in time to see her face contort into an agonized grimace of pain. Then, with one last shuddering breath, the vile woman was dead.

Letting out a sound that was equal parts sob and laughter, Mel felt the stress of an entire lifetime lift off her shoulders. There was a faint tingling in the skin on her wrist, but she ignored it as she walked over to Hal and draped her arms around his neck. Leaning close, telling him how much she appreciated his help, something moved beneath her arm. Mel stepped back. The scales on Hal looked as though they were melting. They slid and shifted together, letting out a soft *crackling* sound as they did.

"What's happening?" Luke asked as he watched in fascination.

Yvette mumbled something incoherent. Delthan and Gwendella

quietly moved closer. Zachoriun shook his head. Mel was too stunned to give any response at all.

As they all stood there, Hal slowly shrank. Scales lost their vibrant colors, transforming into deep brown as they melded together and softened into skin. His tail and wings vanished. Bedraggled clothing revealed itself as dragon gave way to human. His fingers were bent at the wrong angles. Blood poured from the deep gouges that lined his face and neck. Now, the wounds that had been slowly cauterizing just a short while ago were reopening with a vengeance.

Mel's heart raced as she inched forward. She grabbed the man by his shoulder and rolled him onto his back. As soon as her eyes landed on the unconscious man's face, she forgot how to breathe.

Yvette's voice cracked as she inched closer and asked, "Papa?"

The sound of her sister's voice breaking through her stupor, Mel spun toward the group. "I need another healing potion! Now!"

"We've no more left." Gwendella looked on, pity in her eyes.

Running up to him, Yvette fell to her knees beside their father and flung her arms around his shoulders. She sobbed, "Zachoriun! Help him!"

"I cannot." He hesitated as he knelt down at Yvette's side and looked at the wounded and unconscious King Harold. "I am sorry, my love, but there is naught I can do. I am too weakened at present, and this is beyond my abilities."

Luke came over, knelt at Mel's side, and said, "Give me some space. I need to try something."

Moving slightly to let him have more room, Mel stared at him in confusion.

Grabbing the man's hand, Luke closed his eyes tightly and shifted his black hood. His lips moved as he muttered something under his breath over and over.

Mel leaned close, tilting her ear toward Luke. She could finally— barely—make out his words. "Share the heal." Her jaw dropped as she realized what he was attempting to do. She sat back again and stared.

Gradually, the air around Harold and Luke started to shimmer.

The gaping wounds grew smaller, and the flow of blood slowed. On Luke, cuts and bruises and scorch marks resurfaced. Luke wobbled slightly. As Harold suddenly gasped and opened his eyes, Luke broke his hold and shoved his hood backward. The two of them sat there now, both somewhat injured but neither in mortal peril any longer. Yvette and Mel threw their arms around their father, and all three lingered for a long time, laughing and crying together.

Feeling someone grab her hand and turn it over, Mel at last pulled back to see what was happening. Luke was staring down at the spot where the white, crown emblem had once marked her as being under that despised curse. Now, that was gone. In its place was a new crown, this one split into two distinct halves. Between those broken pieces lay a pair of daggers.

Luke held out his own wrist to show a matching design in black. Mel couldn't hold back her smile as she buried her fingers in his hair and pressed her lips to his.

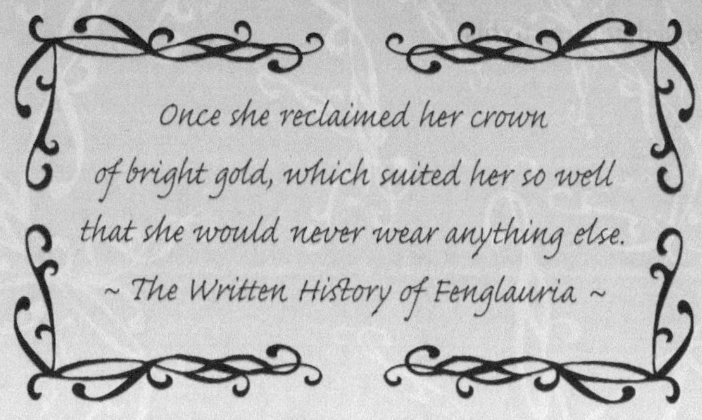

A few puffy, white clouds floated lazily across the sky. Yvette and Mel were seated on each side of their father. Zachoriun and Luke stood nearby, alongside Calista and Fenris. The large balcony where they gathered provided a clear view of several of the rivers and forests that comprised this portion of the Losmehdyan Kingdom.

Breaking the peaceful quiet, Harold cleared his throat and waited until everyone's attention was on him. "Long ago, I..." His voice was hoarse after years of forced disuse. Though his eyes were still crinkled with joy, just as Mel remembered, they also now held a hint of sadness.

He cleared his throat more forcefully this time and started once more. "Long ago, I gave up all hope of ever reclaiming my former life. I've missed so much. For so long, I could watch over my two darling daughters from afar, but I always knew that I would never again truly be part of your lives. I could not be more grateful that I was wrong."

"We all are, papa."

Calista echoed the sentiment and smiled. The long gash that ran from her shoulder to her hand had mostly healed, and the bruises on her face were nearly gone. Fenris was still using a cane as he walked but was hopeful that he would soon return to normal. When the battle had ended, most of the Citrines were dead or gone. Healing potions were now harder to come by than ever before. And while many of the other healers across the continent had offered to lend their services to the royal couple, Calista and Fenris had refused the offers, insisting that all those who had fought on behalf of Westerlands receive care first.

Harold nodded, returning Calista's smile. "I am so proud of both of my daughters and so incredibly pleased to be in your lives once more. And I owe a debt of gratitude to each and every one of you here but perhaps to you most of all, Luke."

Color bloomed across Luke's face. "You don't owe me anything special. I only did what anyone else there would've done to heal you."

"I am, of course, grateful that you were able to heal me. But that is not all to which I am referring. You left your home and life to accompany my daughter into a land you did not even know existed. You braved perils of which you were unaware only a few short weeks ago. You did everything in your power to help and protect Melzia even when you had little reason to believe you would prevail. And for all that, I thank you. I am overjoyed that my daughter found someone as noble and brave as you. I hope that someday I shall be able to repay you for everything you have done for Fenglauria."

The slight pink blush in Luke's face from the attention suddenly turned deep red. With a broad grin plastered across his face, he looked away. "No problem."

"Melzia. Yvette." Harold looked at each of them in turn. "As I said, I am so very proud of the courageous, strong, wise women you have become. And I am so sorry to have been absent from such a vast portion of your lives."

Mel squeezed his hand. Leaning over, Yvette hugged his neck and said, "We've both missed you terribly, Papa. But no one blames you."

"Thank you, dearest. I do not wish to dwell on the sadness of the past today." Harold took a deep breath and smiled. "Today is a day to speak of Losmehdyos's future!"

"What of it?" Yvette tilted her head in question.

"I do not believe it would be right for me to rule it any longer."

"What?" Yvette shot up out of her chair. "Of course it would be! It was stolen from you! You were always good to the people of this land, and you were—*are*— the rightful ruler here!"

Harold reached out and took Yvette by the hand, gently pulling her back down into her seat. "If it weren't for me, that woman never would have found a way into power. And regardless of that, I have—"

"Yes, she would have! A woman such as she does not admit defeat! If she had not married you, she would have found some other way."

"Perhaps. We cannot know for certain either way. However, that does not preclude my second reason. As I was about to say, I have not ruled for decades. I have no rapport with the people. I know little of their lives or their struggles. I scarcely remember *living* as a human, let alone *ruling* as one."

Mel licked her lips and leaned forward. "What are you suggesting?"

"I am suggesting that you, Melzia, take over the kingdom. It was always meant to go to you one day."

"Me?" Mel's voice came out an octave higher than she intended. "Talk about it being a long time since you've ruled. I've *never* ruled!

You've at least done the job before! Besides, the people won't accept me. I haven't lived here for ages. And what about the ones who were loyal to that woman? Or those who still hate me for what I did to Yvette? In fact, you know what? Yvette knows how to do this. It should go to her."

Yvette laughed. "One kingdom is enough, thank you."

Harold smiled as he reached to clasp both of Mel's hands in his own. "There was a time when the job was new to me as well. And I agree. It will take time to earn their trust. I will be at your side throughout, and I will help you be the queen the people of this land deserve."

"Zachoriun and I will help as much as we are able. We have already begun spreading the word of how you defeated that woman. Next, we will work toward assuring our own subjects know that all has been forgiven and there is no ill will toward you."

"In addition, Delthan and Gwendella assured us of the support you have among their people," Calista said. "And you know you have ours as well."

"I need a minute." Mel's eyes found Luke's.

Luke took Mel by the hand and led her downstairs and out into the gardens. At the sound of children's laughter, they both paused. Her nephew, Harry, was beaming as he was chased by Fenris and Calista's two young sons. Her nieces, Anya and Katrín, were toddling together through the tall grass, not yet able to keep up with the older children. Mel's heart warmed as she watched them playing there. Her family had grown significantly while she had been away, and she couldn't wait to get to know her young cousins and her nieces and nephew.

Giving a quick greeting to the nannies who sat in the grass beside the children, Mel pulled Luke further into the gardens until they were alone, surrounded on all sides by neatly trimmed hedges. They found a bench nestled between two large rosebushes and took a seat.

"So. What are you thinking?"

"I'm glad to be back with my family again." She sighed. "And I'm also sorry for not telling you the truth sooner. And for not being able to marry you. And dragging you into all this."

"That's all water under the bridge. I was hurt at first, but I understand why you did it. I know you tried to protect me, and I know the things that happened were beyond your control. But that's not what I mean. Is that really all that's on your mind right now?"

Mel leaned her head on his shoulder. "There are about a billion thoughts running through my head right now. That's only a tiny fraction of it. But I really am sorry."

"Look." Luke held out his wrist and turned her hand over so hers was exposed as well. Their matching emblems were plainly visible. "It's forgiven. And even the fates agree that we're meant to be together. Nothing is going to tear us apart now."

Mel smiled as she lightly ran her fingertips across the dark lines that now showed on Luke's wrist. "Thank you."

He leaned over and kissed her forehead. Straightening up, he wrapped an arm around her shoulders. "So, about that offer to take over. What do you want to do?"

Chewing on her thumbnail, Mel looked up at him. "I don't know. Can I rule an entire kingdom?"

"Listen to me, woman. I watched you take on a damn wyvern with no planning and nothing more than a couple of daggers. You came back to face a sister who you thought would want you dead. You took down a sorceress-tyrant. If there's anyone that I believe is capable of figuring out how to run an entire country, it's you."

Mel laughed half-heartedly. "But you're probably ready to go back to Earth, aren't you? We've been gone quite a while now."

"And give up these fancy new magical powers?" Luke shook the edge of his black cloak in emphasis.

This time, Mel laughed for real. "I'm serious. You never intended to come here in the first place. Everything you've ever known is still on Earth."

Luke turned to meet her eyes, tucking a lock of curly, black hair behind her ear. "The only thing I ever really wanted on Earth is sitting here next to me right now."

With that, Luke buried his fingers in Mel's hair, pulled her close, and kissed her deeply. She relaxed into him with a sigh.

When Mel finally pulled back, she beamed. "Alright. As long as I have you by my side, I'll do it. I'll take over this place. I'll learn to be their queen."

"And I think you'll be great at it."

Mel's cheeks grew warm. She slowly trailed her thumb down Luke's forearm. "What about you? What do you want to be now that we'll be married soon?"

"Aside from becoming king?" He winked at her.

"Aside from becoming *prince consort?*" Mel poked him in the ribs and watched him squirm.

As their laughter faded, Luke reached out to trace Mel's wrist mark with its broken crown and dual daggers. "I just want to be with you, helping you heal this kingdom. I want to be the one who helps you make this world into what it would've been if that woman had never taken over in the first place. What about you? I mean, other than being queen, obviously. What's next?"

"Next? Well." She paused for a beat to let the word hang in the air. "I know exactly what I want to be now."

"What?" Luke tucked a stray lock of hair back behind her ear.

Mel glanced down at the matching emblems on their wrists and slid her hand into Luke's. She smiled at him.

"Yours."

PLEASE LEAVE A REVIEW

Thank you so much for taking the time to read my book! You'll never know how much it means to me.

If you have a few minutes to spare, I would really appreciate if you'd leave a review for this book on Amazon, Goodreads, or any other site where it's listed. More reviews increase the chances of my book finding its way to new readers.

PRONUNCIATIONS

<u>Characters:</u>

Calista ——————— kah - LISS - tuh
Delthan ————————— DELL - thon
Ezmaunda —————— ehz - MON - duh
Fenris ————————— FEN - riss
Gwendella ———————— gwen - DELL - uh
Kyahn ——————————— KAI - yon
Melzia ————————— mel - ZEE - uh
Yvette ———————————— ee - VET
Zachoriun —————— zuh - KOR - ee - uhn

<u>Locations:</u>

Eldévas ——————— el - DAY - vahs
Fenglauria ———— fen - GLAH - ree - uh
Liebrahnt ——————— LEE - bront
Lindenbracht ————— LIN - den - brakt
Losmehdyos ——— los - MEH - dee - ohs
Malkidahn ——————— MAL - kee - don
Nurthahrya ——— nur - THAW - ree - uh

Nurtidahn ————————— NUR - tih - don
Rundish ————————— RUNE - dish
Weidlahnt ———————— WIDE - lont
Whytnaylk ———————— WIT - nailk

Words:

Ostrenia ————— oh - STREEN - yah
Chroma ————————— KRO - mah
Chromaveiled ———— KRO - mah - vailed
Effylz ————————— afe - YEELS
Gleffik ————————— GLEFF - ick
Túls ——————————— TOOLS
Zindt —————————— ZEENT

GLOSSARY

Chromaveiled - A specific type of magic wielder, similar to witches, mages, etc. The magical abilities held by the chromaveiled can vary drastically from one caster to the next; this branch of magic is chaotic and very difficult to control without the aid of enchanted cloaks. When the enchanted cloak binds to its designated spellcaster, its color changes to represent that spellcaster's specific subset of powers. The changing colors of these cloaks are the inspiration for the name of these spellcasters. (Chroma = "intensity of color" / veiled = "covered, concealed, or disguised")

Dracona - A classification of large, scaled, lizard-like creatures. (*E.g. dragons, wyverns, wygons, sea dragons, etc.*)

Drenkth - Curse word similar to "shit" or "damn"

Gleffik - Curse word similar to "damn it" or "hell"

Humanoid - Humans or other creatures having a similar body structure to that of a human. (*E.g. elves, harpies, mermaids, goblins, etc.*

Note: While pixies appear to have a similar type of body structure, they are not considered true humanoids.)

Lycansia - Magical energy found in the bodies of lycanthropes. Allows them to transform into the bodies of wolves and lycans. When this type of energy is depleted, any wolf or lycan transformation is ended, reverting the lycanthrope back into the humanoid form. This energy type cannot be magically restored, it must be regenerated over time.

Lycanthrope - A humanoid who has the gene for lycanism.

Mana - Magical energy found in the bodies of spellcasters (mages, chromaveiled, witches, etc.). This form of energy can be restored either via potions or it will rebuild over time.

Ostrenia zindt - Stars above; used to indicate surprise, add emphasis, or express annoyance

Túls effylz - insulting name, similar to "twice-cursed asshole"

DRACONA ARTWORK

Dragon, Wyvern, and Wygon drawings
By Lizzie DeLano

https://www.instagram.com/boba_theblessed/

Dragons

- Large reptilian creatures with four taloned feet and a pair of wings. They are classified as part of the Dracona order.
- Dragons are covered in scales and have a forked tongue.
- Larger than wyverns. Male dragons are larger than females.
- Nearly all dragons breathe fire, although some breathe ice.
- Unlike most reptiles, dragons are not cold-blooded. In fact, their blood consistently stays extremely hot. (This is true of both fire-breathing and ice-breathing types.)
- Personalities vary greatly between dragons. Some are friendly with humans, elves, fae, etc; other dragons prefer to keep their distance from all humanoids. Regardless, dragons rarely attack humanoids unless provoked.
- Most of the time, adult dragons live alone or in pairs.

Dragon

(Drawing by Lizzie DeLano)

Wyverns

- Large reptilian creatures with two taloned feet and a pair of wings that end in talons. They are classified as part of the Dracona order.
- Wyverns are covered in scales and have a forked tongue. They have an acid-like venom in their bite and in the stingers at the ends of their forked tail.
- Most female wyverns are larger than male wyverns.
- Due to the aggressive nature of wyverns, their blood temperature is not well documented. Most Fenglaurian draconologists believe that wyverns have very hot blood, similar to dragons.
- Personalities are much meaner than dragons. They are extremely aggressive toward any non-wyverns, and they can sometimes be quite aggressive to other wyverns as well.
- Most of the time, adult wyverns are very territorial and live alone.

Wyvern

(Drawing by Lizzie DeLano)

Wygons

- Large reptilian creatures with two taloned feet and a pair of wings that end in talons. They are classified as part of the Dracona order.

- Wygons are a cross between a male wyvern and a female dragon. (A cross between a female wyvern and a male dragon is theoretically possible, but female wyverns are so aggressive toward male dragons, it is unlikely to occur. There has never been a documented case of this happening.)

- Wygons are covered in scales and have a forked tongue. Similar to dragons, they can breathe fire or ice. They also have a single stinger on the end of their tail that can inject their target with its acid-like venom.

- Their blood temperature is not well documented. Most Fenglaurian draconologists believe that wyverns have very hot blood, similar to dragons.

- Wygons grow significantly larger than their wyvern and dragon parents. They grow extremely slowly, but most Fenglaurian draconologists believe the creatures never stop growing. Female wygons grow larger than males.

- Typically, wygons live in packs. They are extremely aggressive toward any creature outside their packs.

Wygon

(Drawing by Lizzie DeLano)

ACKNOWLEDGMENTS

To the readers: *Thank you so much for reading my book! I hope you had as much fun reading it as I had writing it!*

To my husband: *Thank you for your encouragement, for being my first reader, and for allowing me to talk your ear off about all things Fenglauria while writing this book!*

To Indie Bubble: *Thank you for making another great, eye-catching book cover!*

To Lizzie DeLano: *Thank you for bringing my dragons, wyverns, and wygons to life with your awesome drawings!*

To Rhino: *One of our dogs, Rhino, passed away between the time this was completed and when it was published. I'm not ready to take him out of the "About the Author" just yet, but I feel like he needs memorialized in some way. So, to Rhino: thank you for being such a good boy. You'll always have a place in my heart, you bouncy goofball.*

ALSO BY C. BRITT

<u>**Monstra Inter**</u>

The living, the dead, and the monsters in between.

One day, humanity is hurled into chaos as zombies appear throughout the world. These new monsters will chase for miles; they'll stalk and hide in ambush; they don't eat or drink; their singular goal is to spread the infection to everyone–and everything–in their path. The few people who make it through the initial wave struggle to survive in this horrifying new reality. Will anyone learn to live in this new world? Or will this be the end of humankind?

The story follows several different characters in their fight for survival as these cunning and quick new monsters take over the world. Abigail tries to find her family. Nathaniel seeks shelter. Charlie stands her ground and refuses to leave her farm. Evie and Eric face challenges they'd never dreamed of. Brad and his father head west, as far from civilization as they can get. Paths cross and intertwine.

Who will make it out alive? Who won't? And who will end up as the monsters in between?

<u>*Where to find it:*</u>

https://books2read.com/MonstraInter

https://www.cbrdpublishing.com/

ABOUT THE AUTHOR

C. Britt lives in the midwestern United States with her husband, cat, and two dogs. She enjoys spending time sewing, photographing nature, playing video games, and (of course) dreaming up fictional worlds to write about.

This is her second book. The first was a zombie apocalypse story titled **Monstra Inter**.

Follow C. Britt:

https://www.linktr.ee/cbritt

https://www.cbrdpublishing.com/c-britt

amazon.com/author/cbritt

goodreads.com/cbritt

bookbub.com/authors/c-britt

facebook.com/CBrittAuthor

threads.net/@cbrittauthor

tiktok.com/@authorc.britt

instagram.com/cbrittauthor

www.ingramcontent.com/pod-product-compliance
Lightning Source LLC
Chambersburg PA
CBHW011335010826
48972CB00016B/2941